John Carroll Power

Abraham Lincoln

His life, public services, death and great funeral cortege, with a history and

description of the National Lincoln monument, with an appendix

John Carroll Power

Abraham Lincoln
His life, public services, death and great funeral cortege, with a history and description of the National Lincoln monument, with an appendix

ISBN/EAN: 9783337396541

Printed in Europe, USA, Canada, Australia, Japan

Cover: Foto ©Andreas Hilbeck / pixelio.de

More available books at **www.hansebooks.com**

Abraham Lincoln.

HIS

LIFE, PUBLIC SERVICES, DEATH

AND GREAT FUNERAL CORTEGE,

WITH A HISTORY AND DESCRIPTION OF THE

National Lincoln Monument,

WITH AN APPENDIX.

By *JOHN CARROLL POWER.*

THIRD EDITION.

SPRINGFIELD, ILL.:
H. W. ROKKER, PRINTER AND BINDER.
1882.

TO THE

YOUNG MEN AND WOMEN

IN THE

UNITED STATES OF AMERICA,

Of all stations in life, this volume is most respectfully

DEDICATED;

With the earnest hope that they will adopt

ABRAHAM LINCOLN

As their MODEL, and strive

· to conform their lives to his standard of

Truthfulness, Honesty and exalted Patriotism.

THE AUTHOR

MONUMENTAL EDITION

OF THE

LIFE OF LINCOLN.

PREFACE.

In presenting to the reading public a new volume on the life of Abraham Lincoln, I do not claim to have discovered any new mines of truth, but my aim has been to present old truths in a new and attractive dress, to divest the subject of all irrelevant and redundant matter, and give a concise and connected account of the life, public services and tragic death of the wonderful man whose character seems to enlarge and expand the more it is studied.

I have drawn extensively upon other biographers and historians, especially the writings of Hon. I. N. Arnold, Dr. J. G. Holland, J. H. Barrett, Ward H. Lamon, and others. In addition to the published works on the subject, I have derived very great advantage from more than four years residence among the people where Mr. Lincoln spent nearly thirty years of his life, and from a personal acquaintance with every member of the National Lincoln Monument Association.

I have not felt called upon to defend Mr. Lincoln's character against unfavorable criticisms of his religious views. His own words will answer them more thoroughly than anything I could say, and I must confess my astonishment at finding in his writings so

many places where he unqualifiedly gives expression
to his belief in the overruling power of divine providence, and of his reliance on God for support and
guidance.   This feeling evidently strengthened, as he
advanced in life.   I am one of those who believe that
God can and does convert men from the error of their
ways, to be living epistles of the truths contained in
His word; and that He did touch and turn the heart
of Abraham Lincoln, his own words abundantly testify.

That wonderful funeral journey, which has no parallel in human history, except that of the Israelites
carrying the body of the patriarch Jacob up out of
Egypt, is delineated in detail.

The characteristics which distinguish this book from
all others, touching the life of Abraham Lincoln, are:
the Map, showing the course of his life and funeral;
and the full and minute account of the building and
dedication of the National Lincoln Monument, erected by a grateful people as a visible symbol of their
desire to commemorate his virtues.

J. C. P.

Springfield, Ill., Dec. 1874.

TABLE OF CONTENTS.

APPENDIX.

LIFE OF LINCOLN.

.

MONUMENTAL EDITION.

CHAPTER I.

About the year 1752, a family of Lincolns removed from Berks county, Pennsylvania, to Rockingham county, Virginia. In his "Life of Abraham Lincoln," Dr. J. G. Holland speculates, with much plausibility, of the probability that some of the Lincolns among the Massachusetts Friends, usually called Quakers, emigrated, with other New England Puritans, to Pennsylvania, and that in time they, or their descendents, removed to Virginia. From a paper written in December, 1859, by Abraham Lincoln, at the request of Hon. Jesse W. Fell, of Bloomington, Ill., I find that he gives expression to similar views with reference to the Quaker origin of the family, but without anything more definite than the conjectures of Dr. Holland. A fac simile of the paper referred to above may be found covering three pages in Lamon's Life of Lincoln. I have good reason to believe that it was unknown to Dr. Holland at the time he wrote.

Daniel Boone, at the head of a small party of adventurers, left his home on the river Yadkin, in South Carolina, in the year 1769, to explore that part of Virginia, then known as the "Country of Kentucky." After suffering great hardships for about two years, the party returned with glowing accounts of the result of their expedition. In 1775, Boone, with others who were charmed with the reports brought back by the first party, organized another, and with their families went into Kentucky for the purpose of becoming permanent residents.

2

The Revolutionary struggle came on, and the weary
years of war and bloodshed wore away, and still those
hardy frontiersmen held their ground among the savages.   As the war drew to a close, and Independence
was achieved, reports went back from the wilderness
to the colonies, then become States, of the fertility of
the soil, abundance of game and mildness of climate,
in what came to be called the "Dark and Bloody
Ground."

Among those for whom the new country had
charms, was a man in Rockingham county, Virginia,
by the name of Abraham Lincoln.   I shall not attempt to exhibit the Lincoln family tree, but will content myself with following this one branch.   He removed to Kentucky about the year 1781 or 1782,
taking with him a young family.   As near as can be
ascertained, he settled in what is now Bullitt, but
others say Mercer, county.   In the year 1784, while
Abraham Lincoln was at work in his field, unconscious of danger, he was stealthily approached by an
Indian and assassinated, being shot dead.   He left a
widow with five children.   The widow subsequently
removed to a place now in the limits of Washington
county, and there brought up her family as best she
could.   Three of these children were sons, who were
named in the order of their births: Mordecia, Josiah
and Thomas.   The two daughters were named Mary
and Nancy.   Both married in Kentucky and remained
there.   Mordecia lived in Kentucky until late in life,
when he removed to Hancock county, Illinois, where
he left a number of descendants.   Josiah, when young,
removed to Harrison county, Indiana.   Thomas, the
third son, who was born in Virginia in 1778, in consequence of the early death of his father and the poverty of the family, was suffered to grow up in ignor-
ance, and wandered about, laboring whenever and
for whatever wages he could command.   He never received any education from books, but mechanically

learned to write his name. He remained a bachelor
until he was twenty-eight years of age. In 1806
Thomas Lincoln was married to Miss Nancy Hanks, a
young lady who came from Virginia to Kentucky with
some of the early settlers. Previous to his marriage,
Mr. Lincoln had prepared a cabin for his future home
in Hardin county. Into this humble dwelling he took
his young bride, and remained there until three children were born : Sarah, Abraham and Thomas. The
latter died in infancy, leaving only Sarah and Abraham. Abraham, of whose life I am writing, was born
February 12, 1809.

Thomas Lincoln, the father, was a strong, healthy
man, about five feet ten and a-half inches high. From
his circumstances and surroundings he was compelled
to dress plainly, but he was a man who was respected
by all who knew him. Mrs. Lincoln was quite tall,
being five feet five inches high, and was a "slender,
pale, sad and sensitive woman, with much in her nature that was truly heroic, and much that shrank from
the rude life around her."

Poverty was the lot of all in this humble home, but
the father and mother were both pious, and sought at an
early age to impress the minds of their children with
religious truth, but religious institutions were exceedingly rude and irregular. For many years young
Abraham Lincoln never saw a church, but he occasionally heard Parson Elkin preach. He was a Baptist, and Thomas and Nancy Lincoln being members
of that denomination, he was frequently attracted to
their cabin. The first ideas of public speaking Abraham ever received was from the sermons of Mr. Elkin.

Schools were scarce and very inferior. To supply
the deficiency, Mrs. Lincoln, having received more
education than her husband, would read aloud to her
son and daughter from the few books that could be
obtained in the neighborhood.

Young men and women who have enjoyed the advantages of schools as they are now systematized in all the northern and some of the southern States, can not realize the almost entire destitution of the means for developing and improving the mind. Such establishments as the large publishing houses, with their classified series of text books, in almost every branch of learning, were then unknown. The schools were usually kept in houses that would be thought unfit for the protection of horses or cattle at the the present time.

The studies were confined to spelling, reading, writing and arithmetic. Grammar and geography were unknown. Such a thing as a dictionary was seldom or never seen by any person connected with the schools. The books in use were, Dilworth's spelling book, and for reading, any book, on any subject, that happened to fall into the hands of the different families. A country school is remembered by the writer about fifteen years later than the time Abraham Lincoln commenced his studies, and in a better part of Kentucky, when Dilworth's spelling book had given place to Webster's. The following is a partial list of the books used, as the best that could be obtained, by a large number of boys and girls about equally advanced in their knowledge of reading. Almost any Kentuckian, unless his lot was cast in some of the larger towns or cities of the State, has seen its counterpart. There being no possibility of classification, they would be called up to recite in something like the following order: The Bible, Æsop's Fables, Life of Washington, Robinson Crusoe, New Testament, Revised Statutes of Kentucky, Life of Marion by Horry, a book of Western Adventures, English Reader, Charlotte Temple, Columbian Orator, Thaddeus of Warsaw, Debates on Baptism, between Campbell and McCalla, and others about as well selected.

At about seven years of age, Abraham Lincoln was sent to a school, of which the above is, no doubt, a fair description. The only aid in his studies was an old copy of Dilworth's spelling book. He went two or three months to that teacher, and within that year went about three months to another teacher. With the instruction he received from these two teachers, Zachariah Riney and Jacob Hazel, and the aid of his mother, he learned to read and write legibly. The instruction the boy received from his mother was, no doubt more valuable to him than the schools. Later in life, Lincoln, speaking of his education, said: "If a straggler, supposed to understand Latin, happened to sojourn in the neighborhood, he was looked upon as a wizzard."

That part of the country in which Abraham Lincoln was born has since been separated from Hardin and erected into a new county, called Larue, with Hodginsville as the county seat. Hodginsville is about fifty miles south by east of Louisville, thirty-five miles northeast of the Mammoth Cave, and eight or ten miles east of the Louisville and Nashville railroad, either from Glendale or Nolensville stations. The nearest point from Hodginsville to the Ohio river is thirty-five miles northwest, through Elizabethtown, the county seat of Hardin county, to West Point, at the mouth of Salt River.

The cabin in which he was born was situated about one and a-half miles from Hodginsville, on Nolen's Creek. The family remained there a year or two after his birth, and then removed to a cabin on Knob Creek, on the road from Bardstown, Kentucky, to Nashville, Tennessee, at a point three and a-half miles south or southwest of Atherton's Ferry, on the Rolling Fork of Salt river, and six miles east or northeast of Hodginsville. As the family of Thomas Lincoln increased, he became dissatisfied with his situation. The land where he lived was much of it broken, poor and stony, and besides these disadvantages, Kentucky was exceedingly unfortunate in its early settlement on account of the insecurity of its land titles.   From this combination of causes, he determined to sell his small estate and emigrate west of the Ohio river.   The price he asked for his home was $300.   In the year 1816 he found a purchaser, by taking his pay principally in whisky and a small amount of money.   As soon as his sale was effected he built a small flat boat, launched it on the waters of the Rolling Fork, loaded it with his whisky and heavier household goods and farming utensils, and commenced his journey alone. He floated safely down the Rolling Fork into Salt river and entered the Ohio.   Here he met with the misfortune of having his boat upset, by which he lost about two-thirds of his load.   Obtaining assistance, his boat was righted and he continued his voyage until he landed at Thompson's Ferry, now the town of Rockport, Spencer county, Indiana.   He at once procured conveyance for his goods and took them about eighteen miles north, to a point near the present town of Gentryville, in the same county.   He left his goods in the care of a settler, and returned to the river, and after crossing it, proceeded on foot to his Kentucky home, taking as near a straight course as possible.   He at once commenced preparations for removal.   The bedding and clothing for the family was packed upon three horses, and all set out overland for their new home.   They occupied seven days in making the journey, and at the end of that time met with neighborly assistance in erecting a dwelling, and were soon ready to begin life in the wilderness.

The first journey, including the river voyage and land travel, must have been at least two hundred miles; although, on a straight line, the points of departure and destination were less than one hundred miles apart.   He had moved about seventy-five miles west and fifty north and exchanged a slave for a free

State. The removal took place in the autumn of 1816 when Abraham Lincoln was in the eigth year of his age. About two years after their settlement in Indiana his mother sickened and died, in the fall of 1818, leaving her husband, son and daughter to mourn her loss. The ability of Abraham to write was now for the first time found to be an acquisition of real utility. In their affliction, both father and son thought of their old friend Parson Elkin, and it was finally decided that Abraham should write to him imforming him of the death of Mrs. Lincoln, and ask the parson to come and preach the funeral. The preacher wrote them in reply, that he would be there on a certain Sunday and comply with their wishes. Notice was given of the time set for the funeral, and about two hundred persons were collected from an area of nearly twenty miles in diameter. The minister was there at the appointed time, and taking his stand at the foot of the grave, with his congregation seated on logs and stumps, preached a sermon suitable to the occasion. The memory of his mother was always held sacred by Abraham Lincoln. After he had acquired great fame, while in conversation with a friend he said, with tears in his eyes, "All that I am, or hope to be, I owe to my angel mother." It has been said that the foregoing remark was made concerning his step-mother, but that is not very probable, as she was living at the time the remark was made. That he was strongly attached to her there can be no doubt.

A gentleman who resided at Charleston, Coles Co., Ill., was present when Abraham Lincoln visited his step-mother soon after he was elected President, in the fall of 1860, and gave to the writer a description of the parting scene, which, if truly portrayed, would secure fame to the artist who should execute it. He said that when Mr. Lincoln was about to take leave of the aged, white-haired matron who had so faithfully supplied the place of a mother, she approached him with

tottering steps, surrounded by her humble neighbors,
and leaning upon his breast, in faltering tones sobbed
out the words, "Abram, I feel that I shall never see
you again." As Mr. Lincoln stood, his tall form tow-
ering above hers, his left arm around her neck, his
right hand raised and pointed towards Heaven, he uttered the single word, "Mother." He could say no
more, and after standing a few moments in silence,
with his head slightly inclined forward, they slowly
separated to meet no more on earth.

CHAPTER II.

When he was about twelve years of age, one of the neighbors, named Andrew Crawford, commenced teaching a school in his own cabin, and Abraham made diligent use of this opportunity to improve his mind. The same obstacle presented itself here that existed in Kentucky, with reference to books, but such as found their way into the new settlement, were secured for the boy to read. Some of the books read about that time, made a lasting impression on his mind. Among them were the Pilgrim's Progress, by John Bunyan; the life of Washington, both by Weems and Ramsey; the life of Henry Clay; Æsop's Fables, and other books of like value.

In the latter part of 1819, a little more than a year after the death of his wife, Thomas Lincoln returned to Kentucky, and married Mrs. Sally Johnston, of Elizabethtown, a widow lady with three children. She proved to be a kind step-mother, and the two families grew up in harmony.

In 1822, Sarah Lincoln was married to a young man named Aaron Grigsby. She died about a year after her marriage, and thus Abraham was motherless and without a brother or sister.

In the year 1828, when Abraham was nineteen years of age, a neighbor applied to him to take charge of a flatboat and its cargo, and, in company with his own son, run it down the Mississippi river and sell it at the sugar plantations near New Orleans. The business was placed entirely in his hands. They started from the town of Rockport, Spencer county,

and made a successful trip, giving satisfaction to all
parties.   On their return, they walked the greater
portion of the distance.

Abraham Lincoln had, long before his flatboat trip,
ceased to attend any school.   Summing up all the
time spent under his five teachers, it did not amount
to more than about one year, and the most that could
be said of his attainments, was that he could "read,
write and cipher," but he was always reading or
studying at every leisure moment.

After living thirteen or fourteen years in Indiana,
and the children of both families grew to be men and
women, all became dissatisfied with their location.
The country continued to be unhealthy, and to extend
farming required a great amount of labor to remove
the timber.   They had heard of the prairies of Illinois,
and decided to send Dennis Hanks, a relative of Mrs.
Lincoln, to examine the new country.   He returned and
reported very favorable.   Mr. Lincoln disposed of his
interests in Indiana, and on the first of March, 1830,
started in search of a home.   They entered the State of
Illinois by crossing the Wabash river at Vincennes, and
continued their course to the northwest through Law-
renceville, near the site of the present town of Newton, in Jasper county, and through Charleston, Coles
county.   The roads, or rather the country, was very
muddy, and it took them fifteen days to travel about
two hundred miles.   Abraham drove one of the ox
teams, and was afterwards remembered by some of
the citizens along the route on account of his being so
tall.

Thomas Lincoln selected a spot on the north side
of Sangamon river, where timber and prairie were
convenient to each other.   It was in Macon county,
about ten miles west of Decatur.   Abraham assisted
his father in building a log cabin, and in splitting
rails and fencing ten acres of land.   After this, he
worked for hire among the neighbors.   A part of his

work at that time was breaking fifty acres of prairie with four yoke of oxen. The expectation that their new home would be a more healthy location, proved to be a sad disappointment. In the autumn of the first year, nearly all of the new emigrants were afflicted with fever and ague. The winter of 1830–31 is remembered as the winter of the "deep snow." I quote from an address by President Sturtevant, before the old settlers association at Jacksonville: "In the interval between Christmas, 1830, and January, 1831, snow fell over all central Illinois to a depth of fully three feet on a level. Then came a rain, with weather so cold that it froze as it fell, forming a crust of ice over this three feet of snow, nearly if not quite strong enough to bear a man, and finally, over this crust of ice there was a few inches of very light snow. The clouds passed away, and the wind came down upon us from the northwest with extraordinary ferocity. For weeks, certainly for not less than two weeks, the mercury in the thermometer tube was not, on any one morning, higher than twelve degrees below zero. This snow fall produced constant sleighing for nine weeks."

In the spring of 1831, the Lincoln family retraced their steps in part, leaving Macon for a better locality in Coles county, not far from Charleston. That continued to be the home of Thomas Lincoln until his death, which occurred January 17, 1851, in the seventy-third year of his age.

After the removal of the family to Coles county, Abraham never made his home in his father's house. During the winter of the deep snow, he made an engagement for himself, his step-brother, John D. Johnston, and John Hanks, a relative of his own mother, to take a flatboat to New Orleans. They were to meet their employer at Springfield, which they did about the first of March, to learn that the enterprise was a failure, in consequence of the inability of their employer to obtain a boat.

An arrangement was then made for the three to build a boat at Sangamo, on the south bank of the Sangamon river, about seven miles northwest from Springfield. After the boat was finished, it was floated down below New Salem, now in Menard, then a part of Sangamon county, where the boat was loaded for the trip, a part of the cargo being live hogs. The voyage was a success, the running of the boat and selling the cargo being under the direction of Mr. Lincoln. On his return, he became a clerk in the store of Mr. Offutt, who had fitted out the boat. The store was at New Salem, a town now extinct.

In connection with all the hard labor he had performed, Mr. Lincoln was a constant reader, making the best choice he could from the scanty materials to be obtained. While clerking in the store at New Salem, he borrowed a copy of Kirkham's grammar, and mastered its intricacies. It was while he was clerking in this store that the people began to call him "Honest Abe." After spending about one year in the store, his employer failed, and he was thrown out of business.

In 1832, the Indian war, headed by the chief Black Hawk, broke out, and young Lincoln, now twenty-three years of age, enlisted for the fight. When the time came for the election of a captain for his company, a Mr. Kirkpatrick was candidate. Mr. Lincoln had previously worked for Kirkpatrick, and found him so tyranical that he refused longer to remain in his employ. Lincoln was put forward as a candidate for the same office, by a party of young men, without any aspirations for the office on his part. The candidates took positions some distance from the men, and at a given signal they fell to the rear of their favorite. Lincoln received about three-fourths of the votes. In after life he often referred to this incident, and con-

fessed that no subsequent success gave him half the
satisfaction that this election did.   Captain Lincoln's
company did a great amount of marching, but was
not in any battle.   The time for which the men enlisted expired before the closing of the war, and many
of them went home, but Captain Lincoln and some
of the men re-enlisted and served until Black Hawk
was taken prisoner and his followers dispersed.

The rendezvous of the soldiers before starting for the
enemy was at Beardstown.   While in camp, Captain
Lincoln became acquainted with Captain John T.
Stuart, who was soon after elected Major of a spy
battalion. Thus commenced the acquaintance between
these two men which ripened into the closest friendship and continued until the death of Mr. Lincoln.

After his return from the war, Lincoln became a
candidate for the legislature, but failed to be elected,
not for want of personal popularity, but because he
espoused the weakest side in politics, being a Whig.
The official poll-books for New Salem precinct, where
he lived, show that Lincoln received 277 votes, when
at the same time the combined vote of the Whig and
Democratic candidates for congress was only 276.

Being out of business, Lincoln was about to commence learning the trade of a blacksmith, but soon
abandoned the idea, and took an interest in a store.
That proved to be unprofitable, and he abandoned it
in about one year, because he was unable to pay his
debts.   He was postmaster at New Salem during the
time he kept that store, which gave him access to all
the newspapers he could read.   The postoffice at New
Salem was abolished while he was postmaster, and the
business removed to Petersburg. The village of New
Salem in a short time ceased to exist.

Soon after his failure in business, a chance for remu-
nerative employment presented itself.   John Calhoun,
who many years later took part in the Kansas troubles, was, at the time we speak of, surveyor of Sanga-

mon county. He was anxious to have an assistant
whom he could trust. Having observed Lincoln's
studious habits, and knowing him to be honest, he told
him that if he would study surveying, he could have
all the work he desired, and be well paid for it. Calhoun offered the use of the necessary books. Lincoln
accepted them, and in a few weeks was ready for the
business, and followed it more or less for two or three
years. During that time he did the surveying in laying out the town of Petersburg, the county seat of
Menard county. He also surveyed much of the surrounding country.

In 1834, Abraham Lincoln was again a candidate
for a seat in the legislature, and was elected, receiv-
the highest vote cast for any candidate. When the
time arrived for the assembling of the legislature,
Lincoln laid aside his compass, and with a package
of clothing, went on foot to Vandalia, the capital of
the State, about one hundred miles distant. Hon.
Jesse K. Dubois—then a Representative from Law-
rence county, but now of Springfield—and Lincoln
were the two youngest members of the House. That
session commenced in December, 1834. During the
whole time, Lincoln said little but observed all that
was done by others. He was constantly in his place,
and faithfully discharged every duty assigned him on
the various committees. Major John T. Stuart was
one of Lincoln's colleagues from Sangamon county,
and they roomed together at Vandalia. As they were
taking a walk one morning after breakfast, Lincoln
asked Stuart's advice with reference to the study of
law, and Stuart advised him to begin at once. Lincoln
said he was poor and unable to buy books. Mr.
Stuart was already in a successful practice at Springfield, and offered to loan him all the books he would
require. The offer was gratefully accepted, and when
the session closed, Lincoln returned home as he went
—on foot. When he was ready to begin his studies,

he walked to Springfield, a distance of about twenty-five miles, borrowed enough books to make a commencement. and returned with them to New Salem. He would study as long as his money lasted, and as the opportunity to do more surveying presented itself, he would earn all the money he could and return to his studies.

In the autumn of 1836, Mr. Lincoln was admitted to the bar in Springfield, and about the same time re-elected to the State Legislature. Sangamon county was entitled to two Senators and seven Representatives. At that term the entire delegation were so tall that they were then and have always since been called the "Long Nine." Some of them were a little less and some a little more than six feet, but their combined height was exactly fifty-four feet. None were taller than Abraham Lincoln. The statement written by himself, in December, 1859, at the request of Hon. Jesse W. Fell, of Bloomington, contains this paragragh.: "If any·personal description of me is thought desirable, it may be said I am in height six feet, four inches nearly; lean in flesh; weigh, on an average, one hundred and sixty pounds; dark complexion, with coarse, black hair, and gray eyes—no other marks or brands recollected." It was at the session of 1836–7 that the capital was removed from Vandalia to Springfield. At the close of that session, Mr. Lincoln walked home as before. His Springfield friend, Major Stuart, at this time made him an offer to become his partner in the practice of law, which he accepted, and from April 27, 1837, Springfield was his home. Here he was warmly welcomed on account of his efficient aid in securing the removal of the capital to Springfield. The people were still anxious to keep him in the Legislature, and he was elected in 1838 and again in 1840, but after that declined to be a candidate.

The firm of Stuart & Lincoln continued to practice until April 14, 1841, when Mr. Stuart was elected to a seat in the U. S. House of Representatives, which made it necessary to dissolve the law firm. Mr. Lincoln at once formed a partnership with Judge S. T. Logan, then and now a citizen of Springfield. They were partners until 1845. He then formed a partnership with William H. Herndon, as Lincoln & Herndon, which continued to the end of his life.

Mr. Lincoln was married in Springfield to Miss Mary Todd, November 4, 1842. In 1846 he was elected to the U. S. House of Representatives, and when he took his seat in that body was the only Whig from Illinois, all the others being Democrats.

After serving out his two years congressional term, he was for nearly ten years diligently engaged in the practice of his profession, without being a candidate before the people for any office whatever. But he was by no means an idle spectator of the political acts passing in review before him. He was gradually preparing, perhaps unconscious to himself, for the great events in which he was to act so conspicuous a part. By his occasional speeches, he was gaining a national reputation.

In the first Republican National Convention, which assembled in Philadelphia June 17, 1856, he received 110 votes as the candidate for Vice President, to 259 for Dayton. This of course decided the matter against him, but it was complimentary, and was a formal introduction of Mr. Lincoln to the Nation.

His name headed the Republican electorial ticket for Illinois, and he took an active part in the campaign for Fremont and Dayton. From the time of this campaign to the end of his life, Mr. Lincoln was almost entirely absorbed in politics.

Although United States Senators are not elected by the popular vote, events brought the subject as prominently before the people of Illinois in 1858 as if they had been expected to vote upon it. It was known that it would be a part of the business of the General Assembly to be elected that year to choose a United States Senator to succeed Stephen A. Douglas, and that he was a canidate for re-election. The Democratic State Convention of Illinois assembled in Springfield, April 21, of that year, and endorsed the course of Mr. Douglas in Congress on the slavery question. This endorsement was understood by all parties to be equivalent to a nomination for re-election.

The Republican State Convention also assembled in Springfield, on the 16th of June following. There were about six hundred delegates to this convention, and enough of their alternates were present to make about one thousand earnest men from all parts of the State. A banner was borne into the convention from Chicago bearing the words, "Cook county for Abraham Lincoln." The whole convention rose to its feet and gave three cheers. After adopting a platform and transacting all other business, a resolution was brought forward and unanimously adopted on the 17th, "that Hon. Abraham Lincoln is our first and only choice for United States Senator, to fill the vacancy about to be created by the expiration of Mr. Douglas' term of office." Frequent calls were made for a speech from Mr. Lincoln. It was at length announced that he would address the convention at the State House in the evening. In that speech he defined in the clearest language the issue between the friends and enemies of slavery, and gave as his opinion that "a house divided against itself cannot stand," and that the United States would either become all slave or all free; and pointed out so clearly the duty of the friends of freedom that the convention adjourned in the highest state of enthusiasm.

The work now for the two candidates was, to each exert his influence in the choice of members of the

3

Legislature, the slavery question being the only point at issue. At first their appointments were made independent of each other. Mr. Douglas spoke at Chicago on the 9th and Mr. Lincoln on the 10th of July. On the 16th, Mr. Douglas spoke at Bloomington, Mr. Lincoln being present. On the 17th, both spoke at Springfield to different audiences, neither one hearing the other.

Mr. Lincoln, wishing to come to close work on the subject, addressed the following note to Mr. Douglas:

CHICAGO, ILL., July 24, 1858.

Hon. S. A. Douglas :

MY DEAR SIR: Will it be agreeable to you to make an arrangement for you and myself to divide time and address the same audiences the present canvass? Mr. Judd, who will hand you this, is authorized to receive your answer; and, if agreeable to you, to enter into the terms of such arrangement.

Your obedient servant,

A. LINCOLN.

Mr. Douglas replied the same day at some length. Mr. Lincoln addressed Mr. Douglas again on the 29th, and Mr. Douglas replied on the 30th of the same month, accepting the proposition for discussion, and naming the following seven places and times for holding the meetings:

Ottawa, LaSalle county		Aug.	21, 1858
Freeport, Stephenson county		"	27, "
Jonesboro, Union	"	Sept.	15, "
Charleston, Coles	"	"	18, "
Galesburg, Knox	"	Oct.	7, "
Quincy, Adams	"	"	13, "
Alton, Madison	"	"	15, "

Mr. Lincoln addressed Mr. Douglas on the 31st, acquiescing in the arrangement, and the debates were held at the times and places designated.

The principles of each party were thoroughly discussed, and the weak points of both fully exposed. The discussion was fair, open and manly, the warmest friendship being sustained between the disputants throughout the campaign.

A small majority of the members of the Legislature elected as the result of this canvass were in favor of Mr. Douglas. Mr. Douglas was accordingly returned to the U. S. Senate. Notwithstanding Mr. Lincoln was defeated in the immediate object of the canvass, there is little doubt that it was the means of placing him in the Presidential chair. The principles upon which the Republican party asked the confidence of the American people are not so clearly set forth in any other form as in his speeches in this discussion. These speeches took the whole range of the extension and restriction of slavery in the territories, and the manner in which Mr. Lincoln presented the subject was so clear and logical that it commanded the attention of the people, east, west, north and south. During the year 1859, he visited Kansas, Ohio and New York, and made several speeches of great ability. Albert D. Richardson, who accompanied him to Kansas, referring to his speech delivered in a rickety old court house in Troy, Doniphan county, on a cold, windy November night, says that a Democratic speaker present attempted to reply, but did little more than compliment Mr. Lincoln by saying that it was the finest speech he had ever listened to on the Republican side of the question.

A speech delivered by him in Cincinnati, early in 1860, to an audience in which he assumed there were some Kentuckians, discussed the question with the the border slave States in his own peculiar style. It is yet remembered in that city for its extraordinary power.

An elaborate article, prepared by Senator Douglas, appeared in Harper's Magazine, in the latter part of

1859.   It had an immense circulation all over the
Union.   Mr. Lincoln soon had an opportunity to be
heard on a more extended scale before the people of
the Nation.   An invitation was extended to him to
. speak in Brooklyn at Mr. Beecher's church, but it
was thought best by the Republicans of the two cities
the speech should be delivered at Cooper Institute,
New York.   It was delivered in the latter part of
February, 1860.   He had expended an extraordinary
amount of historical research in its preparation, and
it was one of the clearest exhibitions of the policy of
the Republican party ever delivered in one speech.
It was copied in the newspapers east and west, and
printed in pamphlet form and used as a text book in
the succeeding Presidential campaign.

CHAPTER III.

Invitations to speak were received by Mr. Lincoln from many places in New England. On the fifth of March he spoke at Hartford, and was escorted to the City Hall by the first company of "Wide Awakes" ever organized. He had an immense audience and produced a powerful impression. On the sixth of March he spoke at New Haven, on the seventh at Meriden, on the eighth at Woonsocket, Rhode Island, on the ninth at Norwich, Connecticut, on the tenth at Bridgeport. All of these speeches were to immense audiences. The educated and highly cultivated classes of the Eastern States seemed as much charmed with the man and his style of oratory as the people of the west. During this trip he visited his son, Robert, at Harvard College, and spent two Sabbaths in New York City, both times attending Mr. Beecher's church.

All these speeches were read and re-read, from Maine to California, and from the frozen regions of the North to the border slave States on the South, and to a considerable extent even among the orange groves of the extreme South.

Mr. Lincoln had scarcely returned home from his eastern tour before the Democratic National Convention assembled at Charleston, which occurred on the 23d of April. After wrangling among themselves for several days, that body was rent in twain, one part to assemble in Baltimore on the eighteenth day of June, and the other to meet in Richmond on the second Monday in June.

On the ninth of May the National Constitutional Union Convention assembled in Baltimore. This Convention was made up of old Whigs and native Americans. It nominated John Bell, of Tennessee, for President, and Edward Everett, of Massachusetts, for Vice-President. The Richmond Convention met and adjourned to await the doings of the Baltimore Convention, which nominated Stephen A. Douglas for President, and Benjamin Fitzpatrick, of Alabama, afterwards changed to Herschel V. Johnson, of Georgia, for Vice-President. This was done on the 23d of June.

The members of the Richmond Convention, after adjourning, went in a body to Baltimore and re-organized. They then nominated John C. Breckenridge, of Kentucky, for President, and Joseph Lane, of Oregon, for Vice-President. This body completed its work on the 22d of June, one day before the convention that nominated Douglas.

The Republican National Convention assembled in Chicago, May 16th, 1860, for the purpose of selecting candidates for the offices of President and Vice-President of the United States. At first the choice seemed nearly equally divided between Mr. Seward, of New York, and Mr. Lincoln. On the 18th Mr. Lincoln was nominated on the third ballot by 345 out of 465 votes. His nomination was thus secured, but Mr. Evarts, of New York, after expressing his regret that the gentleman from his own State had not been the choice of the convention, moved that the nomination of Mr. Lincoln be made unanimous. Hannibal Hamlin, of Maine, was nominated for Vice-President.

On Saturday, May 19th, the Hon. George Ashmun, of Massachusetts, President of the Convention, at the head of a committee appointed for the purpose, arrived in Springfield and delivered to Mr. Lincoln a letter informing him of his nomination, and a copy of the platform of the principles adopted by the Convention.

On the 23d of May Mr. Lincoln accepted the nomination in a graceful letter addressed to Mr. Ashmun. The election took place on the 6th of November. The electoral vote of all the States combined was 303. Of this number Lincoln and Hamlin received 180; Breckenridge and Lane, the candidates of the pro-slavery democrats, 72; Bell and Everett 39, and Douglas and Johnson, progressive democrats, 12: making a majority of 37, over all competitors, for Lincoln and Hamlin.

Notwithstanding Mr. Lincoln was elected in strict conformity to the constitutional provisions governing the case, the fact that he *was* elected was made the occasion for the conspiracy, which had long been smouldering in the Southern States, to burst forth in full flame. From the time of his election to the day of his inaugeration, wanted but two days of four months. During that time seven States passed ordinances of secession, and appointed delegates to attend a convention at Montgomery, Alabama, on the 4th of February, 1861. These were South Carolina, Georgia, Mississippi, Alabama, Florida, Louisiana and Texas.

This convention assembled at the appointed time and adopted a provisional constitution for what they called the Confederate States of America. They selected Jefferson Davis, of Mississippi, for President, and Alexander H. Stevens, of Georgia, to be Vice-President of the new Government.

All this was done before Mr. Lincoln left his home in Illinois, and nearly a month before he took the oath of office at the capital of the nation. It was not in consequence of anything he had done, for the time had not yet arrived for him to perform any official act; nor was it in consequence of anything which the leaders saw he had the power to do, for they well knew his views of the sanctity of an oath, and that he would swear to maintain the constitution inviolate Secession was a foregone conclusion, to be carried out at this time if it could be made practicable.

At eight o'clock Monday morning, February 11th, 1861, Abraham Lincoln left his home in Springfield to repair to the capital of the nation for the purpose of entering upon his duties as President of the United States. Almost the entire population of the city, without distinction of party, assembled at the depot of the Toledo, Wabash and Western Railroad, then at the crossing of Monroe and Tenth streets, to see him take his departure. He seemed to feel to its full extent the solemnity of the occasion, and before entering the cars took an affectionate leave of his old friends and neighbors by a general hand-shaking and the delivery of the following brief

FAREWELL ADDRESS.

"*My Friends:* No one, not in my position, can appreciate the sadness I feel at this parting. To this people I owe all that I am. Here I have lived more than a quarter of a century; here my children were born, and here one of them lies buried. I know not how soon I shall see you again. A duty devolves upon me which is, perhaps, greater than that which has devolved upon any other man since the days of Washington. He never would have succeeded except by the aid of Divine Providence, upon which he at all times relied. I feel that I can not succeed without the same Divine aid which sustained him, and on the same Almighty Being I place my reliance for support; and I hope you, my friends, will all pray that I may receive that Divine assistance, without which I can not succeed, but with which success is certain. Again I bid you an affectionate farewell."

It was raining at the time but every hat was lifted when he began to speak, and every head bent forward to catch what proved to be his last words to Springfield auditors. When he uttered the sentiment that *with God's help he was sure to succeed*, there was an uncontrollable burst of applause.

The train arrived at Decatur at half past nine. Mr. Lincoln was almost as well known there as at Springfield. An immense multitude assembled at the depot, broke out with enthusiastic cheers as the car bearing the President elect came alongside.

Mr. Lincoln left his car and moved through the crowd of old friends, shaking hands to the right and left. But a few moments stoppage only was allowed and he was borne away, followed by the prayers and good wishes of thousands of loyal hearts. The train passed the junction south of Lafayette. At that and nearly all towns and stations crowds of people waited to catch a glimpse of the man in whom the hopes of the nation were centred. He reached Indianapolis at five oclock, p. m., to find at least twenty thousand people assembled about the depot, and to be welcomed by a speech from Governor Morton amid the firing of thirty-four guns. A procession in which both houses of the Indiana Legislature participated, escorted the Presidential party to the Bates House, from the balcony of which Mr. Lincoln delivered a brief address. On the twelfth Mr. Lincoln and his party proceeded on a special train. Mr. Lincoln showed himself on the platform and spoke a few words to the people at Shelbyville, Greensburg, Lawrenceburg and other places. A family group were assembled near the old home of President Harrison, to whom Mr. Lincoln bowed his respects as the train passed. This was the fifty-second anniversary of Mr. Lincoln's birth day.

At Cincinnati he was greeted by a throng of people estimated at one hundred thousand, and was conducted to a splendid carriage drawn by six white horses, and escorted to the Burnet House, arriving there at five o'clock, p. m. On the balcony of the Burnet House Mayor John M. Bishop delivered an address of welcome, which was responded to at some length by Mr. Lincoln. . He was afterwards waited

on by a delegation of two thousand Germans. A large
number of Kentuckians were among the assembled
multitude.

On the morning of the thirteenth, at nine o'clock,
the Presidential party started from the Little Miami
depot. At all the stations from Cincinnati to Columbus large crowds were collected with banners, bands
of music and artillery, but stoppages were made at
but few places. A brief stay was made each at Milford, Loveland, Morrow, Xenia and London. At
Xenia an immense multitude awaited the arrival of
the train, and after a few words from the President a
scramble was made to take him by the hand, but,
much as he desired to gratify them, he felt compelled
to retreat into the car. At London the demonstration
was fully equal to that at Xenia; the whole population
was out. About three o'clock, p. m., the President
elect was received at the capital of Ohio by about
twenty thousand people amid the firing of thirty-four
guns, corresponding to the number of States of which
the Union was then composed. A correspondent on
the train says the population seemed to be doubled
and all in the streets.

Mr. Lincoln was escorted to the State House and
introduced by Governor Dennison to the two legislative bodies assembled in the hall of the House of
Representatives. He was then conducted to the
western steps of the Capital, where he spoke a few
words to the vast multitude, after which he was conducted to the mansion of Governor Dennison. In
the evening he held a reception at the Capital, where
a general hand-shaking was indulged in for a short
time.

The electorial vote was counted at Washington
that day, and the result made known to Mr. Lincoln
by special telegram that afternoon.

On Thursday morning the fourteenth, notwithstanding the heavy rain, a large number of people

were at the depot to witness the departure of the train at eight o'clock. Large crowds of people were standing in the rain at Newark, Frazeysburg, Dresden, Coshocton, Newcomerstown and many other stations to catch a passing view of their chosen ruler. At Cadiz Junction a sumptuous dinner was in waiting and was eargerly relished by all. At Steubenville about five thousand people were in waiting, to whom Mr. Lincoln delivered a brief address.

It was night when the party arrived at Alleganey City, and passed over into Pittsburg. The continued falling rain interfered with the demonstration it was intended to make. At the Monongahela House Mr. Lincoln addressed a large concourse of people from the balcony that evening and again the next morning. The speaking was done to gratify the intense desire of the people to see and hear him. Personally Mr. Lincoln would have preferred to say nothing until he spoke to the people in his inaugural address.

Friday morning, the fifteenth, rain was still pouring down when the train left Pittsburg, but there was a dense mass of human beings extending several blocks on every side of the depot, who cheered the departing guests with enthusiasm.

As on the previous days, crowds were collected at every station. They were very large and imposing at Rochester, Beaver, Industry, Liverpool, Wellsville, Yellow Creek, Irondale, Franklin, Hanover, Bayard, and nearly all the intervening stations on the line. At many of these the train did not stop, and tired as the President was, he bowed his respects to them from the platform of the cars.

At Alliance another sumptuous dinner was in waiting. As the train moved up a salute was fired, a band played national airs and a company of Zuaves stood guard while the party dined. The train stopped at Ravenna, Hudson, Newburg and other stations where large crowds were assembled, arriving at Cleveland, amid the roar of artillery, at twenty minutes past four o'clock, p. m. Military and fire companies were out, and made a fine display. The President was conducted to a splendid carriage drawn by four white horses, and escorted through snow and mud to the Weddell House, where a speech of welcome was made by the Mayor and responded to by Mr. Lincoln. Boquets and floral wreaths were showered upon him, and hand-shaking followed, until the President elect could endure it no longer, and he was permitted to retire.

Saturday morning, February sixteenth, was bright and beautiful. At nine o'clock the Presidential party left Cleveland, Mr. Lincoln bowing his farewell from the platform of the rear car to the immense multitude of people. Crowds were collected at about forty stations on the line to Buffalo. Stoppages were made at Painesville, Geneva, Ashtabula, Girard, Erie, Westfield, Dunkirk, Silver Creek and a few other points. At Geneva one of the crowd addressed Mr. Lincoln, exhorting him to stand by the constitution and liberty, and assuring him that he would have the support of the people. After dinner at Erie the President spoke a few words to the immense crowd assembled to see him. At Dunkirk, while addressing the citizens, Mr. Lincoln grasped the staff of the American flag and expressed his intention to uphold it, and asked the people to stand by him. The hearty response assured him that he could rely on them for support. On arriving at Buffalo there were twenty thousand people anxiously awaiting to do honor to their chosen Chief Magistrate. A deputation of citizens with Ex-President Fillmore at their head, between whom and Mr. Lincoln a hearty greeting took place, a military company and the police escorted the party to the American Hotel, but the crowd was so dense that Major Hunter, of the U. S. A., had his shoulder dislocated. The buildings along the line of march were nearly all decked with flags. At the hotel Mayor Bemis made a welcoming speech, to which Mr. Lincoln replied, apologizing for not speaking at greater length, and promising to do better when he should arrive at the capital of the nation. A single quotation will illustrate the spirit he manifested in all his speeches. He said: "I am unwilling, on any occasion, that I should be so meanly thought of as to have it supposed for a moment that these demonstrations are tendered to me personally; they should be tendered to no individual, but to the inhabitants of the country and to the perpetuation of the liberties of the country. Your worthy Mayor has thought fit to express the hope that I may be able to relieve the country from the present, or I should say the threatened difficulties. I am sure I bring a heart true to the work. For the ability to perform it I must trust—through the instrumentality of this great and intelligent people—in that Supreme Being who has never forsaken this favored land. Without that assistance I shall surely fail; with it I cannot!"

The rooms of the Young Men's Christian Association were opposite the American Hotel. From these were displayed a large banner bearing the inscription, "We will pray for you."

The Presidential party spent the Sabbath in Buffalo, and on Monday morning, February 18th, were escorted to the depot by a company of the 74th N. Y. militia. The train departed a quarter before six o'clock, amid the cheers of a large concourse of people.

From Buffalo to Albany there are nearly a hundred stations, where crowds were assembled to catch a passing view of the nation's chosen ruler, but we can only give room to a small number of them at which stoppages were made.

At Batavia the train stopped but a few moments, and Mr. Lincoln bowed his acknowledgments to the hearty greeting of the large crowds assembled at the depot.

The train arrived at Rochester at eight o'clock to find a large number of people anxious to see the President elect.   The few minutes stay were occupied by a brief speech of welcome by Mayor Scranton and an equally brief reply by Mr. Lincoln.

At Clyde a large crowd greeted the Presidential party with enthusiastic cheers.

At Syracuse ten thousand people greeted the President elect with cheers.   A platform had been erected and a live eagle placed upon it.   Mr. Lincoln declined to mount the platform for want of time, but spoke a few words of apology.

At Utica thousands of people were standing in a snow storm, and, as the train come up, cheered the President elect, accompanied with the firing of a salute. Here Mr. Lincoln was induced to ascend a platform, where he was introduced by the Mayor. He excused himself from speaking, saying that he simply appeared to thank them for the reception—to see them and give them an opportunity to see him— and humorously expressing the opinion that so far as the ladies were concerned he had the best of the sight.

At Little Falls, as the train stopped, the church bells rang out merry peals, and the crowd clamored for a speech, but had to content themselves by Mr. Lincoln bowing his acknowledgments.

At Fonda, Amsterdam and Schenectady the people seemed to have turned out *en masse* to welcome the President elect.

At twenty minutes past two o'clock, p. m., the train reached Albany, amid the firing of cannon and the cheers of an immense multitude of people.   The President elect was received by Mayor Thatcher in a neat welcoming speech.   Mr. Lincoln replied, excus-- ing himself from extended remarks, as he expected to appear before the Legislative bodies.   The Presidential party were then taken in carriages and, escorted by the military, were driven to the State Capital, where Mr. Lincoln was taken to the Executive Chamber and introduced to Governor Morgan. The two then proceeded to the front of the Capital to find the Park filled with an immense multitude, even loading the trees and covering every available standing place, all anxious to see the President elect and hear him speak. Governor Morgan made a brief welcoming speech, to which Mr. Lincoln replied. The crowd was so vast that he could not be heard and only bowed his response to their enthusiastic welcome. Mr. Lincoln was conducted from here into the Assembly Chamber, where he was introduced to the two Houses of the Legislature of New York, assembled together to welcome him. Mr. Lincoln replied in a brief speech, acknowledging the courtesies received, but declining to go into a detailed statement of the policy he should pursue, preferring to do that in his inaugural address. At the close of these ceremonies the General Assembly took a recess for the exchange of friendly greetings, after which the distinguished guest was conducted to his carriage and escorted to the Delavan House.

When Mr. Lincoln entered the city and was escorted along Broadway, he was greeted by a large canvass extended across the street bearing the inscription, " Welcome to the Capital of the Empire State. No more compromises."

The Presidential party left Albany Tuesday morning, the 19th, at eight o'clock. The train ran up the west side of the Hudson river, crossing at Troy, where a raised platform had been prepared to afford the vast crowd an opportunity to see the President elect. On ascending the platform Mr. Lincoln was welcomed by Mayor McConike, who said : " Mr. Lincoln I have the honor to welcome you on behalf of the citizens of Troy, not as a politician, not as a partisan, but as the chosen Chief Magistrate of thirty millions of people, and to assure you of our respect for you as a

citizen, and for the high office you are so soon to fill."
Mr. Lincoln replied in brief but appropriate terms.
At least fifteen thousand persons were assembled at
the depot.

The stations on the Hudson river railroad each had
their crowds of people anxious to see, if it was but a
passing view of the President elect on his way down
to the commercial metropolis of the nation. Few
stoppages were made, but at Poughkeepsie it halted
long enough for the Mayor of that city to make a
formal address of welcome, which was happily responded to by Mr. Lincoln.

The train reached the city of New York about ten
o'clock. The reception was grand and imposing.
Places of business were closed and flags displayed along
the line of the procession. The family of the President was driven in carriages directly to the Astor
House, but Mr. Lincoln was escorted to the City Hall,
where he was received by an address of welcome from
Mayor Wood, which was responded to in fitting terms
by Mr. Lincoln, both expressing the warmest patriotic
sentiments. After the speeches a general hand-shaking ensued, amid the crashing of hats and tearing of
broadcloth. The millionaire and the bummers and
roughs, who have rendered New York so famous,
were mingled in delightful confusion. The bare
thought of shaking hands with all who came was a
terror to Mr. Lincoln, and about one o'clock he made
his way to the balcony and spoke a few words to the
people. He told them that he came to see them and
to put himself where they could see him, but gave
it as his opinion that, so far as sight seeing was concerned, he had the best of the show. It was estimated
that a quarter of a million of people were in the
streets trying to obtain a passing view of the chosen
ruler of the nation. By unusual efforts on the part
of the police, Mr. Lincoln was escorted to the Astor
House.

The Presidential party left New York on the morning of the twentieth, at eight o'clock, crossing the Hudson river and taking the cars at Jersey City. An immense concourse of people were in waiting at the depot to catch a passing view of Mr. Lincoln. The train reached Newark at half past nine in a snow storm. Mayor Bigelow welcomed Mr. Lincoln in a brief address, who made an equally brief reply. The party were then taken from the cars at the Morris and Essex depot and escorted by a party of about one hundred on horseback to the Chesnut street depot. They passed along Broad street, which was lined with patriotic devices. As the train moved off Mr. Lincoln bowed his thanks to the vast throng for their reception.

At twelve o'clock, noon, the train reached Trenton, amid the cheers of a vast multitude of people. An address of welcome to the chosen Chief Magistrate was extended by Mayor Mills, who introduced him to the members of the city government. The party was then taken in carriages and escorted to the State House by a body of one hundred horsemen. At the Capital Mr. Lincoln was received in a welcoming speech by the President of the Senate. In his reply Mr. Lincoln made a happy allusion to some incidents of the historic struggle for Independence, of which Trenton was the scene of action. He was then conducted to the House of Representatives and was welcomed by its Speaker. In Mr. Lincoln's reply his patriotic utterances with reference to the threatened troubles elicited rounds of applause. He was then escorted to the Trenton House, where he spoke briefly to the crowd outside, estimated at twenty thousand persons. After partaking of a collation the train moved across the Deleware river and proceeded to Philadelphia in charge of a committee from that city. At four o'clock, p. m., February 20th, the train arrived at the Kensington depot, Philadelphia. The

4

Presidential party were escorted in carriages to the Continential Hotel. One hundred thousand persons were in the procession or lined the streets along which the party passed. The Mayor of the city delivered an address of welcome on the balcony of the hotel, to which Mr. Lincoln replied, declining, however, to go into any exposition of his policy, and barely hinting at the possibility that he might never be inducted into office. He said: " It were useless for me to speak of details or plans now ; I shall speak officially next Monday week, *if ever*. If I were not to speak then, it were useless for me to speak now."

CHAPTER IV.

On the day Mr. Lincoln left Springfield, obstructions were placed on the railroad track at a point in the road near the line between the States of Illinois and Indiana, but it was discovered in time to avert the danger. At Cincinnati a deadly missle was found concealed in one of the cars of the train on which he traveled, but was removed before any damage was done. From these circumstances he knew that his life was in danger at every step, but the first allusion to it was in reply to the Mayor of Philadelphia, and that was hinted at so obscurely that it would not have been noticed were it not for subsequent events. It had been whispered, before Mr. Lincoln left home that he would never be permitted to pass through Baltimore alive, and without his knowledge an experienced detective was employed to ferret out the conspiracy. He employed both men and women to assist him. He found out beyond a doubt that a plot was formed for a party of conspirators to crowd around him in the guise of friends, and at a given signal Mr. Lincoln was to be shot or stabbed. A vessel was to be kept in waiting upon which the assassins were to make their escape.

The detective and Mr. Lincoln arrived in Philadelphia nearly at the same time. Some of the President's personal friends were advised of the information he had secured. An interview was at once held between Mr. Lincoln and the detective, in the room of the latter at the Continental Hotel. This was on the 21st. It had been arranged that Mr. Lincoln was to raise the American flag on Independence Hall the following morning, it being the anniversary of Washington's birthday. He had also accepted an invitation to a reception by the Pennsylvania Legislature in the afternoon of the same day. Mr. Lincoln said, "Both of these engagements I will keep, if it costs me my life." Beyond that he left the arrangements for his safe conduct to Washington, to the detective and his friends.

Gen. Scott and Senator Seward, both of whom were in Washington, had learned from separate sources that Mr. Lincoln was in danger of being slain. The two concurred in sending Mr. Frederick W. Seward to Philadelphia to inform him of his danger. Mr. F. W. Seward arrived late on the night of the 21st, after Mr. Lincoln had retired. Being first satisfied that the messenger was indeed the son of Mr. Seward, he admitted him to an interview. Mr. Lincoln was informed of the plan already arranged by the detective for the President to proceed in advance of his family and party so as to pass through Baltimore in the night and arrive at Washington early Saturday morning. On Mr. Seward's return to Washington it was arranged that Mr. Washburn, of Illinois, should meet Mr. Lincoln at the depot on his arrival.

The details of his passage through Baltimore being settled, the next Morning Mr. Lincoln visited Independence Hall, and was formally welcomed to the city. In response he delivered a brief address, in which he discussed the principles embodied in the Declaration of Independence, which had been prepared and promulgated from that Hall. He then said: "Now, my friends, can this country be saved upon this basis? If it can, I will consider myself one of the happiest men in the world, if I can help to save it. If it can not be saved upon that principle, it will be truly awful. But if this country cannot be saved without giving up that principle, I was about to say I would rather be assassinated on this spot than surrender it."

At the close of the speech, he was conducted to a platform outside, and publicly invited to raise the new flag. In responding to the invitation, he addressed a few words to the people, and then ran the flag to the top of the staff, amid the cheers of a vast concourse of people.

These ceremonies being concluded, Mr. Lincoln and his party left the city for Harrisburg, the capital of the State. where he visited both branches of the Pennsylvania Legislature, in response to the address of welcome. he recounted the scenes and incidents of the morning, coupled with the fact that it was the anniversary of the birth of Washington.

Mr. Lincoln was wearied with the fatigue connected with the exercises of the day, and was permitted to retire to his appartments at the Jones House. It was understood by the public that he was to start for Washington the next morning. He remained in his rooms until nearly six o'clock, when he went into the street unobserved, and, with Colonel Lamon, was driven to a special train on the Pennsylvania Central railroad. To prevent the intelligence of his departure from being communicated, if it should be discovered, the telegraph wires were all cut the moment the train left Harrisburg. This train ran back to Philadelphia, arriving at half past ten o'clock. The detective had a carriage in waiting, in which the party were driven to the depot of the Philadelphia, Wilmington and Baltimore railroad. They arrived at the depot at a quarter past eleven o'clock, and found the regular train which should have left at eleven, delayed. The party took berths in the sleeping car, and without change passed directly through Baltimore, arriving in Washington at half past six o'clock on the morning of Saturday, February 23d, and found Mr. Washburn anxiously awaiting him. He was taken into a carriage, and in a few minutes was talking over his adventures with Senator Seward, at Willard's Hotel.

Mr. Lincoln's family left Harrisburg on the train that had been intended for him, and as his arrival in Washington had been telegraphed all over the country, they went through Baltimore without meeting with any disturbance. The number of conspirators was about twenty, all of whose names were known. The plot was a bold one, but the ingenuity of the detective was too much for them. His life was not thought to be safe in Washington, and he was sent away in a day or two. The story that Mr. Lincoln wore the disguise of a "long military cloak and a Scotch cap," was a falsehood, written by a man who knew nothing of the event, and hated Mr. Lincoln, who did not adopt any disguise. The enemies of Mr. Lincoln ridiculed his fears, and his friends were ashamed, and even vexed, that the chosen chief of the nation should consent to sneak into his capital. It was a shameful thing that he should be obliged to do so, but the responsibility was on the other side. None doubt now that if false pride had prevented his acting upon the advise of his friends, the tragedy would have been enacted at the beginning which proved to be the denoument of the rebellion, and the nation and the world would have been deprived of the four years' faithful services of Abraham Lincoln, which terminated in the emancipation of a race, and establishing upon a basis of justice the most powerful nation upon the earth—powerful because it is just.

The ten or eleven days from the time Mr. Lincoln entered Washington, to the day of his inauguration, were full of nervous anxiety to the loyal people of the nation. It would not have been a surprise to them if the papers on any morning had announced his assassination. He knew himself to be surrounded by at least five enemies to one friend, but he went forward quietly and calmly, preparing for the duties before him, supported by the firm conviction that he was a chosen agent in the hands of God, and that He would give him all the support necessary to the accomplishment of His purposes.

The morning of March 4, 1861, opened beautiful and clear. Gen. Scott and the Washington police were in readiness for the day. The friends of Mr. Lincoln had gathered from all parts of the loyal north, determined that he should be inaugurated. In the hearts of all was great anxiety, but outwardly all looked as usual on such occasions, with the exception of an extraordinary display of soldiers. The stars and stripes floated from every flag-staff, the public buildings, schools, and many of the places of business were closed during the day.

At five minutes before twelve o'clock, Vice President Breckenridge and Senator Foote escorted Mr. Hamlin, the Vice President elect, into the Senate Chamber, and gave him a seat at the left of the chair. At twelve Mr. Breckenridge announced the Senate adjourned, and then conducted Mr. Hamlin to the seat he had vacated. The foreign diplomats, of which there was a very large and brilliant representation, then entered the chamber and took the seats assigned them. At a quarter before one o'clock the Judges of the Supreme Court entered, with the aged Chief Justice Taney at their head. At a quarter past one o'clock an unusual stir announced the coming of the President elect, accompanied by the outgoing President. They proceeded to the temporary platform erected for the occasion, on Pennsylvania Avenue, at the east front of the capitol, accompanied by the Marshal of the District of Columbia, Judges of the Supreme Court Sergeant-at-Arms and others holding official positions, which required them to be present on such occasions. On arriving at the platform, Senator E. D. Baker, of Oregon, who had been a long and intimate friend and neighbor of Mr. Lincoln, introduced him to the assembly. Mr. Lincoln then stepped forward and read his inaugural address. He was listened

to with profound attention, and by none more carefully that President Buchanan and Chief Justice Taney,
The latter gentleman, with much agitation, administered the oath of office to Mr. Lincoln, when his address was concluded.

It deserves to be particularly mentioned that Stephen A. Douglas, without a particle of jealousy apparent, and knowing the danger to which he was exposed in the event of an attempt on the life of the
President, stood patriotically by his side, and as he
removed his hat before commencing to read, and finding no place to put it in consequence of the proximity
of the crowd, Mr. Douglas politely extended his hand,
took the hat and held it until the close of the address.
And after Mr. Lincoln had taken the oath, Mr. Douglas was the first to grasp his hand and extend his congratulations.

The Inaugural Address was a plain, straightforward
talk with the people of the nation. The President
exhorted them to stand by the constitution and the
laws, and declared that he took the oath to do so,
without mental reservation. To those threatening the
destruction of the government, he said, in closing:

"If it were admitted that you who are dissatisfied, hold the
right side in this dispute, there is still no single reason for pre-
cipitate action. Intelligence, patriotism, Christianity, and a firm
reliance on Him who has never yet forsaken this favored land,
are still competent to adjust, in the best way, all our present difficulties.

"In your hands, my dissatisfied fellow countrymen, and not in
mine, is the momentous issue of civil war. The government
will not assail you. You can have no conflict without being
yourselves the aggressors. You have no oath registered in Heaven to destroy the government, while I shall have the most solemn one to preserve, protect and defend it.

"I am loth to close. We are not enemies, but friends
We must not be enemies. Though passion may have
strained, it must not break our bonds of affection. The

mystic chords of memory, stretching from every battle-field and patriot grave, to every living heart and hearthstone, all over this broad land, will yet swell the chorus of the Union, when again touched, as surely they will be, by the better angels of our nature."

In this tender strain did he plead with them as a fond father with his wayward offspring, but it was all in vain. In entering upon the duties of his office, President Lincoln found the treasury empty, the credit of the government impaired by the uncertainty of the future, and its navy scattered, leaving less than a dozen ships in servicable condition to guard our costs. The principal part of the small arms and cannon belonging to the government were in the hands of the authorities of the States which had already seceded. Forts, arsenals, mints and vessels were seized by the insurrectionists. The troops of our regular army who would not yield to the seductive influences of traitors, were deprived of their arms and sent home as paroled prisoners of war, by slow and devious routes. The garrison of Fort Sumter, in the harbor of Charleston, South Carolina, was drawing nigh to a point of starvation, and no supplies could be sent to it except by running the gauntlet of rebel batteries. The government, two months before the close of President Buchanan's term of office, made an attempt to send troops and provisions to Major Anderson, by the steamer Star of the West, a merchant vessel, but she was fired upon and compelled to return.

Notwithstanding the provisions in the fort were so near exhausted, the assailants could not wait its surrender for want of supplies, but acting as if they were thirsting for blood, Gen. Beauregard, under directions from the rebel Secretary of War, demanded the surrender of the fort on the twelfth day of April, 1861. Major Anderson declined to surrender. He was then called upon to say when he would evacuate the fort.

He replied that, should he not receive controlling instructions or additional supplies, he would evacuate on the fifteenth of the month. He was then notified that in one hour from the date of the message, which was "April 12, 1864, 3:30 A. M.," the confederate batteries, which he had seen erected without authority to interfere with them, would open on Fort Sumter. At half past four the batteries did open, and after a siege of thirty-three hours, the garrison surrendered on the 14th of April.

Major Robert Anderson, and about seventy men, marched out with their side arms and colors. War was thus forced upon the nation. The overt act had been committed by the traitors, and there was no alternative but to accept the situation. On the following day, April 15th, President Lincoln issued a call for 75,000 volunteers, and an extra session of Congress to assemble at Washington on the Fourth of July.

The north needed just the shock it had received. The fall of Sumter was the resurrection of patriotism. The call for men was responded to cordially and promptly from all the northern States, but the five border States hung back. Virginia soon went over to the Secessionists, and the Governor of Missouri attempted to take that State over and was foiled by the great number of Union-loving Germans within its borders. Governor Jackson then fled to the rebels alone, and died among them. Maryland, Delaware and Kentucky halted long between loyalty and treason, trying to find neutral ground, but finally espoused the Union cause. None of the five border States gave any assistance on the first call. Some of them answered with insolent threats and defiance.

On the 19th of April, 1861, being the 86th anniversary of the battle of Lexington, Massachusetts, which was the beginning of the American Revolution, the first blood of the war was shed in the streets of

the city of Baltimore, Maryland.   The Sixth Regiment of Massachusetts and the Seventh Regiment of
Pennsylvania volunteers were passing through Baltimore, on their way to Washington, and they were at-
tacked by a mob in the streets, with stones, brickbats and
other missles, from which several were wounded. Shots
were fired by the mob and four soldiers were killed :
two of the Massachusetts regiment, Ladd and Whit-
ney, from Lowell, and two of the Pennsylvanians,
Needham and Taylor.   After the killing of their own
men, the soldiers fired upon the mob, killing eleven
and wounding many more.   Communications were cut
off through Baltimore until the 10th of May, when
Gen. B. F. Butler took possession with a strong force.

After actual hostilities commenced, President Lincoln still cherished the hope that the conflict would be
of short duration, but the battle of Bull Run, on the
21st of July, in which the Union forces were defeated,
dispelled all hope of an early settlement of the national troubles.   The cares of the President were now
almost crushing   The raising and maintaining of great
armies, settling the difficulties with England arising
from the arrest of Mason and Slidell on the British
steamer Trent, by Captain Wilkes, of the U. S. frigate
San Jacinto, adjusting the serious and delicate questions connected with slavery, which were constantly
presenting themselves, under the movements of Generals, Hunter, Butler, Fremont, and other army commanders.

The beginning of 1862 was a time of gloom and
despondency for the Union cause.   As the year wore
away, the necessity, as a war measure, for the emancipation of the slaves, was constantly pressed by army
officers and others who were in advance of the mass
of the people.   Gen. McClellan, however, between
his calls for more men, more horses, more shoes, more
everything, when he had all that could be sent, found
time to protest against the emancipation of the slaves.

On the 7th of July, 1862, he wrote a long letter of advice to President Lincoln, in which he told him that he thought the war should not look to the subjugation of the people of any State, *in any event.* That there should be no confiscation, no forcible abolition of slavery.

In the middle of 1862, the events of the war having gone from bad to worse, Mr. Lincoln began to think that he must "change his tactics, or lose his game." Under these circumstances he prepared his original proclamation of emancipation, without consulting his cabinet or giving them any intimation of what he was doing. In the latter part of July, or early in August, he called a cabinet meeting, and all were present except Mr. Blair, who arrived in time for business, but none of them knew the object of the meeting. After all were ready for business, there was a delay. Mr. Lincoln was about to inaugurate the crowning act of his life, and he took his own way of doing it. The pressure upon his mind had wrought it up to a high key. He took from a shelf a copy of "Artemus Ward—His Book," and read an entire chapter of its drollery, laughing so heartily at its contents that some of his dignified advisers were more pained than amused. On closing the trifling volume, the whole manner of the President changed instantly, and rising to a grandeur of demeanor that inspired all with profound respect akin to awe, he announced to his cabinet the object of the meeting. He had written a Proclamation of Emancipation, and had determined to issue it; therefore, he had not called them together to ask their advice upon the main question, as he had determined that for himself. He wished to inform them of his purpose, and receive such suggestions upon minor points as they might be moved to make. Mr. Chase wished the language stronger with regard to arming the negroes; Mr. Blair thought it would cost the administration the fall elections, but he saw no occasion to make any change until Mr. Seward said: "Mr. President, I approve of the Proclamation, but I question the expediency of its issue at this juncture. The depression of the public mind, consequent upon our repeated reverses, is so great that I fear the effect of so important a step. It may be viewed as the last measure of an exhausted government; a cry for help; the government stretching forth its hands to Ethiopia, instead of Ethiopia stretching forth her hands to the government; our last shriek in the retreat." Mr. Seward thought it would be best to postpone it until it could be given to the country after a military success, rather than after the general disasters then prevalent.

Mr. Lincoln admitted the force of the objections, and permitted the matter to be suspended for a brief period. The retreat of the army of the Potomac, under General Pope, on Washington, and the invasion of Maryland soon followed, making the situation still more gloomy, and the proclamation waited, being occasionally taken out and retouched. At last the battle of Antietam came, with victory to the Union arms. The battle of Antietam was fought on Wednesday, the 17th of September, but it was not until Saturday that it was certainly known to be a victory, and it was too late to issue the proclamation that week, but Mr. Lincoln held a cabinet meeting that day, at which he declared that the time for promulgating the emancipation policy had arrived. Public sentiment, he thought, would sustain it; many of his warmest friends and supporters demanded it, and in a low and reverent tone he said: "I have promised my God that I will do it." Mr. Chase said, "Do I understand you correctly, Mr. President." Mr. Lincoln replied; "I made a solemn vow before God that if General Lee should be driven back from Pennsylvania, I would crown the result by the declaration of freedom to the slaves."

On Sunday Mr. Lincoln retouched it a little, and on Monday, September 22, 1862, the proclamation was issued, declaring that, at the end of one hundred days, or on the first day of January, 1863, he would issue another proclamation, declaring that, "All persons held as slaves within any State, or designated part of a State, the people whereof shall then be in rebellion against the United States, shall be thenceforward and forever free."

CHAPTER V.

There was not the slightest attention given to the proclamation, neither was it expected that there would be. The one hundred days expired on the first day of January, 1863, and on that day President Lincoln issued the proclamation of which he had given previous notice. In the proclamation the President pointed out the States and parts of States in which it should take effect. By that proclamation about three millions of slaves were made free. Simultaneous with its publication came the victory to the Union arms at Stone's River, and a general advance on the rebels east and west. From that time forward the Union forces were victorious in almost every engagement. As midsummer approached, the military operations in the west were chiefly concentrated on Vicksburg as the key to the navigation of the Mississippi river. The rebel forces in Virginia, under General Lee, commenced the invasion of Maryland and Pennsylvania in June. They were opposed by the army of the Potomac, under General Hooker. While the two armies were running a race across the State of Maryland, Gen. Hooker was relieved and Gen. Meade placed in command. The two armies came into collision at Gettysburg, Pennsylvania, on the first of July. The battle raged with teriffic fury for three days. On the night of the third it was evident that the rebels were defeated. President Lincoln announced the fact on the Fourth by a dispatch sent over the whole country under control of the government. He alluded to the fact that it was the aniversary of the Declaration

of Independence, and closed by the invocation, that :
" He whose will, not ours, should ever be done, be
everywhere remembered and renewed with profound-
est gratitude." This was only half the work for the
glorious day. On that day the entire rebel force at
Vicksburg, amounting to about thirty thousand men,
200 cannon, and 70,000 stand of small arms, under
Gen. Pemberton, surrendered to Gen. Grant. The recon-
secration of the Fourth of July to freedom was most
grand, and inspired the loyal people of the nation with
new courage to press forward to the task of crushing
the rebellion.

The State of Pennsylvania purchased a piece of land
adjoining the cemetery of the town, where much of
the fighting had been done, among broken monuments
and tombs, and over the graves of those who had died
and been buried in peaceful times, and set it apart as
a burying ground for the loyal soldiers who had there
yielded up their lives a willing sacrifice on the altar
of freedom. The ground was dedicated on the 19th
of November, 1863, by an oration from the Hon. Edward Everett, in the presence of Mr. Lincoln and his
cabinet, and a large concourse of people assembled to
take part in the exercises. After the oration by Mr.
Everett, the President delivered a brief address from
which I take an extract :

"Fourscore and seven years ago our fathers brought forth upon
this continent a new nation, conceived in liberty, and dedicated
to the proposition that all men are created equal. Now we are
engaged in a great civil war, testing whether that nation, or any
nation so conceived and so dedicated, can long endure. We are
met on a great battle-field of that war. We have come to dedicate a portion of that field as a final resting place for those who
here gave their lives that that nation might live. It is altogether
fitting and proper that we should do this. But in a larger sense
we cannot dedicate, we cannot consecrate, we cannot hallow this
ground. The brave men, living and dead, who struggled here,
have consecrated it far above our power to add or detract. The

world will little note, nor long remember, what we say here, but it can never forget what they did here. It is for us, the living, rather to be dedicated here to the unfinished work which they, who fought here, have thus far so nobly advanced. It is rather for us to be here dedicated to the great task remaining before us, that, from these honored dead, we take increased devotion to that cause for which they gave the last full measure of devotion; that we here highly resolve that these dead shall not have died in vain; that this nation, under God, shall have a new birth of freedom, and that the government of the people, by the people and for the people, shall not perish from the earth."

During the latter part of 1863, the success of the Union arms almost everywhere was so grand that the President issued one proclamation after another, calling on the people to assemble in their places of worship and offer up thanks to Almighty God. He called upon the people to honor and reverence God for the success at Gettysburg, himself publicly thanked Almighty God for the fall of Vicksburg, and on the fifteenth of July issued a proclamation setting apart the sixth of August to be observed as a day for national thanksgiving, praise and prayer, inviting the people to render the homage due to the Divine Majesty for the wonderful things he had done in the nation's behalf, and to invoke the influences of His Holy Spirit to subdue the anger which had produced and so long sustained a needless and cruel rebellion; to change the hearts of the insurgents; to guide the counsels of the government with wisdom adequate to so great a national emergency, and to visit with tender care and consolation, through the length and breadth of our land, all those who, through the vicissitudes of marches, voyages, battles and seiges, had been brought to suffer in mind, body or estate; and, finally, to lead the whole nation through paths of repentance and submission to the Divine Will, back to the perfect enjoyment of union and fraternal peace.

5

On the third of October he issued another proclamation of thanksgiving, setting apart the last Thursday of November as the day to be observed. This latter was more in the nature of an annual thanksgiving. But having heard of the retreat of the rebel forces from East Tennessee, he issued a dispatch on the seventh of December recommending all loyal people, on the receipt of the information, to assemble at their places of worship and render special homage and gratitude to Almighty God for this great advancement of the national cause.

The beginning of 1864 found the financial difficulties of the country most formidable, as the national currency had so far depreciated that it required $280 in currency to buy $100 in gold. Secretary Chase, of the Treasury department, resigned the position, and was followed by Mr. Fessenden, of Maine, as his successor. In May, General Grant commenced his campaign in Virginia, where each day's slaughter was almost equal to an army, and Sherman, at the same time, moved against the rebels, from Chattanooga, Tennessee, into Georgia. This was the commencement of his march of a thousand miles to the sea, making pauses only at Atlanta, reaching the sea at Savannah, thence north to Goldsboro he swept as with a besom of destruction through the rebel territory, and at last brought their forces to surrender after almost a year of continuous marching and fighting. After General Sherman left Atlanta, General Thomas skillfully planned his retreat on Nashville, and then hurled his troops against the rebel forces under Hood, at Franklin and Nashville, by which that part of the rebel army was almost annihilated.

During this whole year the Union forces were victorious on almost every battle-field. Notwithstanding the rebel armies were shattered and broken, they still hoped for a favorable turn to their cause by the defeat of Mr. Lincoln in the Presidential election then pending.

The Republican National Convention assembled in the city of Baltimore on the eighth of June, 1864, for the purpose of nominating candidates for President and Vice President of the United States. Mr. Lincoln was in the fourth year of his presidential term, during which time call after call and draft after draft had been made to keep up the strength of the army. He had found it necessary to remove hundreds of army officers high in command, he had given freedom to more than three million of slaves who were regarded as property when he entered the Presidential chair, and in all these transactions he had displeased a large number of influential citizens, which it was thought would make him many enemies. But when the Convention assembled, and after adopting a platform of principles, the next thing in order was to ballot for a Presidential candidate. On the first ballot every vote was given for Mr. Lincoln, except twenty-two from Missouri, which, under instructions, were given for General Grant. On motion of one of the Missouri delegates the nomination was made unanimous. Andrew Johnson of Tennessee was nominated for Vice President. Ex-Governor Dennison of Ohio was the President of the Convention, and he, accompanied by a committee, waited upon Mr. Lincoln, informed him of his nomination, and placed in his hands a copy of the platform which had been adopted. Mr. Lincoln replied:

"Having served four years in the depths of a great and yet unended national peril, I can view this call to a second term in nowise more flattering to myself than as an expression of the public judgment that I may better finish a difficult work in which I have labored from the first, than could any one less severely schooled to the task. In this view, and with assured reliance on that Almighty Ruler who has so graciously sustained us thus far, and with increased gratitude to the generous people for their continued confidence, I accept the renewed trust with its yet onerous and perplexing duties and responsibilities."

Gen. McClellan was the Democratic candidate for President, and George H. Pendleton for Vice President.

During the height of the canvass, President Lincoln, on the eighteenth of July, issued a call for five hundred thousand men, naming the number required from each State, and including a proviso that if the number was not voluntarily made up, drafting should commence on the fifth of September. His friends feared that it would cost him his election, and urged him to delay it. His uniform reply was that the men were needed, and that it was his duty to call for them, and that he should do it whatever the effect might be upon himself.

November came, and with it the day of election. When the electoral vote was counted, at the time fixed by law, it was found that, of 233 votes, Lincoln and Johnson had received 212 as candidates for President and Vice President of the United States. McClellan and Pendleton received the other 21 votes. The total popular vote cast was 4,015,902, and the majority in favor of Lincoln was 411,428. In a few words, courteously spoken to some of his friends who called upon him on the night of the election, he said: "I do not impugn the motives of any one opposed to me. It is no pleasure to me to triumph over any one; but I give thanks to the Almighty for this evidence of the people's resolution to stand by free government and the rights of humanity." On another occasion, soon after his election, he said: "It has demonstrated that a people's government can sustain a national election in the midst of a great civil war. Until now, it has not been known to the world that this was a possibility." This second election of President Lincoln destroyed the last hope of the rebellion. From that time their armies never gained a substantial victory.

The proclamation of President Lincoln, issued January 1, 1863, gave freedom to about three millions of human beings who, until that time, had been slaves; and declared that they might be enlisted in the military services of the United States. Much prejudice existed among Union men, and even with Union soldiers, against enrolling colored troops. Governor Andrew, of Massachusetts, made the initial move in the northern States. He received an order from the War Department, dated January 20, 1863, authorizing him to organize and equip regiments of colored men, to be called United States Colored Troops. As soon as this became known, colored men flocked to Massachusetts from many of the other States. The example of Massachusetts was followed by Rhode Island, Pennsylvania, New York, Ohio and Kansas. In March, the Government sent Adjutant General Thomas to the Southwest for the purpose of organizing colored troops. It was but a short time after enlistment commenced until they were in the field. By their bravery in battle, they, at the same time, assisted in subduing the rebels and conquering the prejudices of the white soldiers.

Regarding slavery as the sole cause of the war, I select the following quotations from the annual message of President Lincoln to Congress, December 8, 1863. Speaking of our foreign relations, he says: "The supplemental treaty between the United States and Great Britain for the suppression of the African slave trade, made on the 17th day of February last, has been duly notified and carried into execution. It is believed that, so far as American ports and American citizens are concerned, that inhuman and odious traffic has been brought to an end." Referring to the condition of the country at the time of their annual meeting a year before, and contrasting it with the present, he said:

"The preliminary emancipation proclamation, issued in September, was running its assigned period to the beginning of the new year. A month later the final proclamation came, including the announcement that colored men of suitable condition would be received into the war service. The policy of emancipation and of employing black soldiers, gave to the future a new aspect, about which hope, and fear, and doubt, contended in uncertain conflict. According to our political system, as a matter of civil administration, the General Government had no lawful power to effect emancipation in any State; and for a long time it had been hoped that the rebellion could be suppressed without resorting to it as a military measure. It was all the while deemed possible that the necessity for it might come, and that if it should, the crisis of the contest would then be presented. It came, and, as was anticipated, it was followed by dark and doubtful days. Eleven months having now passed, we are permitted to take another review. The rebel borders are pressed still further back, and by the complete opening of the Mississippi the country dominated by the rebellion is divided into distinct parts, with no practical communication between them. Tennessee and Arkansas have been substantially cleared of insurgent control, and influential citizens in each, owners of slaves and advocates of slavery at the beginning of the rebellion, now declare openly for emancipation in their respective States. Of those States not included in the emancipation proclamation— Maryland and Missouri—neither of which, three years ago, would have tolerated any restraint upon the extension of slavery into new Territories, only dispute now as to the best mode of removing it within their own limits. Of those who were slaves at the beginning of the rebellion, full one hundred thousand are now in the United States military service, about one half of which number actually bear arms in the ranks."

In the same message, speaking of the mode of reconstructing State governments where they had been overthrown, he advocated the policy of requiring a test oath to sustain the emancipation measures, in the following language :

"But if it be proper to require, as a test of admission to the political body, an oath of allegiance to the United States and to the Union under it, why not also to the laws and proclamations in regard to slavery? Those laws and proclamations were enacted and put forth for the purpose of aiding in the suppression of the rebellion. To give them their fullest effect, there had to be a pledge for their maintenance. In my judgment they have aided, and will further aid, the cause for which they were intended. To now abandon them would be, not only to relinquish a lever power, but would also be a cruel and an astounding breach of faith. I may add at this point that, while I remain in my present position, I shall not attempt to retract or modify the emancipation proclamation; nor shall I return to slavery any person who is free by the terms of that proclamation, or by any of the acts of Congress. For these and other reasons, it is thought best that support of these measures shall be included in the oath. * * * The movements by State action for emancipation in several of the States, not included in the emancipation proclamation, are matters of profound gratulation. And while I do not repeat in detail what I have so earnestly urged upon this subject, my general views and feelings remain unchanged, and I trust that Congress will omit no fair opportunity of aiding these important steps to a great consummation."

An act to repeal all fugitive slave laws passed both houses of Congress, and was approved by President Lincoln, June 28, 1864. During the summer and autumn of that year elections were held in nearly all the loyal States for members of the 39th Congress. and in November for the election of a President and Vice President of the United States, which resulted, as previously stated, in the second election of Abraham Lincoln.

CHAPTER VI.

At the assembling of the second session of the Thirty-eighth Congress, December 6, 1864, President Lincoln referred to the fact that at the previous session a joint resolution passed the Senate to submit an amendment to the constitution of the United States abolishing slavery throughout the Union, to the Legislatures of the several States, but it failed in the House of Representatives for want of a two-thirds majority. He reminded them of the advanced position of the American people on the subject of abolishing slavery; and urged them to reconsider the question, and submit it to the action of the State Legislatures. He assured them that it must come to that, and the sooner it was done the better. In closing that message he says:

"I retract nothing heretofore said as to slavery. I repeat the declaration made a year ago, that while I remain in my present position, I shall not attempt to retract or modify the emancipation proclamation, nor shall I return to slavery any person who is free by the terms of that proclamation, or by the acts of Congress. If the people should, by whatever mode or means, make it an executive duty to re-enslave such persons, another, and not I, must be their instrument to perform it.

"In stating a single condition of peace, I mean simply to say that the war will cease on the part of the Government whenever it shall have ceased on the part of those who began it."

Aside from the three million slaves liberated by the emancipation proclamation, there yet remained in bondage more than one million of the African race.

But a small number of these were held by men who were real friends to the Government in its efforts to crush out the great rebellion. Being in that part of the country bordering on the line between the original free and slave States, which territory was under the control of the civil authorities, and their owners nominally loyal, the Government did not feel authorized to declare them free as a war measure. The conviction, however, steadily gained in the minds of the people, that peace could never be firmly established until slavery was totally and forever abolished. Various plans were proposed and discussed for compensated emancipation, and in the meantime slave property was becoming less secure.

On the 11th of January, 1864, Mr. Henderson, of Missouri, introduced a joint resolution into the Senate, proposing amendments to the constitution of the United States, which was read and referred to the Judiciary Committee. On the 10th of February, the committee made a report through its chairman, the Hon. Lyman Trumbull. The joint resolution was amended by the committee so as to provide for submitting to the Legislatures of the several States a proposition to amend the constitution of the United States so that neither slavery nor involuntary servitude, except as a punishment for crime, shall exist in the United States, or any place subject to their jurisdiction; and also, that Congress shall have power to enforce this article by appropriate legislation. The report of this committee was taken up and discussed as many as thirteen times —some of them occupying whole days—until the 8th of April, when it was adopted, 38 to 8. Its title was amended so as to read—

A joint resolution submitting to the Legislatures of the several States a proposition to amend the Constitution of the United States :

Resolved, by the Senate and House of Representatives of the United States of America in Congress assembled—two thirds of both Houses concurring, That the following article be proposed to the Legislatures of the several States as an amendment to the constitution of the United States, which, when ratified by three-fourths of said Legislatures, shall be valid, to all intents and purposes, as a part of said constitution, namely:

ARTICLE XIII.

SECTION 1. Neither slavery nor involuntary servitude, except as a punishment of crime, whereof the party shall have been duly convicted, shall exist within the United States or any place subject to their jurisdiction.

SEC. 2. Congress shall have power to enforce this article with appropriate legislation.

After having passed the Senate, it was sent to the House, where it was defeated for want of a two-thirds majority. A motion to reconsider, entered by Mr. Ashley, of Ohio, was pending in the House when Congress adjourned. The elections of 1864 demonstrated, by largely increased Republican majorities, that the sentiments of the people were in favor of the entire abolition of slavery. Mr. Lincoln, in his last annual message, December, 1864, referred to the result of the elections as an indication of the popular will, and recommended that the subject be again taken up and passed.

On the 6th of January, 1865, Mr. Ashley called up his former motion to reconsider, and made an able speech in its favor.

The question was discussed at great length. Those speaking in the affirmative were Ashley, of Ohio; Orth, of Indiana; Kasson, of Iowa; Farnsworth, of Illinois; Jenckes, of Rhode Island; Woodbridge, of Vermont; Thayer, of Pennsylvania; Rollins, of Missouri; Garfield, of Ohio; Thaddeus Stevens, of Pennsylvania, and others. Those speaking in the opposition were Townsend, of New York; Holman, Cravens and Vorhees, of Indiana; Mallory, of Kentucky; Fernando Wood, of New York; Pendleton, of Ohio, and others.

Very many eloquent passages might be culled from the speeches delivered on that resolution, but I will only give a few brief quotations from the Hon. Mr. Rollins, of Missouri, and Thad. Stevens, of Pennsylvania. Mr. Rollins had been a slaveholder, until a few days before they were all liberated by an amendment to the State constitution of Missouri. He said:

"I am a believer in the Declaration of Independence, wherein it is asserted that 'all men are created equal.' I believe that when it says '*all men*,' it means every man who was created in the 'image of his Maker,' and walks on God's footstool, without regard to race, color or any accidental circumstance by which he may be surrounded.   *   *   *   *   *   *

"An anti-slavery man in sentiment, and yet heretofore a large owner of slaves myself—not now, however—not exactly with my consent. The convention which recently assembled in my State, I learned from a telegram a morning or two ago, had adopted an amendment to our present State constitution for the immediate emancipation of all the slaves in the State. *I am no longer the owner of a slave*, and I thank God for it. If the giving up of my slaves, without complaint, shall be a contribution upon my part to promote the public good, to uphold the constitution of the United States, to restore peace and preserve this Union, *if I had owned a thousand slaves, they would most cheerfully have been given up.* I say, with all my heart, let them go, but let them not go without a sense of feeling and a proper regard on my part for the future of themselves and their offspring!"   *   *   *

Mr. Rollins concluded by saying—

"Let ours be the 'bright particular star' next to the star that led the shepherds to Bethlehem, which shall lead the downtrodden and oppressed of all the world into an harbor of peace, security and happiness; and let us, kneeling around the altar, all thank God that, although we have had our trials, we have saved our country; that, although we have been guilty of sins, we have wiped them out, and that we at length stand up a great and powerful people, honored by all the earth, 'redeemed, regenerated and disenthralled by the genius of universal emancipation."

The venerable leader of the House arose to close the debate on this great measure, and the members gathered around him, filling the seats and aisles and every available spot near the "old man eloquent." Inteligence was sent to the Senate that Thad. Stevens was speaking on the constitutional amendment. Many of the Senators came in and the Judges of the Supreme Court to hear him speak on a measure that was to crown the labors of forty years with complete success. As soon as the vast audience could get into their places, all were hushed into silence.

Mr. Stevens commenced by narrating the progress of the anti-slavery cause from its feeble beginning. I can only find room for a few extracts from a speech which attracted the closest attention from the first to the last sentence. He said—

"From my earliest youth I was taught to read the Declaration of Independence, and to receive its sublime principles. As I advanced in life, and became somewhat enabled to consult the writings of the great men of antiquity, I found in all their works which have survived the ravages of time, and come down to the present generation, one unanimous denunciation of tyranny and of slavery, and eulogy of liberty.

*   *   *   *   *   *   *   *

"In immortal language all denounced slavery as a thing which took away half of the man and degraded human beings, and sang praise in the noblest strains to the goddess of liberty; and my hatred of this infernal institution, and my love for liberty, was further inflamed as I saw the inspired teachings of Socrates and the divine inspirations of Jesus.

"Being fixed in these principles immovably and immutably, I took my stand among my fellow-citizens, and on all occasions, whether in public or in private, in season, and if there could be such a time, out of season, I never hesitated to express those ideas and sentiments, and when I went first into public assemblies, forty years ago, I uttered this language. I have done it amid the pelting and hooting of mobs, but I never quailed before the infernal spirit, and I hope I never shrank from the responsibility of my language. * * * *

" When, fifteen years ago, I was honored with a seat in this body, it was dangerous to talk against this institution—a danger which gentlemen now here will never be able to appreciate. Some of us, however, have experienced it. * * * And yet, sir, I did not hesitate, in the midst of bowie-knives and revolvers, and howling demons upon the other side of the House, to stand here and denounce this infamous institution in language which possibly now, on looking at it, I might deem intemperate, but which I then deemed necessary to rouse the public attention and cast odium upon the worst institution on earth—one which is a disgrace to man and would be an annoyance to the infernal spirits.

In the course of the debate, the Hon. George H. Pendleton had made a pathetic appeal for the constitution as it was, with all its guarantees for slavery. Mr. Stevens referred to Mr. Pendleton's speech in his closing sentences, in the following language:

" Perhaps I ought not to occupy so much time, and I will only say one word further. So far as the appeals of the learned gentleman are concerned, his pathetic winding up, I will be willing to take my chance when all moulder into the dust. He may have his epitaph, if it be truly written, 'Here rests the ablest and most pertinacious defender of slavery and opponent of liberty;' and I will be satisfied if my epitaph shall be written thus: 'Here lies one who never rose to any eminence, and who only courted the low ambition to have it said that he had striven to ameliorate the condition of the poor, the lowly, the down-trodden of every race and language, and color.' I shall be content with such a eulogy on his lofty tomb, and such an inscription on my humble grave, to trust our memories to the judgment of other ages."

During the delivery of this speech, the circle set apart for the representatives of all the other governments of the world was crowded; the floor of the House was filled, and the galleries were packed with distinguished soldiers, civilians and citizens. The vote on the final passge of the joint resolution was to be taken at its close, and no one knew with certainty what would be the result. It was known that the Republicans alone could not pass it; there must be accessions from the Democratic side of the House, or the measure would 'fail. English, of Connecticut, was the first Democrat who responded *aye*, which drew fourth great applause from the House and galleries. There were enough accessions to foot up the vote, 119 ayes and 56 nays; when the Speaker made the formal announcement: "The constitutional majority of two-thirds having voted in the affirmative, the joint resolution is passed." This was followed by an uncontrolable outburst of enthusiasm. The cheering was commenced among the members and was taken up in the galleries. Finally, Mr. Ingersoll, of Illinois, who was the successor of Owen Lovejoy; in honor of the sublime event, moved that the House adjourn. The motion was carried, amid the roar of artillery, by which it was announced to the people of Washington that the joint resolution submitting to the State Legislatures for their action an amendment to the constitution for the total abolition of slavery in the United States had passed both Houses of Congress.

Personal friends of President Lincoln hastened to the White House and exchanged congratulations with him on the result. His heart was filled with joy, as he saw in this action of Congress the complete consummation of his own great work. He had seen his emancipation proclamation sustained by the victorious Union armies in the field, by the people at the Presidential election, and now the constitutional majority of two-thirds in both Houses of Congress had voted to submit to the people, through their Representatives in the State Legislatures, the constitutional amendment for the final abolition of slavery.

It is a settled principle in National legislation that the approval of the Executive is not necessary to give vital force to a joint resolution of the two Houses of Congress; but during the excitement attending the passage of the joint resolution submitting the amendment for the abolition of slavery, it was presented to and signed by President Lincoln. Although. done in a mistake, it seems to have been appropriate, as it was the last act it was possible for him to do. It then only remained for a majority of the State Legislatures to approve of the resolution, and for the Secretary of State for the United States to proclaim the fact and declare the article so submitted to be a part of the constitution of the United States.

Lest this action of President Lincoln should become a troublesome precedent, Senator Trumbull introduced a joint resolution in the Senate, reciting the facts in the case, and declaring that such approval was unnecessary to effect the action of Congress.

The joint resolution for the extinction of slavery passed Congress, and received the signature of the President, January 31, 1865. The Legislature of Illinois being then in session, took up the question at once, and in less than twenty-four hours after its passage by Congress, President Lincoln had the satisfaction of receiving a telegram from his old home, announcing the fact that the constitutional amendment had been ratified by both Houses of the Legislature of his own State, Feb. 1, 1865. Then came the action of the Legislatures of other States in the order named: Rhode Island and Michigan, Feb. 2; Maryland, Feb. 1 and 3; New York, Feb. 2 and 3; West Virginia, Feb. 3; Maine and Kansas, Feb. 7; Massachusetts and Pennsylvania, Feb. 8; Virginia, Feb.

9; Ohio and Missouri, Feb. 10; Nevada and Indiana, Feb. 16; Louisiana, Feb. 17; Minnesota, Feb. 8 and 23; Wisconsin, March 1; Vermont, March 9; Tennessee, April 5 and 7; Arkansas, April 20; Connecticut, May 5; New Hampshire July 1; South Carolina, Nov. 13; Alabama, Dec. 2; North Carolina, Dec. 4; Georgia, Dec. 9; Oregon, Dec. 11.

This made twenty-eight, one more than the requisite three-fourths of the thirty-six States. Having ratified the amendment, there was nothing wanting to make it a part of the constitution of the United States, except the official announcement, which came in the following:

"PROCLAMATION.

"WILLIAM H. SEWARD, Secretary of State of the United States; to all whom these presents may come—greeting:

"KNOW YE, THAT WHEREAS, The Congress of the United States, on the 1st of February last, passed a resolution, which is in the words following, namely:

"'A resolution submitting to the Legislatures of the several States a proposition to amend the constitution of the United States:

"'*Resolved by the Senate and House of Representatives of the United States of America in Congress assembled—two-thirds of both Houses concurring*, That the following article be proposed to the Legislatures of the several States as an amendment to the constitution of the United States, which, when ratified by three-fourths of said Legislatures, shall be valid, to all intents and purposes, as a part of said constitution, namely:

"'ARTICLE XIII.

"'SECTION 1. Neither slavery nor involuntary servitude, except as a punishment for crime, whereof the party shall have been duly convicted, shall exist within the United States or any place subject to their jurisdiction.

"'SEC. 2. Congress shall have power to enforce this article by appropriate legislation.'

"AND WHEREAS, It appears from official documents on file in this department that the amendment to the constitution of the United States proposed as aforesaid has been ratified by the Legislatures of the States of Illinois, Rhode Island, Michigan, Maryland, New York, West Virginia, Kansas, Massachusetts, Pennsylvania. Virginia, Ohio, Missouri, Nevada, Indiana, Louisiana, Minnesota, Wisconsin, Vermont, Tennessee, Arkansas, Connecticut, New Hampshire, South Carolina, Alabama, North Carolina and Georgia—in all, twenty-seven States;

"AND WHEREAS, The whole number of States in the United States is thirty-six;

"AND WHEREAS, The before specially named States, whose Legislatures have ratified the said proposed amendment, constitute three-fourths of the whole number of States in the United States;

"*Now, Therefore, be it Known*, That I, WILLIAM H. SEWARD, Secretary of State of the United States, by virtue and in pursuance of the second section of the act of Congress, approved the 20th of April, 1818, entitled 'An Act to provide for the publication of the laws of the United States, and for other purposes,' do hereby certify that the amendment aforesaid has become valid, to all intents and purposes, as a part of the constitution of the United States.

" IN TESTIMONY WHEREOF, I have hereunto set my hand and caused the seal of the Department of State to be affixed.

[SEAL.]

"Done at the city of Washington, the 18th day of December, in the year of our Lord, 1865, and of the Independence of the the United States of America the 90th.

" WM. H. SEWARD,
"Secretary of State."

Although no more States were required, the amendment was ratified by California, Dec. 20; Florida, Dec. 28, 1865 ; New Jersey, Jan. 23, 1866, and Iowa, Jan. 24, 1866.

6

CHAPTER VII.

The election for President and Vice-President having taken place in November 1864, both Houses of Congress assembled in the Hall of the House of Representatives, February 8th, 1865, for the purpose of opening and counting the votes. As previously stated in these pages, the whole number of electoral votes cast was two hundred and thirty-three. Of these Abraham Lincoln and Andrew Johnson, as candidates for President and Vice-President, received two hundred and twelve votes, and George B. McClellan and George H. Pendleton, as candidates for the same offices, received 21 votes. Lincoln and Johnson was, of course, declared to be elected.

On the 4th of March, 1865, Abraham Lincoln was inaugurated President of the United States for the second term, amid the acclamations of an immense throng of visitors from all parts of the United States. His inaugural address on that occasion is justly considered one of the most remarkable State papers ever written, and was the last public address he ever delivered. No extract from it could do it justice, and for that reason I give it entire:

"FELLOW COUNTRYMEN: At this second appearing to take the oath of the Presidential office there is less occasion for an extended address than there was at the first. Then a statement somewhat in detail of a course to be pursued seemed fitting and proper. Now, at the expiration of four years, during which public declarations have been constantly called forth on every point and phase of the great contest which still absorbs the attention and engross the energies of the nation, little that is new could be presented. The progress of our arms, upon which all else chiefly depends, is as well known to the public as to myself, and it is, I trust reasonably satisfactory and encouraging to all. With high hope for the future, no prediction in regard to it is ventured.

"On the occasion corresponding to this, four years ago, all thoughts were anxiously directed to an impending civil war. All dreaded it; all sought to avert it. While the inaugural address was being delivered from this place, devoted altogether to saving the Union without war, insurgent agents were in the city seeking to destroy it without war—seeking to dissolve the Union and divide its effects by negotiation. Both parties deprecated war; but one of them would make war rather than let the nation survive, and the other would accept war rather than let it perish. And the war come.

"One eighth of the whole population were colored slaves, not distributed generally over the Union, but localized in the southern part of it. These slaves constituted a peculiar and powerful interest. All knew that this interest was, somehow, the cause of the war. To strengthen, perpetuate and extend this interest was the object for which the insurgents would rend the Union, even by war, while the Government claimed no right to do more than to restrict the territorial enlargement of it. Neither party expected for the war, the magnitude or duration which it has already obtained. Neither anticipated that the cause of the conflict might cease with, or even before, the conflict itself should cease. Each looked for an easier triumph, and a result less fundamental and astounding. Both read the same Bible, and pray to the same God, and each invokes His aid against the other. It may seem strange that any men should dare to ask a just God's assistance in wringing their bread from the sweat of other men's faces; but let us judge not, that we be not judged. The prayers of both could not be answered—those of neither have been answered fully. The Almighty has His own purposes. Woe unto the world because of offenses! for it must needs be that offenses come; but woe to that man by whom the offense cometh.

"If we shall suppose that American slavery is one of those offenses which, in the providence of God, must needs come, but which, having continued through His appointed time, He now wills to remove, and that He gives to North and South this terrible war, as the woe due to those by whom the offense came, shall we discern therein any departure from those Divine attributes which the believers in a living God always ascribe to Him? Fondly do we hope, fervently do we pray, that this mighty scourge of war may soon pass away. Yet, if God wills that it continue until all the wealth piled by the bondsman's two hundred and fifty years of unrequited toil shall be sunk, and until every drop of blood drawn by the lash shall be paid by another drawn with the sword, as was said three thousand years ago, so still it must be said: 'The judgments of the Lord are true and righteous altogether.'

" With malice toward none, with charity for all, with firmness in the right, as God gives us to see the right, let us strive on to finish the work we are in; to bind up the nation's wounds; to care for him who shall have borne the battle, and for his widow and for his orphan—to do all which may achieve and cherish a just and lasting peace among ourselves, and with all nations."

The closing scenes of the war were being enacted in quick succession. The rebel Congress, driven to desperation, enacted a law which was approved by their President, Jeff. Davis, March 15th, 1865, giving freedom to the slaves on condition of their entering the military service of the confederacy. Orders were at once issued from the rebel War Department for the drilling to commence, but it was too late. All their schemes failed, and the only good accomplished by it was to exhibit to the world the complete failure of the effort to establish a government, the chief cornerstone of which should be human slavery. The conspiracy was in its death throes. Gen. Grant "moved upon the rebel works" at Petersburg and carried them; the rebels retreating towards Richmond, which in turn they evacuated, and on the third day of April a corps of U. S. Colored Soldiers, under General Weitzel, took possession of the city which had been for four long years the capital of the rebel government.

On the fourth day of April, just one month after
the second inauguration of President Lincoln, his
feet trod the pavements of the rebel capital, and he
held a levee in the mansion just evacuated by the
rebel President, who was then a fugitive, with $100,-
000 offered as a reward for his arrest.

On the ninth of April the whole rebel army, under General Lee, styled the army of Northern Virginia, and now reduced to about twenty-five thousand
men, surrendered to General Grant at Appomattox
Court House. The news flashed on the wires to all
parts of the loyal States. Victory! Victory!! Peace!
Peace!! were the exclamations from the lips of all,
and the wildest demonstrations of delight were spon-
taneously indulged in by the loyal millions in every
part of the land. The surrender of the rebel General Johnston, with all his forces was only a question
of a few days' time.

The tremendous burden of responsibility which for
four long, weary years rested upon the shoulders of
President Lincoln, was now about to be removed,
and he was looking forward in joyous anticipation to
the day when the clangor of arms should cease, and
with the smoke of battle cleared away, he should enter upon the pacific work of restoring the nation from
the ravages of war to its proper condition in time
of peace.

As a fitting initial to the work of restoration, the
President instituted measures to have the old flag,
which had been lowered at Fort Sumter in the presence of the parricidal sons of the nation, on the fourteenth of April, 1861, elevated to its place on the
fourth anniversary of that event. Orders were issued
by the Secretary of War to Capt. Gadsden to have the
fine ocean steamer, Arago, in readiness to convey a
select party to that historic spot, the mass of ruins
that was once called Fort Sumter.

Of the party who sailed on the Arago, to the number of two or three hundred, it is necessary to men-

tion the names of a few who were assigned to special
duties on that occasion. There was General Robert
Anderson, the hero of the expedition. and the Rev.
Henry Hard Beecher, who had been selected to deliver the oration. Then there was William Lloyd
Garrison, of our own country, and George Thompson,
of England, "life-long co-workers for the abolition
of slavery, each the champion of a great nation."
There was also General, now Governor, Dix, of New
York; Hon Joseph Holt, of Kentucky; Senator Wilson, of Massachusetts; Justice Swayne, of the Supreme
Court of the United States, and a host of others, including Lieutenant Governor Charles Anderson, a
brother to the General, and who soon after became
Governor of the State of Ohio, in consequence of the
death of Governor Brough.

Besides the Arago there were other vessels chartered
for the occasion, each bearing some of the distinguished personages of the land, so that the entire
party numbered about five thousand. A correspondent of the New York Independent, describing the
approach to the battered walls of Fort Sumter, says:
"There was but one strain worthy of the moment; it
was neither the Star Spangled Banner nor our own
grand America. We all broke forth into—

'"Praise God, from whom all blessings flow. "

The vessels had been so well timed that the party
landed about noon on the day they were celebrating,
April 14th. A prayer was offered by the Rev. Mat-
thias Harris—who was Chaplain at the Fort four
years before—and a portion of Scripture read, followed
by the reading of the dispatch sent by Major Anderson to the Government, announcing the evacuation
of Fort Sumter on the 14th of April, 1861. The
Major, now General, Anderson, and Sergeant Hart
then stepped forward and hoisted the well preserved

flag, amid unbounded euthusiasm, and salutes were fired
from the batteries and fleet. Sergeant Hart was the
same man who, when the staff of this flag had been
shot off four years before, rescued and restored it to
its place upon the fortifications. As soon as the flag
was thrown to the breeze, Gen. Anderson delivered
the following brief speech:

"*My Friends and Fellow Citizens, and Brother Soldiers:* By
the considerate appointment of the Hon. Secretary of War, I am
here to fulfill the cherished wish of my heart through four long
years of bloody war; to restore to its proper place this dear flag,
which floated here during peace, before the first act of cruel rebellion. I thank God that I have lived to see this day, and to be
here to perform this duty to my country. My heart is filled with
gratitude to that God who has so signally blessed us; who has
given us blessings beyond measure. May all the world proclaim,
'Glory to God in the highest, on earth peace; good will toward
men.'"

Rev. Henry Ward Beecher then delivered a most
thrilling and eloquent oration of about two hours
duration. A synopsis of that oration can not be
given here, but I must satisfy myself with one or two
quotations:

"When God would prepare Moses for emancipation, He over-
threw his first steps, and drove him for forty years to brood in
the wilderness. When our flag came down, four years it lay
brooding in darkness. It cried to the Lord, 'Wherefore am I
deposed?' Then arose before it a vision of sin. It had strengthened the strong and forgotten the weak. It proclaimed liberty,
but trod upon slaves. In that seclusion it dedicated itself to
liberty. Behold to-day it fulfills its vows! When it went down
four million people had no flag. To-day it rises and [the same]
four million people cry out, 'Behold *our* Flag!'
    *   *   *   *   *   *   *
"From this pulpit of broken stone we speak forth our earnest
greeting to all our land. We offer to the President of these

United States our solemn congratulations that God has sustained
his life and health under the unparalleled burdens and sufferings
of four bloody years, and permitted him to behold this auspi-
cious consummation of that national unity for which he has
labored with such disinterested wisdom."

The kindly words spoken of President Lincoln
were never known to him.   Little did the orator
think that in less than ten hours the hand of an assassin would put an end to that life, for the preservation of which he had been pouring out congratulations.   Rumors of threatened assassination had from
time to time reached the ear of the public, but so
many dark days had been passed in safety that little
or no danger was apprehended of such a calamity,
especially at this time, when the enemies of the nation
were melting away before our armies as mist before
the rising sun.

CHAPTER VIII

Mr. Lincoln saw the storm coming long before it burst upon the nation, and from the time he became satisfied that he was about to be the choice of the people for President of the United States, he never doubted that he was chosen by the Almighty to do some special work. This feeling clung to him all through his presidential career. Running parallel with this was another feeling, that when his work was done he would pass away. On these two points he often conversed, and to his friends he sometimes expressed himself quite freely.

Among the earliest of his utterances on record with reference to these matters, is a series of conversations in the autumn of 1860, with the Hon. Newton Bateman, of Springfield, Superintendent of Public Instruction for Illinois, now President elect of Knox College. After Mr. Lincoln was nominated by the Chicago convention in May, 1860, he for a time received the public at his own residence. This, however, interfered so much with the privacy of the family that the Executive Chamber, a fine, large room in the State House, was tendered to him. In this he received all who had a mind to call on him, until after his election and departure for Washington. The room of Mr. Bateman was adjoining the Executive Chamber, and by a private door the occupants of these rooms could communicate when they desired to do so. This door was frequently open during the seven months the room was occupied by Mr. Lincoln. When he was tired he would often close the outer door against intrusion, and call Mr. Bateman in for a quiet talk. On one of these occasions, after a long conversation about the inconsistency of ministers of the Gospel, and other professing Christians with whom they were both acquainted in their political action, he said: "Mr. Bateman, I am not a Christian—God knows I would be one, but I have carefully read the Bible, and I do not so understand this book," and he drew from his bosom a copy of the New Testament, and continued: "These men well know that I am for freedom in the territories, freedom everywhere, as far as the constitution and laws will permit, and that my opponents are for slavery. They know this, and yet, with this Book in their hands, in the light of which human bondage can not live a moment, they are going to vote against me. I do not understand it at all." He then paused, his features manifesting intense emotion; he arose and walked the room, in the effort to regain his composure. He at length stopped, his cheeks wet with tears, his voice trembling, and he said:

"I know there is a God, and that He hates injustice and slavery. I see the storm coming, and I know that His hand is in it. If he has a place and work for me—and I think He has—I believe I am ready. I know I am right, because I know that Liberty is right, for Christ teaches it, and Christ is God. I have told them that a house divided against itself cannot stand, and Christ and reason say the same; and they will find it so."

He then spoke of those who did not care whether slavery was voted up or voted down, and then said:

"God cares, and humanity cares, and I care; and with God's help I shall not fail. *I may not see the end*, but it will come, and I shall be vindicated; and these men will find that they have not read their Bibles aright."

Much of this was spoken as if he was talking to himself, and in a manner peculiarly sad, earnest and solemn. Resuming the conversation after a short pause, he said:

"Does it not appear strange that men can ignore the moral aspects of this contest? A revelation could not make it plainer to me, that slavery or the government must be destroyed. The future would be something awful, as I look at it, but for this rock on which I stand"—(alluding to the Testament which he still held in his hand)—"especially with the knowledge of how these ministers are going to vote. It seems as if God had borne with this thing—slavery—until the very teachers of religion have come to defend it from the Bible, and to claim for it a divine character and sanction; and now the cup of iniquity is full, and the vials of wrath will be poured out.".

In the course of his conversation with Mr. Bateman he unreservedly expressed his conviction of the necessity of faith in the Christian's God, as an element of successful statesmanship, that it gave calmness to the mind which made a man firm and immovable amid the wildest excitements. After expressing his belief in an overruling Providence, and the fact of God in history, the subject of prayer was introduced. " He freely stated his belief in the duty, privilege and efficacy of prayer, and intimated, in unmistakable terms, that he had sought in that way the divine guidance and favor." When this interview was drawing to a close, Mr. Bateman said: "I have not supposed that you were accustomed to think so much upon this class of subjects. Certainly your friends generally are ignorant of the sentiments you have expressed to me." He replied quickly: " I know they are. I am obliged to appear different to them, but I think more on these subjects than upon all others, and I have done so for years, and I am willing you should know it."
Numerous instances might be cited of his conversations before his election and between that and the time of his inauguration, in which he expressed the

conviction that the day of the wrath of the Almighty
was at hand, and that he was to be an actor in the terrible struggle, which would issue in the overthrow of
slavery, and that he did not believe that he would see
the end, or that he would pass away with that system
of abominations.

An incident well calculated to deepen this conviction in his mind occurred soon after his first election.
He related it to some of his friends, but we believe it
was not made public until after his death. The following account of it, said to be almost in Mr. Lincoln's own words, is part of an article from the pen
of Major John Hay, in *Harper's Magazine* for July,
1865. He says:

" It was just after my election in 1860, when the news had been
coming in thick and fast all day, and there had been a great ' hur-
rah, boys!' so that I was well tired out, and went home to rest,
throwing myself upon a lounge in my chamber. Opposite where
I lay was a bureau with a swinging glass upon it, and looking at
that glass I saw myself reflected nearly at full length; but my
face, I noticed, had two separate and distinct images, the tip of
the nose being about three inches from the tip of the other. I
was a little bothered, perhaps startled, and got up and looked in
the glass, but the illusion vanished. On laying down again, I
saw it a second time, plainer, if possible then before; and then I
noticed that one of the faces was a little paler—say five shades—
than the other. I got up and the thing melted away, and I went
off, and, in the excitement of the hour, forgot all about it—nearly, but not quite, for the thing would once in a while come up
and give me a little pang, as though something uncomfortable
had happened. When I went home I told my wife about it, and
a few days after I tried the experiment again, when, sure enough,
the thing came back again; but I never succeeded in bringing
it back after that, though I once tried very industriously to show
it to my wife, who was worried about it somewhat. She thought
it was ' a sign' that I was to be elected to a second term of office,
and that the paleness of one of the faces was an omen that I
should not see life through the last term.

After the beginning of hostilities, Mr. Lincoln's whole time was so occupied, and his mind so absorbed with his official duties. that he appears to have forgotten, for a time, the presentiments that in his more leisure hours caused him some uneasiness.

When our men were dying by thousands in the army hospitals at the south, many of them from no other disease than general debility, the best remedy for which would have been permission to breathe the pure northern air, a lady who had spent much time in those southern hospitals, called on President Lincoln for the purpose of inducing him to establish hospitals in some of the northern States. She knew before starting that Mr. Lincoln, the Surgeon General and chief surgeons in most of the departments were opposed to the measure. Mr. Lincoln seemed determined from the start not to grant her request. He was worn down by constant application to business, which made him fretful, and at times his answers to her entreaties were quite severe. As a last argument, at one of her visits, she said : "If you grant my petition you will be glad as long as you live. The prayers of grateful hearts will give you strength in the hour of trial, and strong and willing arms will return to fight your battles."

She says that, at these words, the President seemed to think that he had possibly done injustice to the soldiers, and all the severity left him. He bowed his head, and with a look of sadness impossible for language to describe, said : *"I shall never be glad any more."* In reply to his mournful utterances, she said : "Oh! do not say so, Mr. Lincoln, for who will have so much reason to rejoice as yourself when the government shall be restored, as it will be ?" Pressing a hand on either side, he said : "I know, I know, but the springs of life are wearing away, and I shall not last." After six days' perseverance the lady accom-

plished her object—the hospital was established, and
the President seemed to rejoice that he had been led
to another act for the relief of the brave soldiers who
were fighting the battles of the nation.

After Mr. Lincoln was nominated as a candidate
for President the second time, there were some dissensions in the Republican party. Many of the prominent men of the party found fault with him, and even
talked of an opposition convention to nominate
another candidate. The people of the North were
weary of the war, and demagogues were not wanting
in his own party to take advantage of this feeling to
increase the dissatisfaction. It was but natural that
Mr. Lincoln should scan every movement of this kind
closely, and that, added to his other anxieties, made
him look careworn and haggard. In the month of
July, 1864, one of the many newspaper correspondents who called upon him, remarked that he was
wearing himself out with hard work. The President
replied, "I can't work less, but it isn't that; work
never troubled me; things look badly, and I cannot
avoid anxiety. Personally I care nothing about a
re-election, but if our dissensions defeat us I fear for
the country." On being reminded that right must
eventually triumph, he admitted that, but expressed
the opinion that he should not live to see it, and
added: "*I feel a presentment that I shall not outlast the
rebellion.* When it is over, my work will be done."

On the evening of the anniversary of Sumter's humiliation, and the very day of its restoration, a day
which is called Good Friday, and is observed by a
large portion of the Christian world as the anniversary of the crucifixion of the Savior of mankind,
President Lincoln made up his mind to visit Ford's
Theatre as a means of relaxing the tension upon his
physical and mental energies. He entered his carriage at a quarter past eight o'clock, accompanied by
his wife, Miss Clara L. Harris, and Major Henry R.

Rathbone. The two latter have since become man and wife. Hon. George Ashmun, of Massachusetts, was in conversation with Mr. Lincoln until he entered his carriage, and it was agreed that Mr. Ashmun and a friend, Judge C. P. Daly of New York, should have an interview with the President the next morning. In order to guard against any delay, he took a card, and resting it upon his knee, wrote with a pencil:

"Allow Mr. Ashmun and friend to come to me at 9 o'clock A. M., to-morrow, April 15, 1865.

A. LINCOLN."

Handing the card to Mr. Ashmun, he rode away. Those were, without doubt, the last words he ever wrote.

The box occupied by the Presidential party was about twelve feet above the stage, looking directly upon it. The play for the evening was called "Our American Cousin." About half past nine o'clock, at a part of the play when the stage was vacant, and all eyes were intently fixed upon it, awaiting the entrance of the next actor, the report of a pistol startled those in the vicinity of the box occupied by Mr. Lincoln. Major Rathbone turning around, saw through the smoke a man standing in the rear of the President. The Major sprang up and grappled him, but the man dropped his pistol, made a thrust at him with a large knife, inflicting a severe wound in the left arm, and wrested himself away. He rushed to the front of the box, and brandishing the knife theatrically, shouted, "Sic semper tyrannis!"—Such be ever the fate of tyrants. He then put his hands on the railing and leaped over on the corner of the stage. Having provided himself with a spur to assist in his flight, it caught in the folds of an American flag it was necessary for him to pass over. As if conscious of the great crime against freedom, the flag wrenched the spur from his boot which caused him to fall nearly prostrate, by which, it was afterwards ascertained, a bone in one of his legs was broken. Notwithstanding this severe injury he quickly recovered, sprang to his feet, again brandished his dagger, and exclaimed, *"The South is avenged!"* and rushed out of the back door of the Theatre, which he shut after him, mounted a horse which an accomplice was holding, and rode off across the Anacosta bridge into Maryland, where he expected to make his escape by the aid of rebel sympathizers.

When the shot was fired, Mr. Lincoln's head fell slightly forward, his eyes closed, but he uttered no word or cry. Mrs. Lincoln screamed, and Miss Harris called for water. Laura Keene, the actress, having her own feelings under perfect control, entreated the audience to be calm, and entered the box from the stage, bearing water and cordials. Women in the audience shrieked and fainted, men called for vengeance, and the most terrible uproar prevailed. The President was at once conveyed out of the Theatre to a neighboring residence where he lay unconscious for nine hours, and breathed his last at twenty-two minutes past seven o'clock on Saturday morning, April 15, 1865. The house in which he died was No. 453 Tenth street, a plain three story brick building. It was the residence of a family by the name of Peterson.

The ball entered the skull behind the left ear, crashed upward through the brain, and lodged behind the right eye. It is not believed that he ever knew he was shot, or was conscious of suffering. As before stated, he had many times been threatened with assassination through anonymous letters, and had often been entreated by his friends to take some precautions for his own protection, but having "charity for all, and feeling malice towards none," he went along, seemingly unconscious of the malicious and fiendish elements around him.

As soon as the horrid deed was accomplished, the assassin was recognized, while on the stage, as John Wilkes Booth, an actor who was familiar with the Theatre. It was soon ascertained that an attempt had been made, and came very near being successful, to assassinate the Hon. W. H. Seward, the Secretary of State, and his son Frederick Seward. · The whole detective force of the Government, and the police force of the City of Washington, were at once called into requisition to arrest the assassins and unravel the intricacies of the plot.

The greatest efforts were made to arrest Booth, large rewards being offered for himself and accomplices. After many false moves, the detectives, under Col. L. C. Baker, got on the true scent. It was found that Booth had penetrated about thirty miles into Maryland, followed by Harold, who had held the horse for him on the night of the assassination. They learned that Booth's broken leg had been dressed by Dr. Mudd, who had furnished him with a crutch. Crippled as he was, he for ten days eluded his pursuers, hiding in the swamps by day, and at night working his way further South.

About thirty miles south of Washington he crossed over the Potomac river into Virginia, and in a few hours more would have been under the protection of Moseby's rebel guerrillas. By means of information volunteered by the colored people, and in some instances extorted from the whites, they traced him to the point where he was ferried across the river. They then found the ferryman, and by threats compelled him to reveal the hiding place of Booth, which was in a barn belonging to a man by the name of Garratt. It was near the town of Bowling Green, between that place and Port Royal. Bowling Green is the county seat of Caroline county. The pursuing party, twenty-eight in number, were a portion of the Sixteenth New York Cavalry, under Colonel Conger. They surrounded the barn about dusk, on Tuesday evening, and soon ascertained that Booth and Harold were both in the barn. A long parley ensued. Harold finally surrendered, but Booth utterly refused to give himself up, and expressed a determination never to be taken alive. Col. Conger becoming convinced that longer delay was useless, and wishing, if possible, to avoid shooting him dead, ordered fire to be communicated to some loose straw in the barn, hoping to drive him out where he could be captured.

Booth, seeing death or surrender was inevitable, obstinately refused to come out, and leaning upon his crutch, was in the act of taking aim at one of the pursuing party, who were stationed so as to command every point of observation. Lieutenant Dougherty, seeing his movements, ordered Sergeant Boston Corbett to fire, which he did with a large cavalry pistol. The ball entered just below the right ear, and came out about an inch above the left ear. He died after suffering about two and a half hours in great agony. The barn was fired about three o'clock Wednesday morning, April 26th ; Booth received the shot within less than an hour, and died that morning. He was a native of Baltimore, and was twenty-six years of age. The body of Booth was taken back to Washington, and after being fully identified, was disposed of by government authority.

Nine of the more immediate conspirators, including Booth, suffered speedy punishment. Harold, Payne—who attempted to take the life of Mr. Seward—Atzerott and Mrs. Surratt, were hung ; Arnold, Mudd and McLaughlin, were imprisoned for life, and Spangler for six years.

John Wilkes Booth assassinated Abraham Lincoln not because there was any personal animosity between them, but as part of a plot to kill all the leading members of the Government that had conquered the slaveholders' conspiracy to destroy it. While the events connected with the capture, death and burial of the assassin, were transpiring, it was far different with his victim.

The excitement caused by the intelligence of the death of President Lincoln, not only in our own nation but throughout the civilized world, has never been equalled in human history. Cities, towns and villages, were draped in mourning; all classes and conditions of people lamented him as a father, and everywhere the insignia of sorrow was visible.

We left the party who had gone down to Fort Sumter to restore the old flag to its rightful place, at the close of Mr. Beecher's oration, still on that pile of historic ruins. All unconscious of what was transpiring at the capitol of the nation—there being no telegraphic communication between it and the rebel States—the excursionists betook themselves to sight-seeing, and thus spent the entire day of Saturday, the fifteenth, visiting famous localities of the once haughty, but now desolate and ruined city of Charleston. The Sabbath, too, was appropriately spent in religious services among the freed people of the city. Mr. Beecher preached in Zion's Church to an audience of three thousand dusky-skinned but eager and attentive auditors. Thus they spent Saturday and Sabbath, intending to continue down the coast to Florida before their return. As they were about to resume their journey, the appalling news reached them that President Lincoln had been assassinated on the evening of the day they had just been celebrating. All desire to extend their visit vanished, and the prow of the Arago was at once turned homeward that they might the more freely unite with their friends in expressions of sorrow at the loss of him who had piloted our Ship of State safely through the most terrific storm of civil war ever experienced by any government on the globe.

Two scenes are indelibly fixed in my mind, that will illustrate the sudden plunge of the nation from the highest delirium of joy to the lowest depth of sorrow. I was in the beautiful little city of Richmond, . Indiana, during the closing scenes of the rebellion. Monday morning, April 10, 1865, was as bright and beautiful as any that has dawned upon the earth since the creation. After an early breakfast I entered my office and commenced work for the day. I had been there but a short time until there appeared to be some unusual commotion in the streets. I went down, and after a little inquiry learned that a telegram had just been received announcing that the whole rebel army of northern Virginia, that had evacuated the Confederate capitol but a few days before, under General Lee, had surrendered to General Grant the day before, at Appomattox Court House.

All understood that this was virtually an end of the rebellion; men shouted the news to each other. Grant has captured the rebel army! Lee has surrendered to Grant! The rebels are defeated! The war will soon be over, and then Peace! Peace!! Peace!!. Such shouts as these were mingled with all other imaginable expressions of delight. Business houses were closed; in fact, some had not yet been opened for the day. Men and boys snatched each other's hats and coats; some even turned their coats inside out, and ran and shouted as if they had lost their reason. Some laughed, and some shed tears of joy.

The principal street of the town is a beautiful wide avenue, lined on either side for nearly a mile with business houses. These houses nearly all had wooden awnings in front. Some of them were old and delapidated, and even those that were comparatively new, having been built without any effort at uniformity, destroyed the beauty of the street. For several weeks a formidable party had been trying to get an ordinance passed to have them all removed, but they were not successful.   The City Hall was on a cross street, a short distance from this main thoroughfare.   On the morning of which I am writing, and while the excitement was at its highest point, one of these men, with his coat turned inside out, ran from the direction of the City Hall, and yelled at the top of his voice that the City Council had just passed an ordinance that all those wooden awnings should be removed.   Men never stopped to think that it was not possible for the Council to have assembled at such a time.   But all rushed for the awnings, and in less time than it has taken me to write this, every house was stripped from one end of the street to the other.   All the materials, old and new, were piled in the middle of the street.   At night, bonfires were made at every street-crossing, and all the rubbish consumed.   As soon as the work of demolition commenced, an enterprising photographer placed a huge camera at one end of the street, and produced one of the most comic historical pictures on record.

The other scene was enacted at the same place five days later.   I was in my office again, quite early on Saturday morning, April 15th.   A genial, jovial friend, who had stepped in to say good morning, left the office laughing and talking, but very soon returned with the tears coursing down his manly cheeks, and with faltering voice said: "President Lincoln and Secretary Seward were assassinated last night."   After exchanging a few words with him, I went out on the street.   The day was as bright and beautiful as the Monday before had been.   Some houses were open, and others were being opened, but all thoughts of business vanished.   Men gathered in groups, and in subdued language communicated the sad news.   The telegraph office was besieged for more news until it was known that the President was certainly dead, but that Mr. Seward was yet alive and might possibly recover.

Men wandered about in silence, or stood in groups and talked of the horrid crime and its probable effect on the country.   Many were the expressions of sorrow for the martyred President, and from none were these more heart-felt than the many Quakers who reside in that city and vicinity.   Some business houses and private residences were draped in mourning.   Thus the day wore away, and from the beginning to its close sadness and gloom were depicted on every countenance.

CHAPTER IX.

When the sad tidings of the assassination of Abraham Lincoln were conveyed upon the wings of the telegraph to all parts of America on the morning of April 15, 1865, there was no place where it fell with such crushing weight as in the city of Springfield, where his trials and triumphs were personally known to all. This was Saturday morning. Only five days before, Monday morning, April tenth, the news had been received that the largest part of the rebel army, under General Lee, had surrendered to our own General Grant. On the reception of the news of that surrender in Springfield, flags leaped as if by magic from public buildings and private residences all over the city. An hour later, all business was suspended, and the people were assembled in and around the State House square, to congratulate each other on the glorious news. The excitement increased with the crowd, and found expression in hurrahs, songs and grotesque processions, and the church and fire bells all over the city rang out their merry peals. This was continued for hours, and until all classes, old and young, joined in the general jubilee. Flags, large and small were attached to houses, horses, vehicles, hats, coats, and every other place where a flag could be displayed. Business houses and private residences vied with each other in their display of patriotic emblems. A splendid flag was thrown to the breeze from the old home of President Lincoln.

In the afternoon a procession, civic and military, chiefly grotesque and ludicrous, paraded the streets. The principal object of interest was the old dark bay horse that Mr. Lincoln had ridden many hundred miles on professional business and in his political campaigns. " Old Bob," or " Robin," was decorated with a rich blanket, red, white and blue, thickly studded with flags, and bearing the inscription, " Old Abe's Horse." He was soon robbed of his flags, they having been secured by the people as mementoes.

About half past six o'clock p. m. a salute of twenty guns was fired, followed by a fine display of fire-works. Many of the public and private residences were then illuminated. By eight o'clock an immense crowd of citizens had assembled in the State House and grounds surrounding it. Patriotic speeches were made by a number of prominent men, interspersed with music by a fine band. At a later hour the citizens dispersed to their homes; the noise died away, and the city was at rest. It was but a day or two until an order was issued by the Secretary of War for all recruiting and drafting to cease. This assured the people that the government regarded the war to be virtually at an end, and gave a new impetus to the rejoicing all over the land. This description of the way the people acted in Springfield will apply to hundreds and thousands of towns and cities all over our country. The people continued to meet each other, everywhere, with broad smiles and words of congratulation, up to Friday night, April 14.

We will return again to the citizens of Springfield, and describe their actions as an illustration of the sudden change in the feelings of the people all over the land, from almost a delirium of joy, to the lowest depths of sorrow.

On the fatal Saturday morning, April 15, the citizens of Springfield, half dressed, and, perhaps, yawning from the effects of a full night's sleep, as they sauntered out to their front yards and took up the morning *Journal*, saw nothing unusual in the paper at first, but on opening it and finding the rules reversed, displaying heavy dark lines between the columns, they hastened to find the cause. It was the work of a moment to read, in substance:

"President Lincoln shot by an assassin, in Ford's Theatre, last night! Secretary Seward, at the same time, stabbed, as he lay in bed, from the effect of wounds received by being thrown from his carriage a few days before!! Both thought to be in a dying condition!!! Vice President Johnson, Secretary Stanton and Lieut. General Grant were to have been assassinated also, but some of the conspirators failed to perform the parts assigned them!!!! General Grant saved by unexpectedly leaving the Capital!!!!!

By a common impulse, the people assembled about the State House square to talk of the awful tidings. The telegraph office was besieged for more news. It was ascertained at an early hour that the President was DEAD, and later in the day, that Secretary Seward would probably recover. After the first shock, all felt a desire to give some public expression to their feelings. Very soon the sad insignia of sorrow were displayed in profusion from the houses of the wealthy, and by all in proportion to their ability. The very poor in the outskirts of the city were equally anxious with their more favored fellow citizens, to testify their sorrow for the untimely death of him whom all loved. From the doors of many such were displayed a piece of any black goods they could obtain, if it was but a narrow strip and a few inches in length. These demonstrations were made, with very few exceptions, without any distinction, whatever, as to political preferences.

The crime was so diabolical, and so firmly had Abraham Lincoln entrenched himself in the hearts of the people, that many, for the time being were involuntarily disposed to question the wisdom and goodness of God in permitting the awful deed to be consummated. This was doubtless felt in many instances where it failed to find utterance in words; but, in some cases, it was outspoken. A clergyman of Springfield had a niece residing in his family, who, as soon as she heard the news, ran to him, and, with tears streaming down her face, said, " O, uncle, it does seem to me that I can never love God any more." With the more thoughtful, however, it created a feeling of inquiry as to why it was permitted, and with all such,as expressed by the mayor of Springfield to the City Council that morning, the inquiry was, " Lord, what wilt Thou have us to do."

A call was early issued by the Mayor, J. S. Vredenburg, for a meeting of the City Council at ten o'clock. A notice was also circulated, that a meeting of the citizens would be held in the State House yard at twelve o'clock, noon. When the City Council assembled, it passed resolutions to unite with the citizens in their public demonstration, and after appointing a committee to draft resolutions expressive of their feelings, adjourned until four o'clock p. m.

The meeting at the State House was called to order at noon, and after organizing, several of those who had long been intimately acquainted with the fallen chieftain made interesting remarks, calling up many reminiscences of his past life. Hon. John T. Stuart, as chairman of a committee appointed for that purpose, reported a series of resolutions, which were adopted as expressive of the feelings of the meeting. I find space for a single one of those resolutions :

Resolved, That inasmuch as this city has, for a long time, been the home of the President, in which he has graced with his kindness of heart and honesty of purpose, all the relations of life, it is appropriate that its " City of the Dead" should be the final resting place of all of him that is mortal, and to this end we respectfully request the appointment of a committee on the part of the City Council, to act in conjunction with the Governor of the State, with a view of bringing hither his remains for interment.

The City Council assembled, pursuant to adjournment, and adopted the resolution passed by the public assembly relative to the removal of the remains, and appointed the following committee, to proceed to Washington City, for the purpose of co-operating with Governor Oglesby — who was there at the time of the assassination — in bringing the remains of President Lincoln to Springfield: Hon. Jesse K. Dubois, Hon. Lyman Trumbull, Hon. John T. Stuart, Hon. Shelby M. Cullom, Ex-Governor Richard Yates, Gen. I. N. Haynie, Gen. John A. McClernand, Ex-Mayor J. S. Vredenburg and Mayor elect Thomas J. Dennis. Governor Oglesby was informed by telegraph of the action of the City Council. A series of resolutions, reported by Alderman Wohlgemuth, as chairman of the committee appointed for that purpose, were adopted as expressing the feelings of the members of the council. Within a week after the assassination, almost every society in Springfield, religious, political, benevolent and social, passed resolutions expressive of their sorrow for the death of Abraham Lincoln, and horror at the crime of his assassination.

On Sunday, the sixteenth, the people flocked to the churches, as though they were fleeing from some great calamity. Men who had not been seen in the house of God for months, were, on that day, among the earliest, and seemingly the most attentive and devotional worshippers. In some of the churches, the pulpits were draped in mourning, and the services partook of solemnities appropriate to a funeral occasion.

We will once more look upon the scenes being enacted at the capital of the nation. President Lincoln breathed his last at twenty-two minutes past seven o'clock, on the morning of April 15. At half past nine o'clock, the body was removed to the Executive Mansion, and on the afternoon of that day it was embalmed and otherwise prepared for sepulture, by being placed in a wooden coffin, upon which was a plate bearing the inscription :

ABRAHAM LINCOLN,
16TH PRESIDENT OF THE UNITED STATES.
BORN FEBRUARY 12, 1809.
DIED APRIL 15, 1865.

The coffin was then placed on a dais within a grand catafalque, in the East Room, surrounded by the sad emblems of woe and covered with the most rare and costly floral tributes of affection.

On the same day, at eleven o'clock, Chief Justice Chase administered to the Vice President, Andrew Johnson, the oath of office as President of the United States. By this prompt action, the interregnum in the office of President was but a little more than three hours in duration. President Johnson immediately called a meeting of the Cabinet. At this meeting William Hunter was appointed Acting Secretary of State, to serve during the disability of Secretary Seward. On Monday morning the following proclamation was issued and telegraphed to all parts of the nation :

" The undersigned is directed to announce that the funeral ceremonies of the lamented Chief Magistrate will take place at the Executive Mansion, in this city, at 12 o'clock noon, Wednesday, the nineteenth inst. The various religious denominations throughout the country are invited to meet in their respective places of worship at the time, for the purpose of solemnizing the occasion by appropriate ceremonies.'

W. HUNTER,
Acting Secretary of State.

Washington, April 17, 1865."

On the same day, the following order was issued, preparatory to observing funeral rites suitable to the occasion, at Washington :

WAR DEPARTMENT, ADJUTANT GENERAL'S OFFICE, }
WASHINGTON, April 17, 1865. }

The following order of arrangements is directed:

ORDER OF PROCESSION.

FUNERAL ESCORT IN COLUMN OF MARCH.

One Regiment of Cavalry.
Two Batteries of Artillery.
Battalion of Marines.
Two Regiments of Infantry.
Commander of Escort and Staff.

Dismounted Officers of Marine Corps, Navy and Army, in the order named; Mounted Officers of Marine Corps, Navy and Army, in the order named; all Military Officers to be in Uniform, with Side-arms.

CIVIC PROCESSION.

The Surgeon General of the United States Army, and Physicians to the Deceased.

Clergy in Attendance.

PALL BEARERS.		PALL BEARERS.
On the part of the Senate.		*On the part of the House.*
Mr. Foster, of Connecticut.		Mr. Dawes, of Massachusetts.
Mr. Morgan, of New York.	H	Mr. Coffroth, of Pennsylvania.
Mr. Johnson, of Maryland.	E A R S E	Mr. Smith, of Kentucky.
Mr. Yates, of Illinois.		Mr. Colfax, of Indiana.
Mr. Wade, of Ohio.		Mr. Worthington, of Nevada.
Mr. Conness, of California.		Mr. Washburn, of Illinois.
Army.		*Navy.*
Lieut. Gen. U. S. Grant.		Vice Admiral D. G. Farragut.
Major General H. W. Halleck.		Rear Admiral W. B. Shubrick.
Brev. Brig. Gen. W. A. Nichols.		Col. Jacob Zeilen, Marine Corps.

Civilians.

O. H. Browning.		Thomas Corwin,
George Ashmun.		Simon Cameron.

Family.

Relatives.

The Delegations of States of Illinois and Kentucky, as Mourners.
The President.
The Cabinet Ministers.
The Diplomatic Corps.
Ex-Presidents.
The Chief Justice,
And Associate Justices of the Supreme Court.

The Senate of the United States, preceded by their Officers.
Members of the House of Representatives of the United States.
Governors of the several States and Territories.
Legislatures of the several States and Territories.
The Federal Judiciary,
And the Judiciary of the several States and Territories.
The Assistant Secretaries of State, Treasury, War, Navy, Interior,
and the Assistant Postmaster General, and the
Assistant Attorney General
Officers of the Smithsonian Institute.
Members and Officers of the Sanitary and Christian Commissions.
Corporate Authorities of Washington, Georgetown
and other cities.
Delegations of the several States.
The Reverend the Clergy of the Various Denominations.
Clerks and employees of the several Departments and Bureaus,
Preceded by the heads of such Bureaus and their respective
Chief Clerks.
Such Societies as may wish to join the Procession.
Citizens and Strangers.

The troops designated to form the escort will assemble in the
Avenue north of the President's house, and form line precisely at 11
o'clock a. m., on Wednesday, the nineteenth inst. with the left
resting on Fifteenth street. The procession will move precisely at
2 o'clock p. m. on the conclusion of the religious services at the
Executive Mansion—appointed to commence at 12 o'clock meri-
dian—when minute guns will be fired by detachments of artillery,
stationed at St. John's Church, the City Hall, and at the Capitol.
At the same hour, the bells of the several churches in Washington, Georgetown and Alexandria will be tolled.

At sunrise on Wednesday, the nineteenth inst. a federal salute will
be fired from the Military Stations in the vicinity of Washington,
minute guns between the hours of 12 and 3 o'clock, and a national
salute at the setting of the sun.

The usual badge of mourning will be worn on the left arm, and
on the hilt of the sword.

By order of the Secretary of War:

W. A. NICHOLS,
Assistant Adjutant General.

The Governors of several of the loyal States, immediately after the capture of the rebel army under General Lee, issued proclamations appointing days for thanksgiving in their respective States. These were all countermanded after the assassination of the President, and the proclamation of the Acting Secretary of State adopted instead. That proclamation was incorporated into and made the principal part of the proclamations by Governors of States and Mayors of cities throughout the United States, and also in the British Provinces of North America. The proclamations of some of the Mayors in the Dominion of Canada were fully equal in their expressions of heartfelt sympathy and condolence with those from similar officers in the United States.

In the absence of Governor Oglesby from the State, Lieutenant Governor William Bross issued a proclamation to the people of Illinois, recommending them to assemble in their several places of worship, at as early a day as possible, to " devoutly implore Almighty God to have mercy on us; that He will restrain the wrath of man and cause the remainder of his wrath to praise Him."

On the same day that Secretary Hunter issued his proclamation, Governor Oglesby adopted it, and adds:

"Responding to the spirit of the announcement, I call upon the people of the State of Illinois, the home of her martyred son, to meet in their various churches and places of public worship on that day, to observe it in such manner as this painful occasion shall suggest at the solemn hour.

Done at Springfield, April 17, 1865.

R. J. OGLESBY."

Hon. T. J. Dennis having been installed Mayor on the evening of the 17th, his first official act was to issue a proclamation in harmony with that of the Acting

Secretary of State at Washington, and the one by Governor Oglesby, calling on the people of Springfield to assemble at their several places of worship at the time designated to engage in services appropriate to the occasion.

CHAPTER X.

On Wednesday morning, April 19, 1865, the sun arose in splendor on the glittering domes of the nation's Capital. The East Room of the Executive Mansion, where a Harrison and a Taylor had lain in state, now contained all that was mortal of one who was immeasurably greater than either of them, judging by the result of his labors and the grateful esteem in which he was held by the people of the nation. The hour was approaching for the services to commence. None could be admitted without tickets, and there being only room for six hundred persons, that number of cards were issued, of which the following is an imitation:

SOUTH.

Admit the Bearer to the

EXECUTIVE MANSION,

On WEDNESDAY, the
19th of April, 1865.

Near 11 o'clock a body of about sixty clergymen entered the Mansion. Then came heads of Government Bureaus, Governors of States, members of municipal

8

governments, prominent officers of the army and navy, representatives of foreign governments, or what is usually termed the Diplomatic Corps. At noon, President Johnson, in company with his cabinet, except Secretary Seward, of the State Department, approached the catafalque and took a last look at his illustrious predecessor. The religious services were opened by the Rev. Dr. Hall, of the Protestant Episcopal Church, and Rector of the Epiphany, who read portions of Scripture used in the impressive burial service of that church, and prayer by Bishop Simpson, of the Methodist Episcopal Church.

Rev. Dr. P. D. Gurley, of the New York Avenue Presbyterian Church, and pastor of the President and family, then delivered an impressive funeral sermon. I can only give a single quotation, but that will enable us to understand how President Lincoln labored with such untiring patience in the discharge of his official duties:

"I speak what I know, and testify what I have often heard him say, when I affirm that the Divine goodness and mercy were the props on which he leaned. Never shall I forget the emphatic and deep emotion with which he said, in this very room, to a company of clergymen and others, who called to pay him their respects, in the darkest days of our civil conflict: 'Gentlemen, my hope of success in this struggle rests on that immutable foundation, the justness and goodness of God; and when events are very threatening, I still hope that, in some way, all will be well in the end, because our cause is just, and God will be on our side.' Such was his sublime and holy faith, and it was an anchor to his soul. It made him firm and strong; it emboldened him in the pathway of duty, however rugged and perilous it might be; it made him valiant for the right, for the cause of God and humanity, and it held him in steady patience to a policy of administration which he thought both God and humanity required him to adopt."

Rev. Dr. E. H. Gray, Pastor of the E Street Baptist Church, who was at the time Chaplain of the United

States Senate, closed the services at the Executive Mansion by a fervent prayer.

The coffin was then conveyed to the hearse, and at two o'clock the procession began to move.   It took the line of Pennsylvania Avenue, and was one hour and a half in passing the Executive Mansion.   The rooms, porticos and buildings at all elevated points in the city were occupied by spectators.   As the procession moved, all the bells of Washington, Georgetown and Alexandria tolled, and minute guns were fired at the three points named in the order of April 17th.

First in order of procession was a detachment of colored troops, then followed white regiments of infantry, cavalry, batteries of artillery and the marine corps ; army officers on foot, the pall bearers in carriages, and then came the HEARSE, drawn by six white horses.   The coffin was so elevated as to be seen from all points.   The floor of the hearse was covered with evergreens and white flowers.   Then followed President Johnson and his cabinet, the Diplomatic corps, members of Congress, Governors of States, delegations from the various States—that from Illinois having the post of honor as chief mourners—then came clerks of departments, military organizations, fire companies and civic associations, public and private carriages, closing with a large body of colored men and a great concourse of citizens and strangers.

Arriving at the Capitol, the coffin was conveyed to the rotunda, where it was again placed on a magnificent catafalque.   This was incomparably the largest and most imposing funeral procession ever seen in the Capital of the nation.

The nineteenth of April was observed with religious services all over the loyal States and the reclaimed rebel States and parts of States, and in the British Provinces of North America.   In addition to this, the people of hundreds and thousands of towns and cities in the Union turned out in solemn processions, bearing emblems, mottoes and other devices expressive of their love for the memory of Abraham Lincoln, and of their sorrow for his death. Many of these processions are mentioned in the newspapers of the day, as being composed of from five to twenty thousand persons.

Aside from what was done in the city of Washington on that day, I shall only describe the public demonstrations at the old home of Mr. Lincoln, Springfield, Illinois.

Springfield, on the nineteenth, presented the appearance of deep gloom and sadness. On the day of Mr. Lincoln's death all goods in the stores that could be used for draping the buildings in mourning were taken, and more ordered at once by the merchants. Such additions were made that on this day the insignia of sorrow were profusely displayed on the State House, Governor's Mansion, Post Office, Arsenal, the military headquarters of Gen. John Cook, all the State and county offices, and nearly all the business houses and residences in the city. The feelings of the people prompted them almost universally to comply with proclamation of Mayor Dennis, and close their houses of business. Flags on the public buildings were draped with mourning and hung at half mast. Stillness, more profound than that of the Sabbath, reigned throughout the city. Before the hour appointed for assembling, the people began to wend their way to the churches. When the time arrived for the services to commence—at noon—twenty minute-guns were fired, at the Arsenal. The churches were nearly all filled to overflowing, with sorrowing and attentive audiences. The services partook partly of religious condolence and partly of panegyric and eulogium. Laymen, as well as ministers, took part in the exercises.

In the First Presbyterian Church, of which Mrs. Lincoln was a member, and which the family attended while in Springfield, there were several brief but interesting addresses delivered. Rev. Dr. Bergen, a former pastor of the Church, and the Hon. John T. Stuart, the first law partner of Mr. Lincoln, were the principal speakers. The address by Mr. Stuart is spoken of as having been replete with interesting reminiscences of their long and intimate acquaintance, and, as a whole, was such a fitting eulogium on the life and character of the departed Chief Magistrate, as to do honor to the head and heart of the speaker.

In the Second Presbyterian Church, there was a number of speeches also. The Rev. Albert Hale, Rev. Dr. Harkey and Hon. Lyman Trumbull, were the principal speakers. Mr. Trumbull spoke for nearly an hour, in the most eloquent and touching strain, of the virtues, magnanimity and integrity of Abraham Lincoln. His remarks elicted deep responses in every heart. His address is remembered by those who heard it as an elaborate, truthful and pathetic panegyric on the life, character and public services of Abraham Lincoln.

In the First Baptist Church, an address was delivered by the Hon. W. H. Herndon, who had been the law partner of Abraham Lincoln for more than twenty years. The partnership remained until the day of Mr. Lincoln's death. Mr. Herndon spoke in feeling terms of the public and private life of his departed friend and co-laborer. Hon. J. C. Conkling, a long and intimate friend of Mr. Lincoln, at the same church, delivlivered an equally interesting address, in which many reminiscences of the late Cheif Magistrate were called up. Judge Broadwell addressed the people at the same church, also.

Appropriate services were held in the Third Presbyterian Church.

At the First Methodist Church, the Rev. J. L. Crane, the pastor, delivered an able and interesting discourse on the life and public services of Abraham Lincoln.

Services suitable to the occasion were held in the English Lutheran, North Baptist, German Catholic and many other churches throughout the city. It was a day of quiet, subdued and heartfelt mourning for the loss of one whom all could think of as a brother and friend, and at the same time as a Chief Magistrate of a great nation, unexcelled by any potentate of either ancient or modern times.

Several days elapsed after the assassination before it was certainly known that his remains would be brought back to his old home for interment.

The City Council of Springfield assembled, on the nineteenth of April, and passed an ordinance appropriating twenty thousand dollars to be expended in defraying the expenses connected with the funeral of Abraham Lincoln, the sixteenth President of the United States. The ordinance was approved on the twentieth by Mayor Dennis. Artists were put to work to decorate the State House, both on the exterior and interior, with mourning drapery.

A public meeting of the citizens was called, on the twenty-fourth of the month, to make suitable arrangements for the reception of the body, then on its journey from the Capital of the nation to his former prairie home. This public assembly, in order to act more efficiently, appointed a committee of arrangements, composed of men who had all enjoyed a personal acquaintance with the now martyred President. After taking the initial steps for the construction of a temporary vault, to be ready by the time the funeral train should arrive, the committee resolved itself into a

"NATIONAL LINCOLN MONUMENT ASSOCIATION,

for the purpose of receiving funds and disbursing the same, for obtaining grounds and erecting a monument thereon, in Springfield, Illinois, to the memory of our lamented Chief Magistrate, Abraham Lincoln." Hon. James H. Beveridge, then Treasurer of the State of Illinois, was named as the treasurer of the Association, and " the officers, soldiers and sailors in the army and navy, in camps, stations, forts and hospitals ; loyal leagues, lodges of Masons and Odd Fellows, religious and benevolent associations, churches of all denominations, and the colored population," were requested to contribute for the purpose, the second week in May, or as soon thereafter as possible, and remit to the treasurer named. National banks and postmasters were requested to act as agents. The proceedings were telegraphed to all parts of the country, and published in the papers. Two days after the association was organized, its Executive Committee published an appeal to the nation that it would, " by one simultaneous movement, testify its regard for his exalted character ; its appreciation of his distinguished services, and its sorrow for his death, by erecting to his memory a monument that will forever prove that republics are not ungrateful."

The Association at once contracted for a piece of land, containing five or six acres, near the central part of the city, upon which to erect the monument contemplated, and proceeded to construct a temporary vault—at the expense of the city—as a resting place for the remains of the President until the monument could be built. Men labored upon it night and day, in order to have it ready by the time the funeral cortege was expected to arrive.

CHAPTER XI.

We will now return to the city of Washington. Before the departure of the funeral cortege, arrangements were all completed for transportation. The following order was issued :

WAR DEP'T, WASHINGTON CITY, April 18, 1865.

His Excellency Governor Brough, and John W. Garrett, Esq., are requested to act as a Committee of Arrangements of transportation of the remains of the late President, Abraham Lincoln, from Washington to their final resting place. They are authorized to arrange the time tables with the respective railroad companies, and do and regulate all things for safe and appropriate transportation. They will cause notice of this appointment, and their acceptance, to be published for the public information.

EDWIN M. STANTON,
Secretary of War.

Messrs. Brough and Garrett promptly accepted their appointments, and entered upon the discharge of their duties. When they had prepared their report, the following was issued as a special order :

WAR DEP'T, WASHINGTON CITY, April 18, 1865,

Ordered:

First, That the following report, and the arrangements therein specified, be approved and confirmed, and that the transportation of the remains of the late President, Abraham Lincoln, from Washington to his former home, at Springfield, the Capital of Illinois, be conducted in accordance with the said report and the arrangements therein specified.

Second, That for the purpose of said transportation, the railroads over which said transportation is made be declared military roads, subject to the orders of the War Department, and that the railroads and the locomotives, cars and engines engaged in transportation be subject to the military control of Brigadier General McCallum, superintendant of military railroad transportation; and all persons are required to conform to the rules, regulations, orders and directions he may give or prescribe for the transportation aforesaid; and all persons disobeying the orders shall be deemed to have violated the military orders of the War Department, and shall be dealt with accordingly.

Third, That no person shall be allowed to be transferred upon the cars constituting the funeral train save those who are specially authorized by the order of the War Department. The funeral train will not exceed nine cars, including baggage car, and the hearse car, which will proceed over the whole route from Washington to Springfield, Illinois.

Fourth, At the various points on the route, where the remains are to be taken from the hearse car by State or municipal authorities, to receive public honors, according to the aforesaid programme, the said authorities will make such arrangements as may be fitting and appropriate to the occasion, under the direction of the miltary commander of the division, department, or district, but the remains will continue always under the special charge of the officers and escort assigned by this Department.

By order of the Secretary of War.

E. D. TOWNSEND,
Assistant Adjutant General.

REPORT OF MESSRS. BROUGH AND GARRETT.

WASHINGTON CITY, D. C., April 18, 1865.

Hon. E. M. Stanton, Secretary of War:

SIR—Under your commission of this date, we have the honor to report—

1. A committee of the citizens of the State of Illinois, appointed for the purpose of attending to the removal of the remains of the late President to their State, has furnished us with the following route for the remains and escort, being, with the exception of

two points, the route traversed by Mr. Lincoln from Springfield
to Washington:

Washington to Baltimore, thence to Harrisburg, Philadelphia,
New York, Albany, Buffalo, Cleveland, Columbus, Indianapolis,
Chicago to Springfield.

2. Over this route, under the counsels of the committee, we
have prepared the following time card, in all cases for special
trains:

TIME CARD.

Leave Washington Friday morning, April 21, at 8 o'clock, and
arrive at Baltimore at 10 o'clock a. m.

Leave Baltimore at 8 o'clock p. m., and reach Harrisburg at 8:20
p. m., same day.

Leave Harrisburg at 12 o'clock noon, Saturday, 22, and arrive
in Philadelphia at 5:30 p. m.

Leave Philadelphia at 4 a. m. Monday, 24, and arrive in New
York at 10 a. m., the same day.

Leave New York at 4 p. m. Tuesday, 25, and arrive in Albany
at 11 p. m., same day.

Leave Albany at 4 p. m, Wednesday, 26, and arrive at Buffalo
at 7 a. m. Thursday, 27.

Leave Buffalo at 10:10 p. m., the same day, and arrive in Cleveland at 7 a. m. on Friday, 28.

Leave Cleveland at midnight, same day, and arrive in Columbus
at 7:30 a. m. Saturday, 29.

Leave Columbus at 8 o'clock p. m. Saturday, 29, and arrive in
Indianapolis at 7 a. m. Sunday, 30.

Leave Indianapolis at 12 midnight, Sunday, and arrive in Chicago at 11 a. m. Monday, May 1.

Leave Chicago at 9:30 p. m. Tuesday, May 2, and arrive in
Springfield at 8 o'clock a. m. Wednesday, May 3.

The route from Columbus to Indianapolis is via the Columbus
& Indianapolis Central railway, and from Indianapolis to Chicago
via Lafayette & Michigan City.

3. As to the running of these special trains, which, in order to
guard, as far as practicable, against accidents and detentions, we

have reduced to about twenty miles per hour, we suggest the following regulations:

1. That the time of the departure and arrival be observed as closely as possible.

2. That material detentions at way points be guarded against as much as practicable, so as not to increase the speed of trains.

3. That a pilot engine be kept ten minutes in advance of the train.

4. That the special train, in all cases, have the right of road, and that all other trains be kept out of its way.

5. That the several railroad companies provide a sufficient number of coaches for the comfortable accommodation of the escort, and a special car for the remains; and that all these, together with the engines, be appropriately draped in mourning.

6. That where the running time of any train extends beyond or commences at midnight, not less than two sleeping-cars be added, and a greater number if the road can command them, sufficient for the accommodation of the escort.

7. That two officers of the United States Military Railway Service be detailed by you, and despatched at once over the route to confer with the several railway officers, and make all necessary preparations for carrying out these arrangements promptly and satisfactorily.

8. That this programme and these regulations, if approved, be confirmed by an order of the War Department.

Respectfully submitted,

JOHN BROUGH,
JOHN W. GARRETT, } *Committee.*

The following with reference to the
GUARD OF HONOR,

Was next issued:

General Orders, 72. } WAR DEPARTMENT,
ADJUTANT GENERAL'S OFFICE,
WASHINGTON, April 20, 1865.

The following general officers and Guard of Honor will accompany the remains of the President from the city of Washington to the city of Springfield, the Capital of Illinois, and continue with them until they are consigned to their final resting place:

Brevet Brigadier General E. D. Townsend, Assistant Adjutant General, to represent the Secretary of War.

Brevet Brigadier General James A. Ekin, Deputy Quartermaster General.

Brigadier General A. B. Eaton, Commissary General of Subsistence.

Brevet Major General J. G. Barnard, Lieutenant Colonel of Engineers.

Brigadier General G. D. Ramsey, Ordnance Department.

Brigadier General A. P. Howe, Chief of Artillery.

Brevet Brigadier General D. C. McCallum, Superintendent of Military Roads.

Major General D. Hunter, U. S. Volunteers.

Brigadier General J. C. Caldwell, U. S. Volunteers.

Twenty-five picked men, under a Captain.

By order of the Secretary of War:

Official.   E. D. TOWNSEND,
                                        Assistant Adjutant General.

The following officers acted with the Guard of Honor, although I have been unable to find the order assigning them to that duty:

Rear Admiral C. H. Davis, U. S. Navy.

Captain W. R. Taylor, U. S. Navy.

Major T. H. Field, U. S. Marine Corps.

Including them, the Guard of Honor consisted of twelve general officers.

The picked men were all members of the Veteran Reserve corps, and were selected from the following regiments:

Ninth—Captain J. M. McCamley, J. R. Edwards, J. F. Nelson, L. E. Bulock, P. Callaghan, A. K. Marshall.

Seventh—First Lieutenant J. R. Durkee, First Sergeant C. Swinehart, S. Carpenter, A. C. Cromwell.

Tenth—Second Lieutenant E. Murphy, W. T. Daly, J. Collins, W. H. Durgin, Frank Smith.

Twelfth—Second Lieutenant E. Hoppy, G. E. Goodrich, A. E. Carr, F. Carley, W. H. Noble.

Fourteenth—J. Karr, J. P. Smith, J. Hanna,

Eighteenth—F. D. Forehard, J. M. Sedgwick, R. W. Lewis.

Twenty-fourth—J. P. Berry, W. H. Wiseman and J. M. Pardun.

The three gentlemen whose names are annexed accompanied the escort, each acting in the capacity designated below.

Captain Charles Penrose, Quartermaster and Commissary of Subsistence to the entire party.

Dr. Charles R. Brown, Embalmer.

Frank T. Sands, Undertaker.

Congress was not in session at the time of the assassination, but a public meeting was called of all who were members of either house, or who were delegates in Congress from any of the territories, and happened then to be in Washington. This explains why some of the States were not represented on this committee.

The following gentlemen were chosen from those who were present, and the body thus chosen was designated the Congressional Committee:

States.—Maine, Mr. Pike, New Hampshire, Mr Rollins; Vermont, Mr. Foot and Mr. Baxter; Connecticut, Mr. Dixon; Massachusetts, Mr. Sumner and Mr. Hooper; Rhode Island, Mr. Anthony; New York, Mr. Harris; Pennsylvania, Mr. Cowan; Ohio, Mr. Schenck; Kentucky, Mr. Smith; Indiana, Mr. Julian; Minnesota, Mr. Ramsey; Michigan, Mr. Chandler and Mr. Ferry; Iowa, Mr. Harlan; Illinois, Messrs. Yates, Washburn, Farnsworth and Arnold, unless they preferred being considered part of the Illinois delegation; California, Mr. Shannon; Oregon, Mr. Williams; Kansas, Mr. Clarke; West Virginia, Mr. Whaley; Maryland, Mr. Phelps; New Jersey, Mr. Newell; Nevada, Mr. Nye; Nebraska, Mr. Hitchcock.

Territories.—Colorado, Mr. Bradford; Idaho, Mr. Wallace; Dacotah, Mr. Weed.

George N. Brown, Sergeant-at-Arms of the United States Senate.

N. G. Ordway, Sergeant-at-Arms of the United States House of Representatives. Some of the above named gentlemen accompanied the remains, but many of them did not.

NAMES OF THE ILLINOIS DELEGATION.

Gov. R. J. Oglesby; Gen. Isham N. Haynie, Adjutant General of Illinois. Col. J. H. Bowen, Col. W. H. Hanna, Col. D. B. James, Major S. Waite, Col. D. L. Phillips, U. S. Marshal for the Southern District of Illinois; Hon. Jesse K. Dubois, Col. John Williams, Dr. S. H. Melvin, E. F. Leonard, Hon. S. M. Cullom, Hon. O. M. Hatch.

GOVERNERS OF STATES ACCOMPANYING THE ESCORT:

Governor Stone, of Iowa, and the Hon. Mr. Loughridge, of that State, accompanied the escort the entire journey, and rode in the car occupied by the Illinois Delegation.

REPORTERS FOR THE PRESS:

L. A. Gobright, of Washington City, and C. R. Morgan, for the Associated Press; U. H. Painter, for the Philadelphia *Inquirer;* E. L. Crounse, for the New York *Times;* G. B. Woods, of the Boston *Daily Advertiser;* Dr. Adonis, of the Chicago *Tribune;* C. A. Page, New York *Tribune.*

The hearse car was one that had been built in Alexandria, Va., for the United States military railroads, and was intended for the use of President Lincoln and other officers of the Government when traveling over those roads. It contained a parlor, sitting room and sleeping apartment, all of which was fitted up in the most approved modern style. The car intended for the family of the President and the Congressional Committee, belonged to the Philadelphia, Wilmington & Baltimore railroad company, ordinarily used by the President and Directors of the company. It was divided into four compartments, thus: parlor, chamber, dining room and kitchen; with water tanks and gasometer. The whole car was fitted up in the most elegant and costly manner. Both of these cars were richly draped in mourning.

The remains of President Lincoln having been placed in the rotunda of the Capitol on the nineteenth of April, continued to lie there until the time appointed to start on the western journey. A continuous throng of visitors filed past the coffin the entire day of the twentieth. During that day more than twenty-five thousand persons looked upon the face of the illustrious deceased, many of them soldiers who left their beds, in the hospitals, to take one last look at their departed chieftain.

CHAPTER XII.

—

At six o'clock on the morning of April 21, the members of the Cabinet, Lieutenant General Grant and his staff, several United States Senators, the Illinois delegation, and a considerable number of army officers, arrived at the Capitol and took their farewell view of the face of the departed statesman. After an impressive prayer by the Rev. Dr. Gurley, the coffin was borne, without music, to the hearse car, to which the body of his son Willie had previously been removed. Another prayer and the benediction followed.

At eight o'clock, the Funeral Cortege of Abraham Lincoln moved slowly from the depot, for its long and circuitous journey to the western prairies. Several thousand soldiers were in line by the side of the railroad, and presented arms as the train departed amid the tolling of bells and the uncovered heads of the immense assemblage. A scene connected with the departure was so impressive that it will never be forgotten while life endures, by those who witnessed it. A portion of the soldiers in line near the depot were two regiments of U. S. Colored Troops. They stood with arms reversed, heads bowed, all weeping like children at the loss of a father. Their grief was of such undoubted sincerity as to affect the whole vast multitude. Dignified Governors of States, grave Senators, and scar-worn army officers, who had passed through scenes of blood and carnage unmoved, lost their self control and were melted to tears in the presence of such unaffected sorrow.

After leaving Washington there was no stoppage for public demonstrations until the train reached Baltimore, at ten o'clock the same morning. The city, through which Abraham Lincoln, four years before, had hurried in the night, to escape assassination, now received his remains with every possible demonstration of respect. The body was escorted by an immense procession to the rotunda of the Merchants' Exchange, where it was placed upon a gorgeous catafalque and surrounded with flowers. Here it rested for several hours, receiving the silent homage of thousands who thronged the portals of the edifice to take a last look at the features of the illustrious patriot.

Baltimore was then under the control of loyal men, who felt deeply grieved that a plot had been laid there for his destruction when on his way to assume the duties of his office ; and they suffered still greater mortification that it was a native of their own city who had plunged the nation into mourning by the horrid crime of assassinating the President. The city added ten thousand dollars to the reward offered for the arrest of the assassin. Those who accompanied the escort the entire journey say that there was no other place where the manifestations of grief were apparently so sincere and unaffected as in the city of Baltimore, although they admit it was hard to make a distinction when all were intent on using every exertion to do honor to the memory of the illustrious statesman.

At three o'clock p. m. the train left the depot, and making a brief stoppage at York, Penn., a beautiful wreath of flowers was placed upon the coffin by the ladies of that city, while a dirge was performed by the band, amid the tolling of bells and the uncovered heads of the multitude. The cortege arrived at Harrisburg at twenty minutes past eight o'clock p. m. By a proclamation of Mayor Roumfort, all business houses and drinking saloons were closed during the stay of the funeral cortege in Harrisburg. Preparations had been

9

made for a grand military and civic demonstration, but a heavy shower of rain was pouring down when they reached the latter city. Col. Thomas S. Mather, of Springfield, Illinois, was on duty at Philadelphia, at the time President Lincoln was assassinated. He was ordered to proceed to Harrisburg and take command of the United States troops at that place, and make arrangements for giving the remains of the President a suitable reception.

Col. Mather had fifteen hundred soldiers in line, who stood for more than an hour in the rain previous to the arrival of the cortege. The body was conveyed to the State Capitol and placed in the hall of the House of Representatives, amid emblems of sorrow, and surrounded by a circle of white flowering almonds. During a part of that night, and until ten o'clock next day, the people in vast numbers passed through the Hall to look at the silent features of the martyred President. Under orders from Col. Mather, a military and civic procession commenced forming at eight o'clock Saturday morning. Col. Henry McCormic was chief marshal of the civic department. The remains were escorted through the principal streets to the depot. In order to have as much daylight as possible for the procession at Philadelphia, the train moved away from the Harrisburg depot at eleven o'clock—one hour before schedule time. Crowds of people were at the depots of Middletown, Elizabethtown, Mount Joy, Landisville and Dillerville. In many places insignia of sorrow were displayed, and all seemed anxious to obtain a passing view of the mournful cortege.

At Lancaster twenty thousand people awaited the arrival of the train, to make their silent demonstrations of mourning. The depot was artistically decorated with flags and crape. The only words expressive of the feelings of the people were displayed at the side of the depot as a motto:

"Abraham Lincoln, the Illustrious Martyr of Liberty; the nation mourns his loss; though dead, he still lives."

Every place of business was closed, and insignia of mourning were upon every house. At the outskirts of the town the large force of the Lancaster Iron Works lined the road, their buildings all draped in mourning. It was affecting to see old men who had been carried in their chairs and seated beside the track, and women with infants in their arms, assembled to look at the passing cortege.

This city was the home of ex-President Buchanan and of the Hon. Thaddeus Stevens. Mr. Buchanan was in his carriage on the outskirts of the multitude. In approaching the town there is a bridge or tunnel through which the train passed. Under this bridge, standing upon a rock, entirely alone, Mr. Stevens was recognized by personal friends on the train. An eye witness, who related the circumstance to me, says that he seemed absorbed in silent meditation, unconscious that he was observed. When the hearse car approached he reverently uncovered his head, and replaced his hat as the train moved away.

Crowds of people were assembled at Penningtonville, Parkesburg, Coatesville, Gallaghervillc, Downington and Oakland. At each place flags draped in mourning and uncovered heads were the sole expressions of feeling. At West Chester intersection, about a thousand persons were assembled at the stations. As the train approached the city of Philadelphia, unbroken columns of people lined the railroad on each side for miles. Minute guns heralded the news as the train passed on to the depot of the Philadelphia, Wilmington & Baltimore railroad, on Broad street. Here the people were not counted by thousands, but by acres. The train reached the depot at half past four p. m., being one hour in advance of schedule time.

CHAPTER XIII.

It was estimated that half a million people were on the streets. A procession, for which preparation had been making for several days, was already formed; men standing in marching order, from four to twelve abreast. A magnificent funeral car was in readiness, which had been specially constructed for the occasion. The corpse was transferred to this car, the coffin enveloped in the American flag, and surrounded with flowers. The grand procession, composed of eleven divisions, and including every organization in the city, both military and civic, was seven miles in length. It moved through the wide and beautiful streets of the city to the sound of solemn music, by a great number of bands. The insignia of sorrow seemed to be on every house. The poor testified their grief by displaying such emblems as their limited means could command, and the rich, more profuse, not because their sorrow was greater, but because their wealth enabled them to manifest it on a larger scale. It was eight o'clock when the funeral car arrived at the southern entrance to Independence Square, on Walnut street. The Union League Association was stationed in the square, and when the procession arrived at the entrance, the Association took charge of the sacred dust, and conveyed it into Independence Hall, marching with uncovered heads to the sound of a dirge performed by a band—stationed in the observatory over the Hall—the booming of cannon in the distance, and the tolling of bells throughout the city. The body was laid on a platform in the centre of the

Hall, with feet to the north, bringing the head very close to the pedestal on which the old Independence bell stands.

That old bell,' with its famous inscription, rang out on the Fourth of July, 1776, "Proclaim liberty throughout all the land, to all the inhabitants thereof." Leviticus, xxv, 10. As if in sorrow and shame for the degeneracy of mankind, when the curse of slavery crept into and controlled every department of our government, the old bell became paralyzed and broken. The descendants of its early friends gave it sepulture in this Hall, where the mighty deeds were enacted which it proclaimed to the world with such grand peals. These early notes, wafted on the free air of heaven, were heard by one of lowly birth, in his western home. As he pondered over them, they sank deep in his heart, and his whole soul answered to their vibrating touch, as he perused the historic pages of the war for American Independence. The years rolled on, and in his obscurity and poverty, he struggled for light and knowledge, with the love of human freedom for his guiding star. He then learned that our fathers indeed won their independence of a foreign foe, but left a fetter in the land for their children to break. At length he began to dispense light to his fellow men. At first, it was done with such modesty and gentleness that it could be appropriately likened to the moon; but as national events followed each other in quick succession, the wisdom of his words and the fervor of his patriotism were more like the shining of the noon-day sun, and were so apparent as to be known and read of all men. He was called to become the head of the nation, when the spirit fostered by slavery was threatening its destruction. He takes what proved to be a last look at the familiar scenes of his manhood; in feeling language he asks his old friends and neighbors to pray for him, and then sadly bids them an affectionate farewell. In the course of his journey, he stood in this very Hall. While here, in a brief address, he said :

"It was something in the Declaration of Independence, giving liberty, not only to the people of this country, but hope to the world for all future time. It was that which gave promise that, in due time, the weights should be lifted from the shoulders of all men, and that all should have an equal chance. * * * Now, my friends, can the country be saved upon that basis? If it can, I will consider myself one of the happiest men in the world, if I can help to save it. *But, if this country can not be saved without giving up that principle, I was about to say, I would rather be assassinated upon this spot than to surrender it.*"

He passes on, assumes the reins of government as the constitutionally elected president of the United States. A long and bloody war ensues. On the one side, the object was to destroy the government, because slavery could no longer rule it; on the other, it was to save the government. In the course of the war, he proclaimed freedom to the slave, and otherwise administered the government so wisely, that when the time arrived for choosing a man to fill his place, he was almost unanimously elected as his own successor. As soon as he entered upon the second term, the rebellion was so nearly crushed that he commenced the work of restoration where that of destruction began; by ordering the national colors to be replaced at the identical spot where they floated when first assailed by parricidal hands. His happiness seemed almost complete. The authority of government was restored and all men free. But the slave power, in its death throes, slew him by the hand of an assassin, and his body is now again in this Hall, to make its report.

Let us imagine the inanimate clay, and the old bell both endowed with life. We hear the dead President say: "It was from you, Old Bell, as from the tongue of the

Almighty, that I received the command to 'Proclaim liberty throughout all the land, to all the inhabitants thereof.' I have obeyed your orders, but see, I too am broken, like thyself; these acts have cost me my life's blood, but what need we care, our race is run. Is it not enough that four millions of bondmen are free, and the only free government on earth saved, to be an asylum for the down-trodden of all lands? I am content."

Then we hear the old bell say: "Well done, thou good and faithful servant; thou hast been faithful unto the end. Henceforth thou shalt wear a crown, even the martyr's crown."

It was eminently proper that the remains of Abraham Lincoln should rest over the holy Sabbath in what may, without irreverence, be termed the sanctuary of the Republic. The interior of Independence Hall has been decorated on many occasions, but never before had such skill and taste been displayed as on this occasion. The scene was a combination of enchantment and gloom of unexampled brilliancy and splendor. Evergreens and flowers of rare fragrance and beauty were placed around the coffin. At the head were boquets, and at the feet burning tapers. The walls were hung with the portraits of many great and good patriots, soldiers and civilians, who have long since passed away. Among these, in a conspicuous place, was seen the benignant countenance of William Penn, who was the embodiment of peace, and yet he was not a more ardent lover of peace than Abraham Lincoln, who died the commander-in-chief of more than a million of soldiers.

In the procession and on the houses along the line of march, there were many mottoes displayed, some of them touchingly beautiful in their expressions of love and sorrow for the departed statesman. The walls of Independence Hall were adorned with them also. I can only give space for some that were on wreaths of flowers about the coffin.   A cross near its head, composed entirely of flowers artistically intertwined, bore the inscription:

"To the memory of our beloved President, from a few ladies of the United States Sanitary Commission."

A beautiful wreath, presented on Saturday evening, bore the modest words:

" A lady's gift.   Can you find a place?"

An old colored woman managed to find her way into the Hall, and approached the Committee of Arrangements with a rudely constructed wreath in her hand, and with tears in her eyes requested that it might be placed on the coffin.   When her request was granted, her countenance beamed with an expression of satisfaction.   The wreath bore the inscription:

"The nation mourns his loss.   He still lives in the hearts of the people."

One of the wreaths that lay near the head of the coffin contained a card with a quotation from one of Mr. Lincoln's conversations with his cabinet officers, the day before his death.   It was in these words:

" Before any great national event, I have always had the same dream.   I had it the other night.   It is of *a ship sailing rapidly.*"

Arrangements were first made to admit those who desired to view the remains, by means of printed cards, which read:

OBSEQUIES OF ABRAHAM LINCOLN,

LATE PRESIDENT OF THE UNITED STATES,

PHILADELPHIA, APRIL 22, 1865,

AT THE

HALL OF INDEPENDENCE,

FROM 10 TO 12 O'CLOCK, P. M.

Entrance at the Court House, on Sixth street, below Chesnut.

Within the hours designated, a constant stream of men and women poured through the Hall, which was closed at midnight. By three o'clock Sunday morning, a large crowd of persons, of both sexes, were congregated on Chesnut street, between Fifth and Sixth, who patiently waited until six o'clock—the time for again opening the Hall to visitors. When it was opened, the people were formed in lines extending from Independence Hall to the Delaware river, on the east, and to the Schuylkill on the west. Thousands spent from three to four hours in the lines before reaching the Hall. Throughout the entire day and night, men and women, of all classes, continued to move in solid phalanx past the remains of the fallen chieftain. The crowd was so great at times that the people were almost suffocated. On the afternoon of Sunday, many women fainted in the crowd. During the day, about one hundred and fifty soldiers were taken in ambulances from the different hospitals in and around the city; and at a late hour, seventy-five veterans, who had each lost a leg in their country's service, hobbled into the Hall, there, amid the sacred surroundings, to take a last look at the face of him whose heart had always beaten in unison with their own.

Appropriate funeral sermons and orations were delivered in many of the churches of the city during the day. Among them may be mentioned the Rev. Dr. March, of the Clinton Street Presbyterian Church; Rev. Dr. Jeffrey, in the Fourth Baptist Church; Rev. H. A. Smith, in the Mantua Presbyterian Church; Rev. F. L. Robbins, of the Green Hill Church; Rev. N. Cyr, at the French Protestant Chapel, and Rev. J. Hyatt Smith, at Mechanics' Hall.

Both nights in Philadelphia, Independence Hall was brilliantly illuminated, as also the *Ledger, Transcript* and other newspaper offices, and many other public and private buildings. The funeral escort were the guests of the city, and were quartered at the Continental Hotel. While here, the hearse car was additionally decorated, the materials being furnished and the work done by the citizens, who regarded it a privilege to add this testimony of their respect to the memory of Abraham Lincoln.

At two o'clock a. m., Monday, April 24, the coffin was closed and preparations made for the departure. At four o'clock, the funeral train moved out of the Kensington depot. After leaving Philadelphia, the track was lined on both sides with a continuous array of people. At Bristol and Morristown, large crowds stood in silence, with uncovered heads. From the time of leaving Washington, at many points where no stoppage was expected, entire neighborhoods, old and young, men and women, the latter frequently with children in their arms, turned out by the roadside by night and by day, and anxiously watched the gorgeous funeral train as it passed. Flags at half mast, mourning inscriptions and funeral arches, testified the sorrow that was in every heart. Clusters of people were collected at various points between stations. The men reverently uncovered their heads as the funeral train glided by.

The train reached Trenton at half past five in the morning, and was greeted by the tolling of bells, firing of minute guns and strains of solemn music. Crowds of people were assembled, the number estimated at twenty thousand, and the array of mourning inscriptions and other evidences of sorrow were abundant. This is the only State capital passed by the funeral cortege on the entire journey, at which they failed to stop for the people to engage in public demonstrations of respect. Its location between the two great cities, and so near them, is, no doubt, the cause of its being made an exception. Governor Parker and staff, with many citizens were taken on board here, and accompanied the remains to New York. At Princeton, a large number of college students were standing with reverent bearing and in silence.   At New Brunswick, the train stopped for a few moments, to find an immense crowd at the depot.   Minute guns were fired from the time it came in sight until it passed from their view.   Large numbers were assembled at Rahway and Elizabeth City, also.

At Newark, every house seemed to be dressed in mourning.   It appeared as if the inhabitants had turned out *en masse* to pay their respects to the memory of Abraham Lincoln.   Many of the women were shedding tears, and the men stood with uncovered heads.   For more then a mile, those on the train could only perceive one sea of human beings.   The United States Hospital was appropriately decorated, and many of the soldiers on crutches were formed in line near it. Minute guns fired and bells tolled from the time the cortege arrived until it passed out of sight.

At Jersey City the scene was still more impressive. The depot was elaborately draped in mourning, bells tolled and cannon boomed, bringing back sad echoes as the train moved into the depot.   The crowd was not admitted into the vast edifice.   When those on board the train disembarked and the coffin was borne along the platform, the funeral party were startled by a vast choir, composed of German musical associations, which had been stationed in a gallery of the building.   As they chanted an anthem or requiem for the dead, many who were unused to weeping were affected to tears.   As the remains were conveyed from the depot to the boat, the choir chanted a solemn dirge and continued it until the ferry boat reached the opposite side of the Hudson river.   The shipping of all nations in the harbor displayed their flags at half-mast.

CHAPTER XIV.

The ferry boat landed at the foot of Desbrosses street, New York city, at ten o'clock a. m., April 24, and the coffin was at once conveyed to a magnificent hearse or funeral car, prepared especially for the occasion. The platform of this car was fourteen feet long and eight feet wide. On the platform, which was five feet from the ground, there was a dais, on which the coffin rested. This gave it sufficient elevation to be readily seen by those at a distance, over the heads of the multitude. Above the dais there was a canopy fifteen feet high, supported by columns, and in part by a miniature temple of liberty. The platform was covered with black cloth, which fell at the sides nearly to the ground. It was edged with silver bullion fringe, which hung in graceful festoons. Black cloth hung from the sides, festooned with silver stars, and was also edged with silver fringe. The canopy was trimmed in like manner, with black cloth, festooned and spangled with silver bullion, the corners surmounted by rich plumes of black and white feathers. At the base of each column were three American flags, slightly inclined outward, festooned and covered with crape.

The temple of liberty was represented as being deserted, or rather despoiled, having no emblems of any kind, in or around it, except a small flag on the top, at half-mast. The inside of the car was lined with white satin, fluted. From the centre of the canopy, a large eagle was suspended, with outspread wings, and holding in its talons a laurel wreath. The platform around the coffin was strewn with flowers. The hearse or funeral car was drawn by sixteen white horses, covered with black cloth trimming, each led by a groom.

From the foot of Desbrosses street, the remains were escorted by the Seventh regiment New York National Guards, to Hudson street, thence to Canal street, up Canal street to Broadway, and down Broadway to the west gate of the City Hall Park.

The procession which followed the remains was in keeping with the funeral car, the whole being indescribably grand and imposing. As far as the eye could see, a dense mass of people, many of them wearing some insignia of mourning, filled the streets and crowded every window. The fronts of the houses were draped in mourning, and the national ensign displayed at half-mast from the top of almost every building. The procession was simply a dense mass of human beings. During the time it was moving, minute guns were fired at different points, and bells were tolled from nearly all the church steeples in the city. The chime on Trinity church wailed forth the tune of Old Hundred in a most solemn and impressive manner.

On arriving at the City Hall, the coffin was borne into the rotunda, amid the solemn chanting of eight hundred voices, and was placed on a magnificent catafalque, which had been prepared for its reception. The Hall was richly and tastefully decorated with the national colors and mourning drapery, and the coffin almost buried with rare and costly floral offerings. A large military guard, in addition to the Guard of Honor, kept watch over the sacred dust. All day and all night long, the living tide pressed into the Hall, to take a last look at the martyred remains. At the solemn hour of midnight, between the twenty-fourth and the twenty-fifth days of April, the German musical societies of New York, numbering about one thousand voices, performed a requiem in the rotunda of the City Hall, with the most thrilling effect. About ten o'clock,

on the morning of April 25, while a galaxy of distinguished officers were assembled around the coffin, Captain Parker Snow, commander of the Arctic and Antarctic expedition, presented some very singular relics.
They consisted of a leaf from the book of Common
Prayer and a piece of paper, on which were glued
some fringes. They were found in a boat, under the
skull of a skeleton which had been identified as the
remains of one of Sir John Franklin's men. The
most singular thing about these relics was the fact that
the only words that were preserved in a legible condition were " THE MARTYR," in capitals. General Dix
deposited these relics in the coffin. At a few minutes
past eleven o'clock, the coffin was closed, preparatory
to resuming its westward journey. Notwithstanding
such vast numbers had viewed the corpse, there were
thousands who had waited for hours, in the long lines,
to obtain a look at the well known face, who were
obliged to turn away sadly disappointed. This disappointment was not confined to any class or condition
of men. The coffin had just been closed, in the presence of the Sergeants of the Veteran Reserve Corps—
who were in readiness to convey it to the hearse—and
a number of distinguished army officers, whose commissions had been signed by the deceased ; when the
first to realize the disappointment were the representatives of Great Britain, Russia and France. They came
in, glittering with scarlet, gold and silver lace, high
coat collars, bearing embroidered cocked hats under
their arms, with other costly trappings, and high birth
and breeding in every gesture, desirous of seeing the
corpse, but they were too late.

At about half past twelve o'clock, the magnificent
hearse or funeral car, drawn by sixteen white horses,
each led by a groom, as on the day before, appeared
on Broadway, at the west gate of City Hall Park.
The coffin was next conveyed to the car. Then commenced the farewell part of the funeral pageant given

by the commercial metropolis of the nation to the memory of Abraham Lincoln. A military force of more than fifteen thousand men, with the staffs of several brigades and divisions, with their batteries, and the civic societies of every conceivable kind, in a great city, which joined in the demonstration, formed a double line about five miles long—equal to a single column of ten miles. In many parts of the procession, twenty men walked abreast. It was composed of eight grand divisions, each division having a marshal, with aids. It moved through the streets to the tolling of bells, the firing of minute guns and the music of a large number of bands. The animosities and division walls of parties, in politics, and sects and denominations, in religion, if not obliterated, were so far lowered, for the time being, that all parties could shake hands over them. Archbishop McClosky, the highest dignitary in the Roman Catholic church, in this country, walked side by side, in the procession, with Rev. Joseph P. Thompson, D. D., one of the most radical of the Congregational reformers of our land.

I have said that all party lines were, for the time, hidden from view, but it devolves upon me to notice one exception. Notwithstanding the blending of so many hearts in the great national sorrow, the city authorities of New York, true to their Tammany instincts, took measures to prevent the colored people from joining in the procession. They had deferred a procession of their own, on the Wednesday before, in order that five thousand of their number might be ready to show their love and respect for the emancipator of their race, by joining the procession to escort his remains on their way to the tomb. When it was known that the city authorities were trying to keep them out of the procession, Secretary Stanton interfered, and the order was set aside, but it was too late to give them such assurance of protection as to bring out their full numbers.

It is due to Thomas C. Acton, President of the Board of Police Commissioners, that the colored people were not entirely excluded. It was he, who, but a few months, before, enforced the right of the colored people to ride in the street cars. Of the five thousand who intended to turn out, only between two and three hundred could be induced to risk the doubt and uncertainty occasioned by the action of the city authorities. These colored people were placed as an appendage to the eighth division, and to be sure that their rights were respected, Commissioner Acton sent a body of fifty-six policemen, under Sergeant Gay, who marched before and behind them in such a way as to be ready in a moment to quell any attempt at violence. A banner, prepared by the ladies of Henry Ward Beecher's Church, was inscribed on one side,

"Abraham Lincoln, our Emancipator,"

and on the other,

"To Millions of Bondmen, he Liberty Gave."

The banner was carried by four freedmen, just from the south, who were astonished to learn that there were so many more Yankees than colored people. Mourning emblems were displayed in such profusion as to be almost a wilderness of sable drapery, and the mottoes and inscriptions on the houses along the line of march, and those carried in the procession, would, if collected, make a volume of themselves. Space can be given for only a small number of them here.

"The workman dies, but the work goes on."

———

"Your cause of sorrow must not be measured by his worth; for then there would be no end."

"His deeds have made his name immortal."

"Let others hail the rising sun,
We bow to him whose race is run."

"A glorious career of service and devotion, is crowned with a
martyr's death."

"Well done thou good and faithful servant."

"Can barbarism further go?"

The New York Caledonian Club, composed of native Scotchmen, carried a banner inscribed:

"Caledonia mourns Columbia's martyred chief."

A miniature monument, near University Place, bore the name,

LINCOLN.

The panels on the sides of the pedestals had the following inscriptions:

FIRST.

"Good night, sweet prince,
And flights of angels sing thee to thy rest."

SECOND.

"With malice towards none; with charity for all."

THIRD.

"There's a great spirit gone."

FOURTH.

"His life was gentle, and the elements
So mixed in him, that nature might stand up
And say to all the world—
This was a man."

10

"The heart of the nation throbs heavily at the **portals of the**
tomb."

———

"Our country weeps."—"In God we **trust.**"

———

"Behold how they loved him."

———

"The Almighty has His own **purposes.**"

———

"To heaven thou art fled, and left the nation in **tears.**"

———

"His death has made him immortal."

———

"Oh why should the spirit of mortal be proud?
Like a swift fleeting meteor, a fast-flying cloud,
A flash of the lightning, a break of the wave,
He passeth from life to his rest in the grave."

The above is the first verse of a hymn which was a
great favorite with Mr. Lincoln. He committed it to
memory in his younger days, and to repeat its verses
was ever after a source of mournful pleasure to him.
He never knew the authorship of it, but it was written
by Alexander Knox, of Edinburgh, Scotland, in the
year 1778. The following are the third, fifth, eleventh
and twelfth verses:

"The infant, a mother attended and loved;
The mother, that infant's affection who proved;
The husband, that mother and infant who blessed,
Each, all, are away to their dwelling of rest.

"The peasant, whose lot was to sow and to reap;
The herdsman, who climbed with his goats up the steep;
The beggar, who wandered in search of his bread,
Have faded away like the grass that we tread.

> " Yea! hope and despondency, pleasure and pain,
>   We mingle together in sunshine and rain;
>   And the smile and the tear, the song and the dirge,
>   Still follow each other, like surge upon surge.

> " 'Tis the wink of an eye, 'tis the draught of a breath,
>   From the blossom of health to the paleness of death—
>   From the gilded saloon to the bier and the shroud;
>   O, why should the spirit of mortal be proud?"

While the procession was escorting the remains to the depot of the Hudson River Railroad, on Thirtieth street, a vast concourse of people assembled in Union Square. A meeting was opened, with Ex-Governor King as presiding officer. He introduced the Rev. Dr. Stephen H. Tyng, who repeated the beautiful words of the Episcopal burial service, and then offered a fervent prayer, appropriate to the occasion. Hon. George Bancroft was next introduced, who delivered a funeral oration. The following synopsis will give a faint idea of its eloquence and power :

" Our grief at the crime which clothed the continent in mourning, finds no adequate expression in words, no relief in tears. Neither the office with which Mr. Lincoln was invested by the approved choice of a mighty people, nor the most simple-hearted kindness of his nature, could save him from the fiendish passions of the relentless rebellion. Waiting millions attend his remains as they are borne in solemn procession over our great rivers, beyond mountains, across prairies, to their final resting place in the valley of the Mississippi. The echos of his funeral knell will vibrate through the world, and friends of freedom, of every tongue and in every clime, are his mourners.

" Members of the Government which preceded his administration, opened the gates of treason, and he closed them. When he went to Washington, the ground on which he trod shook under his feet, and he left the Republic on a solid foundation. Traitors had seized the public forts and arsenals, and he recovered them

to the United States. The capital which he found the abode
of slaves, is now only the abode of freemen. The boundless
public domain, which was grasped at, and in a great measure
held for the diffusion of slavery, is now irrevocably devoted to
freedom. These men talked the jargon of the balance of power,
in a Republic, between slave States and free States, and now their
foolish words are blown away forever by the breath of a Maryland, Missouri and Tennessee—the only States that adopted voluntary emancipation. The atmosphere is now purer than ever
before, and insurrection is vanishing away. The country is cast
into another mould, and the gigantic system of wrong, which has
been the work of two centuries, is dashed down we hope forever.

"As for himself, personally, he was then scoffed at by the proud,
as unfit for his station, and now, against the usage of latter years,
and in spite of numerous competitors, he was the unbiased and
undoubted choice of the American people for the second term of
service. Through all the business of suppressing treason, he retained the sweetest and most perfect disposition. The destruction
of the best, on the battle field, and the more terrible destruction
of our men in captivity, by the slow torture of exposure and
starvation, had never been able to provoke him into harboring
one revengeful feeling, or one purpose of cruelty. How shall the
nation most completely show its sorrow at Mr. Lincoln's death?
How shall it best honor his memory? There can be but one answer. Grief must, like the character of action, breathe forth, in
assertion of the policy to which he fell a sacrifice. The standard
which he held in his hand, must be uplifted again, higher than
before, and must be carried above everything else. This emanci
pation must be affirmed and maintained.

"For the Union, Abraham Lincoln has fallen a martyr. His
death, which was meant to sever it beyond repair, binds it more
firmly than ever. From Maine to the Southwestern boundary of
the Pacific, it makes us one. The country may have needed this
imperishable grief, to touch its inmost feelings. The grave that
receives the remains of President Lincoln, receives a martyr to
the Union, and the monument which rises over his body will bear
witness to the Union. His enduring memory will assist, during
countless ages, to bind the States together, and to incite a love for

our indivisible country. Peace to the departed friend of his country and his race. Happy was his life, for he was a restorer of the Republic, and he was happy in his death, for the manner of his end will plead forever for the Union of the States 'and the freedom of man.'"

The last inaugural address of President Lincoln was then read by Rev. Joseph P. Thompson, D.D., followed by the reading of the ninety-fourth Psalm, by Rev. W. H. Boole, which was exceedingly appropriate to the occasion. It was addressed by King David to the enemies of his country, and can not be read too often. Prayer was then offered by Rev. Dr. Rogers. It was both concise and comprehensive, enumerating in its petitions all the wants of the people and nation. Rabbi Isaacs, of the Jewish Synagogue, on Broadway, then read a portion of Scripture and offered a fervent and touching prayer, from which I give a single quotation:

"Thy servant, Abraham Lincoln, has, without warning, been summoned before Thy august presence. He has served the people of his afflicted land faithfully, zealously, honestly, and, we would fain hope, in accordance with Thy supreme will. O, that his 'righteousness may precede him and form steps for his way,' to the heavenly abode of bliss; that Thy angels of mercy may be commissioned to convey his soul to the spot reserved for martyred saints; that the suddenness with which one of the worst of beings deprived him of his life, may atone for any errors which he may have committed. Almighty God! every heart is pierced by anguish—every countenance furrowed with grief, at our separation from one we revered and loved. We beseech Thee, in this period of our sorrow and despondency, to soothe our pains and calm our griefs. * * * * Our Father who art in heaven, show us this kindness, so that our tears may cease to depict our sorrow, and give place to the joyful hope that, through Thy goodness, peace and concord may supersede war and dissension, and our beloved Union, restored to its former tranquility, may be enabled to carry out Thy wish for the benefit and the happiness of humanity.

We pray Thee, do this; if not for our sakes, for the sake of our little ones, unsullied by sin, who lisp Thy holy name, with hands uplifted, with the importunity of spotless hearts, they re-echo our supplication. Let the past be the end of our sorrow, the future the harbinger of peace and salvation to all who seek Thee in truth. Amen."

Rev. Dr. Osgood then read a hymn entitled, " Thou hast put all things under Thy feet," which was written by William Cullen Bryant. An " Ode for the Burial of Abraham Lincoln," by the same author, was read by Dr. Osgood, also. It reads as follows:

" Oh slow to smite and swift to spare,
    Gentle, and merciful, and just,
Who, in the fear of God, didst bear
    The sword of power, a nation's trust.

" In sorrow by thy bier we stand,
    Amid the awe that hushes all,
And speak the anguish of a land
    That shook with horror at thy fall.

" Thy task is done; the bond are free;
    We bear thee to an honored grave,
Whose noblest monument shall be
    The broken fetters of the slave.

" Pure was thy life; its bloody close
    Hath placed thee with the sons of light,
Among the noble host of those
    Who perished in the cause of right."

Archbishop McClosky, who was to have pronounced the benediction, having become exhausted by his long walk in the procession, was not present, and that service was performed by Rev. Dr. Hitchcock.

The following is an extract from a sermon by Henry Ward Beecher, at Plymouth Church, Sunday April 30,

1865, with reference to the funeral cortege of Abraham Lincoln :

" And now the martyr is moving in triumphal march, mightier than when alive. The nation rises up at every stage of his coming; cities and states are as pall bearers, and the cannon beat the hours in solemn procession; dead, dead, dead, he yet speaketh! Is. Washington dead? Is Hampden dead? Is David dead? Is any man, that was ever fit to live, dead? Disenthralled from the flesh, and risen to.the unobstructed sphere where passion never comes, he begins his illimitable work. His life is now upon the infinite, and will be faithful as no earthly life can be. Pass on. Four years ago, Oh! Illinois, we took from your midst an untried man, from among the people. Behold! we return to you a mighty conqueror, not thine any more, but the nation's—not ours, but the world's. Give him place, Oh, ye prairies. In the midst of this great continent his dust shall rest, a sacred treasure to the myriads who shall pilgrimage to that shrine, to kindle anew their zeal and patriotism. Ye winds that move over the mighty prairies of the west, chant his requiem! Ye people, behold the martyr, whose blood, as so many articulated words, pleads for fidelity, for law, for liberty."

The funeral cortege remained thirty hours in New York, and about twenty-two of that time, the corpse was exposed to public view. During those hours, it was·thought to be a moderate estimate, that one hundred and twenty thousand persons looked upon the rigid features of Abraham Lincoln. It was also estimated that, on the twenty-fifth of April, from seventy-five to one hundred thousand persons took part in the procession, and that there was at least half a million spectators along the line of the procession. Some newspaper reporters placed the number that viewed the remains at one hundred and fifty thousand, and the spectators of the procession at three quarters of a million.

The more I think of the subject, the more I am

impressed with the inadequacy of language to convey
a correct idea of the intensity of feeling and the magnitude of the demonstration; but take it in all its
bearings, New York paid a tribute of respect to the
memory of Abraham Lincoln, the like of which was
never approached in this country before, and has probably not been excelled in the obsequies of any ruler in
the history of the world.

One incident I can not forbear to mention. Lieutenant General Scott accompanied the escort through the
city, in his carriage. At the Thirtieth street depot, he
paid his last respects to the remains of President Lincoln, and then withdrew from the crowd and stood
alone, waiting for the departure of the train. One of
the Illinois delegation, who was also a member of
Congress, approached the General and introduced himself, offering as an apology for doing so, the fact that
it was his first, and might be his last opportunity.
General Scott assured him that no apology was necces-
sary, and straightening himself to his full height, said,
"You do me honor, Sir.' Notwithstanding he was in
his seventy-ninth year, the gentleman who related the
circumstance to me, says he was the most majestic
specimen of a man he ever saw. After introducing
the other members of the delegation, they all left him
and entered the cars.

CHAPTER XV.

The hearse car and Generals' car, or that occupied
by the Guard of Honor, were transferred from Jersey
City to New York on a tug boat. Those two, with
seven others furnished by the Hudson River railroad,
made up the train to convey the funeral party from
New York to Albany. All things being in readiness,
the train left the Thirtieth street depot at 4:15 p. m.,
April 25, leaving an immense multitude of spectators,
the men with uncovered heads. They then dispersed,
to treasure up the memories of that day to the end of
their lives.

At all the stations were demonstrations of sorrow and
respect. Fort Washington, Mount St. Vincent, Yonk-
ers, Hastings, Dobb's Ferry, Irvington, Tarrytown,
Sing Sing, Montrose, Peekskill, and many other stations, were all passed in quick succession. At many
of them the train was greeted with minute guns and
bands performing dirges. Funeral arches and inscriptions expressive of the sorrow of the people, were
everywhere visible. At some of the stations groups of
young ladies were standing on the platforms, representing the States, dressed in white with mourning badges.
Many of the mottoes seen before were repeated. Among
the new ones, were such as, "He died for truth."
"Bear him gently to his rest."

Garrison's Landing, 6:20 p. m. This is opposite
West Point, with which it is connected by a ferry. A
company of Regular soldiers and all the West Point
Cadets were drawn up in line. The officers of the
Academy stood apart, all with uncovered heads. The

Cadets all passed through the funeral car and saluted the remains of their late Commander-in-Chief. Meanwhile, salutes were being fired from West Point, at the west side of the river.

At Cold Spring, an arch was visible, with a young lady representing the Goddess of Liberty weeping. She was supported by two boys, one representing a sailor, the other a soldier.

Fishkill, 6:55 p. m. The depot was artistically draped in mourning, with the motto, " In God we trust." Newburg is on the west side of the Hudson, opposite Fishkill. A flag draped in mourning was displayed from the house where General Washington had his headquarters in revolutionary times.

Poughkeepsie, 7:10 p. m. A bounteous supper was waiting here for the entire escort. A committee of seven ladies placed a wreath of roses on the coffin of the martyred President. A band, composed of students from Eastman's business college, accompanied the funeral train from New York. Professor Eastman, with the remainder of his twelve hundred pupils, helped to make up the twenty-five thousand assembled here. After a stay of nearly one hour, the train moved on, and from this time it was lighted by bonfires and torches, at the different stations. Passing Hyde Park and Straasburgh, the train reaches Rhinebeck at 8:35, but no stoppage. A torchlight procession enabled the assembled crowds of people to view the imposing funeral cortege as it flitted by. Barrytown, Tivoli, Germantown and Catskill present a scene of mourning, drapery, bonfires and torchlights; reaching Hudson at 9:45 p. m. Thousands of people were assembled, minute guns fired, buildings illuminated and draped in mourning. Stockport, Stuyvesant and Castleton were passed, at all of which were bonfires or torchlights.

Arrived at East Albany 10:55 p. m., to find the depot draped in mourning, bells tolling, cannon firing, soldiers marching, and three companies of firemen bearing torches to light the funeral party across the river to Albany. The remains were taken from the car and placed in a hearse. The entire party passed over on the ferryboat, and were escorted by a midnight torch-light procession to the State Capitol.

The coffin was deposited in the Assembly Chamber on a catafalque prepared for the occasion. Over the Speaker's desk appeared the following inscription : " I have sworn a solemn oath to preserve, protect and defend the Government."

At half past one o'clock on the morning of April 26, all being in readiness, the coffin was opened and the people admitted to view the remains. They passed by at the rate of sixty or seventy per minute from the commencement, and the number increased as daylight approached. When the morning dawned it revealed the fact that the whole city was draped in mourning, with mottoes and inscriptions tastefully displayed at appropriate points. Some of the most touching were quotations from Mr. Lincoln's own words, such as,

" The heart of the nation throbs heavily at the portals of the tomb."

" Let us resolve that the martyred dead shall not have died in vain."

The numbers increased, until the line of those awaiting admission was more than a mile in length, one half of them being ladies, all pressing towards the portals of the stately edifice. The cars and 'steam-boats arriving that morning brought additional thou-sands to the city, many of them coming from one to two hundred miles. From the time of its arrival, the coffin was strewn with flowers of the most rare and costly varieties. · As fast as they exhibited signs of fading, they were removed, and fresh ones put in their places. Solemn dirges were performed at in-tervals by the musical societies and bands. The stream of people continued to pour through the edifice, to take a last look at the distinguished dead, and yet, when the hour arrived for replacing the cover, thousands were still in line pressing their way toward the State House. Governor Fenton met the funeral party at New York, and returned with it to Albany, but could go no further from the fact that the Legislature was about to adjourn, and the business before it required his presence.

While the people were filing through the Capitol of the most populous State of the Union, at the rate of more than four thousand an hour, to do homage to the remains of our martyred President, a far different scene was being enacted, in which his assassin was the central figure. On Monday evening, the twenty-fourth of April, a detachment of the 16th regiment of New York cavalry, numbering twenty-five men, under the direction of Col. L. C. Baker, of the Government detective force, left Washington to visit the southern part of Maryland, in search of John Wilkes Booth. They learned from a colored man that he had crossed the Potomac river into Virginia, and soon ascertained that he and his accomplice, Harold, were well armed, and secreted in a barn, between Port Royal and Bowling Green, the county seat of Caroline county. Lieutenant Dougherty arranged his forces, surrounded the barn about dusk on Tuesday evening, and called upon them to surrender. Several hours were spent in efforts to capture them, but Booth steadily expressed his determination not to be taken alive. Despairing of success in any other way, fire was applied to some straw in the barn, hoping to drive them out and then capture them. Seeing no hope of escape, Harold surrendered, but Booth drew up his gun, and was in the act of taking aim at one of the party outside. At this juncture, Lieutenant Dougherty ordered Sergeant Boston Corbett to fire. The shot took effect in Booth's head, but little differing from the wound he inflicted on President Lincoln. He was shot about four o'clock

Tuesday morning, April 26, and died about seven o'clock, after three hours of the most intense agony.

From the time the funeral party started, they had been astonished to witness the immense throngs of people who, night and day, through sunshine and storm, met them at every point to see the great funeral cortege and view the remains. They feared the people of Springfield would be overwhelmed with numbers before they realized the intensity of feeling on the part of the people. At Albany the Illinois Delegation held a consultation and decided that it was best for one of their number to go at once to Springfield and impress upon the citizens the importance of exerting themselves to the utmost in making suitable preparations for the final ceremonies. Col. John Williams volunteered to discharge that duty, and started immediately for Springfield.

After the remains of the President were taken from the train at East Albany, the hearse car and that occupied by the Guard of Honor, were run up the river five miles, to Troy, where they were taken across the Hudson on the railroad bridge, and run down the west side to the depot of the Central Railroad, at Albany. At two o'clock p. m. the coffin was closed and conveyed to a magnificent hearse, drawn by eight white horses. It was escorted by a vast procession, composed of all the military at Albany and Troy, the fire department, the State and city authorities, about thirty civic associations and the citizens generally, to the New York Central depot, where it was again placed on board the hearse car.

Never before were such multitudes of people gathered at the Capital of the State. Every one seemed fully to realize the solemnity of the occasion. It was estimated that at least fifty thousand men, women and children visited the remains during the twelve and a half hours they were exposed to view. The Central railroad furnished seven of its finest cars, making the same number the train had been composed of before, and at 4 o'clock p. m., April 26, the great funeral cortege resumed its journey westward through the empire State.

CHAPTER XVI.

The train arrived at Schenectady at forty-five minutes past four o'clock, to find a multitude of people assembled. The depot, business and dwelling houses were draped in mourning. The women were much affected, many of them crying audibly, and tears coursed down many manly cheeks. The mechanics of the railroad shops all stood in line, with heads uncovered, and the utmost silence prevailed.

Amsterdam, 5:25 p. m. A crowd of people were at the depot. They were evidently from the country, as it was but a small village, and the line was almost a mile long. The train passed through an arch, decorated with red, white and blue, and draped in mourning. The village bells tolled from the time the train came within hearing until it passed.

Funda, 5:45 p. m. Depot, houses, and an arch across the railroad, all decorated with flags and draped in mourning. Minute guns were fired as the train arrived, and continued until it passed out of hearing.

Palatine Bridge, 6:25 p. m. In passing along the valley of the Mohawk river, the railroad runs under the Palatine Bridge, which was artistically decorated with flags, intertwined with mourning emblems. On approaching the village of the same name, a white cross was erected on a grassy mound. The cross was robed in evergreens and mourning. On each side was a woman, apparently weeping. Inscribed on the cross were the words, "We have prayed for you; now we can only weep." The village buildings were draped in mourning, minute guns fired, and a band was playing most solemn music.

Fort Plain, 6:32 p. m. The depot was draped in mourning, and a large gathering of people looked mournfully at the train as it swept by.

St. Johnsville, N. Y., 6:47 p. m., April 26. The funeral escort were the guests of all the cities where they stopped for public demonstrations of respect to be paid to the remains. At Harrisburg they were quarterted at the Jones House ; in Philadelphia, at the Continental Hotel ; in New York at the Metropolitan Hotel, and in Albany, at the Delavan House. The first place where the services of Captain Penrose, the commissary of subsistence, were brought into requisition, was on the run from New York to Albany, when it was necessary to have supper prepared at Poughkeepsie. Between Albany and Buffalo, the distance being too great to pass over without refreshments, Commissary Penrose made arrangements to have them supplied at St. Johnsville, and when the train arrived, a bounteous supper was in waiting. The depot was elaborately draped in mourning. Twenty-four young ladies, from the most wealthy and refined families of the village and surrounding country, dressed in white with black velvet badges, waited on the tables. After supper, these young ladies assembled, entered the hearse car, and placed a wreath of flowers on the coffin, and then the train moved on in its westward course.

It was now quite dark, and the remaining distance to Buffalo occupied the whole time until daylight.

Those on board the train remember this as having been the most remarkable portion of the whole route for its continuous and hearty demonstrations of respect — if any part could be so designated, where all were without precedent. Bonfires and torchlights illumined the road the entire distance. Minute guns were fired at so many points that it seemed almost continuous. Singing soceities and bands of music were so numerous that, after passing a station, the sound of a dirge or requiem would scarcely die away in the distance, until it would be caught up at the town or village they were approaching. Thus through the long hours of the night did the funeral cortege receive such honors that it seemed more like the march of a mighty conqueror, than respect to the remains of one of the most humble of the sons of earth.

We will notice in detail some of the towns and villages on the line.

Little Falls, N. Y., 7:35 p. m. The train paused here long enough for a wreath of flowers in the form of a shield and cross, to be placed on the coffin. It bore the following inscription.

"The ladies of Little Falls, through their committee, present these flowers. The shield, as an emblem of the protection which our beloved President has ever proved to the liberties of the American people. The cross, of his ever faithful trust in God; and the wreath as a token that we mingle our tears with those of our afflicted nation."

Herkimer, 7:50 p. m. Thirty-six young ladies, dressed in white, with black sashes, and holding flags representing the thirty-six States of the Union, were on the platform, surrounded by a vast multitude. A band was playing solemn music, and wreaths of flowers were thrown on board the train as it moved slowly past.

Ilion, N. Y., 7:56. Remington's gun factory was brilliantly illuminated. A torchlight procession and boy zouaves were in line.

Utica, 8:25 p. m., April 26. The depot and other buildings draped in mourning. Many banners were displayed in mourning and bearing inscriptions. Minute guns were firing and bands playing solemn dirges. A multitude of people were assembled and a gorgeous torchlight procession was in line.

As the train swept by Whitesboro and Oriskany, the people were gathered in crowds around large bonfires, and were waving flags trimmed with mourning.

11

Rome, April 26, 9:10 p. m.   It was raining heavily when the train arrived at this place, but there was an immense crowd assembled at the depot, which was richly draped in mourning.   A band of music on the platform was playing a dead march.

Green's Corners and Verona were next passed, at both of which large numbers of people were standing around bonfires.

Oneida, 9:50 p. m.   An arch draped in mourning, bore the inscription :   " We mourn with the nation." The depot was decorated with flags all draped in mourning.   A crowd of people were at the depot, the men with heads uncovered.   A company of firemen bearing lighted torches were in line.

At Canastota, Canaserga, Chittenango, Kirkville and Manlius, the people stood around bonfires and carried lighted torches to see the funeral cortege on its westward course.

Syracuse, April 26, 11:05 p. m.   The depot and adjoining buildings were almost covered with the insignia of sorrow.   Many dwellings were illuminated and mourning drapery suspended around the windows. Tears coursed down the cheeks of both men and women.   Minute guns were firing and bands playing solemn dirges.   The scene was grand and imposing.

Memphis, N. Y., midnight.   At this place, and Warners, just passed, people stood in groups, with uncovered heads and lighted torches, to see the funeral cortege glide past.

At Weedsport, Jordan, Port Byron, Savannah, Clyde, Lyons and Newark, the depots were draped in mourning, bonfires and torchlights revealed groups of men and women with bare heads standing for hours in the middle of the night to catch a passing view of the great funeral.

Palmyra, N. Y.. April 27, 2:15 a. m.   The depot is nicely decorated, and men, women and children flock about the hearse car.

Meriden was next passed, and a bonfire threw a glare of light on the whole surrounding scene.

Fairport, 2:50 a. m. The people with lighted torches, banners, badges and mourning inscriptions were assembled in large numbers, to view the funeral train.

Rochester, N. Y., 3:20 a. m, Thursday, April 27. Here there were assembled an immense multitude, numbering many thousands. The Mayor, City Council, military and civic organizations were out in full force. The depot was draped in mourning, and inscriptions and mottoes were displayed, expressive of the sorrow of the people. From the time the funeral cortege arrived until it passed out of hearing distance, minute guns were fired, bells tolled and bands performed measured and mournful music.

The towns, Coldwater, Chili, Churchville, Bergen, West Bergen and Byron were passed. At all of these the people were gathered in groups around bonfires, and some were carrying lighted torches, all eager to obtain a view of the funeral cortege of Abraham Lincoln.

Batavia, N. Y., 5:18 a. m., April 27. A large number of citizens were assembled at the depot, which was richly draped in mourning. A choir of male and female voices were singing a requiem. Minute guns were firing and bells tolling from the time the cortege arrived until it passed out of hearing.

At Crofts, Corfu, Alden, Wende and Lancaster, the depots were draped, flags displayed and the people stood in groups with uncovered heads, as the funeral cortege glided by. Soon after daylight, in passing a farm house, a group of children were seen in a wagon waving flags trimmed with mourning, towards the train.

Buffalo, N. Y., 7 a. m., Thursday, April 27. The following editorial appeared in the Buffalo *Daily Express*, a few days after the assassination :

" How reverently Abraham Lincoln was loved by the common people ; how much they had leaned upon the strength of his heroic

character, in the great trial through which he led them; how perfect a trust they reposed in his wisdom, his integrity, his patriotism, and the fortitude of his faithful heart; how great a sphere he
filled in the constitution of their hopes, they did not know before.
The shock of consternation, grief, and horror, which revealed it
to them, was undoubtedly the most profound that ever fell upon
a people. It shook this nation like an earthquake. The strong
men of the nation wept together like children. Never, do we
believe, was there exhibited such a spectacle of manly tears,
wrung from stout hearts, by bitter anguish, as in the streets of
every city, town and hamlet, in these United States, on Saturday
last. Ah! there was a deep planting of love for Abraham Lincoln in the hearts of his countrymen! Noble soul, honest heart,
wise statesman, upright magistrate, brave old patriot, the nation
was orphaned by thy death and felt the grief of orphanage.

It would be natural to expect that where such noble
and sympathetic sentiments were expressed, the remains
of Abraham Lincoln would receive a tender greeting.
An extensive military and civic funeral procession
turned out on the nineteenth, the day the obsequies
took place at Washington. For this reason there were
no preparations for any such demonstration on the arrival of the funeral cortege, but it was met at the depot
by a large concourse of people. An impromptu procession was formed by citizens, headed by the military.
The coffin was taken to a fine hearse, which was covered with black cloth, and surrounded by an arched
canopy tastefully trimmed with white satin and silver
lace. The coffin was elevated so as to be seen at a long
distance. The procession moved along the principal
streets to the sound of solemn music, and reached St.
James Hall about half past nine o'clock. The body
was conveyed into the Hall and deposited on a dais, in
the presence of the accompanying Guard of Honor and
the Union Continentals. As the remains were carried
in, the Buffalo St. Cecelia Society sang, with much feeling, the dirge, " Rest, Spirit, Rest; " after which, the

Society placed an elegantly formed harp, made of choice white flowers, at the head of the coffin, which was overshadowed by a crape canopy, and the space lighted up by a large chandelier in the ceiling.   Ex-President Fillmore was among the civilians composing the escort to St. James Hall.   Large numbers of Canadians came over to Buffalo during the day, to manifest their sympathy by taking part in the procession and viewing the remains.   The funeral party being the guests of the city, were quartered at the Mansion House.   All kinds of business was suspended, and it was estimated that between forty and fifty thousand persons took a parting look at the remains.   At eight o'clock in the afternoon the coffin was closed ; about nine it was taken back to the depot, and at ten p. m. the train resumed its journey.

CHAPTER XVII.

At New Hamburg, North Evans, Lake view, Angola and Silver Creek, the depots were draped in mourning, large bonfires were burning, and the people were assembled in great numbers to see the funeral cortege of the martyred President.

Dunkirk, N. Y., 12:10 a. m., Friday, April 28. The depot was elaborately and artistically decorated with mourning drapery and festoons of evergreens. An immense throng of people were assembled, who stood with heads uncovered as the train moved up. The principal feature of the scene was a group of thirty-six young ladies, representing the States of the Union, dressed in white, with black scarfs on their shoulders. All were kneeling, and each held in her hands a national flag. It was a beautiful tableau, as seen at the midnight hour by the glare of more than a hundred lamps and torches. When the train stopped, the young ladies entered the funeral car and placed a wreath of flowers and evergreens on the coffin. The firing of minute guns, the tolling of bells, and the band performing a requiem, combined with the other parts to present a spectacle such as had never before been witnessed on the shores of Lake Erie.

At Brockton there was a crowd standing with heads uncovered and in silence as the train passed by.

Westfield, N. Y., one o'clock a. m., April 28. The train stopped for wood and water, and a delegation of five ladies placed a cross and wreath of roses on the coffin. It bore the inscription:

"Our's, the Cross; Thine, the Crown."

All of them were affected to tears, and considered it a privilege to kiss the coffin.

Ripley, N. Y. Flags were draped in mourning, bonfires blazing, and the people stood in groops with heads uncovered.

State Line, between New York and Pennsylvania, 1:32 a. m., April 28. A bonfire was blazing, flags were draped, and a large number of people were assembled to look at the funeral cortege of Abraham Lincoln.

North East, Pa., 1:47 a. m. A little girl came on board with a cross and wreath of roses and other flowers, and placed it on the coffin. The cross bore the inscription: "Rest in Peace." Major General Dix took leave of the remains at this place and returned to New York. F. F. Faran, Mayor of Erie, and others, came on board.

Erie, Pa., 2:50 a. m., April 28. The citizens of Erie were making arrangements to give suitable reception to the honored remains, when they were informed by the Superintendent of the Cleveland & Erie railroad that the funeral escort had made a special request that no public demonstration be made at that place, in order to give them an opportunity for repose. The request was unauthorized, but it deprived them of a mournful pleasure. Notwithstanding this, a large number of people were assembled at the depot, where a transparency was displayed, with the inscription :

" Abraham Lincoln may die, but the principles embalmed in his blood will live forever."

Girard, Pa. A large number of people were collected at the depot, which was draped with mourning and illuminated with bonfires.

Springfield, Pa., 2:27 a. m., April 28. A large crowd of people, with lighted torches and drooping flags were assembled at the depot to see the funeral cortege pass by.

Conneaut, Ohio, 3:48 a. m., April 28. This is the first station in Ohio. The depot was draped in mourning and a large number of persons on the platform with heads uncovered.

Kingsville, Ohio. Depot was draped and a crowd of people.

Ashtabula, Ohio, 4:27 a. m. Minute guns heralded the approach of the funeral train. The depot was draped in mourning and flags floating to the breeze. Mottoes and inscriptions were displayed expressing the sorrow of the people for the cruel assassination of Abraham Lincoln.

Geneva, Madison, Perry, Painesville and Mentor were passed as the day dawned, but the depots were all draped in mourning, flags floating, mottoes displayed and large crowds of people, all eager to see the hearse car bearing all that was mortal of Abraham Lincoln, to his rest.

Willoughby, Ohio, April 28, 6:08 a. m. Notwithstanding the early morning hour, a number of very aged men were seen leaning on their staffs with their snow-white locks uncovered. Hundreds of watchers looked longingly at the sable cortege gliding by.

Wickliffe, Ohio, 6:20 a. m. Governor John Brough, on the part of Ohio, received the funeral party. He was accompanied by his staff, consisting of Adj. Gen. B. R. Cowan, Asst. Adj. Gen. John T. Mercer, Quar. Mast. Gen. Merrill Barlow, Sergeon Gen. R. N. Barr, Col. S. D. Maxwell, Aid-de-Camp, and F. A. Marble, Private Secretary. Ex-Governor Tod, Senator Sherman, Hon. Sam. Galloway, and others, accompanied the party.

Major General Joseph Hooker, commanding the department of Ohio, with his staff, came on board the train at Wickliffe, and, under General Orders No. 72, took chief command of the funeral escort. A delegation of about twenty-five citizens of Cleveland met the train at this point and formed part of the escort.

Euclid, 6:32 a. m. More of the citizens of Cleveland came on board the train at this point.

Cleveland, Ohio, 7 o'clock a. m., Friday, April 28. The attention of those on the train, was first attracted by a magnificent arch, bearing, in large letters, the inscription :

"ABRAHAM LINCOLN."

Immediately under the arch was a female, dressed to represent the Goddess of Liberty. She held in her hand a flag, and this, together with her cap, was braided in mourning. An immense multitude thronged the streets. At seven o'clock, as the train arrived, a national salute of thirty-six guns was fired, and half-hour guns from that time until sunset. As the funeral cortege approached, the bells throughout the city commenced tolling, the shipping in the harbor and all the hotels and other public buildings displayed the American flag at half-mast, and all business houses were closed, and remained so throughout the day. At half past seven an immense procession consisting of military and civic associations, was formed at the Euclid street station. It was composed of six divisions, each headed by a band. As soon as the train arrived at the station the coffin was placed in a magnificent hearse, draped with the American flag trimmed with mourning.

The procession moved through Euclid street to Erie street, down Erie to Superior street, thence to a public park, where a beautiful temple had been erected. This temple was twenty-four by thirty-six feet, and fourteen feet high, to the cornice. The roof was in pagoda style. Within this temple was a gorgeous catafalque. The coffin was laid on a dais, about two feet above the floor of the catafalque. The columns were wreathed with evergreens and white flowers, and trimmed with mourning. Black cloth fringed with silver, drooped from the corners and the centre of the canopy, and looped back to the columns. The floor and sides of the dais were covered with black cloth, bordered with silver fringe. The cornice was brilliantly ornamented with white rosettes and stars of silver. The inside of the canopy was lined with black cloth, gathered in folds, and black and white crape. In the centre of the canopy was a large star of black velvet, ornamented with thirty-six silver stars, representing the States of the Union. The dais was covered with flowers and a figure representing the Goddess of Liberty was placed at the head of the coffin. The ceiling of the temple was hung with festoons of evergreens and flowers. Lamps were attached to the pillars of the catafalque, and the columns of the temple, that the remains might be viewed at night as well as by day. This temple seemed, in daylight, as if it was a creation of fairy land, and when lighted up with all the lanterns, and standing out amid the surrounding darkness, looked more like the realization of an enchanted castle than the work of men's hands. The cost of it must have been very great, and I have been thus minute in the description because there was nothing comparable to it at any other place on the whole journey. This large expenditure on the part of the citizens of Cleveland, to prepare a few hours resting place for the remains of Abraham Lincoln, on their way to the tomb, was only a faint symbol of the sacrifices they had already made, and were still willing to make in support of the principles for which he was assassinated.

The religious services were conducted by the Right Rev. Bishop McIlvaine, of the Protestant Episcopal Church. He read a part of the funeral service of that Church, suitable to the occasion. After the religious services, two columns of spectators—one on each side— began filing past the corpse, and, notwithstanding it rained the greater part of the time, about eighty persons per minute viewed the remains of President Lin coln, throughout the day.   At intervals the coffin was freshly covered with flowers by the ladies.   It was estimated that more than fifty thousand persons viewed the remains, and when the coffin closed, near midnight, there were still hundreds in line, disappointed in their efforts to look on the face of the dead.   The funeral party being the guests of the city, were quartered at the Weddell House.

While the funeral party were in Cleveland they were waited upon by Charles L. Wilson, editor of the Chicago *Journal*, as chairman of the Committee of One Hundred citizens, appointed by the City Council of Chicago, " to proceed to Michigan City to receive the remains of President Lincoln, escort them to Chicago, and accompany them to Springfield."   Mr. Wilson tendered the hospitalities of the city to the funeral escort when they should arrive in Chicago, and stated that, up to the time of his departure, forty-one organizations and societies, representing twenty-five thousand men, had reported to the Chief Marshal their intention to form part of the procession.

The saloons of Cleveland were all closed during the stay of the funeral party in that city, by a proclamation from the Mayor; and, in order to control the movements of the vast multitude, all the streets leading to the Park were fenced up and gates placed in the centre. They were guarded by military, and the people admitted no faster than they could view the remains and pass out.   In this way, all crowding about the temple was avoided.   The procession began re-forming about ten o'clock p. m., and escorted the remains to the depot.

CHAPTER XVIII

At midnight, the funeral cortege left Cleveland, to continue its westward course. Rain continued to fall, but that did not abate the anxiety of the people.

Among the towns worthy of special mention, on account of their costly and elaborate demonstrations, were Berea, Olmstead, Columbia, Grafton, Lagrange, Wellington, Rochester, New London, Greenwich, Shiloh, Shelby and Crestline, the latter place being reached at seven minutes past four o'clock a. m. At all these places the depots were draped and the national flag shrouded in mourning. Mottoes and inscriptions expressive of the sorrow of the people were everywhere visible. Through the rain and darkness they came, bearing lanterns and torches, that they might obtain a passing view of the great funeral pageant. Galion, Iberia and Gilead, each presented the same appearance, and the train arrived at Cardington at 5:20 a. m., Saturday, April 29. The largest gathering seen after leaving Cleveland, were collected at this place, about three thousand people being present. The depot was handsomely draped with mourning flags. Over the doorway was an inscription, in large letters,

"He sleeps in the blessings of the poor, whose fetters God commissioned him to break."

The train arrived and departed to the sound of minute guns and the tolling of bells. Ashley, Eden, Delaware, Berlin, Lewis' Centre, Orange, Westerville and Worthington, all presented the same appearance of depots draped in mourning. with mottoes, inscriptions, and increasing crowds of people.   The train arrived at . Columbus, Ohio, at 7:30 a. m., Saturday, April 29. By way of preparing for appropriately honoring the remains of the late Chief Magistrate, the following order had been promulgated at the proper time :

General Order, No 5. }

GEN'L H'DQ'RS, STATE OF OHIO,
ADJUTANT GENERAL'S OFFICE,
COLUMBUS, April 23, 1865.

Major John W. Skiles, Eighty-eighth O. V. I., is hereby appointed Chief Marshal of the ceremonies in honor of the remains of the late President Lincoln, in the city of Columbus, on the twenty-ninth inst.   He will appoint his own aides, and will have entire control of the ceremonies and procession attending the transfer of the remains from and to the depot.   All societies, delegations, or other organizations, wishing to participate in the ceremonies, will report, by telegraph or letter, to the Chief Marshal on or before ten o'clock a. m. of Friday, the twenty-eighth inst.

The headquarters of the Chief Marshal, during Thursday and Friday, twenty-seventh and twenty-eighth inst., will be at the Adjutant General's office, in the Capitol.

By order of the Governor:

B. R. COWEN,
Assistant Adjutant General.

Immediately on the arrival of the train, the funeral party were taken in carriages, the carriages moving three abreast, and the coffin was conveyed to a magnificent hearse.   It was seventeen feet long, eight and a half feet wide, and seventeen and a half feet from the ground to the top of the canopy.   The floor of the hearse was four feet from the ground.   A dais was raised two and a half feet above the floor, making six and a half feet above the ground.   On this the coffin rested, where it was sufficiently elevated for all to see it.   The canopy was formed like a Chinese pagoda. The interior of the canopy was lined with silk flags, and the outside covered with black broadcloth. The dais, main floor,and the entire hearse was covered with black cloth, which hung in festoons from the main platform to within a few inches of the ground. The broadcloth was fringed with silver lace and ornamented with heavy tassels of black silk. Surrounding the cornice were thirty-six silver stars, and on the apex and the four corners were heavy black plumes. The canopy was curtained with black cloth and lined with white merino. On each side of the dais was the name "Lincoln," in silver letters. The hearse was drawn by six white horses, all covered with black cloth, edged with silver fringe. The heads of the horses were surmounted with large black plumes, and each was led by a groom, dressed in black, with white gloves and a white band around his hat.

The flowers of Buffalo and Cleveland were still on the lid of the coffin. The procession was by far the most grand and imposing of any that had ever marched through the streets of the capital of Ohio. It was composed of soldiers, citizens and civic societies, not of Columbus only, but of Cincinnati and other cities and towns for many miles around. At the Soldiers' Hospital, the invalids had adorned the palings in front of the building with national flags, trimmed with mourning, and displayed other evidences of sorrow.

These invalids, made so in the service of their country, gathered flowers and branches, principally lilac, and for several hundred yards, had strewn them on each side of the street, where the procession was to pass. Many of the soldiers appeared on crutches.

Amid the tolling of bells and the booming of cannon, the solemn cortege wended its way to the State Capitol. The pillars of that beautiful white edifice were artisticially draped in mourning, and flags were at halfmast on each side of the dome. Displayed conspicuously, in large black letters, were the following words: "With malice toward none, with charity for all."

Arched over the gate leading to the grounds, were the words, "Ohio Mourns," and over the entrance to the building, "God moves in a mysterious way." The interior of the capitol was draped in the most elaborate and costly style.

The coffin was conveyed into the rotunda, where it was deposited on a mound of moss, thickly dotted with the choicest of flowers, and surrounded by elegant vases of rare exotics. The walls were adorned with Powell's great painting of Perry's victory on Lake Erie; with clusters of battle flags, torn and riddled with bullets, as they were borne by Ohio regiments in suppressing the rebellion. These were festooned with crape, and drooped sadly around the spacious rotunda. As soon as the coffin was properly arranged, the spectators began to pass before the remains.

Solemn dirges were performed at intervals, and guns were fired during the day. In the afternoon, a meeting was held at the east side of the capitol. On the stage were Major Generals Hooker and Hunter, with the clergy of the city. Rev. Mr. Goodwin opened the services with prayer. The Hon. Job E. Stevenson then addressed the vast assemblage, in a most eloquent and thrilling oration. He was listened to with the most profound attention from beginning to end. I can only give a very brief synopsis. He said:

" Ohio mourns, America mourns, the civilized world will mourn the cruel death of Abraham Lincoln, the brave, the wise, the good; bravest, wisest, best of men. History alone can measure and weigh his worth, but we, in parting from his mortal remains, may indulge the fullness of our hearts, in a few broken words, of his life, his death and his fame.

" A western farmer's son, self-made, in early manhood he won by sterling qualities of head and heart, the public confidence, and was entrusted with the people's power. Growing with his State, he became a leader in the west. Elected President, he disbelieved the threats of traitors, and sought to serve his term in peace. The clouds of civil war darkened the land. The President pleaded and prayed for peace, 'long declined the war,' and only when the storm in fury burst upon the flag, did he arm for the Union. For four years the war raged, and the President was tried as man was never tried before. Oh, 'with what a load of toil and care,' has he come, with steady, steadfast step, through the valley and the shadow of defeat, over the bright mountain of victory, up to the sun-lit plain of peace!

"Tried by dire disaster at Bull Run, where volunteer patriots met veteran traitors; at Fredericksburg, where courage contended with nature; at Chancellorville, that desperate venture; in the dismal swamps of the Chickahominy, where a brave army was buried in vain; by the chronic siege of Charleston, the mockery of Richmond, and the dangers of Washington—through all these trials the President stood firm, trusting in God and the people, while the people trusted in God and in him. There were never braver men than the Union volunteers; none braver ever rallied in Grecian phalanx or Roman legion; none braver ever bent the Saxon bow, or bore barbarian battle axe, or set the lance in rest; none braver ever followed the crescent or the cross, or fought with Napoleon, or Wellington, or Washington. Yet the commander-in-chief of the Union army and navy was worthy of the man—filling for four years the foremost and most perilous part unfaltering.

"Tried by good fortune, he saw soldiers of the West recover the great valley, and bring back to the Union the Father of Waters, and all his beautiful children. He saw the legions of Lee hurled from the heights of Gettysburg. He saw the flag of the free rise on Lookout Mountain, and spread from river to sea, and rest over Sumter. He saw the Star Spangled Banner, brightened by the blaze of battle, bloom over Richmond, and he saw Lee surrender. Yet he remained wise and modest, giving all the glory to God and our army and navy.

"Tried by civil affairs which would have taxed the powers and tested the virtues of Jefferson, Hamilton and Washington, he administered them so wisely and well, that after three years no man was found to take his place. He was re-elected, and the harvest of success came in so gradually, that he might have said, ' Now, Lord, lettest Thou Thy servant depart in peace, for mine eyes have seen Thy salvation.' Yet he was free from weakness or vanity. Thus did he exhibit, on occasion, in due proportion and harmonious action, those cardinal virtues, the trinity of true greatness—courage, wisdom and goodness; goodness to love the right, wisdom to know the right, and courage to do the right. Tried by these tests, and by the touchstone of success, he was the greatest of living men.

"But why multiply words of his greatness? We read it in the nation's eyes. What a scene do we witness! Some of us remember when, on the thirteenth of February, 1861, four years and two months before his death, the President was here on his way to Washington, and spoke in the State House. Then, this self-made man was untried, and his friends, and he himself, questioned his capacity to fill the responsible position to which he was chosen. He spoke with misgivings, but placing his reliance on Providence, went forward reluctantly to the chair; and now, after four short years, he returns, borne on the bosom of millions of men, his way watered with tears and strewn with flowers.

"He stood on the summit, his brow bathed in the beams of the rising sun of peace, singing in his heart the angelic song of 'Glory to God in the highest, peace on earth and good will toward men.' 'With malice toward none, with charity for all,' he had forgiven the people of the South, and might have forgotten their leaders— covering with the broad mantle of his charity their multitude of sins. But he is slain—slain by slavery. That fiend incarnate did the deed. Beaten in battle, the leaders sought to save slavery by assassination. This madness presaged their destruction.

"Abraham Lincoln was the personification of Mercy. Andrew Johnson is the personification of Justice. They have murdered Mercy, and Justice rules alone, and the people, with one voice, pray to heaven that justice may be done. The blood of thousands of murdered prisoners cries to heaven. The shades of sixty-two thousand starved soldiers rise up in judgment against them. The body of the murdered President condems them. Some deprecate vengeance. *There is no room for vengeance here. Long before justice can have done her perfect work, the material will be exhausted and*

12

the record closed. Some wonder why the South killed her best friend. Abraham Lincoln was the true friend of the people of the South; for he was their friend as Jesus is the friend of sinners, ready to save when they repent. Ours is the grief, theirs is the loss, and his is the gain. He died for Liberty and Union, and now he wears the martyr's glorious crown. He is our crowned President. While the Union survives, while the love of liberty warms the human heart, Abraham Lincoln will hold high rank among the immortal dead. The imperial free Republic, the best and strongest government on earth, will be a monument to his glory, while over and above all shall rise and swell the great dome of his fame."

The procession of the morning was re-formed, and escorted the remains to the depot, and at eight o'clock p. m. the funeral train resumed its course, amid the firing of guns and the tolling of the bells of the city.

CHAPTER XIX

At Pleasant Valley, Unionville, Milford, Woodstock and Cable, the depots were decorated and draped in mourning, and bonfires and torches enabled the large crowds assembled to see the funeral train. At Woodstock a delegation of ladies entered the hearse car and decorated the coffin with flowers, and at the same time the Woodstock band played a solemn piece of music.

Urbana, Ohio, 10:30 p. m., April 29. Three thousand people were assembled, and a large bonfire lighted up the scene. Ten young ladies entered the car and strewed flowers on the bier, some of them weeping. At the same time a choir of forty male and female voices sang, "Go to thy Rest." The train arrived and departed with minute guns firing and bells tolling.

At St. Paris and Fletcher bonfires were blazing and the people were standing with heads uncovered and in silence as the train moved along.

Piqua, Ohio, 12:20 a. m., Sunday, April 30. Many thousands of people were assembled at the depot, which was draped in mourning. The scene was lighted up with large fires. A delegation from the Methodist Church, with Rev. Granville Moody, sang a funeral hymn. Two bands also discoursed solemn music.

Covington, Bradford Junction and Gettysburg were passed in quick succession, and, notwithstanding it was in the middle of the night, there was a large crowd at each place, with bonfires, flags and mottoes.

Greenville, Ohio, two o'clock a. m., Sunday, April 30. The depot was tastefully decorated, and the scene lighted up by two large bonfires. Thirty-six young ladies, representing the States of the Union, were dressed in white, each waving a star-spangled banner. A requiem was sung by a choir of ladies aud gentlemen. A large number of people were standing at the depot at New Madison.

New Paris, 2:41, Sunday morning, April 30. The depot was artistically draped in mourning. An arch spanned the track. It was adorned with evergreens draped in mourning. The scene was lighted up by huge bonfires. This was the last town on that line of road in the State of Ohio.

Richmond, Ind., 3:10 a. m., Sunday, April 30. This was the first town entered in the State of Indiana. The scene here was imposing and magnificently solemn. The city contains about twelve thousand inhabitants, but there were more than that number present. Arrangements were effected the day before to have all the bells in the city rang an hour previous to the expected arrival of the funeral cortege. At the time appointed they pealed forth their notes on the still night air, and soon the streets were filled with men and women, old and young, all wending their way to the depot. Broad-brimmed hats and Quaker bonnets were liberally sprinkled among the vast concourse—as the Friends are more numerous here, in proportion to the whole population, than they are in the city of Philadelphia. Nearly the whole population of the city came out, and the people in the surrounding country left their homes in the middle of the night and came many miles in wagons, carriages, and on horseback, and it was estimated that between twelve and fifteen thousand were present.

As the train approached the city the bells on the engines of the Airline railroad—a cross road—were tolling, and all the engines were lighted up with revolving lamps and tastefully decorated in mourning. . A gorgeous arch was constructed, twenty-five feet high and thirty wide, under which the train passed. On both sides of the structure American flags were wrought into triangles, down the sides of which were suspended, at equal distances, transparencies of red, white, and blue, alternating with chaplets of evergreens, which clambered up the sides of the triangles and centered at the summit in velvet rosettes. Across the structure, at about eighteen feet from the base was a platform carpeted with black velvet. On the ends of this platform were two flags in drooping folds. In the center of this upper work was a female representing the Goddess of Liberty. She was in a sitting posture, weeping over a coffin. On one side was a boy-soldier and on the other a boy-sailor, both acting as mourners. Governor Morton and suite, with other prominent gentlemen from different parts of the State, about one hundred in all, came on a special train from Indianapolis and joined the funeral party at Richmond. After a brief pause, the train moved slowly away, and the multitude, with sad hearts, dispersed to their homes in silence.

Centerville, Ind., 3:41 a. m. The depot was splendidly robed in mourning. At each end of the platform were two chandeliers, brilliantly lighted. The people were anxious for the train to tarry longer, but of course their wishes could not be complied with. Centerville is the home of the Hon. George W. Julian, and was the home of Hon. O. P. Morton, previous to his becoming Governor of the State.

Germantown, Ind., 4:05 a. m. A number of brilliant bonfires were burning, flags draped in mourning, and other evidences of sorrow exhibited.

Cambridge City, Ind., 4:15 a. m. As the funeral train reached this place, it was received with salvos of artillery. A very tasty arch spanned the railroad track. It was beautifully decorated and appropriately draped in mourning. The darkness was turned into a solemn glare by the burning of Bengal lights, and as the reddish blue met the first streaks of grey on the eastern horizon, the effect was solemn and impressive. It was the unanimous verdict of those who traveled all the journey with the train, that this, and the display at Richmond, was not excelled in taste and appropriateness by anything that had been witnessed. There was a solemn earnestness depicted on the countenance of the Indiana patriots, and the sentence seemed to be written as if in "burnished rows of steel," that though Lincoln had died, the republic should live.

Dublin, Ind., 4:30 a. m., Sunday, April 30. The platform and sides of the track were lined with people whose looks and actions bespoke their deep grief. A neat and beautiful arch, entwined with evergreens and mourning emblems, was erected for the train to pass under. The depot was artistically draped, and on the right was a large flag. In a conspicuous place there was a portrait of the martyred President entwined with evergreens and roses. Dublin is a town of about fifteen hundred inhabitants, and was the last station passed in Wayne county, which has been largely under Quaker influence from its first settlements, and, although you would see but little of the outward sign of that peculiar people, their principles are nowhere more decidedly felt than at this place. There has never been a whisky-shop in the town, and it is a remarkable coincidence that for many years the Republican ticket has been voted unanimously—not a single one on the other side. I well remember the amusement created at Richmond, in the same county, on the evening of the Presidential election, in 1864. As the reports came in by telegraph they were posted on an illuminated bulletin. Among the earliest was,

Dublin,	For Lincoln,	269
"	For McClellan,	0
		—
Majority for Lincoln,		269

At Lewisville, Rayville, Knightstown, Charlottesville, Greenfield, Philadelphia and Cumberland, mourning emblems and other demonstrations of sorrow were everywhere visible.

Indianapolis, seven o'clock, a. m., Sunday, April 30, 1865. The funeral cortege arrived at this hour with all that was mortal of Abraham Lincoln. The avenues leading to the depot were closely packed with people. The military organizations were in line from the depot to the State House. The corpse was taken in charge by a local guard of soldiers, and conveyed to a very large and magnificent hearse, prepared especially for the·occasion. It was drawn by eight white horses, six of them having been attached to the carriage in which the President elect rode, on his way to Washington, four years before. By the time the procession was ready to move, rain commenced falling. The arrival of the train was announced by the firing of artillery and tolling of bells throughout the city, and this continued until the hearse arrived at the State House. The body was conveyed to the interior of the building, and soon after exposed to view.

The Sabbath school children were first admitted, and then ladies and citizens generally passed through the Capitol and viewed the remains. At many of the streets intended to be crossed by the procession were triple arches, adorned with evergreens and national flags. Great preparations had been made in draping the city in mourning. It included public buildings, business houses and private residences of all classes. The threatening rain deterred many from ornamenting their buildings who would otherwise have.done so, and the torrents of water sadly marred what had been done.

The rain prevented many of the organizations from turning out that had provided themselves with banners bearing appropriate inscriptions. The colored Masons, in their appropriate clothing, and colored citizens generally turned out in procession and visited the remains in a body. At the head of their procession they carried the Emancipation·Proclamation. At intervals banners were seen bearing, among others, the following inscriptions:

"Colored men always Loyal."

———

"Lincoln, Martyr of Liberty."

———

"He lives in our memories."

———

"Slavery is Dead!" ·

———

The City Councils of Cincinnati, Louisville and Covington, with Governor Bramlette and many other distinguished personages from Kentucky, and from nearly all the towns and cities of Indiana, were in Indianapolis, to take part in a grand military and civic demonstration. It was expected that the procession would march early in the day, and that Governor Morton would deliver a funeral oration at the Capitol in the afternoon. Every railroad train for the previous twenty-four hours brought in its thousands, but the incessant rain prevented the programme from being carried out. All that could be done was to pay their silent respects to the remains. A constant stream of spectators continued to file past the coffin until near midnight, when it was escorted back to the depot, and, like the star of empire, continued its westward course.

A time table was prepared, and rules and regulations adopted, at Indianapolis, for running the train from that city to Chicago. The paper was signed by an officer of each of the three roads over which the train was to pass—the Indianapolis & Lafayette, the Louisville, New Albany & Chicago, from Lafayette to Michigan City, and the Michigan Central from Michigan City to Chicago. As a sample of the way the train was run during the whole journey, I omit the time table, but insert here the

RULES AND REGULATIONS.

1.   The figures in Table represent the time upon which the Pilot Engine is to be run, and the funeral train will follow, leaving each station *ten minutes* behind the figures of this table.

2.   The funeral train will pass stations at a speed not exceeding *five miles an hour,* the engineman tolling his bell as the train passes through the station and town.

3.   Telegraph offices upon the entire route will be kept open during the passage of the funeral train, and as soon as the train has passed a station the operator *will at once give notice to that effect to the next telegraph station.*

4.   The pilot engine will pass no telegraph station without first getting information of funeral train having passed the last preceding telegraph station, coming to a full stop for that information, if necessary.

5.   Upon the entire route a safety signal will be shown at each switch and bridge, and at entrance upon each curve, indicating that *all is safe for the passage of pilot and train*—each man in charge of a signal knowing personally such to be the case, so far as his foresight can provide for it.   The signal from Indianapolis, until reaching *broad daylight,* to be a *white light,* and from that point to Chicago, a *white flag,* draped.

6.   The engineman in charge of pilot engine will carry two red lights in the night, and an American flag, draped, during daylight, indicating that a train is following, and will also provide themselves with red lights, flags and extra men, to give *immediate notice* to the funeral train, in case of meeting with anything on the route causing delay or detention.

7.   The enginemen in charge of the funeral train will keep a sharp lookout for the pilot engine and its signals.

8.   The pilot and funeral train will have entire right to the line during its passage, and all engines and trains of every description will be kept out of the way.

9.   Each road forming the route will run its train upon its own standard time.

CHAPTER XX.

Notwithstanding the train departed in the middle of the night from Indianapolis, formidable demonstrations were made at Augusta, Zionsville, Whitestown, Lebanon, Hazelrigg, Thorntown, Colfax, Stockwell and many other points. The depots were draped in mourning and other insignia of sorrow were visible, in the light of bonfires and torches; but the people were assembled in large numbers at every point, to witness the great funeral train.

Arrived at Lafayette at three o'clock and thirty-five minutes, Monday morning, May 1. It was known that the train would stop at this place but a few minutes, but it appeared to those on board as if all the inhabitants of the city, and from many miles of the surrounding country, were there. The depot was draped in mourning, and the surrounding scene well lighted. The bells of the city were tolled, and other manifestations of sorrow were visible.

From Lafayette, the stations of Tippecanoe Battle Ground, Brookston, Chalmers, Reynolds, Bradford, Francisville, Medaryville, Kankakee, LaCrosse, Wanatah, Westville, Lacroix and many other towns, the depots were draped, and the people in many ways demonstrated their sorrow for the loss of our Chief Magistrate.

Michigan City, Indiana, eight o'clock a. m., May 1. A bountiful breakfast was prepared for the entire funeral party, in the main station house. Thirty-six young ladies, representing the States of the Union, and one representing the Goddess of Liberty, appeared in appropriate costumes, and with a large number of other ladies, appropriated the time assigned to the funeral party for breakfast, in passing through the hearse car to look on the coffin containing the remains of the martyred President.

The funeral train approached the depot under a large triple arch, which was surmounted by a tall flagstaff, bearing the national colors trimmed with mourning, at half-mast. Portraits of the illustrious deceased were suspended from the centre of each arch, wreathed in evergreens, and surrounded by draped flags and other insignia of sorrow. Among the mottoes displayed, were the following:

"Noblest martyr to Freedom; sacred thy dust; hallowed thy resting place."

"With tears we resign thee to God and History."

"The purposes of the Almighty are perfect, and must prevail."

"Our guiding star has fallen; our nation mourns."

Here the funeral escort were joined by the Hon. Schuyler Colfax and friends, and the citizen's committee of one hundred, who came out from Chicago on a special train. After all had partaken of breakfast, the train started for Chicago, at 8:35 a. m., over the Michigan Central Railroad.

Arrived at Chicago at 11 o'clock a. m., Monday, May 1. The train did not run to the Union depot, but stopped a little more than one mile south, where a temporary platform had been prepared, opposite Park Place, a short street running from the lake shore one square west, to Michigan avenue. Park Place is one square north of Twelfth street, and is between that street and Lake Park.

Across the foot of Park Place a magnificent Funeral Arch had been erected. It was built of wood, in the Gothic style of architecture, and consisted of a central arch thirty feet high in the clear, and twenty-four feet wide, and two side arches, each eight feet wide in the clear, and twenty feet high. The three arches and their abutments, or columns, made a total width of fifty-one feet. The total height of the central arch and turrets was about forty feet.

This grand triple arch had two fronts, one east, the other west. Fifty American flags, with mourning drapery interwoven, were used in decorating the arches. Busts and portraits of Lincoln were placed conspicuously upon the arches. Two figures of an American eagle were placed near the apex of the central arch— that on the east front folding its wings, as if at rest, and the one on the west with wings extended, as if in the act of taking flight. All three of the arches had inscriptions on each front. Those on the east or lake side were :

"Our Union; cemented in patriot blood shall stand forever."

———

"An honest man is the noblest work of God."

———

"The poor man's champion; the people mourn him.'

On the west front:

"We honor him dead, who honored us while living."

———

"Rest in peace noble soul, patriot heart."

———

"Faithful to right, a martyr to justice."

Beneath the central arch was a platform or dais.

The dais was covered with black velvet, ornamented with silver fringe, and fastened with silver stars. Black velvet hung in festoons on all sides, reaching nearly to the ground. It was sufficiently elevated for those at a distance to view it over the heads of the surrounding multitude. The area around the dais was large enough to afford standing room for many thousands. This area was filled to its utmost capacity long before the hour of the expected arrival.

When the funeral train arrived at Park Place, a signal gun was fired, and the tolling of the bell on the Court House announced the news to the citizens, but there were already thousands and thousands of people congregated in the vicinity of the funeral arch. The vast multitude stood in profound silence, and reverently uncovered their heads as the coffin was borne to the dais beneath the grand arch, while the great Western Light Guard Band performed the Lincoln Requiem, composed for the occasion. Thirty-six young lady pupils of the High School, dressed in white and banded with crape, then walked around the bier and each deposited an immortelle on the coffin as she passed. The coffin was then placed in the funeral car or hearse, prepared expressly for the occasion, and the funeral cortege passed out of Park Place into Michigan avenue, and fell into procession in something like the following order:

Police.

Band of music playing the Lincoln Requiem.

Chief Marshal Col. R. 'M. Hough and Major General Joseph Hooker.

Assistant Marshal Col. J. L. Hancock, and Superintendent of Police, William Turtle.

Major General Alfred Sully and staff.

Brigadier General N. B. Buford and staff.

Brigadier General J. B. Sweet and staff; and Military Band.

Eighth Veteran Reserve Corps, Lieut. Col. Skinner, and four
hundred men, with arms reversed, and in mourning.

Military Band.

Fifteenth Regiment Veteran Reserve Corps, Lieut Col. Martin
Flood commanding, with four hundred men, arms
reversed and in mourning.

PALL BEARERS.		PALL BEARERS.
Hon. Lyman Trumbull,		Hon. Thomas Drummond,
Hon. John Wentworth,		Lt. Gov. William Bross,
Hon. F. C. Sherman,		Hon. J. B. Rice,
Hon. E. C. Larned,		Hon. S. W. Fuller,
Hon. F. A. Hoffman,		Hon. T. B. Bryan,
Hon. J. R. Jones,		Hon. J. Young Scammon.

FUNERAL CAR.

Military Escort.

Capt. James McComly, of the 9th Veteran Reserve Corps; First
Lieutenant J. R. Durkee, 7th U. S. I.; Second Lieutenant E.
Murphy, 10th U. S. I.; and twenty-five sergeants of the Veteran
Reserve Corps.

Guard of Honor,

Consisting of the general officers appointed by the Secretary of
War to accompany the remains from Washington to Springfield,
Illinois.

Two carriages contained the relatives and family friends. In
the first, rode the Rev. Dr. Gurley, pastor, and Ninian W. Edwards and C. M. Smith, the two latter brothers-in-law of the President. In the second, rode Judge David Davis, of the U. S. Supreme Court; General W. W. Orme, and W. H. Hanna, Esq.

Illinois Delegation.

Gov. R. J. Oglesby, Hon. Jesse K. Dubois, Hon. Shelby M.
Cullom, Hon. D. L. Phillips, W. H. Hanna, Adjutant General
Isham N. Haynie, Col. James H. Bowen, E. F. Leonard, Dr. S.
H. Melvin, Hon. O. M. Hatch, Col. John Williams.

Congressional Committee.

Senator Nye, of Nevada; Senator Williams, of Oregon; Senator H. S. Lane, of Indiana; Senator J. H. Lane, of Kansas; Senators Howe and Doolittle, of Wisconsin; and George T. Brown,
Sergeant-at-Arms of the U. S. Senate. Hon. Schuyler Colfax,
Speaker U. S. House of Representatives; Hon. E. B. Washburn,

Hon. B. C. Cook; Hon. J. O. Norton, the three latter from Illinois; Hon. J. K. Morehead and Hon. Joseph Bailey, of Pennsylvania; Hon. J. C. Sloan, of Wisconsin; Hon. J. F. Wilson, of Iowa; Hon. J. H. Farquhar, of Indiana; Hon. Sydney Clarke, of Kansas; Hon. Thomas B. Shannon, of California; Hon. Charles E. Phelps, of Maryland; Hon. Samuel Hooper, of Massachusetts; Hon. T. W. Ferry, of Michigan; Hon. W. A. Newell, of New Jersey; Hon. N. G. Ordway, Sergeant-at-Arms U. S. House of Representatives.

Gov. O. P. Morton and staff, of Indiana; Governor W. H. Wallace, of Idaho Territory; and Gov. William Pickering, of Washington Territory.

Representatives of the Press.

L. A. Gobright, of Washington City, and C. R. Morgan, both of the Associated Press; Dr. Adonis, of the Chicago *Tribune;* C. H. Page, of the New York *Tribune;* U. H. Painter, of the Philadelphia *Inquirer;* and G. B. Woods, of the Boston *Daily Advertiser.*

Committee of One Hundred,

Appointed by the City Council of Chicago, "to proceed to Michigan City, to receive the remains of President Lincoln, escort them to Chicago, and accompany them to Springfield." The following catalogue contains the names of all the members of the committee:

Ex-Mayors B. W. Raymond, J. L. Milliken, James H. Woodworth, J. S. Rumsey, Charles M. Gray, John C. Haines, Alexander Lloyd, and A. S. Sherman; Charles Randolph, N. K. Fairbanks, J. S. Brownson, John C. Dore, John F. Beatty, Stephen Clary, C. J. Wheeler, J. Maple, S. S. Hayes, Mancel Talcott, N. W. Huntley, Aaron Gibbs, Judge J. B. Bradwell, Judge E. S. Williams, Judge E. Van Buren, H. T. Dickey, John Kinzie, H. D. Colvin, Thomas Hoyne, Elliot Anthony, Ira Y. Munn, O. S. Hough, Chas. H. Walker, D. R. Holt, W. D. Houghtelling, G. S. Hubbard, R. McChesney, Samuel Howe, I. Lawson, B. E. Gallup, J. K. Botsford, A. B. Johnson, Judge Jos. E. Geary, J. M. Watson, Judge Van H. Higgins, W. B. Brown, Mark Skinner, John Alston, S. P. A. Healey, James H. Goodsell, George M. Kimbark, Wm. Wayman, E. H. Sargent, C. G. Hammond, George C. Bates, Samuel Hoard, Peter Page, W. H. Bradley, L. P. Hilliard, Dr. William Wagner, J. S. Grindell, George Anderson, U. P. Harris, Dr. J. V. Z. Blaney,

J. L. Marsh, J. H. McVicker, W. F. Tucker, Dr. J. P. Lynn, J. H. Burnham, James Nulten, B. J. Patrick, Dr. D. Brainard, Matthew Laflin, John B. Turner, S. B. Cobb, W. W. Boyington, Isaac Speer, James W. Sheahan, Robert Hervey, M. L. Sykes, John B. Drake, John L. Wilson, Luther Haven, George Schneider, W. L. Church, John A. Wilson, Jacob Rehm, H. W. Bigelow, A. H. Blackall, Charles L. Wilson, Joseph Medill, A. C. Hesing, J. H. Field, E. W. Blatchford, T. S. Blackstone, Gen. Julius White, Capt. James Smith, J. V. Farwell, Robert H. Foss, L. Brentano, Wm. James, James Long, S. A. Goodwin, J. M. Van Osdel, M. W. Fuller.

Charles L. Wilson was Chairman of the Committee of One Hundred, and Col. James H. Bowen and U. P. Harris, Marshals.

Next came the Wisconsin Delegation, consisting of Gov. Lewis and other State officers, the Mayor and Councilmen of the city of Madison, and several hundred citizens.

After the Wisconsin Delegation, came a body of about fifty clergymen—all the principal denominations being represented.

The remainder of the procession was separated into five grand divisions, each under a marshal, with a staff or corps of aids. The procession was made up of societies of almost every kind known to the country. Military organizations innumerable; Board of Trade; Mercantile Association; about one thousand Free Masons, and as many Odd Fellows, appeared in the line. Then there were Union Leagues, Fenian Societies, and many Roman Catholic Societies, Hebrew Societies, Trades Societies and Unions, students of Chicago University, Druids and societies belonging to citizens from European countries, such as the Holland and Belgian Society, French Benevolent Society, German Societies in large numbers, Scandinavian, Bohemian, Irish, English and others. About four hundred colored citizens bearing the mottoes:

"We mourn our loss,"

———

"Rest in peace, with a nation's tears."

The Chicago Fire Department brought up the rear.

It is worthy of remark, that of the military who took part in the funeral honors, there was a full regiment of infantry, which was composed of men who had been in the rebel army, and, after taking the oath of allegiance, at the several prison camps, were recruited into the government service.

To attempt a detailed description of the procession would only result in failure. It was a wilderness of banners and flags, with their mottoes and inscriptions. The estimated number of persons in line was thirty-seven thousand, and there were three times as many more who witnessed the procession by crowding into the streets bordering on the line of march, making about one hundred and fifty thousand who were on the streets of Chicago that day, to add their tribute of respect to the memory of Abraham Lincoln.

The line of march was from the Lake shore, at the foot of Park Row, or Park Place, west on that street to Michigan avenue, thence north on Michigan avenue to Lake street, west on Lake to Clark street, south on Clark to the east gate of the Court House square, and inside the square to the south door of the Court House. The remains reached the Court House at a quarter before one o'clock, passing in under the inscription :

"Illinois clasps to her bosom her slain and glorified son."

Over the north door was inscribed :

"The beauty of Israel is slain upon her high places."

A gorgeous catafalque had been erected in the centre of the rotunda, directly beneath the dome. The coffin was placed on the platform or dais within the catafalque, and the entire procession passed through the rotunda in the order observed in marching through the streets. This was done before the coffin was

13

opened. The embalmers and assistants spent a short time in preparing the remains, and the people were admitted. By midnight, it was estimated that forty thousand people passed through the Court House and looked upon the face of the dead President.

Whilst the people are filing past the remains, we will leave them and go back to review the route of the procession from its starting point to the Court House. The whole distance was guarded on either side by strong ropes, stretched along near the outer edge of the side walks. The streets were occupied entirely by the procession, and the side walks by spectators. The grand triple arch, with its inscriptions and mourning decorations, has been described. The residences and business houses, on either side of the streets along which the cortege moved, were among the finest buildings of their kind in the world, and their owners had been lavish in the expenditure of money in draping them with mourning insignia and otherwise decorating them. Language would utterly fail to describe this part of the scene, and I shall content myself by quoting a small number of the hundreds of mottoes displayed and in describing some of these houses.

"Mournfully, tenderly, bear on the dead."

"Our Country's Martyr."

The mansion of Lieutenant Governor Bross was beautifully draped with black and white crape, interwoven with the national colors.

The mansion of Hon. J. Y. Scammon bore on its front a bust of Abraham Lincoln, surrounded with wreaths of immortelles, and surmounted on the back ground by a cherub. The anchor of Hope was beautifully arranged among the mourning drapery.

On another house was displayed the motto:

"We mourn our beloved President."

The residence of Bishop Duggan, of the Roman Catholic Church, displayed the national flags of Ireland and America intertwined.

Other houses bore such inscriptions as the following:

> " In sorrowing grief, the nation's tears are spent,
> Humanity has lost a friend, and we a President."

> " Bear him gently to his rest."

Beneath a marble bust of the President, surrounded by thirty-six golden stars, was inscribed:

> " We loved him much, but now we love him more."

One of the banners bore the inscription:

> " Ours the cross—Thine the crown."

On a banner hanging over a bust of Lincoln was:

> " Freedom's noblest sacrifice."

At the Soldiers' Rest, this quotation was displayed:

> "EMANCIPATION PROCLAMATION."

> " Upon this act, I invoke the considerate judgment of mankind, and the gracious favor of Almighty God."

And there were many others, such as:

> " To Union may our heartfelt call
> And brotherly love attune us all."

> " Nations swell thy funeral cry."

> " Young, old, high and low,
> The same devotion show."

"And over the coffin man planteth hope."

———

"Though dead, he yet speaketh."

———

"He won the wreath of fame,
And wrote on Memory's scroll a deathless name.

———

"Look how honor glorifies the dead."

———

"Know ye not that a great man has fallen this day in Israel."

———

"The great Emancipator."

———

"He left us sustained by our prayers,
He returns embalmed in our tears."

I might continue these quotations almost indefinitely, but I have given enough to indicate the spirit that pervaded all hearts. Thousands and tens of thousands of dollars were expended in decorating the buildings with mourning drapery. The triple arch was designed, constructed and decorated under the superintendence of the well known architect, W. W. Boyington. The decorations at the Court House were designed and executed under the superintendence of the other equally well known architect, J. M. Van Osdel. The catafalque was equal in design, execution and costliness of material, to any that have been described. To attempt a minute description would only bewilder the understanding.

Solemn music, both vocal and instrumental, was performed at intervals during the entire night. At midnight, several hundred German voices chanted a requiem in the rotunda with thrilling effect. Brigadier General Sweet appointed a guard of honor from the

Veteran Reserve Corps, to relieve those who had acted in that capacity from Washington. Their services were not required, for the reason that fifty Illinois officers, formerly serving in the army and navy, had already tendered their services, through Gen. Julius White, to act as Guard of Honor to the remains while in Chicago, and had been accepted by Gen. Townsend. They were appointed as follows :

First relief, Col. Edward Daniels ; second relief, Col. Hasbrouck Davis ; third relief, Lieut. Col. Arthur C. Ducat ; fourth relief, Capt. R. L. Law, U. S. N.

Each officer of relief had nine officers under him, who, for the time, acted as Guard of Honor. The following was the full guard :

Col. Hasbrouck Davis, Col. Edward Daniels, Lieut. Col. Arthur C. Ducat, Capt. R. L. Law, U. S. N.; Lieut. Col. T. W. Grosvenor, Lieut. Col. S. McClevy, Maj. M. Thieman, Maj. John McCarthy, Maj. J. B. Kimball, Chief Engineer, U. S. N.; Maj. Walter B. Scates, Maj. Charles Ehoon, Brev. Maj. L. Bridges; Captains W. S. Swayne, James Dugane, F. Busse, Edward Went, Z. B. Greenleaf, Henry Konkle, John McAssen, Samuel A. Love, G. W. Hills, H. S. Goodspeed, R. N. Hayden, J. M. Leish, B. A. Busse, P. H. Adolph, J. G. Lauggarth, C. G. Adoe, Wm. Cunningham; Lieutenants N. S. Bouton, C. George, W. P. Barclay, M. Shields, J. S. Mitchell, G. S. Bigelow, R. J. Bellamy, R. S. Sheridan, Harry Briggs, F. A. Munge, J. H. Hills, A. Russell, C. H. Gladding.

The skill and cool judgment of Col. R. M. Hough, in handling forty thousand men in the crowded streets of a city like Chicago, was equal to managing twice the number on open ground, and won the praise of all the military men who participated in the procession. A citizen of Chicago, while the people were pouring through the Court House by thousands, to look at the remains of Abraham Lincoln, was heard to say :

" I have seen three deceased Kings of England lying in state, but never have witnessed a demonstration so vast in its proportions, so unanimous and spontaneous, as that which has been evoked by the arrival in the city of the remains of the fallen President."

The three kings referred to were, George the Third, who, after a reign of sixty years, died in the eighty-third year of his age, January 29, 1820; George the Fourth, who died June 26, 1830; and William the Fourth, who died June 20, 1837, and was succeeded by his niece, Queen Victoria.

The Chicago *Times* of May 3, speaking of the manifestations of sorrow and respect, says:

"The bitterest of his political opponents in life, vied with his warmest adherents in speaking words of appreciation and esteem. Some of the most touching and characteristic reminiscences of his personal traits, and of his private deeds, were contributed with tearful eye and broken voice by his former opponents.

"All joined heartily and liberally in preparation for the ceremonies, which yesterday and the day before were to put the seal of the people's approbation on his character and acts in the eye of the world. If men no longer went about their preparations with heavy and o'erburdened hearts, they did so with subdued and kindly ones. All was done with a tenderness more touching than the most uncontrollable passion of grief could be. When the sacred remains were brought through the streets and deposited in the keeping of the people of the city, there were no downcast countenances, but none that were not sad and pitiful. There were no loud voices in the unnumbered throngs. Men expressed themselves in subdued tones, and often nothing would be heard but the indescribable murmur of ten thousand voices, modulated to a whisper, and the careful tread of countless feet on the damp pavement of the streets. It was the entire population of a great city in mourning, conscious of what was due alike to herself and the honored dead."

After having been exposed to view from four o'clock p. m., May 1, to eight p. m., May 2, the scene was closed by the Court House doors shutting out the

throng that was still pouring in.   At half-past eight
the Court House was cleared of all except the guard
and the choir.   The coffin was then closed and borne
upon the shoulders of the Sergeants of the Veteran
Reserve Corps down the south steps to the funeral car.
The Light Guard Band performed a requiem as the
remains were being transferred.   An immense procession, bearing about three thousand torches, was already
in line, to escort the remains to the depot.   At a quarter before nine o'clock, it moved to the time of numerous bands of music.   The route lay west on Washington street to Market, south on Market to Madison,
west on Madison, by the Madison street bridge, to
Canal street, on the west side, thence south on Canal
street to the depot of the Chicago, Alton & St. Louis
Railroad.   While the preparations for starting were in
progress, the choir continued to sing funeral dirges,
and the twenty-five Sergeants of the the Veteran Reserve Corps stood around the funeral car with drawn '
swords.   At half-past nine o'clock, the funeral cortege
moved slowly out of the depot to the strains of a funeral march by the band, while the bells of the city
tolled a solemn farewell to all that was mortal of
Abraham Lincoln.

Some idea may be formed of the princely style of
the reception and passage of the funeral cortege through
Chicago, from the fact that the City Council paid bills
for expenses incurred in erecting the funeral arch at
Park Place, and decorating the Court House, to the
amount of about fifteen thousand dollars.   This was
probably not more than a tithe of the total expenditure by citizens and asssociations.

CHAPTER XXI.

The remains had tarried so long at Chicago, while such extensive preparations were in progress at Springfield, it would not have been surprising if the people along the line had contented themselves with visiting one or the other of those places, and had omitted any demonstrations at the respective towns and cities along the route, but the love in the hearts of the people of Illinois for the memory of Abraham Lincoln would not permit them to be so easily satisfied.

At Bridgeport, in the very suburbs of Chicago, the people had kindled bonfires, and with torches lighted the way as the train moved slowly along. Crowds of spectators were at Summit and Willow Springs stations, and at the town of Lemont.

Lockport, 11:33 p. m., Tuesday, May 2. An immense bonfire was burning, minute guns firing, and the track lined with people holding torches. The glare of light revealed the mourning drapery on almost every building, and many mottoes expressive of the feelings of the people. None elicited more sympathetic feeling than the simple words,

"Come Home,"

Joliet. It was midnight and raining. At least twelve thousand people were assembled at the depot. Bonfires lighted up the scene, and the cortege was greeted by minute guns, tolling of bells, and funeral dirges by a band of music. An immense arch spanned

the track, decked with flags, evergreens and the insignia
of mourning.   The arch was surmounted by a figure
representing the Genius of America, weeping.   Among
the mottoes, the most impressive was,

"Champion, defender and martyr of liberty."

As the train moved away, a number of ladies and
gentlemen, on an elevated platform, were singing,

" There is rest for thee in heaven."

At Elwood and Hampton—both very small places—
the people had kindled large bonfires to enable them to
take a passing view of the funeral train.

Wilmington, one o'clock, a. m., Wednesday, May 3.
Minute guns announced the arrival of the train, and a
line of men with torches was drawn up on each side
of the track.   The depot was draped in mourning and
about two thousand people were present to view the
grand funeral cortege.

At Gardner all the houses to be seen were draped in
mourning and illuminated, while crowds of people were
at the depot.

Dwight, two o'clock, a. m., May 3.   Minute guns
and the tolling of bells announced the arrival of the
cortege.   The American flag was displayed, and all
the buildings in view were draped in mourning.
The entire population appeared to be out of doors desirous to pay their respects to the memory of Lincoln.
Some of the escort recognized this as the place where
the Prince of Wales and his royal party were entertained.

Minute guns, tolling of bells, bonfires, funeral dirges
and the insignia of mourning made up the demonstrations at Odell, Cayuga, Pontiac, Chenoa and Lexington.

Towanda, 4:30 a. m., May 3.   A large assemblage
of people were at the depot anxious to testify their sorrow and respect for the distinguished martyr.   This is
the highest point between Chicago and St. Louis, being

one hundred and twenty-eight feet above the water of Lake Michigan.

Bloomington, five o'clock, a. m., May 3. A large arch over the track bears the inscription, "Go to thy Rest." The depot was handsomely draped in mourning, and about five thousand persons were assembled to testify their respect for the distinguished statesman. There would, no doubt, have been greater demonstrations at Bloomington, but a considerable number of the citizens visited Chicago, and a very large delegation had already gone, or were then on the point of going to Springfield to participate in the procession and other demonstrations of respect and mourning.

At Shirley, a large number of people were present, with sad countenances, to view the imposing funeral cortege as it glided by.

At McLean, minute guns, tolling bells, and singing by a choir of ladies contributed with mournful effect to the occasion, which called out almost the entire population.

Atlanta, six o'clock, a. m., May 3. Minute guns and the fife and muffled drum greeted the funeral cortege at this place, just as the sun arose in splendor over the beautiful prairies. A large number of people had assembled, and portraits of Abraham Lincoln with emblems of mourning were everywhere visible. Among the mottoes were,

"Mournfully, tenderly, bear him to his grave."

"He saved our country and freed a race."

Lincoln, Ill., 7 a. m., May 3. This town was named for Abraham Lincoln, by some personal friends before he was known to fame. The depot was appropriately draped in mourning, and ladies dressed in white, trimmed with black, sang a requiem as the train passed under a handsomely constructed arch, on each column of which was a portrait of the deceased President. The arch bore as a motto:

"With malice to none, with charity for all."

The national colors were prominently displayed, and a profusion of evergreens, with black and white drapings, completed the artistic decorations.

At Elkhart, a beautiful arch spanned the track, ornamented with evergreens and national flags, all draped in mourning. The arch was surmounted by a cross formed of evergreens and bearing the motto:

"Ours the cross, thine the crown."

At Williamsville, the houses were nearly all draped in mourning, with a profuse display of small flags and portraits of the late President. An arch spanned the track here, also, which bore the inscription:

"He has fulfilled his mission."

Springfield, Ill., 9 a. m., Wednesday, May 3, 1865. The train arrived one hour later than schedule time, so little did it deviate from the time table arranged before leaving Washington twelve days previous. The trains on all the roads for the twenty-four hours before the expected arrival of the funeral cortege, brought in passengers by thousands. The greatest anxiety was manifested by the people to be present at the reception of the remains of Abraham Lincoln. Long previous to the time appointed for their arrival, crowds were collected at the depot of the Chicago & Alton Railroad, and extended along the line of the road several squares north. Every building in the vicinity was covered with spectators. Hundreds of men who could not find standing or sitting room near the depot, walked up Fourth and Fifth streets to the crossing near the northern limits of the city. Every class of people was represented in the assembled multitude. Minute guns were fired by a section of Battery K, Second Missouri Light Artillery. A few minutes before nine o'clock, the pilot engine made its appearance. The ten minutes between its arrival and that of the funeral train, were occupied by Gen. Cook in bringing to their proper places the committee of reception, members of the several delegations, the military and the civic societies.

As soon as the funeral car came along side of the depot, the coffin was transferred to the beautiful hearse which had been tendered for the occasion by Messrs. Lynch & Arnot, of St. Louis, through mayor Thomas of that city, and accepted by mayor Dennis of Springfield. The hearse was built in Philadelphia, at a cost of about six thousand dollars, and was larger and longer than the ordinary size. It had been used at the funeral of the Hon. Thomas H. Benton. After the offer was accepted, the proprietors had it additionally ornamented with a silver plate engraving of the initials "A. L." around which was a silver wreath, with two inverted torches and thirty-six silver stars, representing the States of the Union. It was drawn by six superb black horses, draped in mourning, and wearing plumes on their crests. The horses belonged to Messrs. Lynch & Arnot also, and were driven on this occasion by Mr. A. Arnot, without the aid of grooms.

The procession moved in the following order:

Brig. Gen. John Cook and staff.
The 146th regiment Illinois Volunteer Infantry, Col. H. H. Deane;
one company of the 46th regiment of Wisconsin Volunteer
Infantry, Capt. Chase, and Company E. Veteran
Reserve Corps, under Lieut. Cornelius.
The above organizations were acting as a military funeral escort.
Band.
Maj. Gen. Joseph Hooker and staff.

PALL BEARERS.		PALL BEARERS.
Hon. Jesse K. Dubois,		Erastus Wright, Esq.
Hon. S. T. Logan,	H	Jacob Bunn, Esq.
Hon. W. F. Elkin,	E	Chas. W. Matheny, Esq.
Hon. Gustavus Kœrner,	A	Capt. James N. Brown,
Hon. S. H. Treat,	R	Col. John Williams,
James L. Lamb, Esq.	S	Dr. Gershom Jayne.

HEARSE.

Guard of Honor.

Composed of the same general officers who were appointed by the Secretary of War to accompany the remains to Springfield. Also, the Commissary of Subsistence, Embalmer and Undertaker.

Relatives and family friends.

Among the latter were the Rev. Dr. P. D. Gurley, Pastor of the deceased, and Judge David Davis of the U. S. Supreme Court.

Illinois Delegation, named in another place.

Congressional Committee, or Delegation, named in another place.

Gentlemen from Washington, D. C.   Hon. Richard Wallach, Mayor, and Col. Ward H. Lamon, U. S. Marshal for the District of Columbia.

[It is worthy of remark here, that three of the men who left Springfield with Mr. Lincoln, February 11, 1861, returned with his remains, viz.: Major General David Hunter, Judge David Davis and Col. Ward H. Lamon.]

Members of the Illinois State Legislature.

Governors of the different States.

Delegation from Kentucky.

Chicago Committee of one hundred.

Springfield Committee of Reception.

Judges of the several Courts.

The Reverend Clergy.

Officers of the Army and Navy then in service or honorably discharged.

Civic Societies.

Citizens generally.

The procession moved from the depot east on Jefferson street to Fifth, south on Fifth to Monroe, east on

Monroe to Sixth, north on Sixth to the State House
Square, entering through the east gate, and by the north
door of the State House to Representatives' Hall, in the
west end of the building, second story, where the coffin was placed on a dais, within a magnificent catafalque
prepared for the occasion.

A few minutes after ten o'clock all being in readiness, the doors were opened and the vast multitude began to file through the hall to view the remains. They
entered the Capitol at the north door, ascended the
stairway in the rotunda and entered Representatives'
Hall at the north door, passed by the catafalque, out at
the south door, then down the stairway and made their
exit from the Capitol at the south side.

CHAPTER XXII.

We will turn our attention for a time from the crowds of people, and view the preparations for this reception. For ten days a large number of men and women worked almost night and day in decorating the State House. The whole building was draped in mourning on the exterior ; and the rotunda and Representatives' Hall on the interior, and the entrance to the Governor's room, the rooms of the Secretary of State, Auditor of State and Superintendent of Public Instruction. Part of the time there were one hundred and fifty persons at work. The ladies of Springfield bore their full share in these arduous labors. I have been furnished with the following figures by a prominent citizen of this city, who prepared some of the designs for decorations. I shall not attempt a description of the ornamental work, but will give a few facts by which some idea of their gorgeous beauty may be conveyed. About fifteen hundred yards of black and white goods were used in the decorations, exclusive of the catafalque. In its construction and decoration, black cloth, black velvet, black, blue and white silk and crape, with silver stars and silver lace and fringe, were used in the greatest profusion. The canopy of the catafalque was made of velvet, festooned with satin and silver fringe. It was lined on the under side with blue silk, studded with silver stars. Three hundred yards of velvet and mourning goods, and three hundred yards of silver lace and fringe, besides a vast quantity of other materials, were used in its construction. Each of the six columns was surmounted with a rich plume.

Evergreens and flowers interwoven with crape, hung in festoons from capitals, columns and cornices in all parts of the building. Two hundred vases of natural flowers in full bloom, emitted their fragrance throughout the edifice. Nearly all of them were furnished free of cost by Michael Doyle, horticulturist, of Springfield. Mottoes and inscriptions were displayed at various places about the hall, but I can only give place to two of them:

"Washington the Father, Lincoln the Saviour."

"Rather than surrender that principle I would be assassinated on this spot."

The Governor's mansion, the old Lincoln residence, the military headquarters of Gen. Cook and Gen. Oakes, were decorated, externally, similar to the State House. Of the twenty thousand dollars appropriated by the City Council of Springfield, to be expended in preparations for the funeral, less than fifteen thousand were used. Part of it was expended in building the temporary vault on the new State House grounds, paying railroad charges on some carriages from Jacksonville, the hearse from St. Louis, and the expenses of musicians and the orator; but much the largest portion of the whole amount was laid out in decorating the buildings above named. This, however, was only a small part of the money thus expended, for the whole city was draped in mourning, business houses, private residences and all, and in many instances they were as richly decorated as the public buildings.

It was well known that the hotels could not accommodate a tithe of the strangers who would be in attendance, and private families who could do so, made preparations and invited to their houses such as could not otherwise be provided for. The six organizations of Free Masons in Springfield, viz.: four lodges, one chapter and one commandery, made equal appropriations from their several treasuries, procured one of the largest halls in the city, filled it with tables, and kept them supplied with well cooked food prepared by the families of their members.   This dining hall was intended to be free to masons only who should be in attendance, but many others partook of their bounty also.   As for sleeping, there was not much of that done in Springfield on the night the remains of Abraham Lincoln were exposed to view.

Strangers who were in the city on this occasion for the first time, almost invariably visited the former residence of Abraham Lincoln, at the north east corner of Eighth and Jackson streets.   As already stated, it was elaborately and tastefully decorated with the national colors and the insignia of sorrow.   The committee of escort from Chicago, numbering one hundred—although business engagements prevented part of their number visiting Springfield—assembled near the residence and had their photographs taken in a group, in connection with the house, to be preserved as a memorial of their mournful visit.   The photograph was by an artist from Chicago, who accompanied the escort to Springfield for the purpose of taking views of the State House, the closing scenes at Oak Ridge, and other objects of interest.

From the time the coffin was opened, at ten o'clock on the morning of May third, there was no cessation of visitors.   All through the still hours of the night, no human voices were heard except in subdued tones; but the tramp, tramp, of busy feet, as men and women filed through the State House, up one flight of stairs, through the hall, and down another stairway, testified the love and veneration for Abraham Lincoln in the hearts of his old friends and neighbors.   While the closing scenes were being enacted, a choir of two hundred and fifty singers, accompanied by Lebrun's Washington band, of twenty performers, from St. Louis, assembled

14

on the steps of the Capitol, and, under the direction of Professor Meissner, sang

" Peace, troubled soul."

The coffin was closed at ten o'clock on the morning of May 4th, and while it was being conveyed to the hearse the choir sang Pleyel's Hymn :

" Children of the Heavenly King."

The funeral procession was then formed in the following order, under the immediate direction of Major General Joseph Hooker, Marshal-in-Chief:

Brig. Gen. John Cook and staff.
Brig. Gen. James Oakes and staff.
Military.
Funeral Escort.

First Division. Col. C. M. Prevost, 16th Reg. V. R. C., Marshal. AIDS: Lieut. Thomas B. Beach, A. A. A. Gen.; Maj. Horace Holt, 1st Mass. Heavy Artillery; Capt. J. C. Rennison, 15th N. Y. Cavalry; Capt. E. C. Raymond, 124th Ill. Inf.; Capt. Eddy, 95th Ill. Inf.; Lieut. H. N. Schlick, 1st N. Y. Dragoons.

This division consisted entirely of Infantry, Cavalry and Artillery.

Second Division. Maj. F. Bridgman, Pay Department, U. S. Army, Marshal. AIDS: Maj. R. W. McClaughry and Maj. W. W. White.

This division was composed of officers and enlisted men of the Army and Navy, not otherwise assigned, officers in uniform and side arms.

Maj. Gen. John A. McClernand was the chief marshal of the civic department of the procession. AIDS: Lieut. Col. Schwartz, Capt. Henry Jayne, Capt. R. Rudolph, Capt. Benjamin Ferguson, Hon. Charles Keys, W. M. Springer, E. E. Myers, Ed. L. Merritt, N. Higgins.

The command of Gen. McClernand commenced with the

Third Division. Col. Dudley Wickersham, of the 1st Army Corps, Marshal. AIDS: Joshua Rogers, Isaac A. Hawley, W. F. Kimber, J. B. Perkins.

Marshals of Sections—Col. W. S. Barnum, Capt. A. J. Allen, Col. S. N. Hitt, Clinton L. Conkling, Robert P. Officer, W. Smith and Capt. T. G. Barnes.

Orator of the Day and Officiating Clergymen—Rev. Dr. Simpson, Bishop of the M. E. Church and Orator of the Day; Rev. Dr. Gurley; Rev. Dr. N. W. Miner; Rev. Dr. Harkey; Rev. Albert Hale; Rev. A. C. Hubbard, and others.

Surgeons and Physicians of the Deceased.

PALL BEARERS.		PALL BEARERS.
Hon. Jesse K. Dubois,		Erastus Wright, Esq.
Hon. S. T. Logan,	HEARSE.	Hon. J. N. Brown,
Hon. Gustavus Kœrner,		Jacob Bunn, Esq.
James L. Lamb, Esq.		C. W. Matheny, Esq.
Hon. S. H. Treat,		Elijah Iles, Esq.
Col. John Williams,		Hon. John T. Stuart.

"Old Bob." or "Robin," the old horse formerly ridden by Abraham Lincoln in his political campaigns and law practice, off the lines of railroad. He was about sixteen years old, and was led by two colored grooms.

Guard of Honor, in carriages, as follows: Brevet Brig. Gen. E. D. Townsend; Brevet Brig. Gen. Charles Thomas; Brig. Gen. A. B. Eaton; Brevet Maj. Gen. J. G. Barnard; Brig. Gen. G. D. Ramsay; Brig. Gen. A. P. Howe; Brevet Brig. Gen. D. C. McCallum; Maj. Gen. D. Hunter; Brig. Gen. J. C. Caldwell; Brig. Gen. Elkin: Rear Admiral C. H. Davis; Capt. W. R. Taylor, U. S. Navy; Maj. T. H. Field, U. S. Marine Corps.

Relatives and Family Friends, in Carriages.

Fourth Division. Col. Speed Butler, Marshal. AIDS: Maj. Robert Allen, Capt. Louis Rosette and Capt. Albert Williams.

Marshals of Sections—William Bennett, H. W. Ives, Philip C. Latham, William V. Roll, K. H. Richardson, J. E. Williams and J. D. Crabb.

Congressional Committe or Delegation.

Senate—Hon. Messrs. James W. Nye of Nevada, George H. Williams of Oregon, Henry S. Lane of Indiana, John B. Henderson of Missouri, Lyman Trumbull and Richard Yates of Illinois, Howe and Doolittle of Wisconsin, Foote of Vermont, Chandler of Michigan, and George T. Brown, Sergeant-at-arms of the U. S. Senate.

House of Representatives—Hon. Schuyler Colfax, Speaker; Hon. Messrs. Pike of Maine, Rollins of New Hampshire, Baxter of Connecticut, Harris of New York, Cowan of Pennsylvania, Farnsworth, Washburn, Cook, Norton and Arnold, of Illinois, Morehead and Bailey of Pennsylvania, Sloan of Wisconsin, Wilson of Iowa, Farquhar of Indiana, Clarke of Kansas, Shannon of California, Phelps of Maryland, Hooper of Massachusetts, Ferry of Michigan, Newell of New Jersey, Whaley of West Virginia, Schenck of Ohio, Smith of Kentucky, Ramsay of Minnesota, Hitchcock of Nebraska, and S. G. Ordway, Sergeant-at-arms of the U. S. House of Representatives.

Territorial Representatives—Hon. Messrs. Bradford, of Colorado, and Weed, of Dacotah.

A portion of those who are named among the Congressional Delegation did not attend, but of those who were certainly with the funeral cortege from the beginning to the end of the journey, were the Hon. Messrs. Williams, of Oregon, Nye, of Nevada, Washburn, of Illinois, Morehead, of Pennsylvania, Hooper, of Massachusetts, and Schenck, of Ohio. Some of the Members of Congress from Illinois were in the

Illinois Delegation.

Governor R. J. Oglesby, Hons. Jesse K. Dubois, Shelby M. Cullom and D. L. Phillips, Adjt. Gen. Isham N. Haynie, Col. J. H. Bowen, W. H. Hanna, E. F. Leonard, Dr. S. H. Melvin, Hon. O. M. Hatch, Col. John Williams.

Governors of States with their suites, and Governors of Territories: Oglesby, of Illinois; Bramlette, of Kentucky; Morton, of Indiana; Fletcher, of Missouri: Stone, of Iowa; Pickering, of Washington Territory, and Wallace, of Idaho Territory.

Members of the Illinois Legislature.
Kentucky Delegation.
Chicago Committee of Reception and Escort.

Fifth Division. Hon. George L. Huntington, Marshal. AIDS: Dr. S. Babcock, George Shepherd, Charles Ridgley, George Latham, Moses B. Condell.

This division was composed of the municipal authorities of Springfield, and other cities.

Sixth Division. Hon. W. H. Herndon, Marshal. AIDS: P. P Enos, C. S. Zane, Dr. T. W. Dresser, John T. Jones, William G. Cochrane, James Rayborne, Charles Vincent, Edward Beach, John Peters, C. W. Reardon, R. C. Huskey.

Marshals of Sections—Thomas Lyon, B. T. Hill, George Birge, Henry Yeakel, Jacob Halfen,   Sweet, Dewitt C. Hartwell, Hamilton Haney, Fred. B. Smith.

The sixth division was composed of Christian, Sanitary and other kindred Commissions, Aid Societies, etc. and delegations from Universities, Colleges and other institutions of learning.

Reverend Clergy, not officiating for the day.
Members of the Legal Profession.
Members of the Medical Profession.
Representatives of the Press.

Seventh Division. Hon. Harmon G. Reynolds, Marshal. AIDS: George R. Teasdale, John A. Hughes, James Smith, P. Fitzpatrick, Henry Shuck and Thomas O'Conner.

Marshals of sections—Capt. Charles Fisher, Frank W. Tracy, M. Conner, Frederick Smith, M. Armstrong, Richard Young.

This division was composed of the various bodies of Free Masons, Odd Fellows and other kindred fraternities, and the Firemen.

Eighth Division. Hon. John W. Smith, Marshal. AIDS: Capt. Isaac Keys, S. H. Jones, Hon. John W. Priest, O. A. Abel, Maj. H. N. Alden, Wm. P. Crafton, G. A. Kimber, John W. Poorman, Henry Ridgley, J. H. Crow, John W. Davis, Presco Wright, N.

V. Hunt, George Dalby, Alfred A. North, Hon. J. S. Bradford, Samuel P. Townsend.

This division was composed of citizens generally, and all who had not been assigned to some other place in the procession, bringing up the rear with the colored people.

The procession thus formed received the corpse at the north gate of the State House square, and moved east on Washington street to Eighth, south on Eighth —passing the Lincoln residence at the corner of Jackson and Eighth—to Cook, west on Cook to Fourth, north on Fourth, passing between the Governor's mansion—then the home of Governor Oglesby—and the fine residence of ex-Governor Matteson, to Union, west on Union to Third, north on Third to the eastern entrance to Oak Ridge Cemetery, one and a half miles from the State House.

On arriving at the cemetery, the remains were placed in the receiving tomb. The choir then sang the Dead March in Saul:

"Unveil thy bosom, faithful tomb,
Take this new treasure to thy trust," etc.

Rev. Albert Hale, Pastor of the Second Presbyterian Church, of Springfield, then offered a fervent and appropriate prayer, after which the choir sang a dirge composed for the occasion by L. W. Dawes, music by George F. Root:

"Farewell, Father, Friend and Guardian."

A portion of scripture was then read by Rev. N. W. Miner, and the choir sang

"To Thee, O, Lord, I yield my spirit."

President Lincoln's Inaugural Address of March 4, 1865, was then read by Rev. A. C. Hubbard. A dirge was performed by the choir, and then followed the Funeral Oration by Rev. Dr. Simpson, Bishop of the

Methodist Episcopal Church.   It was a review of the life of Abraham Lincoln, more particularly that part from the time he left Springfield, Feb. 11, 1861, until his death.   In drawing the contrast between his departure and return, the Bishop said:

"Such a scene as his return to you was never known among the events of history.   There was one for the Patriarch Jacob which come up from Egypt, and the Egyptians wondered at the evidences of reverence and filial affection which came up from the hearts of the Israelites.   There was mourning when Moses fell upon the heights of Pisgah, and was hid from human view.   There has been mourning in the kingdoms of the earth when kings and princes have fallen, but never was there in the history of man such mourning as that which accompanied this funeral procession.

"Far more eyes have gazed upon the face of the departed than ever looked upon the face of any other departed man.   More eyes have looked upon the procession for sixteen hundred miles and more, by night and by day, by sunlight, dawn, twilight, and by torchlight, than ever before watched the progress of a procession."

In illustration of the universal feeling of sorrow, the orator said:

"Nor is this mourning confined to any one class, or to any district or country.   Men of all political parties and of all religious creeds, have united in paying this mournful tribute.   The archbishop of the Roman Catholic Church in New York and a Protestant minister walked side by side in the sad procession.   A Jewish Rabbi performed part of the solemn services.

"But the great cause of this mourning is found in the man himself.   Mr. Lincoln was no ordinary man; and I believe the conviction has been growing on the nation's mind, as it certainly has been on mine, especially in the last years of his administration, that by the hand of God he was especially singled out to guide our government in these troubled times.   And it seems to me that the hand of God may be traced in many of the events connected with his history.

"I recognize this in his physical education, which prepared him for enduring herculean labors.   In the toils of his boyhood and the labors of his manhood, God was giving him an iron frame. Next to this was his identification with the heart of the great people, understanding their feelings because he was one of them, and connected with them in their movements and life. His education was simple. A few months spent in the school house gave him the elements of an education. He read Bunyan's Pilgrim's Progress, Æsop's Fables and the life of Washington, which were his favorites. In these we recognize the marks which gave the bias to his character, and which partly moulded his style. His early life, with its varied struggles, joined him indissolubly to the working masses, and no elevation in society diminished his respect for the sons of toil. He knew what it was to fell the tall trees of the forest, and to stem the current of the broad Mississippi. His home was in the growing West—the heart of the Republic—and invigorated by the winds that swept over its prairies, he learned lessons of self reliance that sustained him in scenes of adversity. His genius was soon recognized, as true genius always will be, and he was placed in the legislature of his adopted State. Already acquainted with the principles of law, he devoted his thoughts to matters of public interest, and began to be looked upon as the 'coming statesman.' As early as 1839 he presented resolutions in the legislature asking for emancipation in the District of Columbia, while, with but rare exceptions, the whole popular mind of his State was opposed to the measure. From that hour he was a steady and uniform friend of humanity, and was preparing for the conflict of later years.

"It was not, however, chiefly by his mental faculties that he gained such control over mankind. His moral power gave him pre-eminence. The convictions of men that Abraham Lincoln was an honest man, led them to yield to his guidance. As has been said of Cobden, whom he greatly resembled, he made all men feel a kind of sense of himself—a recognized individuality—a self relying power. They saw in him a man whom they believed would do what was right, regardless of consequences. It was this moral feeling which gave him the greatest hold upon the people, and made his utterances almost oracular.

"But the great act of the mighty chieftain, on which his power shall rest long after his frame shall moulder away, is giving freedom to a race. We have all been taught to revere the sacred scriptures. We have thought of Moses; of his power, and the prominence he gave to the moral law; how it lasts, and how his name towers high among the names in heaven, and how he delivered those millions of his kindred out of bondage. And yet we may assert that Abraham Lincoln, by his proclamation, liberated more enslaved people than ever Moses set free—and those not of his kindred. God has seldom given such power or such an opportunity to man. When other events shall have been forgotten; when this world shall have become a network of republics; when every throne shall be swept from the face of the earth; when literature shall enlighten all minds; when the claims of humanity shall be recognized everywhere, this act shall still be conspicuous on the pages of history. And we are thankful that God gave to Abraham Lincoln the decision and wisdom and grace to issue that proclamation, which stands high above all other papers which have been penned by uninspired men.

"Look over all his speeches—listen to his utterances—he never spoke unkindly of any man. Even the rebels received no words of anger from him, and the last day of his life illustrated, in a remarkable manner, his forgiving disposition. A dispatch was received that afternoon that Thompson and Tucker were trying to escape through Maine, and it was proposed to arrest them. Mr. Lincoln, however, preferred to let them quietly escape. He was seeking to save the very men who had been plotting his destruction; and this morning we read a proclamation offering $25,000 for the arrest of these men as aiders and abettors of his assassination; so that, in his expiring acts, he was saying, 'Father forgive them, they know not what they do.' As a ruler, I doubt if any president ever showed such trust in God, or, in public documents, so frequently referred to Divine aid. Often did he remark to friends and delegations that his hope for our success rested in his conviction that God would bless our efforts because we were trying to do right. To the address of a large religious body he replied, 'Thanks be unto God who, in our national trials, giveth us the churches.' To a minister who said he 'hoped the Lord was on our side,' he replied that it 'gave him no concern whether the Lord was on our side or not,' and then added, 'for I know the Lord is always on the side of right,' and with deep feeling continued: 'But God is my witness that it is my constant anxiety and prayer that both myself and this nation should be on the Lord's side.'"

After the oration or eulogy, a requiem was performed by the choir, a prayer offered by the Rev. Dr. Harkey, followed by the singing of

"Peace, troubled soul."

Rev. Dr. P. D. Gurley then arose, made a few remarks and the closing prayer, after which the following funeral hymn, composed by him for the occasion, was sung:

Rest, noble martyr! rest in peace;
  Rest with the true and brave
Who, like thee, fell in freedom's cause,
  The nation's life to save.

Thy name shall live while time endures,
  And men shall say of thee,
He saved his country from its foes,
  And bade the slave be free.

These deeds shall be thy monument,
  Better than brass or stone;
They leave thy fame in glory's light
  Unrivaled and alone.

This consecrated spot shall be
  To freedom ever dear;
And freedom's sons of every race
  Shall weep and worship here.

O, God, before whom we, in tears,
  Our fallen chief deplore,
Grant that the cause for which he died,
  May live forever more.

The services closed by the choir singing the doxology, and the benediction by Dr. Gurley, when the vast multitude melted away and sought the railroad depots, from which the trains bore them to their homes in all parts of the nation—east, west, north and south. Thus ended the most grand and sublime funeral pageant the world ever saw. The injunction so often repeated on the way—

" Bear him gently to his rest "—

was reverently obeyed, and Mr. Lincoln's own words,

" The heart of the nation throbs heavily at the portals of the tomb,"

were realized with a force of which he little thought at the time they were spoken.

In the largest number of places where the escort stopped to give an opportunity for public honors, the local authorities provided guards to relieve the Guard of Honor detailed by the Secretary of War, but in no instance did they all leave the remains. They were acting under orders to guard the body of Abraham Lincoln until it should be deposited in its final resting place at Springfield, Illinois, and during all the journey there was not a moment but one or more of these veteran officers, with bronzed visages and gray hairs, could be seen near the body.

According to the special order issued from the War Department, April 18, 1865, all arrangements by State or municipal authorities for doing honor to the remains, were to be under the direction of the military commander of the division, department or district in which the proposed demonstrations were to take place. In order to see that the provisions of this order were carried out, Major General Cadwallader, commander of the department of Pennsylvania, joined the cortege at the State line between Maryland and Pennsylvania. He continued with the funeral party until it reached Jersey City, when he was relieved by Major General John A. Dix, commander of the department of New York. Gen. Dix traveled with the cortege through New York and across the northern end of Pennsylvania. Major General Joseph Hooker, commander of the department of the Ohio, relieved Gen. Dix at Wick-liffe, Ohio. General Hooker continued with the funeral cortege until the closing ceremonies at Springfield, Illinois.

I have omitted to mention the estimates given in the papers of the numbers who viewed the remains at different points; but summing them all up at the close, I feel justified in saying that more than *one million men and women* must have looked upon the dead face of Abraham Lincoln ;an event which has no parallel in the history of the world.

In the course of the entire journey, there can not be a line or even a word found on record, urging the people to turn out in honor of the deceased. The assembling of such multitudes was, in all cases, spontaneous. Day and night, cold or warm, rain or shine, for twelve long days and nights, it was only necessary for the people to know the time the cortege was expected to arrive at any given point, to bring them together in great numbers.

The annexed table will exhibit the distance traveled by the funeral train that bore the remains of Abraham Lincoln from Washington city to Springfield, Illinois. The distance is also given between the different points at which the remains were taken from the train, in compliance with the desire of the people to do honor to the memory of the martyred President:

	MILES.
From Washington to Baltimore	40
" Baltimore *via* York to Harrisburg	84
" Harrisburg to Philadelphia	107
" Philadelphia *via* Trenton to New York	87
" New York to Albany	142
" Albany *via* Schnectady, Utica, Syracuse, Rochester and Batavia to Buffalo	296
" Buffalo *via* Dunkirk and Erie to Cleveland	183
" Cleveland *via* Crestline and Delaware to Columbus	138

From Columbus *via* Urbana, Piqua, Greenville, Richmond, and Knightstown to Indianapolis................	188
" Indianapolis *via* Lafayctte and Michigan City to Chicago...	212
" Chicago *via* Joliet, Chenoa and Bloomington to Springfield................................	185
Total...	1662

It is but natural that the very best that could be written would appear in those papers of Mr. Lincoln's own way of thinking in politics; but some of the finest articles appeared in papers that had always been opposed to him politically. The *Daily Register*, a Democratic paper published at Springfield, in its issue of Saturday evening, April 15, 1865, after relating the news of the assassination, says :

"Just in the hour when the crowing triumph of his life awaited him; when the result which he had labored and prayed for four years with incessant toil, stood almost accomplished; when he could begin clearly to see the promised land of his longings—the restored Union—even as Moses, from the top of Pisgah, looked forth upon the Canaan he had for forty years been striving to attain, the assassin's hand at once puts a rude period to his life and to his hopes. As Moses of old, who had led God's people through the gloom and danger of the wilderness, died when on the eve of realizing all that his hopes had pictured, so Lincoln is cut off just as the white wing of peace begins to reflect its silvery radiance over the red billows of war. It is hard for a great man to die, but doubly cruel that he should be cut off after such a career as that of him we mourn to-day."

And the same paper of April 18th says :

"History has recorded no such scene of bloody terror. The murder of monarchs has been written. Cæsar was slain in the Senate Chamber; Gustavus was butchered in the ball room; but these were usurpers and tyrants, not the chosen heads of a people, empowered to select their rulers. And, O horrible! that he should have been assassinated when his best efforts to tranquilize the fears and fury of his people were so nearly realized. We are dumb with sorrow."

The *Illinois State Journal*, at Springfield, the oldest
paper in the State north of Edwardsville, was the first
in which Lincoln's name ever appeared in connection
with any office—he having been announced as a candidate for Representative of Sangamon county, in its
issue of March 15, 1832.   It was then Whig and is
now Republican in politics, and supported Lincoln
every time he was ever a candidate.   The *Daily Journal* of Saturday morning, April 15, 1865, gave the
telegraphic announcement of his assassination, without comment.   Monday morning, the 17th, it said :

"ABRAHAM LINCOLN IS DEAD!   These portentious words, as
they sped over the wires throughout the length and breadth of
the land on Saturday morning last, sent a thrill of agony through
millions of loyal hearts, and shrouded a nation, so lately rejoicing in the hour of victory, in the deepest sorrow.   The blow came
at a moment so unexpected, and was so sudden and staggering—
the crime by which he fell was so atrocious and the manner of it
so revolting, that men were unable to realize the fact that one of
the purest of citizens, the noblest of patriots, the most beloved
and honored of Presidents, the most forbearing and magnanimous
of rulers, had perished at the hands of an assassin.   The horrify-
ing details recalled only the scenes of blood which have disgraced
barbaric ages.   People were unwilling to believe that, in our own
time, there could be found men capable of a crime so utterly
fiendish and brutal.   *   *   *   And yet this is
called chivalry."

" President Lincoln died at the hand of *Slavery*. It was Slavery
that conceived the fearful deed; it was Slavery that sought and
found the willing instrument and sped the fatal ball; it is Slavery
alone that will justify the act.   Henceforth men will look upon
Slavery as indeed 'the sum of all villanies.' "

The same paper of Saturday morning, the 22d, says:

"A week ago this morning, the intelligence first startled the
the nation that a crime of the most fearful character had been
perpetrated in Washington.   The spirit of our honored and beloved President, the most genial, patient and forbearing of men,

but the victim of the most atrocious assassination, was then taking its flight to the 'God who gave it.' "   *   *   *

"One week has passed, and such a week was never known in this or any other land. The popular sorrow, instead of abating by time, has grown even more intense, as the people have been gradually enabled to comprehend the terrible facts. The heart of the nation has been moved as it was never moved before. Every village and city of the land, from the Atlantic to the Pacific, have joined in the most heartfelt demonstrations of grief, in view of the national loss. To-day the sorrowful cortege accompanying the remains of our beloved President is at last approach. ing the home whence, four years ago, he set out with many misgivings, but strong in the sense of duty, to assume the reins of government, to which the suffrages of the people had called him. The eyes of the whole nation are upon it, and wherever that dark and sorrow-burdened train appears, it is attended by the lamentations of the people."

Friday morning, 28th, the *Journal* announced the death of the assassin, and said :

"Retribution, swift and sure, has fallen upon his murderer! J. Wilkes Booth, the author of that atrocious deed, lies as lifeless as Abraham Lincoln.   *   *   *   *   It is no compensation for the loss to the nation of such a man as Abraham Lincoln, that judgment has overtaken his murderer.   *   * The only satisfaction we feel is that justice has been done."

The *Journal* of Wednesday morning, May 3d, says :

"To-day all that is mortal of Abraham Lincoln comes back to us to be deposited among a people with whom he spent so many years of his life, and among whom he hoped, his work being done, to spend the evening of his days."

The *Journal*, Thursday, May 4th :

"To-day we lay him reverently to rest, amid the scenes he loved so well. Millions will drop a tear to his memory, and future generations will make pilgrimages to his tomb. Peace to his ashes."

CHAPTER XXIII.

It will be remembered that, on the twenty-fourth
day of April, a public meeting was held in Springfield,
at which a committee was chosen to make arrangements for the sepulture of the remains of President
Lincoln.   It will also be borne in mind that the committee resolved itself into a National Lincoln Monument Association.

A conditional contract had been made for a plat of
ground on which to erect a monument, and the work
of constructing a temporary vault, at the expense of
the city, had been commenced.   It was designed to be
a resting place for the remains until the monument
could be erected.   By the men working night and day,

(Fig. 1.)

VAULT ON THE NEW STATE HOUSE GROUNDS.

through sunshine and rain, it was ready for use at the appointed time, although the work was not quite completed on the outside.   It was ascertained, on the morning of the fourth, that Mrs. Lincoln objected to the body of her husband being placed, even temporarily, in the new vault, on account of the location of the grounds selected.   She having expressed her preference for Oak Ridge Cemetery, it was in compliance with her wishes that the remains were taken

(Fig. 2.)

PUBLIC VAULT AT OAK RIDGE.

there and deposited in the public receiving vault of the cemetery.   The new vault was on the grounds that have since been purchased and donated by the city of Springfield to the State of Illinois, upon which the State is now erecting a Capitol, at an expense of three and a half millions of dollars.   The vault stood about fifty yards north of the new State House.   A cenotaph should, and doubtless will, be

15

erected on the spot, after the edifice is completed and the grounds put in proper order. Figure No. 1 was engraved from a drawing of the vault, preserved by T. J. Dennis, who was at the time Mayor of the city.

For several weeks after the remains were deposited in the public vault of the cemetery, ropes were extended in front of it, and a guard of soldiers kept there day and night. This was done more as a mark of honor and respect, than from any fear that his tomb would be desecrated. Figure No. 2 was engraved from a photograph taken during that time.

Soon after the remains of Mr. Lincoln and Willie were deposited in this vault, the following entries were made in the register kept by the sexton of Oak Ridge Cemetery:

DATE OF INTERM'T.	NAME.	CAUSE OF DEATH.	PLACE OF BIRTH.	REMARKS.
May 4, 1865.	Abraham Lincoln.	Assassinated.	Kentucky.	Receiving Tomb.
May 4, 1865.	Willie Lincoln.		Springf'ld, Ill.	Removed from Washington, D.C. Receiving Tomb.

On the ninth of May, a call was sent out to all Sunday schools, to take up collections the second Sabbath, and all public schools, the first Tuesday, in June.

The Association was without legal authority until the eleventh of May, when it was established according to the laws of Illinois governing voluntary societies, under the following

ARTICLES OF ASSOCIATION.

We, Richard J. Oglesby, Sharon Tyndale, O. H. Miner, James H. Beveridge, Newton Bateman, John T. Stuart, Samuel H. Treat, Jesse K. Dubois, O. M. Hatch, James C. Conkling, Thomas J.

Dennis, John Williams, Jacob Bunn, S. H. Melvin and David L. Phillips, all being of full age, and citizens of the United States, and of the State of Illinois, certify that we do hereby associate ourselves under and by virtue of an act of the General Assembly of the State of Illinois, entitled "An act for the incorporation of Benevolent, Educational, Literary, Musical, Scientific and Missionary societies, including societies formed for mutual improvement, or for the promotion of the arts," approved February 24, 1859, by the following name, and for the purpose herein specified.

ARTICLE I.

This Association shall be called the "National Lincoln Monument Association," and be located at Springfield, State of Illinois, and shall continue in existence for the term of twenty years.

ARTICLE II.

The object of this Association shall be to construct a Monument to the memory of Abraham Lincoln, in the city of Springfield, State of Illinois.

ARTICLE III.

The following persons shall be the Directors of the Association during the first year of its existence: Richard J. Oglesby, Sharon Tyndale, O. H. Miner, James H. Beveridge, Newton Bateman, John T. Stuart, Jesse K. Dubois, O. M. Hatch, James C. Conkling, Thomas J. Dennis, John Williams, Jacob Bunn, S. H. Melvin, Samuel H. Treat and David L. Phillips.

In testimony whereof, we have hereunto set our hands and seals, this eleventh day of May, 1865.

RICHARD J. OGLESBY,	[SEAL.]	SHARON TYNDALE,	[SEAL.]
ORLIN H. MINER,	[SEAL.]	NEWTON BATEMAN,	[SEAL.]
JOHN T. STUART,	[SEAL.]	S. H. TREAT,	[SEAL.]
JESSE K. DUBOIS,	[SEAL.]	O. M. HATCH,	[SEAL.]
JAMES C. CONKLING,	[SEAL.]	S. H. MELVIN,	[SEAL.]
JOHN WILLIAMS,	[SEAL.]	JAMES H. BEVERIDGE,	[SEAL.]
JACOB BUNN,	[SEAL.]	THOMAS J. DENNIS,	[SEAL.]

DAVID L. PHILLIPS, [SEAL.]

These gentlemen were nearly all occupying high official positions at the time, or had previously been. The first five named in the preamble were, respectively,

Governor, Secretary, Auditor, Treasurer and Superin- .
tendent of Public Instruction for the State of Illinois
at the time. Mr. Stuart was the preceptor and first
law partner of Abraham Lincoln, an ex-member of the
U. S. House of Representatives, and is yet one of
the leading lawyers of Central Illinois; Mr. Treat
has been for many years, and is yet, a Judge of the
U. S. Court for Illinois; Mr. Dubois is an ex-member
of the State Legislature, ex-receiver of the U. S. Land
Office, ex-Auditor of State, etc., etc.; Mr. Hatch is an
ex-Secretary of State, and a man of wealth and influence; Mr. Conkling is an ex-Mayor of Springfield, ex-
member of the State Legislature, a leading lawyer,
capitalist, and public spirited citizen; Mr. Dennis was
at the time Mayor of the city, and is one of the foremost architects in the west; Mr. Williams and Mr.
Bunn are, respectively, at the head of two among the
oldest and most wealthy banking houses in the city;
Dr. Melvin is a prominent merchant, banker and railroad man; Mr. Phillips was then United States Marshal for the Southern District of Illinois. All of them
had long been on terms of personal friendship and in-
timacy with Abraham Lincoln.

On the day the Association took a legal form, the
Board of Directors organized by electing

Governor Richard J. Oglesby, President.

Hon. Jesse K. Dubois, Vice President.

Clinton L. Conkling, Secretary.

Hon. James H. Beveridge, Treasurer.

A code of by laws was adopted, agents appointed to
collect funds, agricultural and horticultural societies
called on to contribute, and the Treasurer directed to
invest funds—which were already beginning to reach
the treasury—in United States securities. Until June,
it was the intention of the Association to erect the
monument on the plat of ground where the first vault
had been built, not doubting that Mrs. Lincoln would
give her consent to that arrangement, on a deliberate

consideration of the subject.   In a letter to the Association, dated at Chicago, June fifth, Mrs. Lincoln still objected to that location.   On the fourteenth day of the month, it was decided by a majority of one, in a full Board of Directors, to build the Monument in Oak Ridge Cemetery.   Six acres of land were donated by the city of Springfield, and conveyed to the Asssociation as a site for the Monument.

Measures were at once taken to erect a temporary vault, near that belonging to the cemetery.   The object in building a temporary vault, was that the remains might be deposited there until the Monument could be completed, and thus vacate the public vault.   The temporary vault was completed before winter, and a notice given to Mrs. Lincoln, at Chicago, that the Association was ready to remove the body of her late husband; that it would be done without public display, and asked her to name the time that it would be convenient for her to be present.   She replied, saying that December 21, at three o'clock p. m., would suit her.   A day or two previous to the time fixed for the removal, Mrs. Lincoln, with her son Robert, came to Springfield, and visited the new tomb. She expressed herself well pleased with what had been done, but a sudden indisposition prevented her being present when the removal took place.   In process of transferring the remains, the box containing the coffin was opened, in order that the features of the deceased might be seen, and six of his personal acquaintances filed a written statement with the Secretary of the Association, that it was the body of Abraham Lincoln beyond a doubt.   This was deemed advisable, to keep the evidence of identity unbroken through the changes necessary to be made before the completion of his final resting place.

Mr. Lincoln had one son who died in childhood, many years ago, and was buried in Hutchinson cemetery, near the city.   His body was removed to the temporary vault also, and it then contained the bodies of the father and two sons, Eddie and Willie. Edward was named for Col. E. D. Baker—who was killed at Ball's Bluff—between whom and Mr. Lincoln the warmest friendship always existed. I must digress here, to say that I have been informed by one who knows, that in one of the finest cemeteries of San Francisco, the grave of that pure and eloquent statesman and brave soldier, is the only one that is neglected. Is there no lover of free institutions, and admirer of genius in that city, who will see that the stain is removed?

Figure No. 3 was engraved from a photograph of the temporary vault. It stood on the brow of the hill, about fifty yards northeast of the monument. It was removed late in the autumn of 1871, and the site where it stood graded down about fifteen feet.

Early in 1868, the Association advertised a " Notice to Artists," offering $1000 for the best design for a monument, with the usual conditions, and named the

(Fig. 3.)

TEMPORARY VAULT AT OAK RIDGE.

first of September as the day for the examination. Thirty-seven designs, by thirty-one artists—six of them sending two each—were received and placed on exhibition in the Senate Chamber.

They came from the following States: Illinois—Chicago, John Wesley Hooper, Henry L. Gay, H. Schroff, Cochrane & Piquenard, one each, and from L. W. Volk, two; Mattoon, J. E. Hummell, one; Bloomington, J. R. & J. S. Haldeman, one; Quincy, C. G. Volk, two; Springfield, Joseph Baum and E. E. Myers, one each, making a total of twelve. Wisconsin—Milwaukee, N. Merrill, two. Iowa—Jefferson, Henry Goodman, one. Indiana—Logansport, William Emmett, and Indianapolis, J. H. Vrydagh, one each. Ohio—Toledo, W. H. Macher, one, and Cincinnati, Thomas D. Jones, two. Massachusetts—Boston, C. B. Odiorne and Miss Harriet E. Hosmer, one each. District of Columbia—Washington, Miss Vinnie Ream, one. Kentucky—Louisville, M. S. Belknap, one. Missouri—St. Louis, J. Beattie, Charles Bullitt, R. H. Follenius, McLaren & Baldwin, one each. New York—Brooklyn, Horwan & Maurer, two. Pennsylvania—Philadelphia, J. H. Bailey & H. H. Lovie, A. E. Harwicke, J. H. Hazeltine, E. N. Scherr, one each. Connecticut—Hartford, J. G. Batterson, one. Vermont—Brattleboro, Larkin G. Mead, Jr., two; making a total of thirty-seven.

Some of these designs would have cost a million dollars each to put them into execution. Five days were occupied in studying them, when the board adjourned to meet again on the tenth of the month. They reassembled on the tenth, and continued to the eleventh, when it was

Resolved, That this Association adopt the design—one of them—submitted by Larkin G. Mead, Jr., to be constructed of granite and bronze, and that the whole matter be referred to the Executive Committee, with power to act.

Those voting in the affirmative were, Bateman, Beveridge, Bunn, Conkling, Dennis, Dubois, Hatch, Melvin, Miner, Stuart, Treat, Williams and Phillips. In the negative, Mr. Tyndale. Absent or not voting, Gov. Oglesby.

The Association, then entered into a contract with Mr. Mead, to erect the monument, together with the statuary, and all the accessories necessary to the fulfilment of the design. It was soon after ascertained that it was Mr. Mead's intention to let the contract for the architectural part of the work and return to Italy, where he had been residing for several years. Then it was mutually agreed to annul the existing contract, and a new one was entered into on the thirtieth of December, in which it was stipulated that the Association was to manage the building of the architectural part of the monument, and that it should be done strictly after the drawings and specifications of Mr. Mead. On his part, Mr. Mead was to mould, cast and deliver all the statuary required by and necessary to his design, namely.

1. A statue of Lincoln, not less than ten feet high, for $13,700.

2. A group representing infantry, containing three figures and appropriate accessories, the figures to be not less than seven and a half feet high, for $13,700.

3. A group of cavalry, to contain a horse and two human figures, with appropriate accessories, the human figures to be not less than seven and a half feet high, and the horse in proportion, for the sum of $13,700.

4. A group of artillery, to contain three figures and appropriate accessories, the figures to be not less than seven and a half feet high, for $13,700.

5. A marine group, to contain three figures and appropriate accessories, the figures to be not less than seven and a half feet high, for $13,700.

6. The coat of arms of the United States, as shown in the specifications, for $1,500, making a total of $70,000.

It was a part of the contract, that the Association was to have the right to order one or more of these pieces or groups at a time, to suit its own convenience, and that it was not under obligations to pay for any piece until a written order was given for the work to proceed. When a written order was given, one-third of the stipulated price was to accompany it, one-third to be paid when the plaster model was delivered at the foundry where it was to be cast, and the remaining third when the work was completed and delivered in good order, at Springfield, Illinois. It was also stipulated in the contract, that if cannon were donated to be used in the statuary, the value thereof should be deducted from the price. It was further agreed, that if any donations of freight were made, it should be to the Association, and not to Mr. Mead.

On the back of this contract, Mr. Mead gave the signatures of five business men of New York city, binding themselves in the penal sum of $5,000 each, for the faithful performance of the contract on his part. A note, also an the back of this contract, over the signature of John J. Cisco, of New York, expresses the opinion that the bond is good and sufficient.

On the seventh day of May, 1869, the Board of Directors, under the above contract, instructed the Executive Committee to order the statue of Lincoln and the coat of arms of the United States, and to accompany the order with one third of the money, as per contract.

After advertising for proposals to erect the monument—excepting the statuary—and receiving five or six bids, that of W. D. Richardson, of Springfield, was accepted. A contract was then entered into, between the Association and Mr. Richardson, in which he agreed to erect the National Lincoln Monument, in Oak Ridge Cemetery, according to the plans and specifications adopted by the Association, for the sum of

$136.550. He was to build the foundation during the year 1869, and the superstructure by January 1, 1871. The Association agreed to pay Mr. Richardson the sum above named, and for the purpose designated, by monthly estimates as the work progressed, fifteen per cent of which was to be withheld until the work was completed according to contract, when the total amount remaining should be paid. Mr. Richardson gave ample security, under a penalty of $50,000, for the faithful performance of the contract on his part.

CHAPTER XXIV.

Arrangements having been previously made, the Board of Directors held a special meeting in Oak Ridge Cemetery, September 9, 1869. After calling the roll, a brief but fervent prayer was offered by Rev. Albert Hale, invoking God's blessing on the work they were about to commence. The president of the Association being absent, the vice president, Hon. Jesse K. Dubois, at the request of the board, made the following statement of the financial condition of the Association:

U. S. 5-20 bonds, on special deposit with J. Bunn....	$66,300 00
Premium on said bonds, at present value............	13,260 00
Cash in bank..............	2,023 46
Notes on individuals..............................	80 00
Illinois State bonds, on special deposit with J. Bunn..	17,000 00
Illinois State appropriation........................	50,000 00
Estimated value of cannon donated by Congress.....	5,000 00
Paid to Larkin G. Mead on contract for statuary.....	5,000 00
Total assets.......... ....$158,663 46	

Mr. Dubois also made a statement of all the contracts entered into by the Association, in consequence of which the following liabilities were incurred:

To W. D. Richardson, for building monument.......$136,550 00	
To Larkin G. Mead, for statute of Lincoln and coat of arms..	15,200 00
Total liabilities........ ....$151,750 00	
Balance, after meeting all liabilities.....	$6,913 46

Mr. Dubois said that, if no misfortune befel the Association, it could, by January 1, 1871, have the monument completed, except the four groups of statuary, and be out of debt, with a small balance in the treasury. He expressed the hope that the American people, or separate States or cities, would furnish the means to pay for the remaining groups of statuary, that the monument might stand complete and symmetrical, a fitting emblem of the character and virtues of the man it was designed to honor.

Vice President Dubois closed his statement by saying: " In obedience to the order of your board, and to testify their and my approbation of all that has been done, it is my pleasure now to begin the work, by throwing out the first shovelful of earth."

Mr. Richardson had his materials on the ground, and before winter closed in, had the foundation completed, doing all his contract required for the year 1869.

When the work was about to commence, the Association reorganized its Executive Committee, so that it was composed of the Hon. John T. Stuart, Jacob Bunn and John Williams.

Mr. Stuart, as previously intimated, was the preceptor of Abraham Lincoln, in the study of the law, and furnished him the library for that purpose. They were also partners in practice from 1837 to 1840, when the partnership was dissolved, in consequence of Mr. Stuart being elected to a seat in the United States House of Representatives.

I shall now endeavor to describe the monument. The excavation for the central part, or that on which the main shaft rises, is twenty-three and a half feet deep, and seventeen feet square. The bottom of the excavation is filled with concrete, the whole seventeen feet square, to the depth of eight feet. (See Fig. 7.) On this concrete, the whole seventeen feet square is built up with solid masonry of block stone, to a height of thirty-nine feet and four inches. The stone is all dressed true and square, and is very heavy, some of the pieces weighing several tons each. The excavations for all the outer walls and piers are six feet deep. The walls commence with two feet depth of concrete. There is a round pier, fifteen feet in diameter—at the bottom—at each of the four corners of the central shaft. These piers are built up to a height of twenty-eight feet and four inches above the ground line, and are tapered to form a pedestal of eleven feet diameter at the top.

There are three straight walls on each side of the central shaft, parallel with its sides, and at equal distances from each other. These walls are all joined to the round piers. The central shaft, pedestals, and walls touching the pedestals, form a square of fifty-four feet, with rounded corners. There is another wall outside of all these, nearly ten feet distant, the whole forming a square of seventy-two feet six inches. In addition to these walls, there is an oval room thirty-two and a half feet long and twenty-four feet wide, in the clear. About half of it projects from the south side, and the other half extends inward, nearly to the base of the obelisk. This room is called Memorial Hall, and is designed to be a repository for articles used by, or in any way associated with the memory of Abraham Lincoln. The interior wall is planed Illinois stone, and inside of that, a few inches, is a lining of Vermont marble in panel work, extending in dome groined arches, to form the ceiling, all supported by a series of Doric columns. This Hall is entered from the ground by a door at the south. (See Fig. 4.)

At the north side there is a similar projection, called the Vestibule to the Catacomb. It is finished inside the same as Memorial Hall, except that the floor is of black and white marble instead of Illinois stone. It is entered by a door from the north. (See Fig. 4.)

The ground plan is one hundred and nineteen and a half feet from north to south, and seventy-two and a half feet from east to west. The walls shown in Fig-

(Fig. 4.)

GROUND PLAN OF THE NATIONAL LINCOLN MONUMENT.

ure 4 are all fourteen feet and four inches high.   Arches are sprung from one to another at the top, and heavy iron beams or joists, with flanges on the lower edge, are laid across Memorial Hall and the Catacomb. Arches are sprung from one of these beams to another, beginning on the flanges at the bottom of the iron beams. The upper part of this series of arches is brought to an even surface by filling the depressions with concrete.   On top of this, embedded in cement, is a covering of immense slabs of Illinois stone, planed to a uniform thickness of about eight inches, which brings the whole area of seventy-two and a half feet square, and the half circular projections over Memorial Hall and the Catacomb, up to fifteen feet ten inches in height.   Figure 5 is an illustration of this area, which is called the Terrace.

You can ascend to the Terrace by either of four flights of granite steps, one at each corner.   The two on the south land over Memorial Hall, and the two at the north over the Catacomb.   The flagging stone that makes the Terrace, and at the same time a roof for everything below, is laid with sufficient inclination outward to carry off the water.

A heavy granite balustrade ascends on the outside of each stairway, and is extended so as to form a parapet around the Terrace and over the Catacomb and Memorial Hall.   A small section of the parapet may be seen on each end of Figure 7.

The Catacomb now consists of five crypts, side by side, elevated three feet above the floor of the vestibule. The crypts are three feet square, and seven feet from north to south.   Figure 6, is an elevation fronting north, of the five crypts as they appeared before the marble panel work was put in place.   Now the central crypt is the only one visible.   In it there is a marble Sarcophagus, containing all that was mortal of Abraham Lincoln.

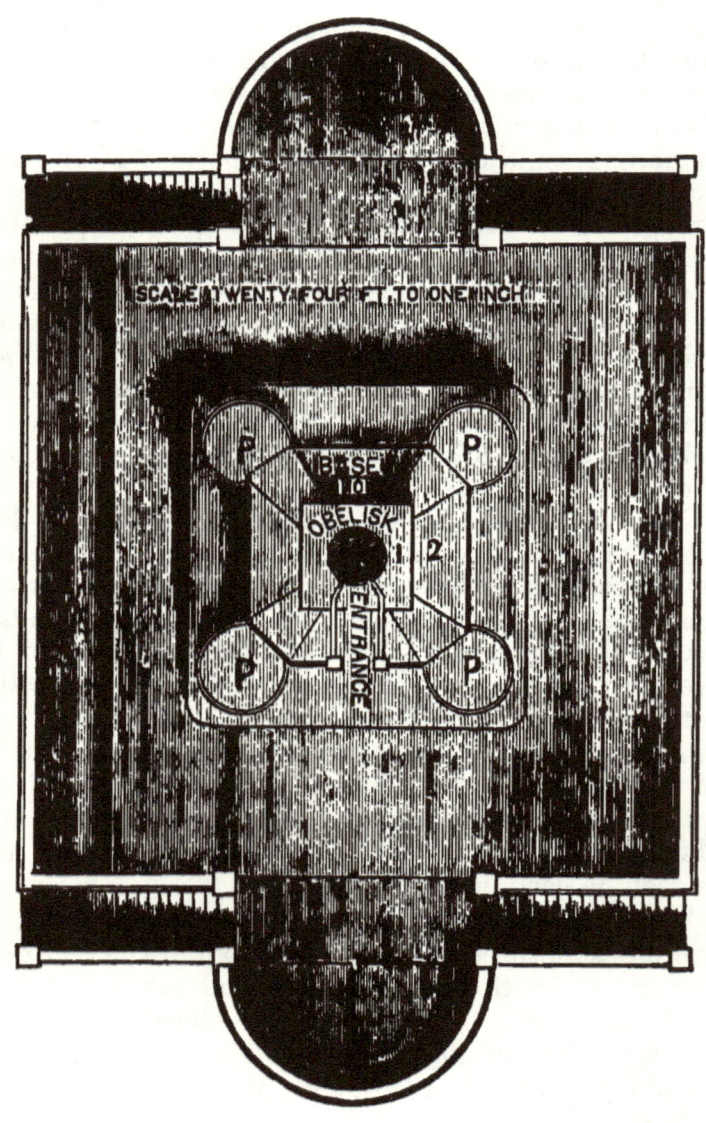

(Fig. 5.)

THE TERRACE.

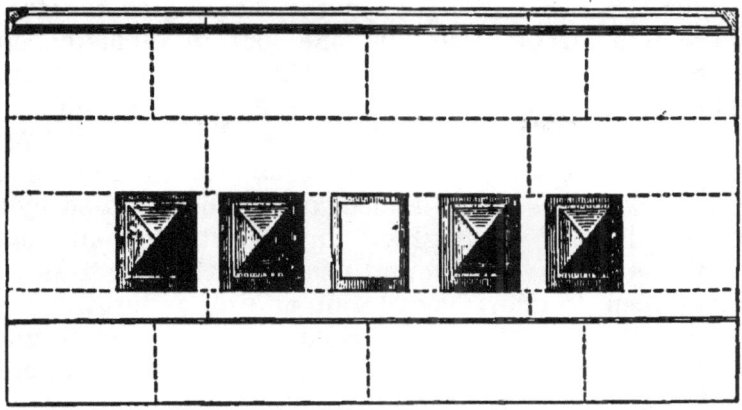

(Fig. 6.)

ELEVATION OF THE CRYPTS.

The Catacomb and Memorial Hall are each lighted by six openings, and each opening is designed to be closed by a single piece of plate glass, when necessary.

The central shaft, being seventeen feet square at the bottom, as it rises is reduced to twelve feet square on the outside, at the top of the Terrace, and tapers to eight feet square at the apex, ninety-eight feet four and a half inches from the ground. The outside is dressed granite, and the inside hard burned brick. The shaft, or obelisk, is hollow from the terrace to the top, eighty-two and a half feet. The opening is six feet in diameter, and perfectly round. Fastenings were built in the wall, as the work progressed, for the support of a circular iron stairway, which ascends from the entrance, over the Terrace, as shown in Figure 5, and ends in a platform of iron, just near enough the cap stone to leave convenient room for standing erect. Each step is fastened to the wall by two iron bolts, the other end is attached to a central iron shaft, which extends from bottom to top. Figure 7 presents an interior view of the construction of the stairway.

16

One-third of the way from the Terrace to the top, there is a circular window, one foot in diameter, on each of the four sides. Two-thirds of the way up, there are four similar windows. At the top, and at a convenient height to stand on the platform and look out, there are twelve of these windows, three on each side. Each one was intended to have been closed by a single piece of plate glass, three-fourths of an inch thick, but it has been found necessary thus far to leave them open, to afford ventilation as well as light.

The study of Figure 7 will enable the reader to understand the interior construction of the monument better than a written description only.

It is as though the monument was cut exactly through the centre, from north to south, and you were standing at the west, facing the east, and looking at the eastern half. You see how the arches are sprung from one wall to another, to support the stone flagging which forms the Terrace. The south end, or that to the right, shows the interior of Memorial Hall, and the north end, or that to the left, shows the interior of the Catacomb, without any attempt to illustrate the crypts. The letter S indicates that the material used is stone, and the letter B, brick. It will be observed that the foundation of the obelisk is sunk much deeper than the other walls. The spiral stairway is seen commencing on a level with the Terrace. A small section of the granite parapet, which extends around the Terrace, is seen at each end of the cut. The small light spots in Memorial Hall and the Catacomb, are the small windows previously described. The elevation at the south side is a profile of the pedestal for the statue of Lincoln. It is thirty-five and a half feet above the ground line, and nineteen feet eight inches above the Terrace.

In preparing the granite for the monument, a series of ashlars, two feet by two feet nine inches, are so dressed that each presents the appearance of a raised

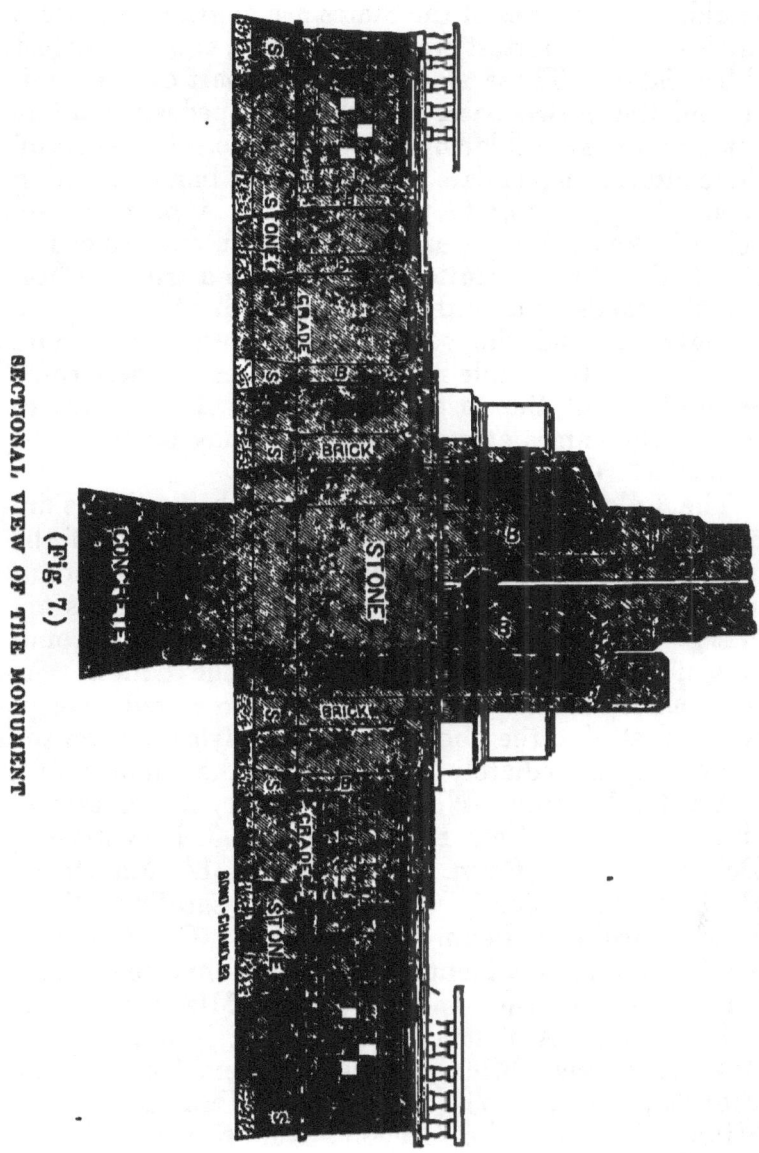

SECTIONAL VIEW OF THE MONUMENT

(Fig. 7.)

shield.   The names of the States are engraved on these shields.   The shortest are given in full, and the longest abbreviated.   These shields form a part of the wall, around the entire base, and the four pedestals, alternating with an ashlar of the same size.   On each of these alternating ashlars, are two raised bands, running horizontally, giving to the States the appearance of being linked together, as it were, by an endless chain. The body of the granite is dressed to a true surface, and the bands and letters are polished.   To complete a course around the edifice, there were three more shields than the whole number of States.   These three are built in at the east side, and left blank, ready to receive the names of any States that may hereafter be admitted.   (See Fig. 10.)

The following is the order in which the States are placed, beginning on the east side, at the right of the blanks, and continuing to the right around the monument.   The names of the original thirteen States are first given, and then the newer States, in the chronological order of their admission into the Union.   As the names of the States are all abbreviated, except two, I first give the abbreviation exactly as it is on the stone, and immediately follow it with the name in full.

Va. for Virginia; N. Y. New York; Mass. Massachusetts; N. H. New Hampshire; N. J. New Jersey; Del. Delaware; Conn. Connecticut; Md. Maryland; R. I. Rhode Island; N. C. North Carolina; S. C. South Carolina; Penn. Pennsylvania; Ga. Georgia; Vt. Vermont; Ky. Kentucky; Tenn. Tennessee; Ohio; La. Louisiana; Ind. Indiana; Miss. Mississppi; Ills. Illinois; Ala. Alabama; Me. Maine; Mo. Missouri; Ark. Arkansas; Mich. Michigan; Tex. Texas; Fla. Florida; Iowa; Wis. Wisconsin; Cal. California; Minn. Minnesota; On. Oregon; Kan. Kansas; W. Va. West Virginia; Nev. Nevada; Neb. Nebraska; ending at the left of the three blank shields.

This cordon of States is twenty-three feet above the

ground, seven feet above the Terrace, and three feet below the top of the pedestals on which the four groups of statuary are to stand, previously described as representing the Infantry, Cavalry, Artillery, and the Navy. The names of the States, as above described, and

LINCOLN,

in raised letters on the front of the pedestal for his statue, constitute the whole of the inscriptions on the monument. Figure 8 is a view of one of the four round pedestals.

(Fig. 8.)

ROUND PEDESTAL.

This is one of the four for the support of the groups of statuary, and is situated at the southwest corner of the monument, showing that part of it above the Terrace. The tablets are all of the same size, but the pedestal being round, as it recedes, Missouri, on the

right, and Illinois, on the left, are apparently diminished in width. The left edge of the tablet—Ill.—
forms the inside of the corner, as it joins the square
base of the obelisk, which brings Mississippi on a
straight surface. The bands or links connecting the
tablets are well illustrated.

(Fig. 9.)

U. S. COAT OF ARMS.

The statue of Mr. Lincoln stands on a pedestal pro-
jecting from the south side of the obelisk, seven feet
higher than the four round pedestals. The pedestal
bearing the statue of Lincoln has the United States
Coat of Arms, in bronze, sunk in a recess on its front.
The Coat of Arms, as shown in Figure 9, is somewhat
modified, and is in bas relief.

It will be observed that the shield, with part of the

stars obscured, supports the American Eagle. The olive branch on the ground shows, that having been tendered until it was spurned by the rebels, it was then cast under foot. Then the conflict began, and raged until the chain of slavery was torn asunder, one part remaining grasped in the talons of the eagle, and the other held aloft in his beak. The coat of arms, in the position it occupies on the monument, is intended to typify the Constitution of the United States. Mr. Lincoln, on the pedestal above it, makes the whole an illustration of his position at the outbreak of the rebellion. He took his stand on the Constitution, as his authority for using the four arms of the war power of the Government—the Infantry, Cavalry, Artillery, and the Navy, which are to be represented in groups around him—to hold together the States, which are represented still lower on the monument, by a cordon of tablets, linking them together, as it were, in a perpetual bond of Union.

The statue of Lincoln is the central figure in the group, or series of groups. There is nothing visible, on all the exterior, except granite and bronze. You enter the shaft, or obelisk, on a level with the Terrace, at the south side, under the statue of Lincoln, and ascend the spiral stairway seventy-seven feet, which brings you to the platform at the top, previously described. The floor of this platform is made of iron, and is ninety-two feet from the ground. The monument being on almost as high ground as any within several miles of the city, affords a fine prospect of Springfield and the surrounding country. Figure 10 is an accurate representation of the monument from the southeast, as it will appear when completed, and as it now appears, with the exception of the statuary. The door on the ground is the entrance to Memorial Hall; that on the Terrace, the entrance to the obelisk. The Catacomb is on the opposite side, and consequently

(Fig. 10.)

NATIONAL LINCOLN MONUMENT, SPRINGFIELD, ILL.

does not appear in this picture, but it is entered by a door on the ground, the same as that to Memorial Hall.

In order to make it more easily understood, I will recapitulate the dimensions. The base is seventy-two and a half feet square, and with the circular projection of the Catacomb on the north, and Memorial Hall on the south, the extreme length on the ground from north to south is one hundred and nineteen and a half feet. Height of the Terrace, fifteen feet ten inches. From the Terrace to the apex of the Obelisk, eighty-two feet six and a half inches. From the grade line to the top of the four round pedestals, twenty-eight feet four inches, and to the top of the pedestal for the Lincoln statue, thirty-five and a half feet. Total height from ground line to apex of Obelisk, ninety-eight feet four and a half inches. The above measurements were taken by T. J. Dennis in January, 1872.

CHAPTER XXV.

I have said that Memorial Hall would be the receptacle for articles that had been used by Mr. Lincoln, or in any way associated with his memory. There is a stone preserved in the Hall, which will furnish food for reflection to all lovers of liberty, but to those whose meditative faculties are fully developed, the study of it will be a rich feast.

All historians are aware that much of the early history of Rome is obscure and traditional, and that some of her reputed rulers are regarded, by a portion of the early historical writers, as mere creatures of the imagination, whilst others who are entitled to equal credence, regard what is related of them as, in the main, true.

Taking all the light that can be obtained on the subject, the following is thought to be a correct version of the life of Servius Tullius: He is said to have been the sixth king of Rome. It is stated that he ascended the throne 578 years before the birth of Christ. He was of obscure origin, and his history mingled with pagan mythology. It is intimated that one or both of his parents were slaves. The policy of his reign was to better the condition of the common people by every means he could devise, and to raise them to an equality with their rulers, so far as the right to life and property was concerned. It is even asserted that he was aiming to qualify them to be their own rulers, with a view to abolishing the kingly office. He discharged the debts of his indigent subjects from his own private revenues, and deprived the creditor of the power of seizing the body of the debtor, restricting him to the goods and chattels for the liquidation of his claims.

At the time his reign commenced, the city was composed of but four hills: the Palatine, the Tarpeian—now called the Capitoline—the Aventine and the Cælian. The king manifested his public spirit by adding the Viminal, the Esquiline and the Quirinal, making Rome, at that ancient date, the city of the seven hills. Having enlarged its boundaries, he enclosed it with a stone wall which was ever after called by his own name. His reign was eminently peaceful and tempered with kindness and benevolence. In his efforts to ameliorate the condition of the common people, and confer upon them the right to take part in the affairs of the State, thus, for the first time, making them politically independent, he established a constitution for their government.

Already jealous of his love for the common people, this last act of the king aroused all the latent malignity of the wealthy classes, or those claiming to be the nobility, and they determined upon his destruction. He had no sons, but two daughters, both of whom were married. His daughter Tullia put her husband to death. Lucius Tarquinius, who had married the other daughter, put her to death and then took her sister Tullia to wife. Tarquinius plotted with the nobles, and at the head of an armed mob, in the summer, when the commoners were gathering their harvests, he entered the forum and seated himself on the throne. The king, unconscious of danger, while going from one part of the city to another, was struck down and assassinated in the streets by some of the followers of his treacherous and ungrateful son-in-law. His body was left where it fell until the chariot of his daughter Tullia was driven over it by her own directions. Thus passed away king Servius Tullius, 538 years before the birth of Christ, in the fortieth year of his reign.

What were called the walls of Servius Tullius, were the walls of Rome for about 700 years, or until the reign of the Emperor Aurelius, which commenced in the year 138 of the Christian era.

The constitution given to the Roman people by Servius Tullius, and which is believed to be historical, never came into force, but was swept away with all his other reforms, soon after his successor ascended the throne. Instead of the happy condition in which the good king hoped and labored to place the Roman people, they were plunged into the deepest abyss of woe by Tarquinius, whose oppressions of the poor were so great that many slew themselves, and the historians say, that "in the days of Tarquinius, the tyrant, it was happier to die than to live."

During all the centuries of oppression and tyranny through which Rome has grown hoary, there has been a chosen few who loved liberty and justice. When suffering under the oppressions of the aristocratic classes, they have kept alive by their traditions, as objects of fond regret, the memory of the just laws of king Servius Tullius.

Some of these Roman patriots evidently watched with intense interest for four long and weary years, the struggle in the new world, between liberty on the one side and tyranny and oppression on the other. They saw it terminate in the destruction of the slave power, and the elevation of four millions of the oppressed and downtrodden of the human family, to an equal right with all other men—to life, liberty and the pursuit of happiness. They kept their eyes steadily fixed on the man whose head and heart and hands wielded the power of the great liberty loving nation to consummate these grand achievements. They believed that they saw in him an embodiment of all the virtues of their ancient king, whose memory they so fondly cherished.

After his election as President of the United States for the second time, and in order to show their appreciation of his character, and the parallel between the lives of Abraham Lincoln and Servius Tullius, these Roman patriots took from a fragment of the wall, where it had been placed by human hands more than two thousand four hundred years before, a stone, and placed upon it an inscription and sent it as a memorial to President Lincoln.   Figure 11 is a *fac simile* of the stone, with its inscription.   It was engraved from a photograph, taken for the purpose after its arrival in Springfield.

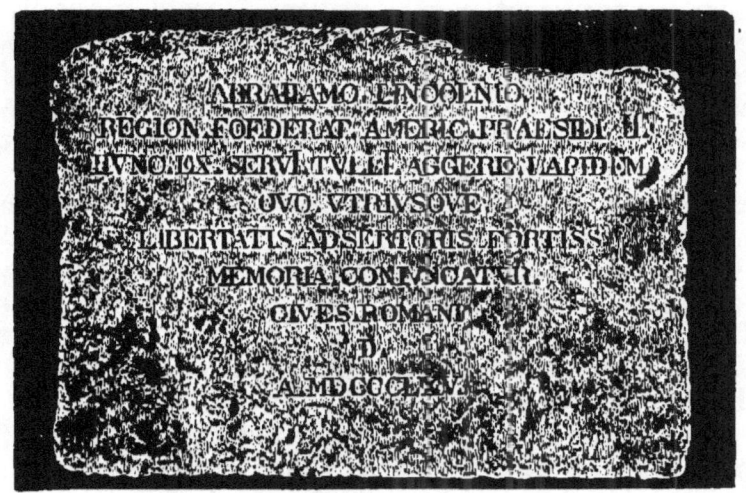

(Fig. 11.)

STONE FROM THE WALL OF SERVIUS TULLIUS.

The following is a translation of the inscription:

" To Abraham Lincoln, President for the second time, of the American Republic, citizens of Rome present this stone, from the wall of Servius Tullius, by which the memory of each of those brave assertors of liberty may be associated.   Anno, 1865."

It is a conglomerate sandstone, and Prof. Worthen, State Geologist for Illinois, says that it is possibly an artificial one.   It is twenty-seven and a half inches long, nineteen inches wide, and eight and three-quarter inches thick.   The lower edge and the side which bears the inscription are dressed true; the opposite side shows the unevenness peculiar to the natural surface of a stone—the upper edge and both ends are broken as if done with a hammer.

By authority of the Hon. Shelby M. Cullom and the Congressional Records, I give the following as the American history of the stone: Something like a year after the assassination of President Lincoln, it was discovered in the basement of the Executive mansion, where it had been run over, covered with rubbish and somewhat defaced. The attention of President Johnson was called to it, and he caused diligent search to be made by the clerks of the Executive mansion, to ascertain if any letters had been received giving a clue as to how or when it came. Not a word of anything connected with it could be found, and all that is positively known of its history is the inscription it bears on its face; yet no person acquainted with the circumstances doubts that it really came from the wall of Servius Tullius at Rome.

It is believed that it arrived before the death of Mr. Lincoln, and to avoid a newspaper furore, he quietly placed it where it was afterwards found. When the stone was discovered it was removed to the Capitol and placed in the crypt in the basement, still depriving the public of any opportunity to see it. Early in June, 1870, a joint resolution was introduced into the House of Representatives at Washington, instructing the architect of the Capitol to transfer it to an appropriate place in a conservatory of the United States Botanical Gardens. Upon its coming before the House, Mr. Cullom moved the following substitute: "Strike out all after the enacting clause and insert that the architect of the Capitol be, and he is hereby directed to cause the stone presented to the late Abraham Lincoln by the patriots of Rome, to be transferred to the possession of the National Lincoln Monument Association, at Springfield, Illinois, to be placed by said Association in the monument now being erected to the memory of Abraham Lincoln."

In a brief speech, Mr. Cullom presented some very forcible reasons why the stone should be placed in the monument, and when he closed, the resolution was adopted. Passing both Houses, this action of Congress was completed on the 17th of June. The stone was boxed and shipped to this city and placed in the office of Vice President Dubois, Sept. 15, 1870, where it remained until August, 1871, when it was removed to Memorial Hall.

That stone was prepared and shipped to Abraham Lincoln because his life had thus far been similar to that of Servius Tullius. Both sprang from the common people; both, in their official capacity, did all they could to elevate and improve the condition of the common people; both incurred the hatred of those claiming to be the nobility, because they were of and for the common people; and both were assassinated because they were endeavoring so to administer their respective governments, as to increase the freedom, happiness and prosperity of the common people. Little did those who put the inscription on that stone think that the parallel in the lives of those two rulers would so soon be complete, even to the closing tragedy of assassination. The death of our martyred President sealed the right to life, liberty and the pursuit of happiness to every human being on American soil; but it required twenty-four centuries for the blood of Servius Tullius to produce its legitimate fruits, in severing the manacles which held in bondage the Roman people. King Victor Emanuel is deserving of all honor for the part he has taken in their elevation; but they must make another stride by educating the masses until they are prepared to set aside a kingly government for that of a republic, and then they will be acting in the true spirit of their ancient ruler.

There is no beauty in that stone to make it attractive, but the association of ideas that cluster around it will always cause it to be an object of interest. Dur-

ing the time that has elapsed since it was placed by
human hands in the wall surrounding the city of Rome,
continents have been discovered; empires have risen
and fallen; and more than seventy generations of human beings have sprung from the earth, acted their
busy parts and sunk back into its bosom.   Servius
Tullius at the beginning and Abraham Lincoln at the
close of that long period of time, were influenced by
the same spirit of humanity.   Both loved and trusted
the common people, and both were loved and trusted
in return; and because of that mutual love, both were
assassinated by the minions of tyranny and oppression.
The object of the Roman patriots is attained—the names
of "those brave assertors of liberty" are and will be
associated from this time henceforth.

CHAPTER XXVI.

In the preceding chapters I have endeavored to describe the appearance which the structure will present when completed. We will now see what has really been done. Mr. Mead, who is a sculptor by profession, does not pretend to be an architect. After studying out the general design for the Monument, he secured the services of Mr. Russell Sturgis, Jr., Secretary of the American Institute of Architects, located in New York city, to prepare his drawings, and after they were completed, Mr. Mead submitted them to that association for criticism by its members, particularly with reference to its proportions, and they gave it their unqualified approval. When the Association was about to adopt it because of its general beauty, they required improvements in some of the minor details. The most important change was made at the suggestion of Mr. T. J. Dennis, one of the members of the Association, who prepared drawings for the purpose. It was that of substituting the present granite balustrade and parapet for the metalic railing originally designed. As soon as arrangements were perfected for going forward with the building, the necessary drawings and specifications for the guidance of the stone cutters were prepared by Mr. Dennis and placed in the hands of the contractor, Mr. Richardson, who, after having some of them redrawn, conveyed them to the stone cutters at Lemont, near Joliet, Illinois, and the granite quarries at Quincy, Massachusetts, where each piece was cut, dressed and numbered before being shipped to its destination.

17

As already stated, ground was broken September 9 1869, and the massive foundation was completed before the close of that year. When the spring of 1870 opened, Mr. Richardson had materials ready to commence the work on the superstructure. He pushed it steadily forward with a full force of men, expecting to finish it during 1870, but there was so much delay on the part of the railroads in bringing the granite on the ground that it was found impossible to finish it within the building season.

Work was resumed early in the spring of 1871, and the cap stone was elevated to its position on the obelisk Monday morning, May 22, without any ceremonials whatever. That did not complete the work, however, for there was still more to do on the Catacomb, Memorial Hall, and other parts of the terrace.

It will be remembered that on the seventh of May, 1869, orders were given by the Association for Mr. Mead to proceed with the work, and prepare the models for the statue of Lincoln and the coat of arms of the United States. A newspaper called *La Riforma*, published in Florence, Italy, in its issue of February 22, 1870, criticises Mr. Mead's work on the model of Lincoln, then far advanced towards completion. The article was translated by Mr. A. Alvey of this city, and published in the *Register*. From his translation I make the following quotations:

"The statue which will arise in colossal proportions from the monument holds in the left hand a scroll upon which is written 'Emancipation,' and in the other the pen with which Lincoln blotted from human history the stain of slavery. As a symbol of Union, to which he devoted his existence, the fasces are placed near the statue, upon which is thrown, in relief, the glorious banner of the republic * * * At the foot of the fasces reclines a crown of laurel, that crown which mankind has unanimously placed upon the head of the great citizen.

"But art stops when life is to be infused into inert matter, and then inspiration must be summoned to express the feeling and sentiment of a soul, which reflects, as in a mirror, the grandeur of the hero whose figure she would model. * * * In this work, Mr. Mead has surpassed our expectations. * * * The Florentines admire the works of Mr. Mead, and desire to do homage to the memory of Lincoln, who no longer belongs exclusively to America, but to the whole world, an honor to the human race."

Hon. W. M. Springer, also of Springfield, while traveling in Europe, spent several weeks in Florence when Mr. Mead was at work on the bust and features of Mr. Lincoln. He sent a translation of the criticism in *La Riforma* to the *Journal* of this place. In his accompanying letter he says: "The comments of the Florentine papers are very complimentary, and you have a right to conclude that the statue merits all that is said of it. Here, where are found the finest works of Michael Angelo and Canova, and the renowned *chefs d'œuvre* of Greek sculpture, every work of this kind must stand upon its own merits. All who have seen Mr. Mead's statue of Mr. Lincoln admire it." The engraving of the coat of arms in this volume is from a photograph by L. Powers, a son of Hiram Powers, who has a gallery adjoining the studio of his father in Florence. It was a present from Mr. Mead to Mrs. Springer.

The models of the statue and coat of arms were completed and shipped to Chicopee, Massachusetts, arriving there in the latter part of October, 1870. Hon. J. C. Conkling of this city, a long and intimate friend of Mr. Lincoln, was at Chicopee in December, and his description of both models are similar to those previously given.

Thomas Lincoln (Tad), the youngest son of President Lincoln, after having spent the greater part of his time in Germany since the death of his father, returned with his mother to America early in 1871. In crossing the Atlantic he contracted a severe cold, which terminated in his death at Chicago, July 15, 1871.

The monument was not completed, but the Catacomb was far enough advanced to be occupied, and on Monday, the seventeenth of July, the remains were brought to Springfield and deposited in the west one of the five crypts—that which is at the extreme right on entering the vestibule.

At a meeting of the Association August 22, Governor Oglesby was instructed to confer with Judge David Davis of Bloomington and Robert T. Lincoln of Chicago, and they three were to agree upon a day for the removal of the remains of President Lincoln. After consultation they named September 19, at three o'clock p. m. The removal was intended to be done privately, a few personal friends only being notified. At the time appointed there were about two hundred persons at the monument to witness the event. Of the fifteen members of the Association, thirteen were present, namely, Oglesby, Dubois, Miner, Stuart, Conkling, Williams, Bunn, Bateman, Treat, Hatch, Melvin, Beveridge and Phillips.

When the remains were removed, December, 21, 1865, Jesse K. Dubois, Newton Bateman, D. L. Phillips, O. M. Hatch and O. H. Miner, members of the Association, signed a paper stating that it was the body of Abraham Lincoln beyond a doubt. In making their preparations for removal on the forenoon of September 19, 1871, it was thought that the embalming was a failure, and the remains were changed from the wooden coffin in which they were brought from Washington and placed in a metalic casket. The same members of the Association viewed the corpse, and again signed a paper testifying to the identity of the body. About four o'clock in the afternoon, the casket was conveyed to the Catacomb and deposited in the central crypt. As the time approached for the dedication, the Association made arrangements for transferring the remains to a marble Sarcophagus. They had all things in readiness, and on Friday evening, about seven o'clock, Oct. 9, 1874, the body was removed from the casket to a red cedar coffin lined with lead. The remains were found to be in a good state of preservation, and readily recognized as the true body of Abraham Lincoln. The transfer was made by Thomas C. Smith, undertaker, and soldered air tight by Col. A. J. Babcock. The coffin was then placed in the Sarcophagus, which was deposited in the central crypt of the catacomb, and the evidence of identity preserved unbroken by the same six gentlemen signing a paper similar to the two previous ones.

All three certificates are on file with the Secretary of the Association. The central crypt is lined with fine polished marble. The bodies of Willie and Eddie were placed together September 19, 1871, in the crypt to the right, or west, of that in which Mr. Lincoln rests. The body of Thomas (Tad), as previously stated, is in the crypt to the west, or extreme right, on entering the vestibule. The father and three sons are reposing near each other in this National Mausoleum. The two crypts on the left, or to the east, are unoccupied, and are intended for the only two remaining members of the family. They are closed as though they were occupied. Figure 6 presents the appearance of the crypts before the marble panel work, supported by Doric columns, and extending in dome groined arches to form the ceiling, were put in. Now the central crypt only is visible, with the Saracophagus bearing on its front the inscription—

"With malice towards none, with charity for all."

LINCOLN.

The name is surrounded by a wreath of oak boughs.

CHAPTER XXVII.

The reader will doubtless be interested in knowing how the money was raised to accomplish so much. By the courtesy of the treasurer, the Hon. James H. Beveridge, it has been my privilege to examine his books, and a little explanation will be of some advantage. As the money came in, an entry was made in a journal, prepared expressly for that purpose, of each contribution, giving the date of its reception, number on the journal, name of the person or society contributing, place of residence or location, and amount. For everything, except Sunday schools, this is all the record. The whole number of entries in the journal is 5145, and of these 1697 are Sunday schools. Besides entering the Sunday schools on the journal, there is another book prepared for them alone. The names of more than sixty thousand children are enrolled in this book. The total amount of their contributions is about twenty thousand dollars. Every superintendent was requested to send a roll of the names of the children, with the amount contributed by each. The record begins with the name of the school, where located, and the name of the superintendent, followed by the names of the children and amounts of their contributions. After the design was adopted, those who contributed not less than fifty cents, received in return a fine steel engraving of the monument, as it will appear when the statuary is placed on it.

The following extracts from the journal of the Association, taken at random, will give some idea of the great variety of persons and organizations contributing to the fund:

The first entry was made May 8, 1865, and was from Isaac Reed & Co., New York city, $100; Excelsior Lodge, No. 97, F. & A. Masons, Freeport, Ill., $25; St. Annes's Council, U. L. A., No. 1234, Kendall county, Ill.; Big Thunder Lodge, No. 28, I. O. of Good Templars, Belvidere, Ill.; Olive Branch Lodge, No. 15, Independent Order of Odd Fellows, Canton, Ill.; Third Presbyterian Church, Springfield, Ill.; Second Presbyterian Church, Springfield, Ill; German Lutheran Church, Springfield, Ill., and nearly all the other churches in Springfield; First Universalist Church, Sugar Grove and Blackberry, Ill.; First M. E. Church, Springfield, Ill.; 118th Mounted Infantry, Baton Rouge, La.; Cumberland Presbyterian Sunday School, at Lincoln, Ill. This is the first contribution from a Sunday school, and it is remarkable that it comes from a town named by some personal friends for Abraham Lincoln, when his only fame was that of being a good and honest lawyer. Congregational Church, Clifton, Ill.; Baptist Church, Towanda, Ill.; Ladies' Aid Society, Fairfield, Iowa; St. Mary's Church, Protestant Episcopal, Bloomington, Ill.; Citizens of Chelsea, Mass.; M. E. Church, Altoona, Penn.; Presbyterian Church, Omaha, Neb.; Colored Citizens of Cairo, Ill.; Hebrew Citizens of Alton, Ill; Hobart Church, Oneida Indians, Oneida, Wis.; United Brethren Church, Dayton, Ohio. The 73d Regiment U. S. Colored Troops, at New Orleans, La., contributed $1437, a greater amount than was given by any other individual or organization, except the State of Illinois.

It was not until the latter part of June that the Sunday schools began to report in large numbers, when page after page of the journal was filled with their contributions. At the same time, reports would come from a U. S. war steamer, with a long list of contributions; then from a U. S. army hospital, then Sunday schools, another U. S. steamship, a regiment in Mississippi, another at Washington, then one in Tennessee, still another from Arkansas, some white and some colored. Then more Sunday schools, Naval Hospital at Portsmouth, Virginia; a colored regiment, Sunday schools, a Hebrew congregation at St. Joseph, Mo.; Sunday schools, M. E. Church in Massachusetts, from a Congregational Church in Wisconsin, a Presbyterian Church in Pennsylvania, Baptist Church in Michigan, Episcopal Church in Illinois; roll of contributors from a colored regiment fills twenty-three pages; Hebrew congregation in Philadelphia, and a Presbyterian Sunday school at Aurora, Indiana. An American missionary, from his far-off field in Hong Kong, China, sends his contribution, to help build the monument to the memory of Abraham Lincoln. A Methodist Sunday school, away up in Seattle, Alaska, sends twenty dollars for the same purpose. Then comes a contribution from the superintendent of public instruction at Memphis, Tennessee. More Sunday schools, more Masonic, Odd Fellows, and Good Templars' lodges. More Sunday schools, from the east, west, north, and some from the south, of almost every denomination of Christians. Citizens of New York city contributed nearly five thousand dollars. Citizens of Boston and Stockbridge, Mass., contributed nearly fifteen hundred dollars. More Sunday schools—Sunday schools, lodges, churches, Sunday schools, and so it continues, page after page, throughout the journal.

Much the largest part of the money was contributed during the year 1865, but contributions continued to come, decreasing in number, until the early part of 1870. A contribution came, February 2, 1870, from a Methodist Sunday school at Smithtown Branch, Mass. On the sixty-first anniversary of the birth of Abraham Lincoln, namely, February 9, 1870, a contribution of $500 in gold was received from the State of Nevada, by her large hearted Governor, Henry G. Blasdel. One hundred dollars in gold was received on the eleventh of March, following, from the Secretary of the State of Nevada, as the contribution of the members of the Legislature and officers of that State. For a long time it appeared as if no more voluntary offerings would come into the treasury, but in December, 1870, a contribution of $10 was received from a gentleman in St. Louis, and on the twenty-second of the month $15.22 was received from a Presbyterian Sunday school at Princeton, Illinois.

Another pause ensues, until May 12, 1871, when $25 was received from a citizen of Sangamon county, Illinois, and on the fifth of June, $5, from a citizen of Belvidere, Illinois. On the twenty-fourth of June, $5 was received from a Methodist Sunday School at Greenwich, New York, and on the same day, $198 was reported as the contribution of the Second Presbyterian Sunday School of Springfield, Illinois. November 25, 1871, a contribution of $50 is recorded from a citizen of Geneva, Illinois. A report of the contributions for procuring the groups of statuary can be seen in the twenty-eighth chapter, and for ornamenting the monument grounds, in the twenty-ninth chapter.

Only three States have made contributions to the fund, without reserve. Illinois, by an act of the General Assembly, approved January 29, 1867, appropriated fifty thousand dollars. The money was not to be drawn from the State treasury until it was needed to pay out on the work. It has been drawn and applied as contemplated in the law. The State of Missouri appropriated one thousand dollars—a draft from Governor Fletcher, for that amount, came into the hands of the treasurer of the Association, April 18, 1868— and the State of Nevada $500, as already stated.

Men may object to giving assistance, and say it is an enterprise that belongs to Illinois. That State has acknowledged the honor of having been the chosen home of Abraham Lincoln, by her contribution of fifty thousand dollars, and has put her name in the most obscure place on the monument. If any other four

States were to combine, and do as much as Illinois, they would justly be regarded as liberal, and yet it is not a State, but a National Monument. As evidence of this, I need only refer to the great extent of country from which the contributious already received have come. They were made up, too, by all classes of people, and by organizations of almost every kind.

There can be but *one* National Monument to the memory of Abraham Lincoln, and that only can be a National Monument which contains his remains; who, at the time of his death, was the head of the nation, and was slain because he was its Chief Magistrate. This is even more than a National Monument, it is cosmopolitan in its character. His love included all mankind, and all the liberty loving portion of the human family extended their love to him. I might fill page after page with quotations from articles written in all parts of the world, expressing sorrow for his death. These expressions were so numerous that the United States Congress, in order to preserve them in a separate form, by a joint resolution of both houses, approved March 2, 1867,

Resolved, That, in addition to the number of copies of papers relating to foreign affairs now authorized by law, there shall be printed for distribution by the Department of State, on fine paper, with wide margin, a sufficient number of copies of the appendix to the diplomatic correspondence of 1865, to supply one copy to each Senator and each Representative of the Thirty-ninth Congress, and to each foreign government, and one copy to each corporation, association or public body, whose expressions of condolence or sympathy are published in this volume; one hundred of these copies to be bound in full Turkey morocco, full gilt, and the remaining copies to be bound in half Turkey morocco, marble edged.

Under this resolution, a volume of nine hundred and thirty quarto pages was published, making a book almost as large as Webster's unabridged dictionary. It contains " expressions of condolence and sympathy," on account of the assassination of Abraham Lincoln, from the governments, associations or individuals, in some official capacity, from the following countries, in alphabetical order. I give the name of each country, and the number of parties from whom documents were received :

Austria, nine; Argentine Republic, nine; Belgium, seven; Brunswick, one; Baden, Duchy of, four; Brazil, six; Bolivia, one; Chili, seventeen; Costa Rica, six; China, two; Denmark, four; Equador, five; Egypt, two; France, one hundred and fifty—forty-seven of which were from the press; Great Britain and her dependencies, including both houses of Parliament and Queen Victoria, many cities and towns throughout the kingdom, the island of Nassau, the Bahamas, Bengal and Calcutta, India, Cape Town and the gold coast of Africa, Dominion of Canada, with many of her cities east and west, Ireland, Scotland, Australia, islands of Guernsey, Bermuda, Jamaica and Vancouver, New South Wales and Nova Scotia. The addresses received from all these sources were four hundred and sixty-five, including twenty-nine from the press. Greece, one; Honduras, one; Hanseatic Republics, including the free cities of Bremen, Hamburg and Lubec, seven; Hesse Darmstadt, Duchy of, two; Hawaian Islands, four; Hayti, one; Italy, seventy-two, outside of Rome; Japan, two; Liberia, five; Mexico, six; Morocco, one; the Netherlands, including the Hague, four; Nicaragua, three; Prussia, seventeen; Portugal, eighteen; Peru, eleven; Russia, eight; Rome, four; Spain, nineteen; Sweden and Norway, nine; Saxe Meiningen, one; Switzerland, one hundred and thirty-six; San Salvador, three; United States of Columbia, twenty-three; Uraguay, three; Venezuela, six; Wurtemburg, three; United States of America, sixty-eight. These latter were, to a great extent, made up of societies composed of foreigners residing in the different cities of the Union. The total number, from all sources, is eleven hundred and sixty-eight. They contain some of the finest sentiments that words can express. They are nearly all written in prose, with a small number in poetry. I insert a single communication of the latter class. It was written by Miss Grace W. Gray, an invalid lady of Northampton, England, and sent to Charles F. Adams, our minister to that nation, with a request that it be forwarded to Mrs. Lincoln. It is an accrostic, and in the number of lines, it would also be a sonnet, if the versification had been arranged for that purpose:

"A nation—nor one only—mourns thy loss,
Brave Lincoln, and with voice unanimous
Raise to thy deathless memory
A dirge-like song of all thy noble deeds.
High let it rise; and I, too, fain would add
A loving tribute to thy priceless worth,
More widely known since banished from the earth.

"Laurel shall now thy brow entwine,
In memory's ever-faithful shrine;
Nor shall it fade when earth dissolves.
Caught up to meet thee in the air,
Old age and youth shall bless thee there;
Love shall her grateful tribute pay,
Nor cease through heaven's eternal day."

Resolutions and other expressions, by legislative bodies, corporations, voluntary societies and public assemblies called for the occasion, one and all, expressed in unmistakable terms their horror at the crime, and the warmest sympathy and condolence with the bereaved family of the President and the American people; but from the very nature of things, they partook too much of formality to express the finer feelings of the heart. These latter could only be found in the public journals. Of the former class, I make a

single selection of part of an utterance in four where-
ases and six resolutions, from the government of Liberia:

*Resolved, By the President of the Republic of Liberia and his
Cabinet, in council,* That it is with sincere regret and pain, as well
as with feelings of horror and indignation, the government of Liberia has heard of the foul assassination of Abraham Lincoln, late
President of the United States of America.

Resolved, That the government and people of Liberia deeply
sympathize with the government and people of the United States,
in the sad loss they have sustained by the death of so wise, so
just, so efficient, so vigorous, and yet so merciful a ruler.

Resolved, That while with due sorrow the government and people of Liberia weep with those that mourn the loss of so good and
great a chief, they are, nevertheless, mindful of the loss they themselves have experienced in the death of the great philanthropist
whose virtues can never cease to be told so long as the Republic
of Liberia shall endure; so long as there survives a member of
the negro race to tell of the chains that have been broken; of the
griefs that have been allayed; of the broken hearts that have been
bound up by him who, as it were a new creation, breathed life into
four millions of that race whom he found oppressed and degraded

From a large number of French papers, I select a
single paragraph, from the *Siecle* of April 30, 1865:

"I pause to pay a tribute of homage to the memory of Abraham
Lincoln; he will have been the apostle and the martyr of freedom.
The cause of slavery could only be put an end to by assassination.
It dies as it has lived, the dagger in hand. What a lost cause!
What a dishonored cause! The frightful drama of Golgotha is the
purchase of the disinherited. , The blood of the just is invariably
the ransom of the slaves."

We have heretofore regarded the people of South
America as not more than half civilized, but in all the
hundreds of papers on the death of Abraham Lincoln,
there is none that exhibits more accurate and discrim-

inating knowledge of our history, and that for sub-
limity of thought and deep pathos, excels that written
by the Hon. Salvador Camacho Roldan, and translated
from *La Opinion*, Bogota, June 7, 1865 ; from which I
make some brief extracts.   After stating in the most
clear and concise language, the causes of our civil war
and the difficulties in the path of President Lincoln,
the writer says : "There is in his last words something
of the fire of the old prophets," and then proceeds to
quote from his inaugural address of March 4, 1865:

" Fondly do we hope, fervently do we pray, that this mighty
scourge of war may soon pass away.   Yet if God wills that it continue until the wealth piled by the bondman's two hundred and
fifty years of unrequited toil shall be sunk, and until every drop
of blood drawn by the lash be paid by another drawn with the
sword, as was said three thousand years ago, so still it must be
said, 'the judgments of the Lord are true and righteous altogether."

The writer continues :

"And that nothing should be wanting to complete the grandeur
of his life, the hand of crime snatched it from him in the midst of the
triumph of his cause, and bound his temples, already pale from the
vigils and anguish of four years, with the resplendent crown of
the martyr.

"Abraham Lincoln is dead, but his work is finished and sealed
with the veneration which God has given to the blood of martyrs.
He who was yesterday a man, is to-day an apostle ; he who was the
centre at which the shots of malice and hatred were aimed, is to-day
a prestige, sacred and irresistible.   His voice is louder and more potent from the mansion of martyrs, than from the Capitol, and the
cry which was loudly raised among the living, is mute before the
majesty of the tomb.

"Abraham Lincoln passes to the side of Washington—the one
the father, and the other the saviour of a great nation.   The traditions, pure and stainless, of the early times of the republic,
broken at the close of the administration of the second Adams,
were restored in the martyr of Ford's Theatre ; and the predomi-
nance of material interests which has heretofore obscured the
country of Franklin, will abdicate the field to the prelacy of

moral ideas, of justice, of equality, and of reparation. The whip has dropped from the hand of the overseer; the bloodhound will hunt no more the fugitive slave in the mangrove swamps of the Mississippi; the hammer of the auctioneer of negroes has struck for the last time on his platform, and its baleful sound has died into eternal silence. The sacred ties of love which unite the hearts of slaves will not again be broken by the forced separation of husbands and wives, parents and children. The unnatural and infamous consort between the words liberty and slavery is dissolved forever; and liberty! liberty! will be the cry which shall run from the Atlantic to the Pacific, and from the northern lakes to the Gulf of Mexico. This great work has cost a great price. Humanity will have to mourn yet many years to come the horrors of that civil war; but above the blood of its victims, above the bones of its dead, above the ashes of desolated hearths, will arise the great figure of Abraham Lincoln, as the most acceptable sacrifice offered by the nineteenth century in expiation of the great crime of the sixteenth. Above all the anguish and tears of that immense hecatomb will appear the shade of Lincoln as the symbol of hope and pardon."

These expressions of condolence and sympathy were written in not less than twenty-five of the leading languages of the world, but when translated into our own, they one and all convey such true appreciation of the motives that governed the life of Abraham Lincoln, as leads us to believe that the language of freedom is everywhere the same. I believe it may be truthfully said, that there is not a man under the whole canopy of heaven, that loves liberty for liberty's sake, who does not feel that, when Abraham Lincoln was struck down, he lost a brother, for his love included all mankind.

A copy of the book containing these expressions of condolence and sympathy, also the books, papers and letters of the Monument Association will be placed in Memorial Hall. A package of the original documents sent to Mrs. Lincoln and the officers of the United States government, after the death of Mr. Lincoln.

was forwarded by Robert T. Lincoln to the Hon.
John T. Stuart in December, 1871, are framed and
placed in Memorial Hall.   A small number of them
are on paper, but much the largest number are on either
parchment or vellum.   They are of all sizes, from
eight by ten inches to eighteen by twenty-four.   Among
them are some very fine specimens of pen-printing.
They will be highly valued for their ornamental appearance.   Twenty-two of them are the originals of
those contained in the book published by Congress.
I will mention them in something like the order in
which they appear in that book.

In the borough of Blackburn, county of Lancaster,
England, a meeting was held May 2, 1865, and an address issued to Mrs. Lincoln, Mr. Seward and their
families.   In this address the sentiment is expressed,
that when the exigencies of a nation demand a great
leader, God always sends the man for the time, and that
Abraham Lincoln was raised up for the special purpose of leading our government through the perils of
the rebellion, and to let the oppressed go free.   Although
the language varies, there is a similarity in the sentiments running through them all, therefore I shall
simply give the dates and places from whence they
came :

Belfast, Ireland, May 8, 1865.
Dublin, Ireland, May 1, 1865.
Borough of Lancaster, England, May 3, 1865.
City Council of Liverpool, England, May 3, 1865.
City of Leeds, England, May 1, 1865.
' Workingmen of London, England, May 4, 1865.
Their words of patriotism and love of freedom are so
clear, that they seem to be Americans.   Their address
comes on a large piece of parchment, with fifty-five
signatures.

The Emancipation Society, at St. James Hall, London, April 29, 1865.

British and Foreign Anti-Slavery Society, London, May 5, 1865.

Temple Discussion Forum, of London, without date.

Atlantic Telegraph Company, from the London office, May 8, 1865.

New England Society, of Montreal, Canada, April 19, 1865.

Municipal Council of Northampton, England, May 1, 1865. Two copies, on vellum; one to the government archives at Washington, the other to Mrs. Lincoln.

Municipal Council of Oldham, England May 1 and 3, 1865.

Town Council of Paisley, Scotland, May 6, 1865.

The inhabitants of Plaistow, England, without date.

Municipal Council of Rochdale, Scotland, May 4, 1865.

Sheffield Secular Society, England, without date.

The inhabitants of Southport, England, May 6, 1865.

Parish of St. Pancras, county of Middlesex, England, May 10, 1865.

Chamber of Commerce of the State of New York, New York city, April 22, 1865.

Board of Managers of the Missionary Society of the Methodist Episcopal Church, 200 Mulberry street, New York, April 24, 1865.

The following do not appear in the book published by Congress, but on the parchments only :

From the Aldermen and Burgesses of the city of Liverpool, England, May 3, 1865.

The inhabitants of Gateshead, England, May 4, 1865.

Ladies of the London Emancipation Society, to Mrs. Lincoln, without date.

St. George's Society, Quebec, Dominion of Canada, April 24, 1865.

Montgomery Lodge No. 19, Free and Accepted Masons, Philadelphia, May 4, 1865.

Friends, or Quakers, of Kendall, England, to the

18

widow and children of Abraham Lincoln, without date. This parchment contains sixty-seven autograph names, about one-third being women.

Mercantile Library Company sent a piece of parchment, with some very neatly expressed sentiments and fifteen signatures, but it is without date or location.

The St. Andrew's Scottish Benevolent Society of San Francisco, California, April 17, 1865. Their expressions are recorded on a fine piece of vellum, and attached to a roller, heavily plated with gold.

Declarations of the Bishop and Clergy of the Protestant Episcopal Church, in the Diocese of Illinois, April 19, 1865. These are neatly engrossed on a piece of vellum, eighteen by twenty-four inches, and signed by Bishop Whitehouse and fifty-one of the clergy of his diocese.

Among the number there is one very fine piece of parchment, which has nothing on its face to show whether it was prepared before or after Mr. Lincoln's death. It is a series of joint resolutions of the Select and Common Councils of the city of Philadelphia, inviting Abraham Lincoln to visit that city on his way to Washington, to be inaugurated President of the United States. It contains the names of the committee of invitation, consisting of six members of each council, and was approved by the Mayor, Alexander Henry, February 14, 1861.

On the morning of Saturday, April 29, 1871, the Hon. Sharon Tyndale, of Springfield, arose from his bed about one o'clock, took an affectionate leave of his family, and started to the depot of the Chicago and St. Louis Railroad, with the intention of visiting Belleville. At daylight his body was found, about a square from his residence, lying on its face, with a pistol shot through his head. The wound was almost like that which caused the death of Mr. Lincoln. Large rewards were offered for the arrest of the assassins, but there has never been the slightest clue as to who they were.

At the annual meeting of the Association, May 11, 1871, a committee was appointed who reported the following resolutions, which were adopted and ordered to be spread upon the record :

Resolved, That in the death of the Hon. Sharon Tyndale, one of the corporators of the National Lincoln Monument Association, and the first of that number who has departed this life, this Association has lost one of the most earnest, faithful and valued members—one who cherished the memory of Abraham Lincoln with sincere and patriotic devotion, and who gave his time and thought, gladly and without stint, to promote the success of the enterprise for which this corporation was created.

Resolved, That we recall with grateful emotions the unvarying courtesy and kindness of the deceased, as a member of this body ; his exalted conception of the historic significance of the proposed monument; his strong desire that the structure should be worthy of the great name to be honored and perpetuated by it, and his many valuable services and suggestions as the work was begun and carried forward.

Resolved, That the cruel assassination of Mr. Tyndale derives a blacker coloring of atrocity from his singularly benevolent and philanthropic nature, and his well known kindness of disposition, and that we earnestly join in the general wish that his inhuman murderers may yet be arrested, convicted and punished.

Resolved, That a copy of these resolutions be forwarded, with assurances of our deep and respectful sympathy, to the afflicted widow and family of the deceased.

NEWTON BATEMAN, ⎫
DAVID L. PHILLIPS, ⎬ Committee.
JAMES C. CONKLING, ⎭

At the same meeting, upon the suggestion of Hon. O. M. Hatch, Gov. John M. Palmer was elected a member of the Association, to fill the vacancy occasioned by the death of Mr. Tyndale. With this exception, there has never been any change in the membership, from the organization of the Association.

Clinton L. Conkling, the first secretary, was never a member of the Association, but served as secretary until December 28, 1865, when he tendered his resignation, which was accepted January 18, 1866. Hon. O. M. Hatch was then elected secretary, which he accepted, and has continued to serve until the present time. The Association is at present composed of ex-Gov. R. J. Oglesby, President; Hon. Jesse K. Dubois, Vice President; Hon. James H. Beveridge, Treasurer; Hon. O. M. Hatch, Secretary; Hon. O. H. Miner, Hon. John T. Stuart, Hon. James C. Conkling, John Williams, Thomas J. Dennis, Jacob Bunn, Hon. Newton Bateman, Hon. S. H. Treat, Hon. D. L. Phillips, Dr. S. H. Melvin, and Gov. John M. Palmer.

The Executive Committee, appointed when the work commenced, namely, the Hon. John T. Stuart, Jacob Bunn, and John Williams, has continued to superintend it to the present time.

CHAPTER XXVIII.

Soon after the National Lincoln Monument Association was organized, it announced its intention to raise two hundred and fifty thousand dollars for the purpose of building a monument to the memory of Abraham Lincoln. There was but one contribution made, the payment of which was dependent on the amount named being raised. The Legislature of the State of New York, at its first or second session, after the Association was organized, appropriated ten thousand dollars, to be paid to the National Lincoln Monument Association at Springfiield, Illinois, when two hundred and forty thousand dollars were raised from other sources. As that amount was never collected, the appropriation lapsed, but another law was enacted in February, 1872, appropriating the same amount, to be paid when a sworn statement of the amount expended by the Association was placed in the hands of the Comptroller of the State of New York. That statement was duly forwarded, and a draft for the amount was received by the Treasurer of the National Lincoln Monument Association, November 15, 1872.

A single incident will illustrate how easy it would have been to raise money in many other places, with the proper exciting cause. An aged colored woman, Charlotte Scott, who had received her freedom in Virginia by the Emancipation Proclamation, was living at Marietta, Ohio, when President Lincoln was assassinated. She at once said: "The colored people have lost their best friend on earth; Mr. Lincoln was our best friend, and I will give five dollars of my wages towards building a monument to his memory." This circumstance being related in the Missouri *Democrat*, of May 2, 1865, caused more than sixteen thousand dollars to be raised by the colored people. The fund was held in St. Louis by Hon. James E. Yeatman for several years, but was pledged to the National Lincoln Monument Association at Washington City.

From the time ground was broken in the autumn of 1869, until the spring of 1871, the structure arose steadily and quietly, and the work, both on the Monument and statue, was so far advanced that the Association began to prepare for some public demonstration connected with the enterprise, without waiting for the four groups of statuary. On the eleventh day of May, at the sixth annual meeting of the Association, a committee was raised consisting of President Oglesby, D. L. Phillips, J. C. Conkling, Newton Bateman and S. H. Treat, to make the necessary preparations. They were expected to visit Chicopee, Massachusetts, and "examine the Statue of Lincoln and the Coat of Arms, suggest to the Association the name of a suitable person to deliver the oration upon the occasion of the unveiling of the Statue when placed upon the Monument, and to select and suggest a day upon which the ceremonies should take place."

On the nineteenth of July, four days after the death of Thomas Lincoln, at a meeting of the Association, that committee reported progress. A few days after that, Governor Oglesby and Mr. Phillips, of the before mentioned committee, started East.

A meeting of the Association was called on the twenty-second of August, to hear the report of the committee, of which the following is the substance:

Messrs. Oglesby and Phillips went by the way of Chicago, for the purpose of availing themselves of the counsels—particularly in the selection of an orator—of some of the prominent gentlemen of that city, who had been the personal and political friends of President Lincoln. Upon making their business known to the Hon. J. Young Scammon, Col. James H. Bowen,

Chauncey T. Bowen, Esq. and others, they learned that several of these gentlemen, on their visit to Springfield with the remains of Thomas Lincoln, became deeply interested in seeing the monument completed. When the subject was more fully discussed, the committee received what they regarded as ample assurances that Chicago would furnish the means to purchase one of the groups of statuary. They went so far as to select the Infantry Group as the one they would prefer to have placed to the credit of their city. The whole question was left open, with the understanding that whenever the Association desired it, the money would be forthcoming.

The committee next visited New York city and called on ex-Governor E. D. Morgan, Hon. Russell Sage, Hon. George Opdyke, Winthrop S. Gilman, Esq. Geo. T. M. Davis, Esq. A. D. Shepherd, Esq. and others, and received assurances that New York would furnish the Naval Group. They left the matter of raising the money there open also, for the reason that it was in the heat of summer, and they were assured that many gentlemen who would cheerfully contribute to the fund were then absent.

On visiting Boston they called on Governor Claflin, and after a long consultation with him, were gratified to find that he entered heartily into the spirit of the enterprise, and although he declined, alone, to make a positive promise, he assured the committee of his sympathy with the movement, and gave it as his opinion that Boston would furnish the means to pay for one of the groups.

The committee would have visited Philadelphia but did not think it advisable to go while the weather was so hot, and that it would be better to defer it until winter.

On visiting Chicopee the committee found the Coat of Arms finished, and the work on the Statue of Lincoln in a good state of progress. They took ample time to study it, and unhesitatingly pronounce it as perfect a reproduction of Abraham Lincoln as it is possible to transfer from life to inert matter.   In their opinion Mr. Mead has proven himself a true artist, in the fact that he has made no effort to improve on nature.   Mr. Lincoln stooped in the shoulders, just enough to spoil the fit of a coat about the breast, and the Statue shows this to perfection.   The peculiar contour of the features, the full lower lip, the mole on the cheek, the wrinkles on the forehead, and the nose, unlike any other except Lincoln's, are all faithfully reproduced.   His long, bony fingers, as they grasped the Emancipation Proclamation, and all his other angularities, are brought out with great accuracy.   They regard the work a signal success, and think it a fortunate circumstance that the casting and finishing was placed in the hands of the Ames Manufacturing Company.   Mr. James T. Ames, as President of that Company, became intimately acquainted with Mr. Lincoln during the four years of the rebellion.   His business relations in manufacturing cannon and other arms for the government, led to many personal interviews with the President.   His recollection of these events was of great value when he came to finish up the statue, which he seemed to regard more as a labor of love and patriotism, than a mere matter of business.

It appeared to them as if the work was almost done, but Mr. Ames declined to name a time when it would be completed.   Being satisfied that it could not be done and put in position on the Monument in time to be unveiled during 1871, the committee did not make a selection of an orator, neither did they name any day for the ceremony of unveiling to take place.

Although the committee found it inexpedient at that time to do all they were appointed for, they did that which was much more important.   They developed the fact that the movement on the part of the people to build a monument to the memory of Abraham Lincoln was not a mere impulse, to be abandoned when the novelty wore away, but that the people are firmly resolved to complete it in all its parts. Thus matters connected with the Monument stood when the great tornado of fire swept over Chicago on the eighth and ninth of October. Hundreds of thousands of dollars' worth of property, belonging to the men who had united in pledging the money to purchase the Infantry Group of statuary, were reduced to ashes in a day.

When this great calamity befel the commercial metropolis of the Northwest, it was about the close of the building season for 1871. The Monument proper was then nearly completed. The Association had the means to pay all bills for this part of the work, also for the United States Coat of Arms and the Statute of Lincoln. But the Monument would still lack what was necessary to give vital force to the design of the artist. It would be an apt emblem of our government at the beginning of the great rebellion. The constitution was there as a pedestal, and Abraham Lincoln took his position upon it. The States were there, but threatening dissolution, and he had neither Infantry, Cavalry, Artillery or a Navy, without which he would have been compelled to look on and see them crumble away beneath his feet. At this juncture the loyal people of America rallied to his support, and placed at his disposal the means necessary to organize all the forces required for the preservation of the government. The members of the Association, when assembled on the twenty-ninth of November, felt that the time had arrived for an earnest appeal to be made to the American people, to again furnish the means to organize the Infantry, the Cavalry, the Artillery and the Navy—*in bronze*—to be marshaled around his Statue, in imitation of the support the loyal people of the nation gave him in its hour of greatest peril.

The feeling was unanimous among the members that the magnanimity which always characterized

Abraham Lincoln, should restrain them from holding those gentlemen in Chicago to their promises made before the fire. In consideration of the munificent liberality manifested by them in so many ways when in prosperity, all felt that they should be consulted before calling on any other city to take their place in supplying the Infantry Group. It was decided that, as the initial step to further proceedings, Governor Oglesby should visit Chicago and ascertain their feelings on the subject. After spending a day or two there, the Governor wrote a letter to the Hon. O. M. Hatch, Secretary of the Association. The letter was dated Chciago, Dec. 8, and when it was received Mr. Hatch informed Vice President Dubois, who called a meeting Dec. 11, 1871, for the purpose of hearing a report from the Governor.

He said that at an interview with the Hon. J. Young Scammon, he opened the conversation about the future purposes of the Association, and suggested that it might be under the necessity of calling upon some other city to take the place of Chicago in supplying one of the groups of statuary. Mr. Scammon said he thought not, and inquired into the terms of the contract with the sculptor, as to the time of payments. The Governor informed him that one-third of the price was to be paid when the order was given for the work to proceed; but then added very explicitly, that the Association did not, under the present circumstances, expect Chicago to contribute anything, and assured him of the profound regret felt by the members at the necessity of looking somewhere else for the Infantry Group. Mr. Scammon said he thought that unnecessary, and then to the surprise and gratification of the Governor, proceeded to say: "Your Association may give Mr. Mead the order to proceed at once to prepare the cast for the Infantry Group, and I will furnish you in cash one-third of the $13,700; and I think by the time the second payment becomes due, we shall be able to meet that and the last also." The Governor conferred with Mr. Chauncey T. Bowen, and other gentlemen, who heartily approved of the action of Mr. Scammon, and expressed the determination of Chicago to have one of the groups if no other city did so.

One of the rules of the Association is, never to order any work until they have the money in hand to pay the whole amount; but the Governor recommended a deviation from that rule in the case of Chicago. The other members adopted his views, and on motion of Dr. S. H. Melvin, it was

"*Resolved:*   That, in consideration of the proposition—magnanimous under the circumstances—made by the Hon. J. Young Scammon to President Oglesby, as detailed in his letter just read, the Executive Committee be, and they are hereby directed to request or order Mr. Mead to proceed to execute the work upon the Infantry Group, and prepare the same for the Monument, as stipulated and contemplated in his contract with the Association."

The following order was then issued, with instructions to Mr. Mead to draw on Mr. Scammon for $4566.66⅔ :

SPRINGFIELD, ILL. U. S. A. Dec. 11, A. D. 1871.

Mr. Larkin G. Mead, FLORENCE, ITALY.

SIR—You are hereby directed to proceed to the construction of the Infantry Group for the National Lincoln Monument, as specified in your contract with the Association, this order being given upon a resolution of the Association, a copy of which is herewith transmitted.

Respectfully yours,

JOHN T. STUART,
 JOHN WILLIAMS, } Executive Committee.
 JACOB BUNN,

Ex-Governor Oglesby and D. L. Phillips, of the committee appointed May, 1871, again started east *via* Chicago about the eighth of February, 1872, for the purpose of completing their labors and of enlisting the patriotic citizens of some of the eastern cities in the laudable work of supplying the means to secure the remaining groups of Statuary, and to make arrangements for having the Statue of Lincoln placed upon the Monument when completed ; also, to secure the consent of some distinguished American citizen to deliver the oration on that occasion.

At a meeting of the Association on the fourteenth of March, the committee made their report, of which the following is the substance :   One or both of them visited New York, Philadelphia, Boston, Chicopee, Albany and Auburn.   At New York, Boston and Philadelphia, each, they received positive assurances from gentlemen eminent for their love of country, that the money would be raised to pay for a group of statuary.   At each place the parties giving this assurance had a book prepared for recording one hundred and thirty-seven subscriptions, of one hundred dollars each, making $13,700, the amount required.   When the subscriptions are completed, the books are to be forwarded to Springfield and placed in Memorial Hall, as an additional attraction to the contributors, or their friends, when visiting the Monument.

New York being the largest seaport in the United States, the Naval Group was very appropriately assigned to that city.   The assurances that the money would be raised for that group was supported by ex-Gov. E. D. Morgan, Russel Sage, Col. G. T. M. Davis and Winthrop S. Gilman.   Gov. Morgan went to work among his friends and very soon became convinced that he would have no difficulty in raising the money.   The following letter, written the day before Messrs. Oglesby and Phillips made their report, explains itself:

NEW YORK, March 13, 1872.

Hon. R. J. Oglesby, Decatur, Ill:

MY DEAR GOVERNOR—I have been at work since Thursday last upon the matter of obtaining the autographs of one hun-

dred and thirty-seven of our citizens, for the purpose of contributing one of the Bronze Groups for the monument to Abraham
Lincoln. I have gone far enough to enable me to assure you,
and the Association represented by you, that I am certain to be
successful; so certain that I will be responsible for raising the
sum of thirteen thousand seven hundred dollars, being the amount
necessary to pay for the group representing the Navy. Each
autograph on my book means a check for $100, and it may be
until the middle of April before the matter will be complete, and
the certificate of deposit in the United States Trust Company forwarded to you. Therefore, that no time should be lost in ordering
the modeling to be done by the artist (Mr. Mead), I want you to advise him and get him to work *without delay*. My subscribers are all
chosen, and none refuse, while many *thank me* for giving them
the privilege; and yet, time is required to see so many gentlemen. Some are not in town, and others not always at their place
of business when I call; but be assured that success is certain,
and that there ought not to be any delay in forwarding the order.
The artist may get engaged in some other heavy work.

I am very truly yours,

E. D. MORGAN.

The letter was transmitted by President Oglesby to
Secretary Hatch, with instructions to call a meeting
at once. The meeting was called for March 22d.
When the Association was convened, and the letter
read, the following resolution was unanimously
adopted:

Resolved, That in consideration of the letter from Hon. E. D.
Morgan, just read, we hereby request and direct Larkin G.
Mead, Esq., to proceed without delay to prepare and construct the
Naval Group for the Monument, as contemplated and specified
in his contract with this Association, and draw upon them for
one-third of thirteen thousand seven hundred dollars. The Secretary is hereby directed to cause to be transmitted to Mr. Mead
a copy of this order.

The order was at once forwarded to the artist at Florence, Italy. The money was all paid, and received by the Treasurer of the Association at Springfield, October 4, 1872. The models for the Infantry and Naval Groups were completed and shipped to Chicopee, Massachusetts. In crossing the Atlantic ocean both Groups were somewhat injured, but in such a manner as not to affect the work when completed. A letter from the Association inquiring into the progress of the work, elicited the following response :

CHICOPEE, MASS., Oct. 10, 1874.

National Lincoln Monument Association, Springfield, Ill.

GENTLEMEN: By request of O. M. Hatch, for the Association, on the 7th inst., would say that the amount of cannon on hand is 44,511 pounds; have purchased similar stock at twenty cents per pound. We are in receipt of the models of the Navy and Infantry Groups. The models for Navy Group are repaired, and the moulding in a good state of forwardness in the foundry, part of the castings being in a finished state. The models for Infantry Group are not all repaired, but will be ready to follow Navy Group when out.

Yours Truly,
AMES MFG. CO.

The Cavalry Group was assigned to Boston, and the assurance that the money will be raised is supported by such names as ex-Gov. Claflin, Nathaniel Thayer, Alpheus Hardy, J. Wiley Edmonds, Horatio Harrison and others. Hon. Henry Wilson, Vice-President of the United States, was so pleased with the monument, while on his first visit to Springfield to participate in the ceremony of unveiling the Statue of Lincoln, that he expressed his decided opinion that when the people of Boston were informed of the progress of the work, they would no longer delay, but would raise the money at once to pay for the Cavalry group.

At Philadelphia some parties proposed raising the $13,700 by subscriptions of $1000 each, but it was afterwards decided to adopt the plan pursued in New York. The following are the names of some of the parties who entered heartily into the spirit of the movement, upon the object being presented by Gov. Oglesby: Col. John W. Forney, Morton McMichael, G. W. Childs, Henry Cary. —— Comly, the collector of customs, and James L. Claghorn.

Pennsylvania being the largest iron producing State in the Union, and Pittsburgh the city where the greatest quantity of heavy ordnance was manufactured during the war to suppress the rebellion, it seemed appropriate for the commercial metropolis of that State to furnish the Artillery Group. The proposition made by Gov. Oglesby that this should be done, was very heartily acceded to by the gentlemen above named. Now that Boston and Philadelphia can see that it only depends on the fulfilment of their pledges to complete the monument in all its parts, they will doubtless vie with each other in seeing which shall be first to fill its quota. As soon as the money is in the treasury the Association will order the work to proceed on the two groups together. If it is done soon the Association may hold the two groups, now so near completed, until they can have all four placed on the Monument at the same time, when it will be completed and symmetrical in all its parts.

Previous to the departure of the committee for the east in February, 1872, the feeling was almost unanimously expressed by members of the Association and others, that in view of the historical associations connected with the death of President Lincoln, and the attempt to assassinate his Secretary of State, it would be eminently proper that the latter should take the leading part in the approaching demonstration at the tomb of the former. With the view of making such arrangements as would lead to the consummation of

the wishes of the Association, Gov. Oglesby visited
Auburn, New York, on the seventh of March, and on
behalf of the Association, extended to the Hon. William H. Seward an invitation to visit Springfield and
deliver the oration at the unveiling of the statue of
Lincoln.   After taking one whole day to consider the
matter, and consult with his physician and family,
Mr. Seward felt compelled to decline the invitation
on account of the precarious condition of his health.

CHAPTER XXIX.

After the death of William H. Seward, October 10, 1872, no definite steps were taken towards dedicating the monument, until July 24, 1874. At a meeting of the National Lincoln Monument Association, held on that day, it was decided, by the passage of a resolution to that effect, that the ceremony of unveiling the Statue of Abraham Lincoln, and dedication of the Monument, should take place October 15, 1874. The principal reasons for selecting so early a day for the ceremonial, and without waiting for the groups of Statuary, was that the work was substantially completed, and the members of the Association being nearly all men of advanced age. Of the fifteen original members, one only has passed away—Mr. Tyndale —and he died by violence. It was felt by many of the members that this remarkable Providential preservation could not reasonably be expected to continue. In addition to this, they each cherished a very commendable desire to witness a formal public recognition of their almost ten years' labor of love. Another reason why they selected that particular time, was that the Society of the Army of the Tennessee had decided to hold its Eighth Annual Reunion at Springfield, Illinois, October 14 and 15, 1874.

The citizens of Springfield commenced raising subscriptions August 18, 1874, to defray the expense. Nearly $3,000 were raised, and committees organized on Finance, Decorations, Printing, Banquet, Salute, Music, and one each on the part of the Society of the

19

Army of the Tennessee and of the National Lincoln
Monument Association, on Invitations.

Six grand triumphal arches were erected across the
principal streets. They consisted each of a central
arch, thirty-three and a half feet high, and thirty feet
between the pedestals, each of which had a flag staff
rising in the centre to the height of forty feet. The
central arches had arches on each side, seventeen feet
four inches high in the centre, and nine feet between
the pedestals. One of these compound arches was
placed at each side of the State House Square, on Adams, Washington, Fifth and Sixth Streets. Two others were erected on Sixth Street, one opposite the Leland Hotel and one at the Opera House. The arch
west of the Square, on Fifth Street, was devoted to
mottoes, each expressing some sentiment with reference to Lincoln. That on the south, to distinguished
soldiers, deceased. The others were covered with patriotic devices, utterances and names of distinguished
living soldiers. All were decorated with evergreens
and flowers. The meetings of the Society of the Army
of the Tennessee were held at the Opera House
through the day and evening of the fourteenth, and
an oration and many brilliant speeches delivered. On
the morning of the fifteenth the Society held a closing
meeting at the Opera House, and then joined the procession and marched in a body to the National Lincoln Monument and participated in the services of unveiling the Statue of Lincoln. The closing part of the
services of the Army Society Reunion was a grand
banquet at the Leland Hotel, commencing at nine
o'clock on the evening of the fifteenth.

The Monument Association having decided upon
the time for unveiling the Statue of Lincoln, the next
thing in order was the selection of an orator for the
occasion. That was a delicate question. It had from
the first been the subject of great solicitude with the
Association, that a member of Mr. Lincoln's cabinet

or some one connected with his administration should deliver the oration. The death of Seward, Greeley, Chase, Sumner and others, more especially identified with Mr. Lincoln in the political events before and during his administration, reduced the number of his distinguished compeers, and in proportion increased the difficulty of making a selection that would give general satisfaction. At the meeting of July 24, a resolution was passed, inviting the President of the United States to deliver the oration. Upon its being communicated to him by Gov. Oglesby, President Grant replied, under date of July 31, 1874, and says:

"I have kept the letter two days without answering, to fully consider whether I can undertake a task so different from anything ever attempted by me before. My great admiration for Mr. Lincoln's character, talents, and public services, would tempt me, if I felt able to do justice to the subject, but I do not; therefore decline the honor, thanking the Association of which you are the President for conferring it and hope you will make a selection of some one who can and will do full justice to the memory and public services of our noble martyred President."

The Association held a meeting on the tenth of August, at which the following was offered by Governor Palmer:

Resolved, That the President of this Association be requested to communicate with the following gentlemen in the order herein named, with the view to obtaining the services of one of them to deliver an oration at the unveiling of the Statue of Mr. Lincoln, to-wit: Gov. John A. Dix, Hon. Gideon Welles and Hon. O. P. Morton.

Mr. Hatch offered the following amendment:

"And in the event that neither accept, that the President of this Association, Gov. R. J. Oglesby, be requested to deliver the address upon that occasion."

Governor Dix declined, pleading official engagements.

A special messenger, D. L. Phillips, visited Ex-Secretary of the Navy, Welles, at his home. Mr Welles did not come to an immediate decision, but afterwards declined by letter. Previous to receiving the invitation, Mr. Welles had written some very able and kindly articles on the administration of President Lincoln, in reviewing the Memorial Address on the life, character and public services of William H. Seward, by Hon. Charles Francis Adams, at Albany, N. Y., in April, 1873. We believe that is the only instance where a cabinet officer, who, during the entire struggle for the life of the nation was daily on the most intimate terms with President Lincoln, has so freely commented on the peculiar traits of his character and of the events connected with his administration. This is my apology for digressing here to quote some passages from those articles, which were first published in the *Galaxy*, and afterwards in book form, entitled "Lincoln and Seward."

On page 32, Mr. Welles says :

"Mr. Lincoln was modest, kind, and unobtrusive, but he had, nevertheless, sturdy intellectual independence, wonderful self-reliance, and, in his unpretending way, great individuality. Though even willing to listen to others, and to avail himself of suggestions from any quarter which he deemed valuable, he never for a moment was unmindful of his position or of proper relf-respect, or felt that he was "dependent" on any one for the faithful and competent discharge of any duty upon which he entered. He could have dispensed with any one of his cabinet, and the admin istration not been impaired, but it would have been difficult if not impossible to have selected any one who could have filled the office of Chief Magistrate as successfully as Mr. Lincoln in that troublesome period. In administering the government, there were details in each department which the Secretaries respectively discharged. Of these the President had a general knowledge, and the executive control of each and all. In this respect the Secretary of State bore the same relation to the President as his colleagues in the other departments."

On page 206, he says:

"When the Republicans, in convention at Chicago, chose their standard bearer, they wisely and properly selected as their representative the sincere and able man who had no great money power in his interest, no disciplined lobby, no host of party followers, but who, like David, confided in the justice of his cause, and, with the simple weapons of truth and right, met the Goliath of slavery aggression before assembled multitudes in many a well contested debate. The popular voice was not in error, nor its confidence misplaced, when it selected and elected Lincoln. After his election, and after the war commenced, events forced upon him the emancipation of the slaves in the rebellious States. It was his own act, a bold step, an executive measure originating with him, and was, as stated in the memorable appeal at the close of the final proclamation, invoking for it the considerate judgment of mankind, warranted alone by military necessity. He and the cabinet were aware that the measure involved high and fearful responsibility, for it would alarm the timid everywhere, and alienate, at least for a time, the bold in the border States, who clung to the Union. * * Results have proved that there was in the measure profound thought, statesmanship, courage and far-seeing sagacity—consummate executive and administrative ability, which was, after some reverses, crowned with success. The nation, emerging from gloom and disaster, and the whole civilized world, united in awarding honor and gratitude to the illustrious man who had the mind to conceive, and the courage and firmness to decree the emancipation of a race."

On page 214, Mr. Welles says:

"Mr. Lincoln was in many respects a remarkable, though I do not mean to say an infallible, man. No true delineation or photograph of his intellectual capacity and attributes has ever been given, nor shall I attempt it. His vigorous and rugged, but comprehensive mind, his keen and shrewd sagacity, his intellectual strength and mental power, his genial, kindly temperament—with charity for all and malice towards none—his sincerity, unquestioned honesty and homely suavity, made him popular as well as great."

In his letter, dated Hartford, Ct., August 31, 1874, to the Monument Association, through Hon. D. L. Phillips, declining the invitation to deliver the Oration, Mr. Welles says :

"The intellect and capability of Mr. Lincoln, are, I apprehend, not fully understood and appreciated by those who knew him before entering upon his great public career. His vigorous mind was continually expanding, the horizon enlarging, so that, on the day he was murdered, he was better qualified to discharge the duties of Chief Magistrate than any man living. Well may the nation deplore his loss."

After the Secretary of the Navy declined, Gov. Oglesby waited on Gov. O. P. Morton in person, at Indianapolis, who declined on account of the state of his health. At a meeting of the Monument Association, September 8, on motion of Col. D. L. Phillips, it was—

Resolved, That the Association adhere to its original resolution of August 10th, that Hon. R. J. Oglesby, at the unanimous request and hearty concurrence of the Association, will deliver the Oration.

At a later period it was decided by the Association to relieve Gov. Oglesby of the work of preparing a history of the Monument, and Hon. Jesse K. Dubois, Vice President of the Association, was invited to discharge that duty. Both accepted the positions assigned them.

A committee of invitation and arrangements was appointed, consisting of Ex-Governor John M. Palmer, Dr. S. H. Melvin and Col. John Williams. One thousand invitations were sent out to all parts of the Union. Much the largest number of those invited responded in person on the day of dedication, and those who, from any cause, were unable to be present, they very generally answered by letter, expressing their sympathy with the object of the meeting, and regrets at their inability to attend. Among these were letters *from* Hon. L. F. S. Foster of Norwich, Ct. ; R. H. Dana, Jr., of Boston, Mass. ; Judge G. L. Cranmers, of Wheeling, W. Va. ; Prof. Noah Porter, of Yale College ; Hon. John G. Palfrey, Cambridge, Mass. ; Hon. Reverdy Johnson, of Baltimore, Md. ; Gov. W. P. Kellogg, of Louisana ; Maj.-Gen. George D. Ramsey, Washington, D. C. ; Gen. James Longstreet, New Orleans ; Gov. Thos. A. Hendricks, of Indiana ; Governor J. A. Campbell, of Wyoming Ter. ; George Wm. Curtis, Editor of *Harpers' Weekly;* Rear Admiral Th. Rogers Taylor, Newport, R. I. ; Adjutant General E. D. Townsend, Washington, D. C. ; Hon. James T. Fields, Boston, Mass. ; Maj.-Gen. Andrew B. Eaton, Washington, D. C. ; Gov. Thomas Talbott, Boston, Mass. ; Ex-Gov. J. D. Cox, Toledo, Ohio ; Henry C. Bowen, of the New York *Independent;* Hon. Cassius M. Clay, of Whitehall, Ky. ; Q. M. General M. C. Meigs, Washington, D. C. ; Alexander T. Stewart, New York ; General A. E. Burnside ; General George Cadwallader, Philadelphia ; Mrs. Madeline Vireton Dahlgren, widow of Rear Admiral Dahlgren. Andrew Johnson, the only living ex-President of the United States, was invited, but neither came nor responded to the invitation in any way.

The work of preparation for the grand event was everywhere visible in Springfield for weeks before. The telegraphic reports in the morning papers began to announce the approach of distinguished personages and delegations from every point of the compass, for

thousands of miles distant in our own country, and
some of the English nobility who were traveling in
this country, so timed their movements as to be present at the unveiling also. By Monday evening, October 12, the number of strangers began to increase' in
the city. The earliest arrivals were of distinguished
ex-soldiers and army commanders, in attendance on
the meetings of the Society of the Army of the Tennessee. Every train on Wednesday came loaded with
strangers, and on that night and Thursday morning it
seemed as though the entire adult population of central Illinois came pouring into the streets of the Capital. The hotels were crowded to overflowing, and
private houses were everywhere thrown open to receive the throng of visitors.

In addition to the grand arches, the Capitol building, Court House and Postoffice building, and other
public buildings and business houses and private residences were decorated most tastefully with drapery,
evergreens and flowers. The old home of Abraham
Lincoln, now the residence of Col. Geo. H. Harlow,
Secretary of State, was one among those most tastefully decorated.

On the morning of October 15, the streets of the
city presented the appearance of a moving mass of human beings, and as the hour approached for the procession to form, strains of music from the various bands
in attendance began to swell out on the breeze.

THE PROCESSION.

The Grand Marshal of the day, Gov. John L. Beveridge, with his aids, appeared on north Sixth street
at ten o'clock A. M. on Thursday, Oct. 15, 1874, and
commenced forming the procession in the following
order :

FIRST DIVISION—Gen. John Cook, Marshal, with
aids. This division was composed of Elwood com-

mandery Knights Templar, of Springfield, Ill., mounted, followed by a commandery each, from Mt. Pulaski and Decatur, a band of music and three independent military companies.

SECOND DIVISION—Col. DudleyWickersham, Marshal, with aids. This division was headed by a military band from Newport Barracks, Ky., and was composed of the Governor's Guard of Springfield, the President'and Vice President of the United States, and other distinguished guests; the Orator of the day and other speakers; the Chaplain and other clergymen, the whole division being in carriages.

THIRD DIVISION—Gen. E. B. Harlan, Marshal, with aids; was composed of independent orders and benevolent societies, with two bands of music.

FOURTH DIVISION—Gen. R. N. Pearson, Marshal with aids; was led by the St. Louis Arsenal Band, and was composed of a volunteer company, the "Sherman Guards," of Pawnee, acting as an escort to the Society of the Army of the Tennessee. The Society was led by its President, Gen. W. T. Sherman.

FIFTH DIVISION—Gen. John McConnell, Marshal; consisted of Springfield Fire Department, and citizens in carriages.

THE LINE OF MARCH,

was south on Sixth street to Adams; east on Adams to Eighth, south on Eighth—passing the old family residence of Abraham Lincoln—to Cook; west on Cook to Sixth; north on Sixth to Adams; west on Adams to Fifth; north on Fifth to Washington; east on Washington to Sixth; north on Sixth to North Grand Avenue; west on North Grand Avenue to Second street; north on Second street to Oak Ridge Cemetery.

The line of march was so ordered as to pass the Lincoln family residence, and under each of the six Grand Triumphal Arches.

AT OAK RIDGE CEMETERY

the people began to collect at a very early hour, and the crowd about the Monument was so great that the procession could only reach it by the aid of the military in opening up an avenue. When all were assembled, it was estimated that there were between twenty-five and thirty thousand people present.

Gov. John M. Palmer, Chairman of the Committee of Arrangements, acted as Master of Ceremonies. The exercises opened with music by the Newport, Ky., band. Gov. Palmer then introduced Bishop Wayman, of the African M. E. Church, who offered the opening prayer. He was specially invited, and came from Baltimore for that purpose.

A choir of ladies and gentlemen sang an ode composed for the occasion by Mrs. Mary Riley Smith; music by Mr. George A. Sanders—all of Springfield. I quote one verse, with the chorus:

"We sing to him whose soul, on heights divine,
    Has reached the stature of the undefiled;
In whom a judgment ripe and honor fine
    Were blended with the nature of a child;
Whose pen, with patient toil and God-like grace,
    Picked out the puzzled knot of Slavery;
Unloosed the gyves that bound a hapless race,
    And dared to write, "The bondman shall be free!"

CHORUS:—

"Then sing to him from whom these sweet words fall:
    'With malice towards none—with charity for all;'
And write this epitaph above his grave:
    'He bound the nation, and unbound the slave.'"

After the singing, the Hon. Jesse K. Dubois, Vice President of the Association, delivered the

HISTORICAL ADDRESS.

When Abraham Lincoln fell by the hand of an assassin, April 14th, 1865, after the first expressions of horror and grief, and a partial recovery from the shock which for the instant had paralyzed the nation, a spontaneous feeling arose demanding that some memorial should be erected, to convey to future generations the estimate placed by his contemporaries upon the life, virtues and public services of the martyr President.

While the funeral cortege was slowly proceeding from Washington to Sringfield, letters were received daily by our men in public life, from all parts of the country and from people of every station, suggesting that a great National Monument be erected over his remains, and in many cases tendering contributions.

For some days nothing was said on the subject at his own home, where his lifelong neighbors were bending all their energies to prepare for the funeral ceremonies.

The first mention of the subject in Springfield was in the STATE JOURNAL on the morning of April 24th, in the following words: "We suggest that our citizens assemble at the State House at an early day, and organize an association for the purpose of selecting officers from the State Officials and other leading citizens of the State, and taking immediate steps for the collection of the necessary funds. The sooner done the better. Our idea is, that the Treasurer of the State should be made the Treasurer of the Association, and that every postmaster and every national bank in the country should be requested to act as agents." The editorial closed with the words, "Let us move in the matter at once."

The same day the Committee of Arrangements that had been previously appointed by a public meeting of the citizens of Springfield, to prepare for the reception of the remains of President Lincoln, held a meeting, and, among other items of business,

Resolved, That Gov. Richard J. Oglesby, Lieut. Gov. William Bross, Hon. Sharon Tyndale, Secretary of State; Hon. O. H. Miner, Auditor of State; Hon. N. Bateman, Sup't Public Instruction; Hon. John S. Stuart, Hon. S. H. Treat, Hon. Jesse K. Dubois, Hon. O. M. Hatch, Hon. John A. McClernand, Hon. Wm. Butler, Hon. James C. Conkling, Hon. Thomas J. Dennis, Mayor, etc , and such others as they may select, constitute a Lincoln Monument Association, for the purpose of receiving funds and disbursing the same; for obtaining grounds and erecting a monument thereon, in Springfield, Ill., to the memory of our lamented Chief Magistrate, Abraham Lincoln.

Resolved. That Hon. James H. Beveridge, Treasurer of the State of Illinois, be the Treasurer of said Association.

A call was at once issued by the Association to "The officers, soldiers and sailors in the army and navy, in camps, stations, forts and hospitals, loyal leagues, lodges of Masons and Odd Fellows, religious and benevolent associations, churches of all denominations, and the colored population," requesting contributions by the second week in May, or as soon thereafter as possible.

National banks and postmasters were requested to act as agents. The proceedings were telegraphed to all parts of the country and published in the newspapers. Two days after the Association was organized, its Executive Committee published an appeal to the Nation that it would, "by one simultaneous movement, testify its regard for his exalted character, its appreciation for his distinguished services, and its sorrow for his death by erecting to his memory a monument that will forever prove that Republics are not ungrateful."

The first work of the Association was to secure, conditionally, the plat of ground where the new State House is now being built, and the building of a temporary vault thereon. But when the remains of President Lincoln arrived, it was ascertained that Mrs. Lincoln objected to the body being placed there, even temporarily, and at her request it was placed in the public receiving vault of Oak Ridge Cemetery, May 4th, 1865.

On the 8th day of May, a call was sent out by the Association requesting all Sunday Schools to take up collections the second Sunday, and all public schools the first Tuesday, in June, 1865.

The Association was without legal authority until May 11th, 1865, when it was organized under the general incorporation laws of the State of Illinois, with the following

"ARTICLES OF ASSOCIATION:

"We, Richard J. Oglesby, Sharon Tyndale, O. H. Miner, James H. Beveridge, Newton Bateman, John T. Stuart, Samuel H. Treat, Jesse K. Dubois, O. M. Hatch, James C. Conkling, Thomas J. Dennis, John Williams, Jacob Bunn, S. H. Melvin, and David L. Phillips, all being of full age and citizens of the United States and State of Illinois, certify that we do hereby associate ourselves under and by virtue of an act of the General Assembly of the State of Illinois, entitled "An act for the incorporation of benevolent, educational, literary, musical, scientific and missionary societies, including societies formed for mutual improvement or for the promotion of the arts," approved February 24th, 1859; by the following name and for the purpose hereafter specified.

Article I.

This Association shall be called the "National Lincoln Monument Association," and be located at Springfield, State of Illinois, and shall continue in existence for the term of twenty years.

Article II.

The object of this Association shall be to construct a monument to the memory of Abraham Lincoln, in the city of Springfield, Illinois.

Article III.

The following persons shall be the directors of the Association during the first year of its existence: Richard J. Oglesby, Sharon Tyndale, O. H. Miner, James H. Beveridge, Newton Bateman, John T. Stuart, Jesse K. Dubois, O. M. Hatch, James C. Conkling, Thomas J. Dennis, John Williams, Jacob Bunn, S. H. Melvin, S. H. Treat, and David L. Phillips.

In testimony whereof, we have hereunto set our hands and seals this 11th day of May, 1865.

[Seal.]	RICHARD J. OGLESBY,
[Seal.]	ORLIN H. MINER,
[Seal.]	JOHN T. STUART.
[Seal.]	JESSE K. DUBOIS,
[Seal.]	JAMES C. CONKLING,
[Seal.]	JOHN WILLIAMS,
[Seal.]	JACOB BUNN,
[Seal.]	SHARON TYNDALE,
[Seal.]	NEWTON BATEMAN,
[Seal.]	S. H. TREAT,
[Seal.]	O. M. HATCH,
[Seal.]	S. H. MELVIN,
['Seal.]	JAMES H. BEVERIDGE,
[Seal.]	THOMAS J. DENNIS,
[Seal.]	DAVID L. PHILLIPS.

On the same day, viz: the 11th day of May, 1865, the Association perfected its organization by electing Gov. R. J. Oglesby, President; Jesse K. Dubois, Vice President; Clinton L. Conkling, Secretary, James H. Beveridge, Treasurer. A code of by-laws was adopted, agents to collect funds were appointed, and the treasurer directed to invest the funds in United States securities.

It was still the intention to erect the monument on the ground where the first vault was built, but a letter was received from Mrs. Lincoln, dated at Chicago, June 5, 1865, in which she repeated her objections to that locality.

On the 14th of June, 1865, it was decided by a majority of one in a full board of directors, to build the Monument in Oak Ridge Cemetery.

Six acres of land were given by the city of Springfield to the Association as a site for the Monument. Measures were at once taken to erect a temporary vault near that belonging to the Cemetery, in which to keep the remains until the monument should be ready to receive them.

The body of Mr. Lincoln was removed from the public receiving vault to the temporary vault belonging to the Association, Dec. 21st, 1865.

In the process of transferring the remains, the box containing the coffin was opened, in order that the features of the deceased might be seen and identified; and six of his personal acquaintances: R. J. Oglesby, O. H. Miner, Jesse K. Dubois, Newton Bateman, O. M. Hatch, and D. L. Phillips, filed a written statement with the Secretary of the Association that it was the body of Abraham Lincoln.

On the 28th of December, 1865, Clinton L. Conkling, Esq., tendered his resignation as Secretary of the Association, which was accepted, and Hon. O. M. Hatch elected to fill the vacancy.

· Early in 1868, the Association published a "Notice to Artists," offering, with the usual conditions, $1,000 for the best design for a monument, and named the first of September as the day for the examination of designs.

Thirty-seven designs by thirty-one artists, six of them sending two each, were received and placed on exhibition in the Senate Chamber.

After patient and careful consideration, on the eleventh of the same month the Board announced its decision in the following resolution:

Resolved, That this Association adopt the design submitted by Larkin G. Mead, Jr., to be constructed of granite and bronze, and that the whole matter be referred to the Executive Committee, with power to act.

Ample time was taken to discuss the details of a contract, care being had to fully protect the interests of all parties thereto. By the terms of the proposals for designs, the successful competitor was entitled to the contract to build the entire monument. When Mr. Mead's design was accepted, he at once commenced arrangements to· build the architectural portion of the monument, and caused full plans and specifications to be prepared. Afterwards, by agreement between the Association and Mr. Mead, he surrendered his right to build the architectural part of the monument, and the Association, for good reasons, released him, and agreed to pay the expenses he had incurred up to that time.

On the 30th of December, 1868, a contract was concluded between the Association and Larkin G. Mead, Jr., in which it was stipulated that the Association was to manage the building of the architectural part of the monument, and that it should be done strictly after the drawings and specifications of Mr. Mead.

On his part, Mr. Mead was to mould, cast and deliver all the statuary in bronze, according to his design, namely:

1. A statue of Lincoln, not less than ten feet high, for $13,700.

2. A group representing infantry, containing three figures and appropriate accessories, the figures to be not less than seven and a half feet high, for $13,700.

3. A group of cavalry, to contain a horse and two human figures, with appropriate accessories, the human figures to be not less than seven and a half feet high, and the horse in proportion, for the sum of $13,700.

4. A group of artillery, to contain three figures and appropriate accessories, the figures to be not less than seven and a half feet high, for $13,700.

5. A marine group, to contain three figures and appropriate accessories, the figures to be not less than seven and a half feet high, for $13,700.

6. The coat of arms of the United States, as shown in the specifications, for $1,500—making a total of $70,000.

It was part of the contract that the Association should have the right to order one or more of these pieces or groups at a time, to suit its own convenience, and not be under obligations to pay for any piece until a written order was given for the same. When a written order was given, one-third of the stipulated price was to accompany it, one-third to be paid when the plaster model was delivered at the foundry, and the remaining third when the work was completed and delivered in good order at Springfield, Illinois.

It was also stipulated in the contract that if cannon were given to be used in the statuary, the value thereof should be deducted from the price.

It was further agreed that if any donations of freight were made, they should be to the Association, and not to Mr. Mead.

Five business men of New York, of known responsibility, gave security for the performance of the contract on the part of Mr. Mead.

On the seventh day of May, 1869, the Board of Directors, under the aforesaid contract, instructed the Executive Committee to order the statue of Lincoln and the coat of arms of the United States.

After advertising for proposals to erect the monument—excepting the statuary—the bid of W. D. Richardson, of Springfield, was accepted.

A contract was then entered into between the Association and Mr. Richardson, in which he agreed to erect the National Lincoln Monument, in Oak Ridge Cemetery, according to the plans and specifications adopted by the Association, for the sum of $130,550.

He was to build the foundation during the current year 1869, and complete the superstructure by January 1, 1871.

The Association agreed to pay Mr. Richardson the sum above named on monthly estimates as the work progressed, 15 per cent. of the same to be withheld until the work was completed according to contract.

Ground was broken September 9, 1869, and the massive foundation was completed before the close of that year. When the spring of 1870 opened, materials were ready to commence the superstructure. There was so much delay on the part of the railroads in bringing the granite to the ground, that it was found impossible to finish within the building season of 1870.

Work was resumed early in the following spring, and the capstone was elevated to its position on the obelisk May 22, 1871.

The monument was so far advanced that the remains of Thomas Lincoln, a son of President Lincoln, who died in Chicago on the 15th of July, 1871, were brought to Springfield and deposited in the crypt at the extreme west, on the 17th of that month; and the remains of the President, and of his two sons, William and Edward, were removed from the temporary vault to the monument September 19, 1871.

The six personal friends of Mr. Lincoln, who identified his remains on the occasion of their being deposited in the temporary vault, again viewed them, and again certified in writing that it was the body of Abraham Lincoln.

Both papers are on file with the Secretary of the Association. The evidence of identity is thus unbroken.

20

The total contributions to the general fund of the
National Lincoln Monument Association have
amounted to....................................$144,448 45
To this add the sum realized for interest and prem-
iums.................................. .... 35,672 45

Giving a total of............................$180,120 90

Which has been appropriated as follows:

L. G. Mead, for design............................ $1,000 00
Paid Larkin G. Mead for drawings, specifications and
all details connected with the architectural part of
the Monument.................................... 5,500 00
L. G. Mead, statue and coat of arms................ 15,200 00
W. D. Richardson, on contract 136,550 00
Temporary vault.................................... 1,612 97
Expended on grounds............................... 3,546 60
Iron steps on grounds.............................. 892 00
Paid for steel engraving of the Monument for Sunday
school children, as per agreement................ 1,150 00
Superintendence, printing, expenses of soliciting
agents, commissions to agents, etc., etc........... 7,830 13

Total appropriations........................$173,282 70

The balance unappropriated is $6,838.20, which will all find
profitable use in the future improvements of the grounds.
The contributions may be classified as follows:

Received from States......................... $61,500
As follows:
State of Illinois............................$50,000
State of New York........................ 10,000
State of Missouri........................ 1,000
State of Nevada.......................... 500

The next largest item is the contributions of the soldiers and
sailors, which amount to $27,682.12.
These contributions by companies, regiments, ships and separate commands, will average $1 per man, and in nearly all cases
a record is preserved of the name of each contributor

About $8,000 of the sum is the contribution of the colored soldiers of the United States Army.

Contributions credited to Sunday schools amount to $18,320.38.

This represents the contributions of 1,700 schools; and the names of the individual contributors, embracing more than 60,000 children, are enrolled in a separate book.

The contributions taken up in churches amount to $3,893.03. The contributions of benevolent societies amount to $2,542.39. This sum is contributed by Lodges of Masons, Odd Fellows and Union Leagues. Among many contributions received from public schools, the public schools of California contributed, through the State Superintendent, $1,780.44. In addition to the before mentioned, the contributions to the general fund of other societies and organizations, and of individuals, amount, in the aggregate, to $28,730.09.

A considerable sum, some thousands of dollars, is credited to boxes which were put up in banks and post offices, and other public places. The large amount of these anonymous contributions is the best evidence of the interest of all classes in the undertaking.

It has been the rule of the Association never to order work nor make any contract involving absolute payment of money until the money is in hand to pay the whole amount.

The contract with Mr. Mead was drawn in recognition of this rule. As already shown, the proceeds of contributions, public and private, had been sufficient to pay for the architectural portion of the Monument, and the statue of Lincoln and the coat of arms; but until the summer of 1871, no special effort had been made to raise funds for the four groups.

In July, 1871, citizens of Chicago, through Hon. J. Young Scammon, voluntarily pledged themselves to raise $13,700 to pay for the infantry group of statuary. In December of that year the one-third of this sum was paid to Mr. Mead, and he was ordered to construct the model of the infantry group.

Messrs. Oglesby and Phillips, acting under instructions of the Association, visited New York, Philadelphia and Boston, and submitted to prominent gentlemen in each of those cities the proposition that the three cities should assume the cost of the three remaining groups—that New York should furnish the naval group, Philadelphia the artillery group and Boston the cavalry group. This proposition met with favor and encouragement in each city. In the city of New York, under the leadership of Gov. E. D. Morgan, 137 gentlemen have subscribed and paid $100 each, amounting to $13,700, and the naval group has been ordered in accordance with the terms of the contract.

It is proposed to raise the same amount, in a similar manner, in Philadelphia and in Boston; and the Association has the pledge of prominent and influential gentlemen in each city that it shall be done.

The Monument is finished and paid for. The means are provided for the completion of two of the groups; and we hope, from the assurances from Boston and Philadelphia, that the two others are also provided for. If, however, we fail in that, we doubt not a generous people will make up the deficiency. The work stands to speak for itself. The materials are granite and bronze—than which none can more successfully defy the elements. The foundations are laid deep and strong, and in all the details of construction, the work is well and faithfully done.

Of the original members of the Association, all survive to see the result of their labors, except the Hon. Sharon Tyndale, whose sad taking off by violent hands is still fresh in our recollection. The vacancy caused by the death of Mr. Tyndale was filled by the selection of Governor John M. Palmer.

While all the members of the Association have worked with zeal and fidelity, and without pecuniary reward, the most labor has devolved upon the Secretary, Hon. O. M. Hatch; the Treasurer, Hon. James H. Beveridge, and the Executive Committee, Messrs. John T. Stuart, Jacob Bunn and John Williams.

The Association and its contributors are under especial obligations to Hon. John T. Stuart, Chairman of the Executive Committee, and to Hon. O. M. Hatch, Secretary, for the wise and energetic manner in which they have performed the many duties of their offices.

The members of the Association congratulate the artist upon the success which has crowned his efforts to give a faithful rendering of the face and form of the beloved dead whose remains rest beneath this Monument. Every member of the Association was a neighbor of President Lincoln, and most of them had known him intimately since his early manhood. It is their unanimous opinion that this statue is a truthful likeness, and will serve to give to future generations a perfectly accurate conception of Abraham Lincoln.

Here ends what has been to the members of the Association, for almost ten years, a labor of love and duty.

By the liberal contributions of a grateful nation, we have been enabled to provide a suitable place for the remains of one of the wisest, purest men known to our national history.

There may they rest in peace.

After music by the Band the master of ceremonies, Gov. Palmer, introduced the President of the Association, ex-Gov. R. J. Oglesby, who proceeded to deliver

THE ORATION.

The tenth of a century is about taking its departure since the close of the great rebellion—an epoch in the history of our country marked by glowing associations, and fraught with grave and imposing consequences—a rebellion, in its inception and upon its inauguration, which found a contented and prosperous people enjoying the fruits of long years of peace in a government of their own choice, guaranteed in a constitution upon principles so just and a basis so firm, it was believed it could enter into the hearts of none seriously to contemplate its destruction. This government had descended to us from the revolution, well-shapen by the hands of our fathers, clothing in plain and simple language powers general and national as to the union, ample and local as to the states. Under its broad shield liberty sought and found repose. There was no citizen in its broad domain who was not unfettered in conscience and thought, and not consulted and represented in all its actions— a government the freest, the mildest and the strongest on the face of the earth. It had, by a long career of prosperity, unsettled if not destroyed the dogma of the old school of publicists, "That the durable establishment of a democratic government was not possible in a country of great extent and with a numerous population." There was one stain upon it—all men were not free. The curse of slavery had taken deep root in an unnatural soil.

The consciences of a large majority of the American people were not at rest with the scourge of mankind in their midst, and a new political party was openly protesting against its claims for more general recognition. It had been the source of much disquiet, and was the prolific agent of endless discussion and dissension. At last, halting upon safe ground, with the lights then around us, the friends of freedom said to the friends of slavery, " We will arrest the further spread of it and place it where the public mind shall rest in the belief that it is in the course of ultimate extinction. " Its advocates argued, "We will push it forward until it shall become alike lawful in all the states, old as well as new, north as well as south. "

The rebellion closed, leaving in its wake broken hopes, blasted anticipations, ruined fortunes, desolated homes, and thousands of dead and wounded soldiers—states dissevered, civil governments dethroned, discord in the place of order, and social and political devastation. The soldiers of its vast armies, victors for a time on many fields, with a valor, courage and discipline in a just cause which would have earned for themselves the praise of all men, stacked their arms, parked their artillery, turned over the public property to the officers of the union, and returned to their homes on paroles of honor, prisoners of war in a lost cause.

Again : The rebellion closed with the union maintained in all its strength and majesty, and with liberty preserved. The long years of toil and taxation ; of human patience and human suffering ; of war, bloody, destructive war, shrouded in clouds of bitter anguish, or lighted by the torch of angry passions, were at last rewarded by the return of peace. A heroic people, that good government might not perish from the earth, had conquered the most formidable enemy of modern times, and that enemy its own internal, domestic home people. The return of peace was hailed as the return of only such a peace could be, with unspeakable joy, gratitude and thanksgiving. The great words of the great president were still lingering upon the tongues of men and ringing through the hearts of all people. The British parliament and the British people caught them up, as they were caught up by all the civilized nations of Europe, and applauded them as the noblest of human utterances:

" Fondly do we hope, fervently do we pray, that this mighty scourge of war may speedily pass away; yet if God wills that it continue until all the wealth piled by the bondsman's two hundred and fifty years of urequited toil shall be sunk, and until every drop of blood drawn by the lash shall be paid by another drawn by the sword, as was said three thousand years ago, so still it must be said, the judgments of the Lord are true and righteous altogether.   With malice toward none, with charity for all, with firmness in the right as God gives us to see the right, let us strive to finish the work we are in; to bind up the nation's wounds; to care for him who shall have borne the battle, and for his widow and his orphans; to do all which may serve to cherish a just and lasting peace among ourselves and with all nations."

" A just and lasting peace. "   Late even as February, eighteen hundred and sixty-five, so earnest was the president in his desire for peace, to stay if possible the further effusion of blood, and bind up the nation's wounds, that he went in person to meet messengers from the camp of the enemy, and submitted these general propositions:

First, the restoration of the national authority throughout all the states.

Second, no receding by the executive of the United States on the slavery question from the position assumed thereon in the late annual message to congress and in preceding documents.

Third, no cessation of hostilities short of an end of the war and the disbanding of all forces hostile to the government.

Fourth, all propositions of theirs not inconsistent with the above, would be considered and passed upon in a spirit of sincere liberality.

These generous terms were not accepted, and nothing came of the meeting.   A fatality hung over these deluded people not to be propitiated without an unconditional surrender of their arms and armies.   In the interest of universal humanity, to the credit of the highest civilization known to the world, and especially that our own blessed country might escape the impending humiliation, would to God that then and there, upon the four years wild carnival of passion, the curtain had fallen. It could not be so. I have no heart, even at this late day, to speak of the sad event. America is blackened with the crime of assassination : Abraham Lincoln is the martyr. Badges of mourning covered the whole land; the very air was heavy with sighs, and nature seemed to hang her head in sorrow. Grief—deep, bitter grief—filled the whole land, and malice at last, with its victim before it, closed its repentant lips and skulked away disarmed and discomfited forever. The sad news of his death filled the world with consternation. Condolence poured in upon our people from every land and tongue. Distinctions of nationality and all forms of power, forgetting animosities, obliterating all lines of separation, came together at the bier of Lincoln. Beautiful in life, comely in death, he was annointed with the tears of all nations. There is in the hands of the people, published by authority of the national congress, a volume of 930 quarto pages, containing expressions of condolence and grief over the national bereavement, from the governments and people of almost the entire world.

His people took up his body, and a funeral procession one thousand miles long followed his remains to his old home. Here his body lies, under the trees and amid the people who knew him in poverty and honored him in obscurity, and here it will lie so long as dust shall mark the spot where man has fallen. The friends of his youthful manhood and the children of those who knew and loved him when he was yet unknown to the world, will stand, one generation after another, sentinels over his body. His fame, breaking through the boundaries of his state and nation, has gone abroad over a boundless world, and will descend with the march of time down the illimitable age of the hereafter.

- The generous contributions of an admiring people have erected over his remains this monument—an imposing and lasting testimonial to his great worth. I must be spared the task of passing in detail upon its merits as a work of art. A member of the association from its organization, heartily uniting with it in selecting the design of Larkin G. Mead—a young native artist of more than national reputation, who connects his own rising fame in this structure with the name of his great subject—I turn it over to the impartial criticism of the students, the lovers and the creators of art. Only this I say, after a long and somewhat intimate personal acquaintance with him, the colossal statue unveiled in your presence to-day is the very similitude and likeness of Abraham Lincoln. Republics are not unlike other nations in contemplating the character and cherishing the memory of the illustrious dead. What they have said, what they have done, is quoted over and over again, to impress upon the living the importance of like action. We create honorable customs, to bring them again and again to our remembrance. Addresses, eulogies and orations are made the willing instruments of their praise; and at last, in the hope of some way bearing their fame further along down the course of time, half doubting that civilization will continue and history hold its own faithfully in recording great events and the lives of distinguished citizens, we erect monuments of granite, marble and bronze, that the remotest time may know such men lived.

A great life draws after it the ceaseless attention of the living, and if it be good also, is held up in history, poetry and song for the imitation of all men. Such was the life of Abraham Lincoln. His birth and early life at once excite our attention. Born in a forest, out of the range of school houses, on the margin of civilization, where nature yet almost held primeval dominion, of parents poor and without education, he heard no music but the music of birds—he saw no wonders but the wonders of nature. At the early age of eight years his father moved from the old home in Hardin county, Kentucky, to Spencer county, Indiana. Part of the journey was a ride down the Ohio river on an ordinary raft—something less than a flat-boat, but common enough in those early days of western navigation. The change of homes was simply the exchange of one forest for another, but it was a change from a slave to a free state. It was possibly the unfettering of a young and pure soul from what might have been a thralldom. Soon after the settlement in Indiana his mother died—she who had taught him to read. In time a step-mother entered the cabin door, and soon there sprang up between the boy and his new mother an interest and a love that never died. He went to school about one year, learned to "read, write and cipher," and finished all of education received in that way. From this time until he had grown to manhood, to all those who care to watch the development of mind and the growth of character

under such circumstances, with one destined to fill so large a
share of the public attention and to control so much in public
affairs, the young life of Lincoln presents much that is interesting,
instructive and novel, not however altogether unusual in the first
settlement of a new country, and especially in America. He was the
most diligent student in the neighborhood. The Columbian Orator,
the Life of Washington, Burns' Poems, the Pilgrim's Progress
and the Bible he read and studied over and over again. Clad in
the rustic raiment of the times, as he went from cabin to cabin,
from the gatherings of the pioneers for frolic, and the frequent tests
of physical strength so common in those early times, to the spelling school and debating club, for the higher test of mind in study
and discussion; a prompt attendant upon all occasions either of
frolic or debate; seldom if ever second best in any encounter; a
moderator in the settlement of disputes and the prevention of
quarrels; and, when all other remedies failed, putting all angry
passions to flight by a ludicrous story or a good joke—he came
in time to be looked upon by his admiring companions as a
prodigy. The basis of his moral structure—laid in those early
days, out of reach of the ordinary temptations of vice, away from
the seductive influences of mere fashion, where the rules for the
administration of justice were few and easy of application, un-
haunted by the vexatious speculations of metaphysics—was broad
and deep. And here he laid the foundations of a faith that were
to lead him through life: "Thou shalt not make unto thyself any
graven image or any likeness of anything that is in Heaven
above or in the earth beneath, or that is in the waters under the
earth. Thou shalt not bow down thyself to them nor serve them"
—and he did not. He worshiped the image of neither the living nor
the dead in the material world. Truth he did worship. Truth
and Justice he did bow down to. Truth, Justice and Mercy he
did serve, and he had no other master in the moral world. He could
look up into the clear blue sky of Heaven and descry God everywhere. In the procession of the worlds and the grand laws that
produce uniformity, continuity, order, beauty and justice,
throughout all space and through all time, he beheld the benigni-
ty of universal and divine intelligence. "Therefore, all things
whatsoever ye would that men should do to you, do ye even

so to them," and, "Thou shalt love thy neighbor as thyself," he comprehended as christian precepts and lived up to them daily.

At the age of twenty-one he again moved with his father's family still further west. In 1830 the historical family came to Illinois and settled on the Sangamon river in Macon county. There are still standing the visible marks of his toil upon the inclosure around the home where the family settled. His old friend and near relation, his steady and faithful companion at home and on the long journey to New Orleans on a flat-boat, who assisted in felling the trees, splitting the rails and making the improvements upon the new home in Illinois, now venerable in years, though still blessed with health and the promise of a lengthened life, an ever watchful sentinel along the line of life of his great and good friend, comes to drop another tear on the grave of one he always loved. John Hanks, who stood by the cradle of the mysterious boy, shares his humble part in dedicating a monument to the departed statesman. At the close of his twenty-first year he left the paternal home, and found his way into Sangamon county, not many miles from this city. Again locating on the Sangamon river, he made another trip to New Orleans, and upon his return, in 1832, volunteered as a private, but was immediately chosen captain of a company, and served three months in the notable Black Hawk war. At the expiration of his service in this Indian war he became a candidate for the legislature, and although not successful, of the 207 votes cast at his home, New Salem, he received every one, and this notwithstanding there were several popular candidates in the field. Better fortune however was awaiting him. At the next election he was successful, and was returned every two years from 1834 to 1842, making a continuous service of eight years in the legislature. In the meantime he had turned his attention to the study of the law, and at the age of twenty-seven was admitted to the bar. The Hon. John T. Stuart, with whom he read law, is a member of the association having in charge this monument.

By this time the name of Lincoln began to be known throughout the state. In the great campaign of 1840 he was chosen by the whig party to bear the brunt of its heaviest work. After due consideration and a trial contest in the capital of the state, between the ablest debators of both political parties, which lasted for a week, and which was in the nature of a political skirmish,

Lincoln was selected to meet Douglas, who at that early period of his life was put in the front rank to uphold democracy. To those still living, favored with the privilege of listening to the joint debates of these strong young men, it cannot be forgotten how interesting and able they were. The place of each was at once fixed in the confidence of his party. They met, to be in some way held together before the public eye, for twenty years; met as political antagonists and personal friends. to share in political policies, and to shape political principles in the public mind, uniting their names with measures of the highest significance and broadest influence upon American institutions. Douglas, four years the younger, with fair education, high resolves, and a purpose to do for himself in the world, left his eastern home and worked his way to the great west. Lincoln had preceded him in the same journey. Each selected Illinois for his future home. In the centre of this young state, with a population at that time of one hundred and fifty-seven thousand, they located at no great distance apart. Both studied law, and both attained to some distinction in the profession. Douglas rose to the bench, and was for two years one of the judges of the supreme court of the state. Lincoln gave his whole attention to the practice of law when not engaged in politics, and I am warranted in the statement, upon the uniform testimony of all the great lawyers who practiced at the bar with him, several of whom are here to-day, testifying by their presence the great respect in which he was held by them, that he ranked among the first lawyers of the state. Both entered political life about the same time. Douglas came from Vermont, where liberty early took shelter from tyranny, and where slavery found no friends; Lincoln from the "dark and bloody ground" where slavery was already a planted institution; one from the north, the other from the south; one from a free, the other from a slave state. From 1840 down to 1858 they met at intervals in public discussion, and time and again had debated all the political questions of those times. Both had steadily grown in public favor, and both had been laborious and faithful students of the history of their country, and of every public interest concerning that country. In the interval Lincoln had served one term in congress. One circumstance, not sufficiently considered, had much, I think, to do with forming the political character of these two men, and of giving them prominence before the country—at least upon the subject of slavery. It was one of location. Living between the thirty-ninth and fortieth parallels, where the mighty currents of population flowing ceaselessly west from the north and south first met—where men with anti-slavery and men with pro-slavery views came together, compared ideas and freely discussed the subject, for the first time, on equal terms and out of its presence; where there could be no campaign and no election to choose officers for the ordinary purpose of civil administration that did not bring together at the polls voters of opposing convictions upon this question, it could not be otherwise than that these prominent men should be brought to ponder upon it and to sift and weigh all the feelings and sentiments involved, and all the arguments brought to bear, one way or the other, upon the whole subject. Out of the range of extreme views either way, yet meeting the subject as other public men in the north or south could not, they possessed advantages for its fullest consideration. Both were for a long time inclined to compromise. By 1854 Douglas' position may be perhaps most fairly and correctly stated as one comparatively of indifference—he would leave it to the people to decide for themselves. Lincoln, on the contrary, had come to look upon slavery as a great wrong, a wrong to be dealt with, and, if possible, to be got rid of. Ripe age and riper experience were preparing these men to appear once more on the popular forum. Eighteen hundred and fifty-eight must come, whether hidden beyond the discernment of man or the range of the demonstrable relations of cause and effect, whether attributable to the mysterious movement of the finger of Providence over the affairs of nations, or coming rationally out of the covetous and grasping nature of man in his greed of gain to lay foundations of fortune in disregard of moral precepts and against conscience; the event, the time must come, when slavery in the United States must be met as a national question— must be considered as a domestic institution, and must, in the end, be plucked up by the roots and eradicated from the soil of the republic.

These two great leaders met in joint debate in August, eighteen hundred and fifty-eight. The whole country were spectators, for now both were men of renown.

Douglas, well fortified with natural gifts, a strong intellect, a clear understanding, broad views, a most tenacious and tireless memory, bold in thought, deep in conception, with a robust constitution, and though in physical stature by no means a giant, had come, by his sixteen years of public service in congress, his many admirable speeches and his shining mental qualities, to be regarded as the "little giant"—entirely familiar with the political history of the country, a life-long democrat, true to his party, and resting with undoubting confidence upon its fealty, while it was warm in its attachment to him and proud of his leadership, popular in his manners, genial and warm-hearted by nature, but austere and courageous in the presence of his adversary;·with a faculty, excelled by no American statesman, of clothing in the most exact and forcible language political definitions; clear, logical, fluent, and at times eloquent, and withal exceedingly ingenuous,—he was a man on the stump, before the people, in a campaign, greatly to be dreaded.

Lincoln—calm, self-possessed, contemplative by nature, his mind capable of the deepest penetration, able to grasp any proposition and to analyze every element it contained; cautious, taking no position until every step leading to it had been tested, measured and planted in its appropriate place, but, once resolved upon, not to be driven from it by open denunciation or specious exposition; by no means dogmatic, but exceedingly tenacious of a conviction; shrewd in discovering the weak parts of an argument, and capable of unraveling the most complex sophistry; clear in statement, powerful in argument, forcible in illustration, bringing home to the learned and unlearned alike, by reasoning the simplest and purest, a clear understanding of the subject in debate; rich in raillery, prolific of anecdote, fond of apothegm; in his presence the pretender finding no quarter and the pretense no mercy; seeking no advantage, but hoping to make the right appear to all men as the right by addressing himself to the reason; the people who listened were lifted up and made to feel, by his appeals to their understanding and higher natures, that they were a part of the country and rightfully responsible for its laws and morals; with a humanity that included all races and nations; an honesty that extracted praises from his adversary, touched by the conviction that a great wrong was about being done, or moved by the consciousness of impending evil to his country,—he ranked high above the standard of ordinary debate, and at times was truly eloquent.

The debate covered the entire ground of the slavery question, and developed the views held by each at that time. Douglas—notwithstanding he was perplexed with the Dred Scott decision, which, in some way, he held himself bound to respect as a judicial interpretation of the constitution, although it carried slaves as property, entitled to no less protection than any other property, into the territories against the will of the people, or any law of congress or a territorial legislature to exclude it, and to that extent seemed destructive of the great principle of popular sovereignty to which he was so heartily devoted, and which in his party he had at one time nationalized—continued boldly to defend his favorite doctrine, and still held the people might exclude slavery from the territories by unfriendly legislation. Lincoln, regarding the decision as fixing the status of Dred Scott for the time being, fervently denied that it was a just exposition of the constitution, earnestly denounced it as violative of human rights, and pledged himself to oppose it as such until a just public sentiment should legally provide the means to reverse it. He held slavery to be a moral, social and political wrong, and protested against the further spread of it into the territories. At the election which followed, Lincoln received a majority of the popular vote—Douglas a majority in the legislature, and was re-elected to the United States senate for a third term.

A strange destiny seemed to hang over these two men; they were once more to be opposed in a contest for earthly honors, for the position of highest usefulness to the truly patriotic—for the highest prize within the gift of the American people. Lincoln, fresh from the late contest with Douglas, and, though defeated, occupying higher ground in the public esteem than ever before, now more generally known throughout the country, honored for the dignity of his course and the wonderful abilities he had shown in that debate, was nominated by the republican party in 1860 its candidate for the presidency.

Douglas, to whom the democratic party was more indebted than to any living man for zeal in defending its principles, and for the wisdom he had shown in finding ground on the slavery question upon which it could stand with any hope of success, who had been repeatedly named for president, who was in fact looked upon as the only man entitled to its candidacy, but who at the last moment was forsaken by that branch of it which owed him far more than his more faithful followers of the north, and whose defection closed his chances of an election, faithful to the constitution and the union, became the candidate of the national democracy. I will not dwell for a moment upon the great campaign. It is enough to say Lincoln was elected president of the United States. The charmed circle woven by the slave oligarchy around the temple of liberty was broken, and the great advocate of human rights placed at the helm of the enfranchised policy of the future. Douglas, calm and dignified in defeat, awaited the inaugural of the president for his new policy. The moment the address of the president was closed he arose, expressed satisfaction with its tone, and gave promise of a cordial support to all measures looking to the preservation of peace and the perpetuation of the union. "I take great- pleasure," he said, in January, 1861, "In saying, however, I do not believe that the rights of the south will materially suffer under the administration of Mr. Lincoln." His last utterances in the senate were for the preservation of the constitution, the union and the country. At a later day in yonder capitol, in sight of the spot where I now stand, his last words were words of flaming patriotism, his last admonition was to traitors, his last appeal to patriots. "The shortest road to peace lies through the most magnificent and stupendous preparations for war." United in the high resolve to maintain the dignity, the honor and the glory of their country, both fell victims in the same cause, and both lie buried in the same state.

Who of living men shall forget, and when shall history cease to recount the awful circumstances in rapid succession forming all along the horizon of our unoffending country's long career of peace, in the December of 1860? One by one states were falling away from the union; treason, rank and foul, was plying its envious arts; passions long pent up were breaking over the restraints of prudence; the piled clouds of long years of wrath were making ready to burst in torrents of devastation upon a people not aroused, and not capable of being aroused for months, to the fatal destiny in store for them. Congress, as the winter wore away, unable to solve the difficulties, at last gave up all hope of a settlement, and adjourned on the 4th of March, 1861.

To the administration of the affairs of a nation in such plight, Abraham Lincoln had just been chosen by his grateful countrymen. With that large class of men in the west who knew him personally—were more familiar with his many qualities for such a trial—it was believed he would be equal to the gravity of the situation. The world did not know him so well, and might well enough question his capacity. He knew this and felt it. Lincoln had many advantages to fit him for his great work. He was a man of great personal courage and so moulded by nature as to endure any amount of physical labor. His habits were unexceptionably good—he indulged in none of the vices of society, sometimes carried to extremes in public men. He had no tastes that were not simple and pure—he was born and lived among the common people—he was of them, and in deep sympathy with them—he had no wishes, no ambitions, to lead him away from nor to make him forget their best interests—he had seen nothing of the world outside of his native land, and as he had prospered and grown into distinction under its benign institutions, he loved his country intensely, and wished to see it strengthened and perpetuated. Wholly unsuspecting and most indulgent of views and sentiments opposed to his own, he was slow to believe that men would seriously combine and deliberately conspire by force of arms to destroy the union. With the greatest humility and self-abnegation he set out from his home in February, 1861, to enter upon the great work to which he had been dedicated. His own parting words will best express his feelings at that moment:

"My friends, no one not in my position can realize the sadness I feel at this parting. To this people I owe all that I am. Here I have lived more than a quarter of a century; here my children were born, and here one of them lies buried. I know not how soon I shall see you again. I go to assume a task more difficult than that which has devolved upon any man since the days of Washington. He never could have succeeded except for the aid of Divine Providence, upon which at all times he relied. I feel that I cannot succeed without the same Divine blessing which sustained him, and on the same Almighty being I place my re-

21

liance for support, and I hope you, my friends, will pray all that I may receive that Divine assistance, without which I cannot succeed, but with which success is certain.   Again I bid you all an affectionate farewell."

His journey to Washington was one continued ovation.   He spoke at many places, but his addresses were all marked by the same sad spirit.   At Philadelphia, in Independence Hall, touched by the memory of revolutionary times, and dimly catching a glimpse of his own sad end, he said:

"All the political sentiments I entertain have been drawn, so far as I have been able to draw them, from the sentiments which originated in and were given to the world from this Hall.   I never had a feeling politically that did not spring from the sentiments embodied in the Declaration of Independence.   That *sentiment* it was which gave promise that in due time the weight would be lifted from the shoulders of men.   Now, my friends, can this country be saved upon that basis?   If it can I will consider myself one of the happiest men in the world, if I can help to save it. If it cannot be saved upon that principle, it will be truly awful; but if this country cannot be saved without giving up that principle, I was about to say, I would rather be assassinated on the spot than surrender it.   I have said nothing but what I am willing to live by, and if it be the pleasure of Almighty God, to die by."

He found the national capital smothered with seditious and treasonable sentiments.   It was even seriously doubted that he would be peaceably inaugurated.   On March 4th he sent forth to an anxious country his inaugural address.   It was marked by wisdom, dignity and forebearance.   The whole north accepted it as the emanation of a patriotic heart, and as a just and true exposition of the constitution and his duty.

"I hold that in contemplation of universal law, and of the constitution, the union of the states is perpetual.   I therefore consider that in view of the constitution, the union is unbroken, and to the extent of my ability I shall take care that the laws of the union be faithfully executed in all the states.   In doing this there need be no blood shed nor violence, unless it be forced upon the national authority.   In your hands, my dissatisfied fellow-countrymen, and not in mine, are the momentous issues of civil war. The government will not assail you—you can have no conflict without being yourselves the aggressors.   You have no oath registered in heaven to destroy the government, while I shall have the most solemn one to preserve, protect and defend it. I am loth to close. We are not enemies, but friends. We must not be enemies. Though passion may have strained, it must not break our bond of affection. The mystic chords of memory, stretching from every battle field and patriot grave to every living heart hearthstone all over this broad land, will yet swell the chorus of the union, when again touched, as surely they will be, by the better angels of our nature."

In the light of the intervening and sad experience between that day. and this, we now see how fatal the mistake that would not heed such words of warning and hope. No suggestions of amicable settlement, no appeals to love of country, no imploring for peace, could stay the mad current of events. War we must have—long, cruel, fratricidal war.

We shall fail, if any attempt be made to compare his administration with that of any other president. It has no standard of comparison. The circumstances are in no respect similar, save in the most formal parts. The first and older presidents came to the discharge of their great duties after the close of a war, and the experiment of a temporary government between that war and the establishment of a constitutional government, surrounded with peace and the warm attachments of a people co-operating from all parts of the country in zealous efforts to settle the foundation of an empire of free people. Their successors had wars, but they were foreign wars. Save in one instance, there was not even the serious threat of civil war. The thoughts of the great men who preceded him in the office of president of the United States were directed almost wholly to the establishment of good government under a constitution to be interpreted and applied to the multifarious wants and circumstances of a rising agricultural, planting, manufacturing and commercial people; to fixing in the public mind the just relation existing and to continue to exist between the states and the new nation, and to extending and cultivating peaceable and commercial relations with the civilized nations of the earth Those who have succeeded him in the great office, found the country at peace with the world and free from civil war, rebellion or insurrection—encumbered, it is true, with dismembered fragments, and poisonous with the smell of civil war and bloodshed, requiring talents of the highest order, and the greatest firmness and prudence, to properly remould them into the union. Tested by the circumstances of either, no standard will be found.

He entered upon the performance of his duties like one feeling his way amid precipices in the darkness of night. Habitually regardful of the rights of all, with a sincere respect for the constitution, he would exercise no doubtful power unless absolutely in the interest of the union. His guiding star, his last hope, was the union. When it was believed to be in peril, from whatever cause, he would arrest that cause, and appeal to the people and to congress to sustain him. He would suspend the writ of *habeas corpus*, increase the regular army, and call out volunteers to preserve, if possible, the union, and await the approval of congress, which was sure to come. Day by day, as the storm was raging, month by month, as the cause of the union seemed more doubtful, he grew and strengthened and expanded, steadily gaining a stronger hold upon the country. Year after year, as his messages were laid before congress, with the mournful statement, "the war still continues," the people, with a never-failing confidence in his wisdom, held to his policy, and stood firm in his support.

These messages will stand, as state papers, the test of time and all criticism. His arguments against peaceable and forcible secession, and his admirable and exhaustive reasoning on the whole subject of our domestic troubles, will stand as monuments of intellect, logic and learning, as models of purity and vigor, for all time in American political literature. He became the great central figure in the mighty panorama of war. All eyes were turned upon him, and he was by no means exempted from the severest criticism, from the bitterest complaints, and from the general discontent, when some fault was discovered or some unexpected calamity overtook the country or our arms. Those who craved peace blamed Lincoln that it did not come; those who clamored for a more vigorous prosecution of the war, blamed him equally without just cause. When those conflicts of words were raging around him he was usually silent, or if he replied, it was always in good temper, and always with complete effect. In the fall of 1863, to a storm of this kind which had been raging for some time, he replied: "There are those who are dissatisfied with me; to such I would say: You desire peace, and you blame me that you do not have it, but how can we obtain it? There are but three conceivable ways. First to suppress the rebellion by force of arms. This I am trying to do—are you for it? If you are, so far we are agreed. If you are not for it, a second way is to give up the union. I am against that—are you for it? If you are, you should say so plainly. If you are not for force nor yet for dissolution, there only remains some imaginable compromise. I do not believe any compromise embracing the maintenance of the union is possible. Peace does not appear to be so distant as it did. I hope it will come soon, and come to stay, and so come as to be worth the keeping in all future time. Still, let us not be over sanguine of a speedy, final triumph. Let us be quite sober; let us diligently apply the means, never doubting that a just God, in his own good time, will give us the rightful result."

Deeply impressed with the conviction that he was presiding over a "government of the people, by the people and for the peo ple," and that such government has no safe foundation, except as it shall rest upon the will, the free, outspoken opinion and will of the people, he studied with never ceasing industry not only to find out public opinion, but how also to enlighten and advance it. He was a tower of strength in aiding popular opinion to move forward from old to new, from good to better and advanced positions. He listened attentively to the popular voice, and what is more, and now was greatly to his advantage, from long association with the people, and having had much to do for most of his life in materially aiding in giving direction to public opinion, he knew how to discriminate between bluster and earnestness—between the ceaseless rattle of a vast amount of floating wisdom, the immature suggestions of the meddlesome few, and the more solid convictions of an earnest and patient people taking time to come to just and reasonable conclusion.. But once discovered, once known to be honest, reliable and definitely formed public opinion, he graciously and firmly moved forward with it, taking the right step at the right time, in the right direction; and upon the consummations of his administration, who shall look back and find an error? Therefore it was, his opinions were all pow-

erful with the people, with the congress, and in the deliberations
of his cabinet.

Profoundly absorbed with the great events around him, deeply
penetrated with the sufferings of his country, superintending the
operations of a million of men on land and sea, watching with
ceaseless vigilance the movements of the enemy, deliberating
with his able cabinet, consulting with the generals of his armies
and the commanders of his fleets, keeping a constant watch upon
our somewhat delicate foreign relations, and ever faithfully weighing the suggestions coming to him from the great body of the people, he did not descend into the details of administration, and perhaps did not consider it of serious importance who were appointed to subordinate positions in the civil service, or possibly who
was sent as minister to a foreign court. Who now shall go carp-
ing about the country, and what good shall come of it, intimating
that he was of humble origin, without education, unlearned in
the philosophy of government and the polite literature of diplo-
macy, and that therefore he was not the master of his council?
Leaving, and wisely leaving, to the heads of the various departments the management and direction of the ordinary and formal
duties of each, which are never unimportant, but in a great civil
war of the highest significance, in the higher and graver responsibilities of his office, as to what policy should control in measures for the prosecution of the war, the preservation of the union
and the emancipation of a race, it is not true, and therefore ought
not to be history, that he was not the leading spirit of his admin.
istration. It is altogether true to say, and this without disparagement to the distinguished men who composed it—respected, honored and loved as they ever will be by a grateful country, that in
his cabinet he was premier and without peer.

It is but repeating history to state the rebellion was organized
and fought upon the idea of founding a confederacy upon the
corner stone of human slavery. It was the counter purpose of
the friends of the national government to resist the dissolution of
the union for this or any other purpose, and to leave the institution of slavery to state control, where it then existed, and to
trust to time and the growth of a better sentiment for its final extinction. It was, therefore, alike the cause of the war and the
curse of the country. From the first it was an element to be

dealt with, and in those times, with the views of many of our friends, not yet reconciled upon its many aspects, to be cautiously and wisely dealt with. Lincoln knew this, knew it better than the many earnest and impatient friends of emancipation, and was perhaps better qualified to manage it than any other living man. His views upon the subject were known to the whole country at the time of the inauguration, for they had undergone no change since the election. If the south would remain in the union, he would not disturb the institution in the states. If they would dissolve the union, he would be released from that policy. The war raging, and the enemy utilizing these very slaves to still more firmly rivet their own chains, those of them escaping from the lines of the enemy or captured in his posts or garrisons were permitted to remain inside of ours, and being neither slave or free, to their utter amazement became contrabands. Next they were given employment in subordinate positions with our armies in the field. The war still raging, and prejudice against these unhappy people measurably giving way, a few were permitted to garrison our forts, and finally, good sense and patriotism, conquering hesitation and doubt, they were regularly enlisted, armed, equipped and mustered into the service of the United States as defenders of the republic.

That no experiment might remain untried, that no expedient might go untested, early in the war Lincoln favored colonization upon consent of the colored race and of the country to which they might prefer to go. This proving unexceptable and impracticable, the president next proposed, and with great earnestness urged upon the border states, in the hope that all might ultimately accept the plan, compensated emancipation. But all these schemes and projects failed. One other was waiting, which, in the providence of God, could not fail. The conviction was steadily growing in the public mind that it was the true and only one— that justice, mercy and fair dealing between man and man demanded it, and that final success to our arms could not and ought not to come without it. Lincoln, tired of expedients, chastened and strengthened by the woes of his country, patiently awaited the coming of the hour when a divided and hesitating public opinion, united at last upon its justness and expediency, would hail with joy the great deed. Responding to the instincts of his

own nature, arrayed in the full development of all the powers
that God had given him, with resolution unalterable and purpose
irrevocable, he announced to the world his proclamation of emancipation. It was "the new birth of freedom." Thenceforward
the issue was not doubtful. The last great remedy had been applied. It was the true one. It brought victory to our arms and
safety to our country. It falls to the lot of few men to connec.
their names with great events, but here was a great event and
a great principle—the principle of universal emancipation; the
principle that no man is so low that he should be cut off from
freedom and citizenship in a great republic. His name is linked
forever with both.

If history shall become ungrateful and moral obligations cease
to respond to the calls of justice and patriotism in that race to
which he was born, his fame will still be safe. Another race of
four millions, with their countless descendants of free-born children, holding his memory in precious reverence, will sing anthems of praise and gratitude to his name forever.

The commencement of his second term as president of the
United States, and the close of the rebellion, came closely together.
I do not know that the time or the place is fitting for an examination of the course likely to have been taken by him upon the
question of what is now known as reconstruction. It is true to
say, from the great hold he had upon the hearts of the people,
and their immovable confidence in him—a confidence· perhaps
enjoyed by no president from Washington down to his own time—
any plan maturely considered and seriously put forward by Lincoln would have met with favor, and it is probable would have
been adopted by the people. He was a merciful and forgiving
man. He promptly ratified the generous terms of surrender
dictated to the armies of the rebellion by his humane and victorious general. His proclamation of pardon and amnesty, of December, 1863, granted, with restoration of all property rights, the
right to vote to all, with certain specified exceptions as to classes,
who had been in rebellion, and who would subscribe an oath to
support the constitution of the United States and the union
thereunder, and faithfully abide by and support all acts of congress and proclamations of the president having reference to
slaves. This, it must be remembered, was during the war. But

now that peace had come, by surrender and not by compromise, as in 1861, actual rebellion had released him from the policy of leaving slavery to the states, and in time allowed him to move forward to emancipation, so in 1865 compulsory submission would have released him from terms proposed in 1863, and permitted him to move forward to higher and broader grounds. In addition to the two great facts that the circumstances of the white and colored population had, at the close of the war, entirely changed, and the glimpses on several occasions given out of a purpose on his part to favor a most enlightened and liberal policy as to all, so as to reunite the country upon a just and enduring basis, stood the great fact that in 1861 he had said he would rather be assassinated than surrender the sentiment in the Declaration of Independence that "all men are created equal." It is not likely
• at the close of a contest in which that principle had been saved, and for the first time applied to the whole country, he would have favored any plan which would deny to either those who had laid down their arms against the government, or those who had used them in its preservation, the fullest rights implied and covered by the broad declaration that all men are equal.

Who shall forget that memorable scene in the city of Richmond, which ought to be cherished and perpetuated forever as part of the history of the closing days of the unhappy strife, where the great and good man—his heart swelling with modest pride, leading his little son by the hand through the deserted streets of the once proud capital of treason, and beholding once more the flag of his country in place of a strange and usurping one, restored to its rightful dominion over an undivided union; grateful to Almighty God that in His own good time peace had returned to a divided and sorrowing people; cheered and animated by the hope of a long future of prosperity and happiness to the country—gave assurance to the scattered and remaining few of those who were but yesterday in arms against that flag, as they eagerly gathered about him, of forgiveness and an early restoration to all rights in the old government; and to the humble and long oppressed, rescued from a servitude dishonorable alike to humanity and to that flag, of freedom and citizenship in the great republic forever! Who shall measure the usefulness of the life of such a man? and who shall hope to do his memory justice? In the long range and course of time, come what may—whether a republic grounded on the immovable foundations of justice and freedom, approved after long experience and ages of human happiness as the best form of human government still standing, or whether a republic, torn into factions and rent by the mad ambitious of men, in ruins—this monument, an enduring testimonial to the humble life, glorious deeds and the shining example of the great citizen and martyr, will stand for the illumination of all men of every clime, nationality and condition, who, in search of the highest aims and loftiest purposes of life, shall come to this fountain for inspiration and, hope. Here the humble may take new courage, the proud learn humility, the ambitious that the true way to greatness lies through industry, integrity and patriotism, and all men that only the truly good can be truly great. In no other country under the sun could the obscure boy have found his way through the long succession of mysterious and grave events to such eminence and power; and where and in what land can one be found who wielded power with such grace, humanity and wisdom? The living assign him his proper place in the affections of all men. Posterity, profoundly moved by the simplicity of his private life, elevated and enlightened by the purity and splendor of his administration and public services, cannot fail to fix his place amongst those who shall rank highest in their veneration. He has gone to the firmament of Washington, and a new light shines down upon his beloved countrymen from the American constellation.

And now, by the authority and under the direction of the National Lincoln Monument Association, in the presence of this vast assemblage, who bear testimony to the fact, and under the gracious favor of Almighty God, I dedicate this Monument to the memory of the obscure boy, the honest man, the illustrious statesman, the great liberator, and the martyr President, Abraham Lincoln, and the keeping of time.

Behold the image of the Man!

As the closing words fell from the speaker's lips,

THE STATUE WAS UNVEILED

By two nuns, of the order of St. Dominic, Mother Josepha and Sister Rachel, from Jacksonville, who had been specially invited to perform that duty in consequence of the respect felt for their order by the many soldiers who had witnessed their self-sacrificing labors in the camps and hospitals during the war for the Union.

As. the veil of red and white silk slowly moved down before the statue, the vast multitude stood for a moment in breathless silence, followed by a gentle clapping of the hands and a subdued murmur of applause. The choir then sang, " Rest, Spirit, Rest."

The following

DEDICATION POEM.

BY JAMES JUDSON LORD.

Of Springfield, Illinois, was then read by Richard Edwards, LL. D., President of Illinois State Normal University at Bloomington:

> We build not here a temple or a shrine,
> Nor hero-fane to demigods divine;
> Nor to the clouds a superstructure rear
> For man's ambition or for servile fear.
> Not to the Dust, but to the Deeds alone
> A grateful people raise th' historic stone;
> For where a patriot lived, or hero fell,
> The daisied turf would mark the spot as well.
>
> What though the Pyramids, with apex high,
> Like Alpine peaks cleave Egypt's rainless sky,
> And cast grim shadows o'er a desert land
> Forever blighted by oppression's hand?
> No patriot zeal their deep foundations laid—
> No freeman's hand their darken'd chambers made—
> No public weal inspired the heart with love,
> To see their summits tow'ring high above.
> The ruling Pharaoh, proud and gory-stained,

With vain ambitions never yet attained;—
With brow enclouded as his marble throne,
And heart unyielding as the building stone;—
Sought with the scourge to make mankind his slaves,
And heaven's free sunlight darker than their graves.
His but to will, and theirs to yield and feel,
Like vermin'd dust beneath his iron heel;—
Denies all mercy, and all right offends,
Till on his head th' avenging Plague descends.

Historic Justice bids the nations know
That through each land of slaves a Nile of blood shall flow:
And Vendome Columns, on a people thrust,
Are, by the people, level'd with the dust.

Nor stone, nor bronze, can fit memorials yield
For deeds of valor on the bloody field,
'Neath war's dark clouds the sturdy volunteer,
By freedom taught his country to revere,
Bids home and friends a hasty, sad adieu,
And treads where dangers all his steps pursue;
Finds cold and famine on his dauntless way,
And with mute patience brooks the long delay,
Or hears the trumpet, or the thrilling drum
Peal the long roll that calls: "They come! they come!"
Then to the front with battling hosts he flies,
And lives to triumph, or for freedom dies.

Thund'ring amain along the rocky strand,
The Ocean claims her honors with the Land.
Loud on the gale she chimes the wild refrain,
Or with low murmur wails her heroes slain!
In gory hulks, with splinter'd mast and spar,
Rocks on her stormy breast the valiant Tar:—
Lash'd to the mast he gives the high command,
Or midst the fight, sinks with the Cumberland.

Beloved banner of the azure sky,
Thy rightful home where'er thy eagles fly;
On thy blue fields the stars of heav'n descend,
And to our day a purer luster lend.
O, Righteous God! who guard'st the right alway,
And bade Thy peace to come, "and come to stay:"
And while war's deluge fill'd the land with blood,
With bow of promise arch'd the crimson flood,—
From fratricidal strife our banner screen,
And let it float henceforth in skies serene.

Yet cunning art shall here her triumphs bring,
And laurel'd bards their choicest anthems sing.
Here, honor'd age shall bare its wintery brow,
And youth to freedom make a Spartan vow.
Here, ripen'd manhood from its walks profound,
Shall come and halt, as if on hallow'd ground.
Here shall the urn with fragrant wreaths be drest,
By tender hands the flow'ry tributes prest;
And wending westward, from oppressions far,
Shall pilgrims come led by our freedom-star;
While bending lowly, as o'er friendly pall,
The silent tear from ebon cheeks shall fall.

Sterile and vain the tributes which we pay—
It is the Past that consecrates to-day
The spot where rests one of the noble few
Who saw the right, and dared the right to do.
True to himself and to his fellow men,
With patient hand he moved the potent pen,
Whose inky stream did, like the Red sea's flow,
Such bondage break and such a host o'erthrow!
The simple parchment on its fleeting page
Bespeaks the import of the better age,—
When man, for man, no more shall forge the chain,
Nor armies tread the shore, nor navies plow the main.
Then shall this boon to human freedom given

Be fitly deem'd a sacred gift of heaven;—
Though of the earth, it is no less divine,—
Founded on truth it will forever shine,
Reflecting rays from heaven's unchanging plan—
The law of right and brotherhood of man.

After music by the band, Gen. U. S. Grant, President of the United States, was introduced, and delivered the following brief, but for him lengthy,

ADDRESS.

Mr. Chairman, Ladies and Gentlemen:

On an occasion like the present I feel it a duty on my part to bear testimony to the great and good qualities of the patriotic man whose earthly remains rest beneath the monument now being dedicated. It was not my fortune to make the personal acquaintance of Mr. Lincoln until the last year of the great struggle for national existence. During the three years of doubting and despondency among the many patriotic men of the country, Abraham Lincoln never for a moment doubted that the final result would be in favor of peace, union, and freedom to every race in this broad land. His faith in an All-wise Providence directing our arms to this final result was the faith of the Christian that his Redeemer liveth. Amidst obloquy, personal abuse, and hate undisguised, and which was given vent to without restraint through the press, upon the stump, and in private circles, he remained the same staunch, unyielding servant of the people, never exhibiting a revengeful feeling towards his traducers, but he rather pitied them, and hoped, for their own sake, and the good name of their posterity, that they might desist. For a single moment it did not occur to him that the man Lincoln was being assailed, but that a treasonable spirit—one willing to destroy the existence of the freest government the sun ever shone upon, was giving vent to itself upon him as the Chief Executive of the nation, only because he was such Executive. As a lawyer in your midst he would have avoided all this slander—for his life was a pure and simple one—and no doubt would have been a much happier

man, but who can tell what might have been the fate of the
nation but for the pure, unselfish and wise administration of a
Lincoln ?

From March, 1864, to the day when the hand of the assassin
opened a grave for Mr. Lincoln, then President of the United
States, my personal relations with him were as close and intimate as the nature of our respective duties would permit. To
know him personally was to love and respect him for his great
qualities of heart and head, and for his patience and patriotism.
With all his disappointments from failures on the part of
those to whom he had intrusted command, and treachery on the
part of those who had gained his confidence but to betray it, I
never heard him utter a complaint, nor cast a censure for bad
conduct or bad faith. It was his nature to find excuses for his
adversaries. In his death the nation lost its greatest hero. In
his death the South lost its most just friend.

Hon. Henry Wilson, Vice-President of the United
States, on being introduced, spoke as follows :

Mr. Chairman and Fellow-Citizens:

After listening as we all have to-day to eloquent voices, I am
sure that nothing can be added to your gratification. I came
from my Eastern home from a sense of public duty and from
affection and regard for the memory of Abraham Lincoln, to
participate in the services of this day. I thank God that he has
spared my life to join with you in paying this tribute to the
great man that Illinois gave to the country and the nation gave to
the world, and I shall return to my home, regarding it as among
the great occasions of my life, and among the blessings of provi
dence that I have lived to witness what I have witnessed here to-
day; and to bear my affectionate tribute and my grateful memory
to Abraham Lincoln.

The following is an extract from a speech by Hon.
U. F. Linder:

Fellow Citizens:

I regret that the snows of 66 winters that have fallen upon my
head have extinguished a great deal of my fervor and eloquence,

if I ever had any. I am sorry, fellow-citizens, that I have not prepared something short, worthy of the occasion. I am one of the aged men.   *   *   *   *   *   *   *

(Turning and pointing to the statue) I served in the Legislature of 1836 with that venerated man. We didn't always agree in politics, but we always agreed to disagree as friends. I met him in early life, when he first came to the State in 1830, in my own town, Charleston, Coles county, Illinois. He was dressed in plain jeans clothes. I had no idea, then, that he would ever be President of the United States, nor did I believe that there was any man in the State of Illinois, or that there would ever come into the State any man that would be President of the United States.   *   *   *   *   *   *   *   *

Mr. Lincoln and myself—to be serious—came from the same county, and were born within ten miles of the same place. He came to Indiana—and to a wilderness; I was educated in Kentucky, and though mine was not an extensive library, it stood out of reach of anything Lincoln had, and in his presence I considered myself always a learned man. And when I contemplate a boy like that, for I do suppose his breeches were patched at the knees and his arms out at the elbows, starting with his old mother to Indiana, then a forest, and passing on with his step-mother into Illinois, to be a day laborer and a flatboater; a man way down in the valley of humility, working his way up and on through all the phases of that eventful life, his brave and indomitable earnestness, fearlessness and honesty—never swerving from his honesty—finally fighting his way to the Presidency, where we trace him from that humble cabin in Kentucky to yonder monument, where he stands to-day. I say it is a miracle—fellow-citizens it is a miracle which only a Republican people can work. Merit will always meet its reward, and whenever another Washington shall make his appearance, another monument will go up. Yet that monument, however firm its base may be, the mouldering tooth of time will eat away; but there is another monument dedicated to Lincoln, one built in the memory and with words graven in the hearts of his countrymen, and till the last of them shall cease to live, and the English language cease to be spoken, that monument shall stand firm and unfailing until Gabriel blows his trump on the morning of the resurrection.

While Mr. Linder was speaking, Gen. W. T. Sherman stepped quietly away to look at the sarcophagus and catacomb containing the body of Mr. Lincoln. On being called for he came forward and spoke briefly, from which I make the following extracts:

I came here with feelings of great devotion, desirous to see and hear all that could be said, and I did listen with intense patience to that most admirable and eloquent speech of our friend, General Oglesby, and I turned and looked at the statue of Lincoln, when the flag dropped from it, I gazed upon it long and well, because I loved that form most well in life. I can bear him no greater affection than I do. I turned and went with uncle Jesse Dubois to see the spot where his body rests. I also met the artist of the statue, Mead, whom I knew in Florence, Italy, and went with him to various points, and viewed his work. Now, therefore, I think I have at last done full justice to the subject, and I have responded promptly to you. If you will have it so, with feelings of kindness for the call to appear in your presence, and if I could add one word or utter one single thought that would add a particle to the fame of Mr. Lincoln, I would say it now; but Mr. Lincoln's writings, his speeches, and his proclamations all bear the stamp of an honest, fearless, great, good man, and nothing is truer or better than what General Oglesby has said, that "true fame lies solidly only on a pure character and blameless reputation." I believe Mr. Lincoln's fame does so rest as that of Washington, and that it will always be classified side by side with that of Washington. Surely no man ought to hope for a higher fame on the earth, and such fame will be Lincoln's.

Mr. Larkin G. Mead, the artist, was called for, and on being introduced to the audience, was greeted with applause. He made his bow as graceful as he could under the circumstances, and retired.

Hon. Schuyler Colfax, ex-Vice-President of the United States, was called for, and spoke briefly and eloquently, quoting from Mr. Lincoln's words, spoken

22

on the battle field of Gettysburg, Nov. 19th, 1863, and applied then to Oak Ridge Cemetery.

Hon. —. Forster, M. P., of England, congratulating Gov. Palmer on the success of the arrangements and carrying into execution the dedication exercises, took occasion to say that the most noticeable feature of the assemblage was in the appearance of intelligence, thrift, neatness, health and decorum, and expressed the opinion that it could not be excelled in these respects anywhere in the world. Hon. Schuyler Colfax expressed the same views.

At the conclusion of Mr. Colfax's speech, the doxology was sung, and the benediction pronounced by Rev. Albert Hale, of Springfield, which concluded the exercises.

The procession reformed and returned to the city. The vast multitude gradually melted away, each and all carrying to their homes memories of the day and of the occasion that will be cherished while life endures.

CHAPTER XXX.

It seems peculiarly appropriate that the dedication services should have been held in connection with a reunion of the surviving veterans of one of the grand divisions of the army that saved the nation. In the fallen condition of our race, no government, human or divine, has ever commanded respect that was not sustained by force against internal as well as well as external foes.

Abraham Lincoln, as President of the United States, was Commander-in-Chief of its armies. As such, during the time he was at the head of the nation, he commanded more than one million of citizen soldiers. War was forced upon the nation with the avowed purpose of destroying it. He was compelled to submit to the dissolution of the Union, or accept war to prevent it. By turning to the engraving of the Moument and studying it, the reader will see that it teaches the lesson that the war was for the preservation of the Union. When Lincoln became President, March 4, 1861, war was threatened, and he plead with his dissatisfied fellow-countrymen not to commence hostilities, thus holding out the olive branch of peace. The reply was an attack on Fort Sumter, which was equivalent to casting the olive branch under foot, as shown in the engraving of the coat of arms. The Statue of Lincoln placed above all those emblems, with the coat of arms—which is emblematic of the constitution of the United States—beneath his feet as a pedestal, gave him authority for using the infantry, cavalry, artillery and navy, placed below and around him ; for holding the

States—built in the Monument still lower—in a perpetual bond of Union.

It became imperative for him, as a military necessity, to emancipate four millions of slaves, which is indicated by the pen in his right hand, and the emancipation proclamation which he had just written, in his left. The broken chain of Slavery, part in the talons of the eagle and part in his beak, indicates that the contest is ended. As the closing scene to all this, the Commander-in-Chief dies by a bullet from the hand of a rebel fanatic ; thus dying the death of a soldier as truly as any of the thousands who gave their lives on the field of battle for the preservation of the Union.

Vice President Dubois, in his address, attests the zeal and fidelity with which all the members of the Association discharged their several duties, but makes special mention of Hon. O. M. Hatch, Secretary of the Association, Hon. James H. Beveridge, Treasurer, and Hon. John T. Stuart, Chairman of the Executive Committee. It is no disparagement to the other members to mention these three as deserving special honor.

Mr. Hatch has conducted the correspondence of the Association and recorded its transactions for nearly nine years. To have done this in a private business amounting to nearly $200,000, would have commanded a liberal salary, and yet Mr. Hatch has done all this without fee or reward, except the consciousness of having discharged a pleasing but mournful duty.

Mr. Beveridge has not only faithfully accounted for every dollar that came into his hands, without retaining a farthing for his services, but has added to it many thousands in accrued interest.

The name of John T. Stuart is indissolubly associated with that of Abraham Lincoln, but the parallel between them has never been drawn that I am aware of. Mr. Stuart was born in 1807, in Fayette county,

near Lexington, the very richest part of Kentucky—
of a Scotch-Irish family, distinguished for learning
and refinement ; his father having been a professor of
languages in Transylvania University, and after that
for several years a minister of the gospel in the Presbyterian church.

John T. Stuart was educated at Centre College,
Danville, Ky., having graduated there in 1826, and
after that spent two years studying in the office of his
uncle, Judge Breck, in Richmond, Ky. Thus prepared
to enter upon the duties of life, he turned his back upon home and early friends, and pushing his way to
the very frontier of civilization in the fall of 1828,
hung out his sign as an attorney at law in the little collection of log huts, in what was then almost a quag-
mire, called Springfield, Sangamon county, Illinois.

Abraham Lincoln was born in 1809, in Hardin
county, almost the poorest part of Kentucky, being in
the cavernous limestone region of the Mammoth Cave.
He came of a Virginia family also, but the very anti-
podes of the Stuarts in education, refinement and social position, being of that class that has, from time
immemorial, in all slave States, been denominated
"poor whites." He grew up through the pinchings of
poverty, without schools or any other elevating social
influences, but, like the bee that gathers honey from
every flower, he drew knowledge from any and all
sources. Unlike Stuart, who chose his theatre of action and went to work with well matured plans, Lincoln merely drifted along, snatching the means to satisfy the cravings of hunger and to clothe himself in
the plainest of homespun, by a day's work here and
another there, until he finds himself in the more un-
promising village of New Salem, in the same county
with Stuart. Not having any regular business, Lincoln was ready to turn his hand to building a flatboat
and running it; doing a day's work at chopping, or

farm labor, or acting as a "sort of clerk" in a country store.

Both being on the verge of civilization, the call for fighting men to repel the savages who were scalping their neighbors, brought these two men together for the first time at what is now Beardstown; Stuart as Major of a battalion, and Lincoln as Captain of one of his companies. They stood on common ground. There was a foe before them, and both being young and fond of adventure, were intent on meeting him. Danger, and a willingness to face it, made them equal, and they both felt it. The war passed away and they met in the State Legislature, Lincoln for his first, and Stuart for his second term. They roomed together and while taking a morning walk at Vandalia, Lincoln asked Stuart's advice whether it would be best for him to study law or not. Stuart advised him to commence at once. Lincoln said he was poor and unable to buy books, and Stuart replied with an offer to loan him all the books he needed, and to act as his preceptor. At the close of the session, Lincoln visited Stuart at Springfield, obtained the books, with the necessary instructions, went to New Salem, twenty-five miles, and commenced the study of law. Two years pass on, and the preceptor offers to take his student into partnership, which brings Lincoln to Springfield. Three years later, Stuart is elected to Congress and the partnership ceases.

They both started out Whigs in politics, and continued so until the dissolution of the Whig party, when both, yielding to the force of early associations, formed new political relations; Stuart affiliating with the Democratic party, though never in full sympathy with its principles, and Lincoln aiding in the organization of the Republican party, but this divergence of political views did not in the least affect their personal friendship.

From that to the present time, the history of Lincoln is known to all the world. While he was serving his first term as President of the United States, Stuart was elected by the Democratic party to represent his district in Congress. This brought them together at the Capital of the nation. There is little doubt that Lincoln, left to the promptings of his own heart, would gladly have conferred office and honors, with their emoluments, on his early friend and benefactor, but to have tendered them might have been misconstrued. Stuart heartily reciprocated Lincoln's friendship, knowing that his own position was one of self-sacrifice, as he could not conscientiously place himself in a position to expect or receive official patronage. He quietly and conscientiously served out his term in the House of Representatives and returned home.

When the news came that President Lincoln had fallen by the hand of an assassin, there was no more sincere mourner in Springfield than John T. Stuart. As Chairman of a committee appointed at a public meeting of citizens on the day of Mr. Lincoln's death, Mr. Stuart reported a series of resolutions, the principal one of which was a request that the City Council appoint a committee to co-operate with the Governor of the State in bringing the remains of the fallen President back to his old home for sepulture. On the 24th of April, Mr. Stuart was one of those named by a public meeting of the citizens to form a National Lincoln Monument Association. When that body had raised funds, matured plans and commenced the work of building the Monument, Mr. Stuart was selected as one of the Executive Committee, and by his colleagues, Bunn and Williams, was made Chairman of the same.

During the time the Monument has been building, he has acted as President of the Springfield City Railway Company, President of the Springfield Watch

Company, also as one of the commissioners for building the new State House. He has, for many years, been the senior member of the law firm of Stuart, Edwards and Brown, and is now the third oldest practicing lawyer in the State. Notwithstanding he has been thus engaged, the building of the Lincoln Monument has been to him so emphatically a labor of love, that, without fee or reward, from the time ground was broken in September, 1869, his vigilant eye has watched every movement connected with the same, entering into all the minutia of detail until he saw it completed, and witnessed, in the presence of more than twenty thousand citizens, the unveiling of the bronze imitation of his military comrade, legislative colleague, law student and partner, whom he had seen rise to the highest official position on earth, become the emancipator of a race, and a martyr in the cause of liberty and good government. That he has witnessed all these changes and been more active than any other man in erecting this Masoleum, the like of which is no where else to be found on the continent of America, must be difficult for him to realize. Stretching like a panorama over so many years of his life, it must seem to him more like some strange vision of the mind than the veritable events of real history.

The case of Mr. Stuart presents the interesting and extraordinary spectacle of a man who was in successful law practice before Abraham Lincoln ever set foot on the prairies of Illinois; who advised and encouraged him to the study of law; witnessed his upward steps until his fame filled the whole civilized world; now, in the year 1874, nearly ten years after the tragic death of Lincoln, practicing his profession within a stone's throw of where he commenced, and who has not yet reached his three score years and ten, but, still strong in body and mind, is slowly and gracefully descending the sunset slopes of life.

The Executive Committee made a report October 28, 1874, showing that the architectural part of the Monument is completed, and every obligation paid. The report was received and approved. On the same day, the Association adopted a resolution appointing J. C. Power, author of this volume, Custodian, and on the 29th of October it was first regularly opened for the reception of visitors.

The Association now owns nine acres of land in a central and commanding position in Oak Ridge Cemetery, with right of way to and from it. According to the terms of the charter, the Association terminates its existence May 11, 1885. That gives ample time, and none too much, for completing the groups of Statuary, building a residence for the Custodian, and ornamenting the grounds. At the termination of the charter, the Monument and grounds pass to the care of the State of Illinois, a sacred trust to be transmitted to posterity.

It will thus be seen that the effort to build a Monument to the memory of the Illustrious Patriot, Abraham Lincoln, has proved a grand success. It is a magnificent structure, far surpassing every other work of the kind on the continent of America. In beauty of design it is unique. For all coming time it will be a Shrine at which patriots will delight to renew their vows to Truth, Justice and Liberty.

CHAPTER XXXI.

OAK RIDGE CEMETERY.

When Springfield was only a village, four acres of land about half a·mile west of the old State House was donated by Elijah Iles for a " grave yard," and a few years later another was laid out immediately west of it, called Hutchinson Cemetery. It consisted of about four acres also, and was regularly laid out. Lots were sold, and considerable effort made to ornament the grounds. As the town emerged from its village condition and manifested signs of larger growth, it became evident that some other arrangement should be made for the burial of the dead. With this object in view, Alderman Charles H. Lanphier, on the twenty-eighth of May, 1855, introduced the subject of purchasing land for a permanent grave yard outside the city limits.

After it was decided by the city council to purchase grounds for the purpose designated, two sites were proposed, and on bringing the subject of location to a vote, it was found that the aldermen were equally divided. Gen. John Cook, then and now of Springfield, was mayor of the city. The position of the aldermen threw the responsibility of giving the casting vote on the mayor. The friends of the successful locality awarded to Mayor Cook the honor of naming the ground, and he called it Oak Ridge Cemetery. On the fourth of June the city received of A. G. Herndon and wife, a deed to a fraction less than seventeen acres of land, for which it paid three hundred and fifty dollars. On the fourteenth of May, 1856, eleven and a half acres more we're purchased as an addition to the cemetery. At the same time—May 14, 1856—an ordinance was passed by the city council prohibiting interments in the old town grave yard, and forbidding the enlargement of any cemetery within half a mile of the city limits, which latter provision could only apply to Hutchinson Cemetery. An additional ordinance was passed at the same time, setting apart the twenty-eight and a half acres as a place of burial for the dead, under the name given it by mayor Cook. The cemetery was enclosed with a substantial fence at the expense of the city, and for two or three years it was used as a place of burial for the poor only. There being no sexton, parties dug graves wherever they pleased, of which there was no record preserved.

On the eighteenth of April, 1858, and from that time, a register has been kept of all the interments. The grounds began to present a more orderly appearance, but it required a great amount of labor to remove the under-brush. Up to this time the ground was directly under the control of the city authorities, but it was thought desirable to identify lot owners more closely with it, and make them, to some extent, responsible for its management. In 1859 the Legislature was applied to for some charter amendments, which were granted, authorizing the city council to elect annually a board of five managers, each one of whom should be a lot owner, and whose duty it should be to take charge of all the funds set apart for the use of the cemetery, and direct all the improvements in the grounds.

On the nineteenth of March, 1860, the first selection of managers took place, and on the ninth of April the board organized and entered upon the discharge of the duties assigned them. On the twenty-sixth of that month, the board resolved to set apart the twenty-fourth of May for the purpose of consecrating and dedicating the grounds of Oak Ridge Cemetery for the exclusive purpose of a burial place for the dead. The eighth day of May, a meeting was held, consisting of the managers, a committee of the city council and the clergymen of the city, to make arrangements for the ceremonies. On the twenty-fourth, a procession was formed and marched to the cemetery, where the exercises took place. They consisted of singing, prayer, instrumental music, an oration by the Hon. J. C. Conkling, and the formal dedication by the Hon. G. A. Sutton, mayor of the city.

Upon the recommendations of the board of managers, the city continued to make additions to the grounds, so that in 1865 the cemetery consisted of seventy-six and a half acres. Soon after the remains of President Lincoln were deposited in the public vault, May 4, 1865, the city donated six acres of land, or so much of it as might be thought desirable to occupy, to the National Lincoln Monument Association, and it is upon this ground that the Association has erected the monument. By referring to the map, the form and extent of the grounds may be distinguished by the dark lines a short distance from the monument. It is well to remark here that, although the cemetery contains but seventy-six and a half acres, there are about ninety-seven acres included in the boundaries given on the map, but it is understood that the additions can be made whenever it is thought to be desirable.

For several years the city council appropriated one thousand dollars annually to be used in improving the grounds, but in 1866 the revenue from the sale of lots was such that it was not thought to be necessary to continue the appropriations. In order to create a permanent fund to bring in revenue sufficient to keep up the improvements, the board of managers recommended and the city council set apart two thousand dollars, saved from the sale of lots, as a sinking fund, or rather as an endowment fund, and invested it in bonds bearing ten per cent. interest. In 1867, another thousand dollars was added, and additions have since been made, so that the cemetery fund now amounts to about four thousand dollars.

The four acre plat occupied by the old grave yard, donated by Elijah Iles, reverted to him when it ceased to be used as a place of burial. Mr. Iles then deeded it to Springfield in trust for the benefit of Oak Ridge Cemetery. The land is to be divided into lots and sold in the year 1883, and the proceeds of the sales kept as a fund forever, the interest to be used in embellishing the grounds of Oak Ridge Cemetery. There is a proviso in the deed favorable to the city purchasing the land in a body to be used as a public park, if it should be thought desirable to do so.

With a view to extinguishing Hutchinson Cemetery, the city, in 1866, commenced giving lots in Oak Ridge in exchange for lots of equal size in Hutchinson Cemetery, the lot owners there transferring their lots by deed and receiving deeds in Oak Ridge in return. In this way the city has already received the title to more than half of Hutchinson Cemetery, and the time is not far distant when it will receive it all, and then it will be sold and added to the endowment fund of Oak Ridge. The land in these two old cemeteries amounts to about eight acres, and both are near the new State House, where land is rapidly rising in value. By the time they are to be sold, they will bring such prices as to swell the endowment fund of Oak Ridge to such an amount that the grounds can be ornamented in the very highest style and preserved in that condition.

The Lincoln Monument grounds being a part of Oak Ridge Cemetery, it is proper to state in this place that, in September, 1871, a citizen of Bloomington contributed $500, to be used in grading the grounds around the monument. Another contribution for the same purpose was made under the following circumstances:

The Illinois State Sanitary Commission, organized during the war for the suppression of the rebellion, was composed of John P. Reynolds, President; Col.

John Williams, Treasurer ; Col. Woods, Robert Irwin, Esq., E. B. Hawley, Esq., and Hon. Wm. Butler. They were all citizens of Springfield at the time, but Mr. Reynolds has removed to Chicago, Col. Woods to Winchester, and Mr. Irwin is deceased.

In addition to the sanitary work, the commission attended to the collection of the claims of soldiers against the government. At the close of the war, the services of the commission being no longer necessary :n the field, it turned over the claim business in its hands to Col. Woods and Edward J. Eno, now of St. Louis, with the understanding that a certain per cent. of their fees should be paid into the treasury of the commission. By this arrangement the commission was enabled to relieve the wants of many widows and families of soldiers, and about the close of the war, it donated $5000 to the Soldiers' Orphans' Home at Springfield, before the State commenced providing for that class of sufferers.

More funds accumulated, which remained in the treasury until January 1, 1872. At that time it amounted to $2459.83. By a resolution of the commission, the whole amount was placed in the treasury of the National Lincoln Monument Association, to be expended in embellishing the grouuds. The resolution contains a proviso that not less than $500 were to be· used in erecting a slab or shaft on the monument grounds, which is to contain the names of the Union soldiers buried in Oak Ridge Cemetery. This leaves $1959.83 for ornamenting the grounds. This work is under ·the superintendence of Mr. Samuel Hood, the warden of the cemetery, who is an experienced landscape gardener. Mr. Hood became sexton or warden of the cemetery in the spring of 1867. His books show the total number of interments from the beginning of the register, in 1858, to the first of January, 1872, to be 2134, removals from Hutchinson Cemetery 319, and removals from other places 133, making a total of

2586. The remains of Governor Ninian Edwards, the first territorial governor of Illinois, were removed from Hutchinson to Oak Ridge, October 30, 1866. Governor William H. Bissell, who died in office in 1860, was buried in Hutchinson Cemetery. A very fine monument, at a cost of $5000 to the State of Illinois, was erected to his memory in Oak Ridge, under the supervision of Hon. Jesse K. Dubois and Hon. O. M. Hatch, who filled the offices of Secretary and Auditor of State while he was Governor. The remains of the Governor and his wife were removed to Oak Ridge, with imposing demonstrations and an oration by Governor Palmer, May 30, 1871. A fine marble shaft stands in a conspicuous place over the remains of General Isham N. Haynie, who died while he was Adjutant General of Illinois. Twenty-one other Union soldiers are buried in different parts of the grounds.

Oak Ridge Cemetery is situated near the northwest corner of the city of Springfield, and is one and a half miles due north of the new State House. A deep ravine runs from east to west through the cemetery, dividing it into almost equal parts. The original cemetery was altogether north of this ravine, and for that reason the oldest and best improvements are in that part of the grounds. The entrance to the original cemetery is at the east side, from the northern extension of Third street, the gate being just north of the ravine. By consulting the map, the reader will observe that the entrance is by a wide avenue that branches off in various directions so as to extend over all the northern part of the cemetery. The map also shows that the south entrance is nearer the city than that on the east. Funerals, and parties visiting the cemetery in carriages, usually enter at the south gate, while those who wish to visit the monument and other parts of the cemetery on foot go out Fifth street on the City railway, to the railway park, which is seen on the east side of the map.

Going due west from the east gate, you are soon on the south side of the ravine, which brings you to the receiving tomb, where the remains of Abraham Lincoln were placed May 4, 1865. It is a solid stone structure, built in the south bank and faces north. About fifty yards southeast of this vault, and about half way to the top of the bluff, stood the tomb which was built for the temporary sepulture of the remains of the President, and in which they rested from December 21, 1865, until September 1871, when they were removed into the monument. After their last removal, the tomb vacated was torn down and the ground where it stood graded down about fifteen feet, as previously stated. The relative position of the receiving vault, the temporary tomb and the monument is all shown on the map. Just east of the monument there is a new avenue, beautifully graded and graveled. Following that south leads to the south gate, at the northern extension of Second street, which, at that point, is called Monument avenue.

For a cemetery so new, and for a city of such limited population, the improvements are unusually good. The grounds, naturally beautiful, have been very much improved by art, and are susceptible of the highest ornamentation. The great attraction that will draw visitors from all parts of the world for all coming time, is the Mausoleum containing the remains of the martyred President.

APPENDIX.

CHAPTER XXXII.

The preceding part of this book closed with the dedication of the Monument, and the appointment of a Custodian to open the same for the reception of visitors.

The Infantry and Naval groups of statuary had been modeled at Florence, Italy, the models transferred to Chicopee, Massachusetts, and the work of casting and finishing was satisfactorily progressing, by the Ames Manufacturing Company.

Assurances were given by prominent gentlemen in Boston that the money would be raised in that city to pay for the Cavalry group.

Pennsylvania being the largest iron producing State in the Union, and Pittsburgh the city where the greatest quantity of heavy ordnance was manufactured to be used in suppressing the rebellion, it would have been a fitting recognition of this fact for the commercial metropolis of the State to furnish the Artillery group. When the proposition was made by Governor Oglesby that this should be done, it was heartily acceded to, by some prominent gentlemen in Philadelphia.

The National Lincoln Monument Association having been notified that the Naval group of statuary had been completed and was ready for shipment from

23

Chicopee, Massachusetts, to Springfield, a meeting of
the Association was called for November 25, 1875.
At that meeting, upon motion of Hon. John T. Stuart,
it was,

Resolved, That the whole matter in relation to the Naval group,
as also the settlement with Mr. Mead for bronze used, is hereby
left with the Treasurer and Secretary of this Association, under
direction of the Executive Committee.

Mr. Dubois laid before the Association a photo-
graphic copy of a letter written by Mr. Lincoln to
Mrs. Eliza P. Gurney. The letter was ordered to be
spread upon the records. The circumstances under
which it was written gives it a charm that it would not
otherwise possess. Among the delegations from
religious bodies who visited President Lincoln early
in the war to suppress the slaveholders' rebellion, a
large number of women belonging to the Society of
Friends gave him a call. One of their number, the
widow of Joseph John Gurney, a distinguished Quaker
preacher, of England, though herself an American,
afterwards wrote him a letter. His reply will ever be
highly prized, because it contains such emphatic and
unequivocal expressions of his belief in the over-ruling
providence of God. The following is the letter:

Executive Mansion,
Washington, September 4, 1864.

Eliza P. Gurney:

My Esteemed Friend:—I have not forgotten—probably never
shall forget—the very impressive occasion when yourself and
friends visited me, on a Sabbath forenoon, two years ago; nor has
your kind letter, written nearly a year later, ever been forgotten.
In all, it has been your purpose to strengthen my reliance on God.
I am much indebted to the good Christian people of this country, for
their constant prayers and consolations; and to no one of them more
than to yourself. The purposes of the Almighty are perfect, and
must prevail; though we erring mortals may fail to accurately perceive them in advance. We hoped for a happy termination of this
terrible war long before this; but God knows best, and has ruled
otherwise. We shall yet acknowledge His wisdom and our own
error therein. Meanwhile we must work earnestly in the best
light He gives us, trusting that so working still conduces to the
great ends He ordains. Surely, He intends some great good to
follow this mighty convulsion, which no mortal could make and
no mortal could stay.

Your people, the Friends, have had, and are having a very great trial. On principle and faith, opposed to both war and oppression, they can only practically oppose oppression by war. In this hard dilemma, some have chosen one horn and some the other. For those appealing to me on conscientious grounds, I have done, and shall do, the best I could and can, in my own conscience, under my oath to the law. That you believe this I doubt not; and believing it, I shall still receive, for our country and myself, your earnest prayers to our Father in Heaven.

Your sincere friend,

A. LINCOLN.

The Secretary laid before the Association a communication from Mr. J. C. Power, the Custodian of the Monument, in relation to the purchase of the surveying instruments formerly owned and used by Mr. Lincoln, but then owned by a Mr. Bean, of Petersburg, Illinois. This led to the purchase of them for one hundred and seventy-five dollars,—the Executive Committee paying seventy-five dollars, and the Custodian one hundred dollars from the receipts at the Monument. The instruments are preserved in Memorial Hall.

I find the following letter as part of the records of the proceedings of the Association for this meeting, transcribed there, "that its beautiful sentiments may be preserved." For the same reason I insert it here:

EXECUTIVE MANSION,
WASHINGTON, November 21, 1864.

DEAR MADAM:—I have seen in the files of the War Department, a statement of the Adjutant-General of Massachusetts, that you are the mother of five sons, who died gloriously on the field of battle. I feel how weak and fruitless must be any words of mine, which should attempt to beguile you of the grief of a loss so overwhelming. But I cannot refrain from tendering you the consolation that may be found in the thanks of the Republic they died to save. I pray that our Heavenly Father may assuage the anguish of your bereavement, and leave you only the cherished memory of the loved and lost, and the solemn pride that must be yours, to have laid so costly a sacrifice upon the altar of Freedom.

Yours very sincerely and respectfully,

A. LINCOLN.

To MRS. BIXBY, Boston, Mass.

Hon. Jesse K. Dubois, Vice-President of the Association, died November 22, 1876, and at a meeting of the Association, November 23, 1876, Hon. Shelby M. Cullom, Governor-elect of the State of Illinois, was chosen to fill the vacancy.

Judge Charles S. Zane was chosen in place of Thomas J. Dennis, who had removed to Chicago, thus vacating his seat in the Association.

Hon. Milton Hay was chosen in place of Dr. S. H. Melvin, who had removed to California, thus vacating his seat in the Association. The two latter were chosen November 23, 1876, also.

NAVAL GROUP.

When the Naval group of statuary was completed in the autumn of 1875, it was not shipped direct to Springfield, but was taken to Philadelphia and exhibited at the Centennial Exposition, which was opened July 4, 1876. At the close of the Centennial it was shipped to Springfield, arriving in the spring of 1877. The Naval group represents a scene on the deck of a river gunboat or ship of war. The mortar is poised ready for action, the gunner has rolled up a shell ready to put in it; the boy, called in nautical phrase the powder-monkey, climbs to the highest point, and is peering into the distance, he and the gunner believing that they are on the eve of a battle, but the officer in command, having examined the situation through his telescope, and finding that there is no preparation for battle on the part of the enemy, dismisses the subject.

INFANTRY GROUP.

The Infantry group was shipped from Chicopee, Massachusetts, direct to Springfield, arriving in the spring of 1877, also. Both groups were placed in position on the Monument in September, 1877. The

Infantry group represents a body of infantry soldiers with all their arms and baggage, on the march, not in immediate expectation of battle, but they are supposed to have been fired upon by an enemy in ambush, and the color-bearer killed. The officer in command raises the flag with one hand, and pointing to the enemy with the other, orders a charge. The private with the musket, as the representative of the whole line, is in the act of executing the charge. The drummer boy has become excited, lost his cap, thrown away his haversack, and drawn a revolver to take part in the conflict, and then looks as though he was not sure whether to fight or get behind the officer.

From a letter written by Mr. A. C. Woodworth, President of the Ames Manufacturing Company, which was placed on the records of the Monument Association, I learn that the Coat of Arms was cast in 1870, the statue of Lincoln in 1871 and 1872, the Naval group in 1874 and 1875, the Infantry group in 1874 and 1876, and that the weights of the different pieces are as follows:

Coat of Arms, - - - -	284 pounds.
Statue of Lincoln - - - -	4,862 "
Naval Group, - - - -	7,826 "
Infantry Group, - - - -	7,609 "

I also learn from the same letter that the Ames Manufacturing Company had received sixty-five old bronze cannon, donated by the United States Government to the National Lincoln Monument Association.

Weight of guns, - - - -	49,974 pounds.
Amount used in the statuary, - -	9,261 "
Balance on hand, Nov. 7, 1876, -	40,713 "

The efforts in Boston and Philadelphia to raise money to pay for the Cavalry and Artillery groups, proved to be a total failure, principally for want of some influential citizen to lead off in each city, as Governor Morgan had done in New York. In order to supply that deficiency, the Legislature of Illinois made an appropriation of twenty-seven thousand dollars for the purpose, which became a law in May, 1877. May 17, 1877, the Lincoln Monument Association, at a special meeting:

Resolved, That this Association hereby request and direct Larkin G. Mead, Esq., to proceed without delay, to prepare and construct the Artillery group, as contemplated and specified in the contract with this Association, and draw upon them for one-third of thirteen thousand seven hundred dollars, payable on or before the tenth day of July next.

Resolved, That the Executive Committee be and they are hereby instructed to make and transmit to Mr. Mead an order for the Cavalry group, at such time as they in their discretion may dictate.

At a meeting of the Association December 11, 1878, Jacob Bunn tendered his resignation as a member of the Executive Committee, and the Hon. J. C. Conkling was appointed to fill the vacancy.

At the same meeting Governor Shelby M. Cullom was elected Vice-President of the Association.

A letter from Mr. Mead, dated Florence, Italy, March 4, 1879, and directed to the Secretary of the Association, conveys the intelligence that the models in plaster for the Artillery group were completed and ready for shipment.

At a meeting of the Association, September 12, 1879, it was

Resolved, That we hereby request and direct Larkin G. Mead to proceed without delay to prepare the model and cause the construction of the fourth or Cavalry group for the Monument, as specified and contemplated in his contract with the Association, and that he is hereby authorized to draw upon the Treasurer for the sum of four thousand five hundred and sixty-six dollars and sixty-six cents.

Resolved, That the Secretary is hereby directed to transmit to Mr. Mead a copy of the foregoing resolution.

The following is the formal order of the Executive Committee:

SPRINGFIELD, ILL., September 12, 1879.

Larkin G. Mead, Esq., Florence, Italy:

SIR:—We enclose you herewith a copy of a resolution, this day passed by the Lincoln Monument Association.

In obedience to that resolution, and in compliance with the contract between the Association and yourself, referred to in said resolution, we, the Executive Committee, give you hereby the formal order to proceed and complete, as soon as practicable, the fourth or Cavalry group.

You are hereby authorized, in pursuance of said contract, to draw upon the Association for four thousand five hundred and sixty-six dollars and sixty-six cents, the first payment for said group.

JOHN T. STUART,
JAMES C. CONKLING, } Executive Committee.
JOHN WILLIAMS,

At a special meeting of the National Lincoln Monument Association, November 16, 1880, the death of two of the members of the Association was announced, namely:

Orlin H. Miner, died May 27, 1880.
David L. Phillips, died June 19, 1880.

Their vacancies have not been filled.

The Association having been notified that the models for the Artillery and Cavalry groups of statuary had been shipped from Florence, Italy, and arrived at Chicopee, Massachusetts, in October, 1880, and that Mr. Mead had drawn on the Association for the second payment on each, which, according to the contract, was four thousand five hundred and sixty-six dollars and sixty-six cents each, therefore a formal order was passed that the two several drafts be paid.

At a meeting of the National Lincoln Monument Association, Debember 19, 1881, Hon. John T. Stuart, on the part of the Executive Committee, made a report including various subjects. From that report I make some extracts concerning the Monument grounds.

It will be remembered that the original grant of land in 1865, from the city of Springfield, to the National Lincoln Monument Association, was about six acres. In October, 1877, the Executive Committee applied to the city council for a modification of the south line of the Monument grounds, to make it conform to the lay of the land, but they did not ask for anything additional. In response to this request, and after having a committee examine the land and make a report thereon, October 27, 1877, the city council acceded to the request to change the line, by adding about one and one-third acres on the south of the Monument grounds, making a total of about seven and one third acres, for which a deed of conveyance was made, by the proper authorities of the city, to the National Lincoln Monument Association.

The Citizens' Street Railway Company having purchased eight acres of land immediately west of the Monument, and built a railway to land passengers within less than one hundred yards of the same, there was danger that some of the land belonging to said railway company might be so used as to be objectionable to visitors at the Monument. In order to avert this danger, the Executive Committee applied to the Board of Directors of the Citizens' Street Railway Company and received a title deed, September 1, 1880, to one acre or more of said land, for a nominal sum, making it practically a donation. So that now the Monument Association has the title to between eight and nine acres of land.

Information was before the meeting of December 19th that the Artillery group of statuary had been completed and was subject to the orders of the Association. The Secretary was directed to notify Mr. Mead or his agent, Mr. A. D. Shepherd, to have the group forwarded to Springfield. It was shipped at Chicopee, February 4, 1882.

ARTILLERY GROUP.

A meeting of the Association was held February 24, 1882. The Artillery group having arrived the day before, the draft of Mr. Mead for four thousand five hundred and sixty-six dollars and sixty-six cents, being the last payment on that group, was ordered to be paid. The Executive Committee was authorized to put the group in position without delay. It was accomplished April 13, 1882. The Artillery group represents a section of artillery in battle. The enemy has succeeded in directing a shot so well as to dismount the gun. The officer in command escapes unhurt, mounts the wreck of his gun and carriage, and with drawn sword is looking defiance at the approaching enemy, probably a cavalry or infantry charge. The youthful soldier in front seems oblivious to danger from an approaching charge, but is horrified at the havoc beneath and around him. It is probably his first battle, and the flying pieces from the gun carriage may have killed and wounded half a dozen of his comrades, which could not be made to appear on the small platform allotted to the group. This would be a sufficient cause for him to feel as his looks would indicate.

CAVALRY GROUP.

The model for the Cavalry group was shipped with that of the Artillery, from Florence, Italy, and arrived at Chicopee in October, 1880. The casting and finishing is well under way, and will be placed on the monument early in 1883. The Cavalry group consists of two human figures and a horse, and represents a battle scene. The horse, from whose back the rider has just fallen, is frantically rearing. The wounded and dying trumpeter, supported by a comrade, involuntarily assumes a prayerful and tragic attitude. The Artillery and Cavalry groups seem to represent defeat; but they are truthful, because it was through many such scenes that the Union cause became victorious.

The following column on the left contains the names of the original members of the National Lincoln Monument Association. That on the right the present members. Names of deceased members are marked with a star. Names of those chosen to fill the vacancies are in the column on the right opposite the names of the deceased ones, and of those who have vacated their seats by removal. Two vacancies are unfilled :

Gov. R. J. Oglesby, *President*.	Ex-Gov. R. J. Oglesby, *Pres't.*
*Hon. J. K. Dubois, *Vice-Pres't*.	Gov. S. M. Cullom, *Vice-Pres't.*
Hon. J. H. Beveridge, *Treasurer.*	Hon. J. H. Beveridge, *Treasurer.*
Hon. O. M. Hatch, *Secretary.*	Hon. O. M. Hatch, *Secretary.*
Hon. John T. Stuart,	Hon. John T. Stuart,
Col. John Williams, } *Ex. Com.*	Col. John Williams, } *Ex. Com.*
Jacob Bunn,	Hon. J. C. Conkling, }
Hon. J. C. Conkling.	Jacob Bunn,
Judge S. H. Treat.	Judge S. H. Treat.
*Hon. Sharon Tyndale.	Ex-Gov. John M. Palmer.
Hon. Newton Bateman.	Hon. Newton Bateman.
*Hon. O. H. Miner.	
*Hon. D. L. Phillips.	
T. J. Dennis.	Judge C. S. Zane.
Dr. S. H. Melvin.	Hon. Milton Hay.

The above was the status of the membership of the National Lincoln Monument Association when this edition was put in press in June, 1882.

In the autumn of 1876, P. D. Tyrrell, the chief operative of the United States Secret Service for the district in which Chicago is situated, had his suspicions aroused that a certain drinking saloon in that city was a rendezvous for counterfeiters. He could not learn anything by going there himself, because some of the men whose presence excited his suspicions knew him personally, and for him to appear would only put them on the alert. In order to obtain the desired information, he employed a young man unknown to those parties, and instructed him in the manner he should proceed to gain their confidence. He was first to convince them that he was the same kind of man they were, which he did, by gradual approaches, so thoroughly that they revealed to him the fact that they were not only engaged in putting counterfeit money in circulation, but were then preparing for a speculation on a much larger scale. They told him that they expected to steal the remains of President Lincoln from the monument in Springfield, bury them in some secure place, and then disperse, probably leave the United States, and watch the accounts in the newspapers for a favorable time to enter into negotiations for the return of the body. They expressed the utmost confidence that they could in that way obtain at least two hundred thousand dollars and the release of a celebrated counterfeit engraver who is serving a ten years' sentence in the Joliet penitentiary for engraving and printing counterfeit money. Wishing to avail themselves of the remarkable shrewdness of the young man, whose acquaintance they thus were forming, they proposed that if he would join them and assist, he might have a share in the profits.

As he had only started out to obtain information about their counterfeiting operations, this discovery was quite startling to him. He made some pretext for time to consider, and at the earliest opportunity reported to the officer who employed him, and asked for instructions. The officer then authorized and instructed him to accede to their proposition, join them and keep with them in every movement and report to him daily or more frequent, as circumstances seemed to indicate. The young man did not lose any time in letting the conspirators know that he would take part with them. After that he was at every meeting of the gang, numbering several others besides the two whose confidence he first gained. It was at length decided that the stealing should be done Tuesday night, November 7, 1876, the night after the day on which the Presidential election was to be held. That time was chosen for the reason that if they were seen out unusually late, each party would be likely to conclude that the other was in search of election news, and in that way they hoped to disarm suspicion.

The two conspirators and the young man who had been sent to ferret out their counterfeiting operations, by which he was led to the discovery of the plot, started from Chicago at nine o'clock on the evening of November sixth, by the Chicago, Alton and Saint Louis railroad. The operative of the Secret Service was kept fully posted, and with two assistants boarded the rear sleeping car of the same train as it moved out of the depot. All parties arrived in Springfield at six o'clock on the morning of November seventh, the train being two hours behind time. The day was spent by the conspirators in perfecting their plans, and by the operative of the Secret Service and his assistants in watching the conspirators and perfecting their plans also. Meanwhile, balloting for President and Vice-President of the United States, was going on over the entire Nation. At five o'clock that afternoon the train brought two other assistant detectives from Chicago, one of them an ex-Chief of the United States Secret Service for the whole Nation. There was not a ray of sunshine reached the earth in Central Illinois that day, and in consequence of the thick clouds, night came on early. About six o'clock the operative of the Secret Service, with four trained detectives, including the ex-Chief, also a reporter for a Chicago paper, approached the Monument, two miles north of the city. They were admitted to Memorial Hall at the south end, by the writer as Custodian of the Monument. The outer door was then locked and the entire party conducted through the back door to a point where lights could not be seen from the outside. There lamps were lighted and one man placed inside against the solid wall, opposite the sarcophagus at the north end of the Monument. He was instructed to remain in that position until he heard sounds as if work was being done on the sarcophagus. In that event he was to find his way back to Memorial Hall—lighted lamps having been placed as guides—and report to the officers. The five officers and the writer kept their positions, in darkness that could almost be felt, from two and a half to three hours, when footsteps were heard approaching the outer door, which is closed by two shutters, one of wood and glass, the other of iron rods. Two men appeared, one bearing a lighted bull's eye or dark lantern. They soon found that both doors were locked, and seemed satisfied that there was not any person about the Monument. They then went around to the north end, one hundred and twenty feet distant, and by sawing and filing, broke the padlock to the grated door at the entrance to the Catacomb, and commenced taking the marble sarcophagus to pieces. The man who was placed inside to listen, passed through among the labyrinth of walls to Memorial Hall, and reported that he could hear the conspirators at work on the sarcophagus. For several minutes hurried and excited whisperings were going on between the five officers in the Hall. The writer was greatly puzzled to know why they did not go out and move upon the enemy at once. It subsequently transpired that the officers never expected to go out on the report of the one who was listening inside. Placing him there was merely an extra precaution that they might know when the work commenced. The young man who had discovered the plot in Chicago, was with the conspirators, under instruction from the operative of the Secret Service who was in the Hall, that he was to remain with the conspirators until the door was forced and they began to work on the sarcophagus. Then he was to go around outside and give a signal at the entrance to Memorial Hall. The officers expected then to leave the Hall, move quickly around to the Catacomb and capture the miscreants at their work.

It was afterwards learned that when the lock was forced, and before they commenced work on the Sarcophagus, the conspirators pushed the young man into one corner of the half-circular Catacomb and gave him the lantern to hold. He at once recognized the movement to mean that they would shoot him dead, should he attempt to dispose of the light and pass out of the door. Therefore, he could do no less than to hold it until they had taken the marble sarcophagus apart and drawn the wooden and lead coffin, with the body

24

partly out, that they might conveniently take it up and carry it away. The conspirators then stepped outside and started the young man off for a horse and wagon to haul the body away, they agreeing to remain at the door until his return. He had not secured a team, but made them believe he had one at the east gate. He started in that direction, as though he was going for the team, but the night was cloudy and exceedingly dark, and as soon as he passed from their sight he turned to the right, ran to the door of Memorial Hall and gave the signal agreed upon. The officers went quickly around, expecting to capture the conspirators, but they had escaped. They were too shrewd to remain at the door of the Catacomb, lest others might be looking for them, and so withdrew about thirty-five yards from the Monument, and lay down by a small oak tree, from which they saw the officers enter the Catacomb, and heard their exclamations of disappointment. They afterwards told the young man that they then thought it would be more prudent for them to make their escape. For ten days the conspirators could not be found. At the end of that time, the young man having retained their confidence, informed the officers that the two were together at the same drinking place where he entered into the scheme with them. The officers entered the saloon, one or two at a time, until they were in sufficient force to overpower and handcuff them in a few seconds. They were brought to Springfield, tried and sent to the penitentiary for one year. Only one year, because there was no law in Illinois that made it a penitentiary offense to steal a dead body. A law was enacted and approved May 21, 1879, which came in force July first of the same year, under which a party convicted of the crime is subject to a penalty of not less than one nor more than ten years in the penitentiary.

I have thus given a bare recital of the main points in a case that created the greatest excitement and

indignation at the time.   A full account of the event
and all the incidents preceding, and that have grown
from it, would read like a romance from the dark ages.
It will, probably, be written and published separately
at some future time.

There are persons who oppose the policy of requiring a small fee from each visitor on their first entrance
to the Monument.   The city of London or the English
government might defray the expense of showing visitors through the Tower of London, but every one has
to pay.   The Brock monument at Queenston, Canada,
can be entered only on the payment of a shilling.   The
Washington monument, at Baltimore, was built by the
State of Maryland, but each visitor pays.   The Bunker
Hill monument might be made free by the State of
Messachusetts or city of Boston, but all visitors pay.
The tomb of Washington can only be reached by the
payment of one dollar to a steamboat, and it cannot
land at the wharf except under a contract to pay twenty-
five cents to the Mount Vernon Ladies' Association for
each visitor.   Many of us cannot visit the Tower of
London, nor Bunker Hill, nor Mount Vernon, not
because of the admittance fee, but the expense of time
and travel.   Requiring a fee is the best possible police
regulation.   Those who pay seldom violate rules.   It
is those who do not pay that trespass most upon
forbidden ground.   The State of Illinois has appropriated in all $82,000 to the Lincoln Monument.   Let
her continue to keep it in repair, and ornament the
grounds.   For each one of her citizens who visit it
annually, five hundred and ninety-nine stay at home.
It would not be just to require those who stay at home
to pay the expense of the one who travels.   If so, why
not include his hotel bills and railroad fare?   If the
Custodian cannot interest the people so as to collect
sufficient funds to defray the expense, he is not the
man for the place.   If the people are not sufficiently
interested to contribute, it should be taken as evidence
that it was time to close its doors.

CHAPTER XXXIII.

When Robert Burns wrote:

"Oh, wad some power the giftie gie us
To see oursel's as ithers see us;"

he expressed in his quaint way what every person feels
who desires to improve mentally and morally.   There
are, unfortunately, many shams in the world ; persons
who do not wish to improve, but to appear better or
more wise or more learned than they are.   They aim
to deceive, but as a rule deceive themselves more than
all others.   The most effectual cure for such persons
is ridicule, but should they bring upon themselves
open and pointed rebuke, they are little deserving of
sympathy.   But the shams in society may be likened
to the tares among the wheat, and all must grow until
the great harvest.   It is refreshing to know that there
is pure wheat, that the highest style of Christian ladies
and gentlemen are not at all rare.   In this chapter I
shall treat of all sorts, as part of my experience here.

Mark Twain, in his inimitable book, "The Innocents
Abroad," has made the guides, conductors and custodians of places where pilgrimages are made in Europe,
the laughing stock of the English speaking people all
over the world.   If the guides and custodians could be
heard, they would doubtless turn the tables, and give
us such a record of the doings of Americans traveling
in Europe, on suddenly acquired wealth, as would
make us ashamed of our countrymen and country-
women.   To a limited extent the position of Custodian
here is one of the very best for studying human nature,
therefore, I propose, as far as my experience goes, to
relate the story of the guides.

My conflicts here to maintain my rights and self-respect have not been with the every day common people, nor with those who are denominated roughs, but it has been with those who by the advantages of schooling,—I will not say education, for it is possible to be very extensively schooled, and not educated,—and wealth, ought to be more scrupulous in respecting the rights of others not so highly favored. But there is so much of the first Adam in us all that men and women, even professing Christians, take advantage of those very favors to tyrannize over others. The fact that a man or woman is a professing Christian should be conclusive evidence that he or she is a gentleman or a lady, but my experience here is that the profession is of itself very slender evidence. The actions of some I have encountered here fully explain to my mind why we so frequently hear of the coarse vulgarity of Americans traveling abroad.

I regard the National Lincoln Monument as the grandest school of patriotism on the continent, or in the world, and worth an hundred-fold more than all it costs, to the American people. It has been a great source of pleasure to me to impart its lessons to all men and women, high and low, rich and poor, who visit it from patriotic motives. But for those of either sex who, by their words or actions forfeit all claim to respect, I have no mercy, and the more intense the dislike of such shams for me, the more I feel honored.

When I took charge of the Monument, a set of rules and regulations were prepared by the Executive Committee, and a printed copy placed at each of the three entrances, that all might take notice thereof and govern themselves accordingly. The main points in the rules are, that I am to show all parts of the Monument, and give all the information about it to such visitors as desire it, and in order to defray the expense I am to collect from each visitor who goes inside, the sum of twenty-five cents. The first thing that surprised me was the great number of persons who would go around with me and seem charmed with my outside descriptions, and when it came to paying the small fee would suddenly find themselves so limited for time that they could not go any further.

I call to mind an incident of this kind. A woman who occupies a prominent position in society and missionary meetings, and whose husband is reputed to be worth more than a hundred thousand dollars, rode up in her carriage with a lady friend, both richly dressed. They followed me as I showed another party around on the Terrace and into the Catacomb, asking more questions than all the others. When we came to Memorial Hall, pausing at the entrance to collect the small fee, they suddenly became too limited for time to go inside and at once started for their carriage. The weather was warm and I used only a grated door with a screen before it. When I reached the back part of the Hall, several minutes later, the door became darkened and I stepped quickly around the screen to drive away what I supposed was a lot of boys filling the space, and behold my two nice ladies who were so limited for time, had returned, each with an ear close to the grating, in a listening attitude!

A merchant came with two ladies. Knowing that he understood the rules with reference to paying, I readily admitted them. After giving a moment's attention to visitors who had previously entered, I returned to him, and said: "I suppose you understand the rule requiring a small contribution from each visitor who enters here?" Springing up on his toes, assuming an air of defiance, and with a most contemptuous manner, he said: ":If I choose to." Putting my face almost touching his, I replied, "Sir, if you do not choose to comply with the rules when you .come here, get out of that door as quick as you can, and never enter it again while I am here." He went out on the double quick and never has entered it since.

I prepared a descriptive pamphlet of the Monument to sell for twenty-five cents. So many objected to paying a fee, that I conceived the brilliant idea of pleasing everybody by taking one fee, conducting them through and giving a pamphlet to each one, thus giving double the value for their money. I was soon informed that a newspaper man was going to annihilate me because I compelled each visitor to buy a book as a condition of admittance to the Monument. In order to make his article unanswerable he went to a member of the Monument Association for some strong points, when he found I had authority for collecting all the money I did without giving the pamphlet. The article never appeared, but whenever the writer of it comes in contact with me, I always think I can see his hair turning the wrong way, but perhaps as to the latter part my imagination is somewhat vivid:

There were those who claimed to be of so much distinction as to ignore me, and if they could gain admittance, would undertake to do the talking themselves. One woman high in church, society, and official circles, of fine presence and always richly dressed, practiced this upon me two or three times. I saw her approaching one day accompanied by two distinguished divines. She signified her desire to enter Memorial Hall, did not make the slightest pretense of introducing or placing her friends in my care, but the moment she entered the Hall began to talk about the objects of interest, not so much to give information concerning them as to say in each alternate sentence something of what she had seen in Europe. I walked up by the side of the visitors, quietly saying that I was the Custodian, and as she commenced a description, I began talking about the same article, and thoroughly understanding the subject as it is my duty to do, I talked so much faster and more to the purpose than she could, caused her to turn abruptly to another article. I followed as quickly and soon drowned her voice, being very careful to preserve a gentlemanly demeanor. She soon abandoned the contest, and ever after left me to entertain her friends in my own way. I am not under the necessity of drawing on my imagin-

ation, but these are actual occurrences, and many
more similar to them might be given.   I choose only
such as have the wealth to travel in Europe and make
the name American a by-word.

——————

Of all the classes of people who visit the Monument,
there are none who afford me more pleasure, by their
outspoken loyalty to the principles for which Lincoln
died, and sympathetic interest in all that pertains to
his life and death, than the Methodists, both lay and
clerical.   In the autumn of 1875, the annual meeting
of Illinois Conference was held in Springfield. Before
the business of the conference commenced many of
the delegates visited the Monument, and, of course,
spoke of it to those still arriving.   That was previous
to the attempt to rob the tomb.   On the second or
third day a company of about twenty came and
expressed a desire to obtain all the information they
could.   I took them to the Catacomb and explained
the situation there, showed where the bodies of the
children lay, and the location of the crypts prepared
for the living members of the family.   I then conducted them to the Terrace and explained that the
names of the States were so arranged as to represent
a bond of union, took them to the best point from
which to view the statue of Lincoln, then went to the
south front and summed up the lesson of patriotism
in the whole combination, and after that a few minutes
were devoted to those who wished to ascend the
Obelisk.

The whole party was then conducted to Memorial
Hall, where a running explanation was given of the
relics on the walls and the tables.   I then opened a
book and gave an opportunity for those who desired
to register their names, and took advantage of their
being thus occupied for a brief respite from the continuous talking.   I did not then, as I do now, take the
contributions at the door, and had not said a word
about money, although I knew from some remarks on
their part that they understood there was a regulation
requiring it, and that they had probably read the same

as there is a copy of the regulations kept at each door. While some were writing and others looking at this and that relic, one of the ministers approached me with a pleasant smile and said: "We ought to license you to preach while we are here. So good a talker should certainly be a preacher." This attracted the attention of others and quite a number of them gathered around me. Reflecting a moment, I replied: "Gentlemen, you are better judges of my qualifications for a Methodist preacher than I am, and perhaps you would like to have a test," at the same time removing my hat and holding it out with both hands, added the words: "Suppose we take up a collection." The shout of laughter that followed showed that they appreciated the hit, and each man brought forth his pocket book. As they threw in the twenty-five cent postal currency—silver change not having arrived since the war—accompanied their contributions with such remarks as "That will do." "That test cannot be excelled." "That will carry you through." "Come on, we will license you," etc., etc.

Near the close of the same meeting of Conference, Bishop Ames made a visit, accompanied by Rev. Dr. Edwards, of the *Northwestern Christian Advocate.* When I was explaining that the three blank ashlars on the east side in the cordon of States, were put in to make it more symmetrical, because thirty-seven was an awkward number to build in, Doctor Edwards said quickly, put on the letters U. S. A., United States of America.

After that I frequently alluded to the suggestion of Dr. Edwards, and found that it met with almost universal approval. Quite a ludicrous incident, however, once occurred in connection with it. About the time General Grant was being talked of for a third Presidential term, I was explaining to a company of seven or eight, and when I spoke of the probability of those letters being put on, one of the company became very much excited, and accompanied his demonstrations with some violent expletives, which quite surprised myself and his fellow visitors. A little further on it was discovered that the man had misunderstood me. He thought I said U. S. G., and at once interpreted it to mean that we were going to put Grant's initials on Lincoln's Monument.

On another occasion, an incident of quite a different character occurred, in connection with the arrangement of the initials of the States. I was explaining to a company of preachers—not Methodists. One of them, a doctor of divinity, with a lofty wave of the hand and a pompous air, said: "We do not want to hear anything about that,—we know all about the States," and started on as though he expected to take me and all the company with him, asked what was to go on the next pedestal. I stepped back, reclined against the balustrade and said nothing. The Doctor looked back, called to me to come on, saying we want to know about these things. I said, "Very well, sir, go on; you have no use for me." He insisted that I should go on, and I positively refused to have anything more to do with him, assuring him that I knew my business as well as he did his own. The other ministers and some ladies were all anxious to hear, and the Doctor beginning to realize the awkwardness of the situation, changed his whole demeanor, saying he really desired to obtain the information, and would not interrupt me again. After a few more passes, mixed with a little asperity on both sides, he became quite genial, and by the time we got through, the whole party were in the best of humor. I doubt if the thought ever occurred to the good Doctor, what he would have done if I had gone to hear him conduct religious services, and he had commenced by reading the Ten Commandments, and I had told him I did not want to hear that, I knew all about it.

On one occasion, when a party of seven or eight persons, who had ascended the Obelisk, were coming down, I saw a well-dressed lady and gentleman standing at the most favorable point, and looking at the statue of the President. I approached them, and asked if they desired to be shown around and through the monument. Neither made any reply, and I was about repeating the question, when I became aware that the lady was tossing her handkerchief almost in my face. I looked at her inquiringly, and saw that her bosom was heaving, and her eyes, steadily fixed on the statue of Lincoln, seemed almost ready to send forth a flood of tears. Just then her husband said in a low tone, "She does not wish you to speak." Always entertaining the most profound respect for feelings too deep for utterance, as I have time after time witnessed them here, I quietly withdrew. A few minutes later I made the announcement that all who desired could go with me into Memorial Hall. Those who had been in the Obelisk went with me, and after about ten minutes spent there we were in the act of going out, in order to visit the Catacomb, when the couple I had left on the Terrace appeared at the door of the Hall. Reminding them that there was a small contribution required, the gentleman handed me the money. At the same time the lady said, "Give him the money, but we do not want to hear another word." She seemed surprised at finding so many objects of interest there, and made remarks inquiringly as though the information from me would be acceptable, notwithstanding I had been distinctly told not to talk. I never permit myself to be catechised under any such circumstances, and the only direct question and answer I remember was when she asked: "Where does all the money collected here go to?" The reply was equally abrupt: "It goes into my pocket, Madam!" They soon passed out, and regarding the show of deep feeling as a mere sham, I gave them no further attention, and in a short time they departed, without entering either the Catacomb or Obelisk.

Something like three months passed, when, on a very warm morning, I was superintending some work on the grounds, I saw two ladies ascend the steps to the Terrace and take a seat over Memorial Hall, in front of the statue of Lincoln. I went up and inquired if they were visiting the monument for the first time. One of them, pointing to the other, said : "It is the first time for her, but I have been here before."   I looked and recognized my friend with whom I had parted so unceremoniously a few months previous. There was no time lost in giving me to understand that she had come to have it out with me. I shall not attempt to report *verbatim,* for all the stenographers in the State could not have done that; but will let the reader imagine a section of Dante's Inferno, the Aurora Borealis, and a tropical cyclone, with their electric coruscations and deep reverberations, all in one, and each part doing its utmost for about five minutes, as the best description I can give of what followed. I had no time to look up, but I think Lincoln's statue must have laughed at the ludicrous scene.   When we were becoming exhausted, she demanded admittance to both places she had paid for, but failed to gain at her former visit. "Very well, madam, you shall have it; not because you demand it in the way you have, but because I admit every person who has paid once. I first conducted them to the Obelisk and then to the Catacomb. Looking at some withered flowers on the Sarcophagus, she said to the other lady that she would like very much to take something from there. Overhearing it, I said, "Help yourself, madam." "O," she said. "I meant something living; something that will grow."   I then placed a small pot-plant before her, and said, "take that." She looked at me in amazement, and then said, "Mr. Power, I have been too hard on you." The battle was over. I then conducted them to Memorial Hall, which she seemed to enjoy with redoubled interest. In there I handed her a copy of the second edition of this book, and told her I was the author of it.   She seemed still more surprised. Gradually the whole secret of her actions came out.   She had been told before her first visit, by some person possessed of the spirit of the Evil One, the absurd story that I had once been a servant of Lincoln's, that I was in the position I am as an act of charity, that all my talk was mere nonsense, that I could not give her any information worth listening to, and that she would do well to treat me accordingly. It did not prove successful, and I venture to say that in all her European travels—for she was a lady of refinement and culture and had traveled extensively—she had not a more valuable, and, in the end, a more pleasant experience, for we parted the best of friends.

Of all the classes of people who visit the monument, there are none more gentlemanly and lady like than the members of the theatrical profession. I have never known an actor nor an actress to be rude or boorish here. An actor may bear evidence of having "tarried long at the wine when it is red," but he never fails to be a gentleman while here, and all, both male and female, manifest the highest respect, amounting almost to reverence for anything associated with the memory of Lincoln. Their respectful demeanor may be influenced by his having received his death wound in a theater, but there is another reason why they shou ld and do make themselves generally agreeable. Their profession is a life-long effort to please, which brings immediate returns. Herein their example might be adopted by many professing christians with much farther reaching results.

On a pleasant day in January, 1880, hearing foot-steps on that part of the Terrace over Memorial Hall, I went out, and, ascending the steps, found a very intelligent-looking gentleman quietly studying the statue of Lincoln. When I asked him if he was taking his first look at the Monument, at the same time informing him that I was the Custodian and would render him any service desired, he failed to show the slightest signs of recognition. Leaving him to his meditations, I waited his pleasure, and finally, without taking his eyes from the plain, homely face, he said :

"I have been an infidel all my life, but I was just wondering if it could be, that that great heart is dead."

I thought the best reply would be to leave him to his thoughts until he was ready to hear and see all, which he did with an intelligent interest such as those can best do who have fought for the preservation of liberty, for I found that he had been an officer in the Union army.

———

Of all professions, there is none the privileges of which are so mercilessly abused as that of the newspaper reporter. I have been in the profession and can truthfully say that I never wrote a sentence about any man that I would not have preferred to speak in his hearing, and at the same time look him in the eye. If this rule was strictly observed, there would be little cause for heart burnings from correspondents. But there is a class of guerrillas who crowd into the ranks of decent men, and with brazen affrontery claim every courtesy. Having received them, they have no more scruples than the cowardly and treacherous Cossack, and often stab in the back those who have treated them most kindly. Many of this kind find it convenient to get off some insipid attempts at wit at the expense of the Custodian, but I seldom notice them. I rather like a little contest occasionally with one who is able and willing, in a gentlemanly way, to give and receive hard blows. A single specimen of that kind will be sufficient. In April, 1880, "The Woman's Presbyterian Board of Missions for the Northwest," composed of about six hundred delegates, held their annual meeting in Springfield. This naturally drew representatives of Presbyterian newspapers and other parties identified with the interests of the church. The meeting lasted more than a week, and during that time many of the lady delegates visited the Monument in small companies, but at the close of the meeting, and as a farewell to Springfield, they came to it something like an avalanche. Memorial Hall was soon crowded until it was barely possible to move around. It is oval in form with a ceiling supported by dome-groined arches, making the very worst form for acoustics. If two persons talk in it at the same time, neither can be understood. In order to save time and talking, my custom is to go rapidly over the entire list of articles, saying but a few words about each one, occupying from three to five minutes and parrying all attempts at catechising until I have gone the rounds. On this particular occasion fully seven-eighths of the ladies were desirous of obtaining the information I was endeavoring to impart. But about one-eighth of them were deaf to every appeal from me, and to all entreaties from the other ladies, and talk they would. I had never experienced the like before, and if I could have passed out unobserved, I think now I would have done so and ran away, but in sheer desperation I determined to out-talk them. Just at this time, when it would seem as though bedlam was holding high carnival, Doctor W. C. Gray, of Chicago, managing editor of the *Interior*, then personally unknown to me, appeared at the door and was admitted. We will take an editorial in his paper as a report of the scene, although there is a very strong impression in Springfield that a woman wrote it, but, as an act of chivalry, the Doctor accepted the responsibility. It appeared in the paper of May 6, 1880.

"The Lincoln Monument is situate in a cemetery which has unusual natural beauty, with its fine, smoothly shapen hills and deep ravines. The emblematic groups representing the army and navy are in place, and together with the great statue of the emancipator, are noble works of the sculptor's art. The Monument is worthy of all the commendations given it for massiveness, harmonious design and imposing effect. It has been criticised, of course, —that being the way to demonstrate one's superior artistic knowledge, and the more perfect the object criticised, the finer critical acumen it shows.

"There is a gentleman in charge of the Monument whom they call the Custodian. On leaving the scene, one of the missionary ladies suggested that for the sake of brevity he should be called simply Mr. Cus. The eloquence of Mr. Custodian is wonderful. He addresses visitors in a lofty, uninterrupted Demosthenian strain, from the time they arrive until they depart. It is not a good place to rest, not even if one were dead. Within the Monument is a fine marble-lined apartment, in which are numerous relics of the departed—letters of sympathy and mourning over his death from the governments and magnates of the world. Conspicuous in a glass case are a pair of dilapidated gaiter shoes. We looked on them with veneration—doubtless the shoes which he wore on the night of his assassination. A lady in a sympathetic and low tone ventured to say as much, whereupon the loud voice of Mr. Cus-todian was heard commanding silence. A party of us started for the grating door, but found it pad-locked. It was evident that the orator had us. He had cut off retreat from the very muzzle of his double-shotted oratorical columbiad; so we went back to look at the shoes. In due time he approached that part of his subject. 'These shoes,' he said impressively, 'are the shoes worn by the thief who tried to steal the body of Abraham Lincoln.' Women, you know, are irrepressibly curious—likewise logical. So up spoke a meek-eyed missionary, and said, 'If you got the shoes, how did it happen that you did not get the thief?' Mr. Cus—we insist on giving him his full title—todian, withered her with the sage remark, 'I will explain that, madam, when I come to it.' So we had been paying homage to the foot-furniture of a foot-pad! Another effort was made to get out, when Mr. Cus—we never did believe in nick-names, even for the sake of brevity—todian was at the exit, and in a mild, sweet voice, in beautiful contrast with his oratorical style, said, 'Twenty-five cents each, if you please—were you not aware that there was an admission fee?' We were not aware. 'If you please,' was a figure of speech. It was not the pleasure that we were to pay for. Twenty-five cents might have been a protective tariff as an *admission* fee, but as a fee for *getting out*, there is no other way in which that small sum can be invested so as to secure more pleasure. Mr. Cus—we adhere to his full title—todian, receives this fee 'for his support,' we understand. It is a modest price for the stentorian power exhausted in earning it. But perhaps it is not fair to measure Mr. Custodian's corn in our half-bushel. He really has a fine reputation as an orator. Audiences of ladies and gentlemen hang upon his lips like bees on the under side of the leaf just before swarming time. Amid such daily triumphs, he can look down upon his critics with lofty indifference, and smile as he thinks of the pad-locked door.

"Springfield is a very pleasant city, and is worthy of its suggestive name. It is a city of beautiful homes, located in broad grounds and on wide streets. It is so abundantly shaded by fine old trees as to be largely hidden from view, from any elevated point of observation. The houses are clean and fresh looking; the lawns are neat and not gaudily over-decorated. The universal neatness reminds one of Saratoga. There is the greatest variety in the architecture of the residences—a mingling of the solid-comfort style of building, which marks the colder climate of the more northern cities, with the verandahs and porches of the warmer latitudes. In hotels, it has not much to boast. One of them, surnamed the 'Inter-Ocean,' was disowned by the representative of that aristocratic paper. The new State House—well, we must not criticise it, unless we are willing to suffer the displeasure of all

loyal Springfielders. It is not complete. The great portico awaits
an appropriation before it can be in place. It will greatly add to
the symmetry of the whole work."

I received the paper containing the article the same
day it was published, but did not open it until my
attention was called to the subject. I nursed my wrath
an hour or two, and if I had attempted to answer
during that time would, doubtless, have given cause to
suspect that the play upon my title as Custodian was
not far wrong. Becoming more cool, I reflected that
the best way to vanquish an assailant is to turn the
laugh on him. Following that line, the reader will
judge of my success. The Doctor had the Christian
manliness and spirit of fair-play, not only to publish
my reply, but to add an appreciative postcript, all of
which appeared in the *Interior* of May 20th, of which
the following is a copy:

MEMORIAL HALL, NATIONAL LINCOLN ⎫
MONUMENT, May 8, 1880. ⎭

DEAR DOCTOR: How could you? Here I have been, lo, these many
years, reading *The Interior*, and thinking how happy I would be to
meet and take you by the hand, and you have come and gone, and
I never knew when I met you, and would not have known except for
the sting you thrust back in your paper of the 6th instant. Then,
to think, Doctor, how you slurred us all over, in speaking of the
Illinois Capitol, as though we Springfielders claimed it all for ourselves. True, we have been sufficiently blackmailed on account of
it to justify us in claiming it, but we do not.

Then, you say: "In hotels it has not much to boast." Doctor,
where were your eyes, your ears, to say nothing of your palate?
Did you, or did you not learn of the palatial Leland, where may be
found luxurious rooms, and tables loaded with a bill of fare good
enough for a pope, emperor, king, president, yourself, or any other
man. Then you pass the Revere, St. Nicholas, and other good
houses, and pounce upon a third-class boarding-house, not recognized at all by citizens of Springfield as a hotel, and name that as
your only specimen of capitolian hotels.

Doctor, only think of your report of a visit to this Monument. I
am here under direction of an association of fifteen gentlemen, any
one of whom is the peer of yourself in integrity and gentlemanly
deportment. They are organized under the laws of the State of
Illinois. I make monthly reports to that Association, and at any
hour am subject to their supervision or removal. In the absence of
prescribed orders, I exercise my own judgment, and have never
been censured by them for disobedience, or any other cause, so that

25

it is reasonable to presume my transactions are satisfactory to them. The probability is that you have traveled sufficiently to know that there is something to pay at all places similar to this.   At the Washington monument in Baltimore, you would have to pay fifteen cents; at Bunker Hill twenty cents; at Mount Vernon, one dollar to the steamboat that takes you there,—twenty-five cents of which goes to the Ladies' Association having it in charge,—and you can not gain access to it in any other way.   Then, if you were to cross the Atlantic and visit the Tower of London, you would not only have a fee to pay, but would be compelled to tarry in a waiting-room until a certain number of visitors arrived, and have doors locked after you wherever you went.   If you did not know all that, you certainly can read, and the rules by which I am governed are plainly printed and put up at each of the three doors.   If you did not intend to comply with them, you ought to have remained outside.   If you did, why snarl at the pad-lock, which is only intended as a matter of economy, in the absence of sufficient income to defray the expense of a door-keeper.   I trust, Doctor, that you may never be on the wrong side of any worse pad-lock than you found here!   It would be a pleasure to me, Doctor, even though it were something of a torture to you, if I could make you realize how many pleasant things you overlooked, about which you might have written, and the best you could do was to find a pretext to swear, and then lay the suggestion of the thought to a woman.   You said a lady, but a lady never swears.   Adam could not have done worse than that.   When detected in a wrong act, he only skulked behind Eve, and whined out to the Lord, "The woman whom thou gavest to be with me, she gave me of the tree and I did eat."

Doctor, you speak of my lofty eloquence.   I was constrained to employ the altitudinous variety in self-defense.   How could I have risen above the din of twenty or more female voices in any other way?   In imagination I hear you say, why talk at all?   Let each one look for him or herself.   I have tried that to my heart's content.   With such a company as you saw, there would be silence for about one-tenth of the time there was in heaven on a certain occasion we read of, and then more questions than ten men could answer in an hour, and all expected to be answered by one man in five minutes.   That is the reason why I require silence until I get through.   The great mass of people come here to learn the most they can in the shortest time.   If there are many who wish to hear and one or two who do not, I sometimes have occasion to show that one or two the door, and insist that they shall go out or keep silent, just as you would do in any service you was expected to be responsible for.   It is said that order is heaven's first law.   If I can not preserve it here, I prefer being thrust out myself.   I aim to preserve order because it is right of itself, and in my own self-defense.   I have been acting in self-defense all my life.   I am writing this article in self-defense.

One of my weaknesses from boyhood has been sleeping in church. I was compelled to do it in self-defense. Perhaps you ask, how? For fifteen years or more, I was required to attend services one Saturday and Sunday in each month, at a genuine, simon-pure, old-fashioned, Hardshell Baptist church, in the State of Kentucky. Such a church was never known to exist north of the Ohio river, and I doubt if it can exist in the South much longer. During all that fifteen years I sat under the same sermon, from the same man, Rev. Joel M. It was full three hours long, all in that blessed tone so dear to the heart of the elder sisters of his congregation. It made no difference whether his text was in Genesis or Revelation, the sermon was always the same, with the exception of a sentence or two at the opening and closing. It abounded in stereotyped phrases, such as "mourning like a dove," and "chattering like a swallow," accompanied with tones and gestures as though he was trying to imitate the birds. These long sittings were more than my youthful flesh could endure, hence it became absolutely necessary, as a means of self-dense, for me to wear away part of the time in sleep. I never realize so fully at any other time, that I am a monument of mercy, as when thinking of that sermon, and how I survived it. But it was not all evil. There was one redeeming feature in it, the benefit of which I am enjoying to the present time. I used to preach that same sermon on odd Sundays to congregations of boys and negroes, assembled behind barns and under shade trees, and that is the way I acquired that Demosthenian eloquence which you so much admire.

[*Although the habit of sleeping in church was acquired strictly in self-defense, it has sometimes proved to be quite annoying. After marriage, myself and wife became members of a Presbyterian church less than one hundred miles from Cincinnati, and at one time made our home in the family of the pastor, Rev. L. R. B. He could not fail to observe my weakness, and would occasionally remind me of it. I would retort by saying that it was his duty to preach such sermons as would keep me awake. He would usually speak my name as though it had a plural termination, which it has not. The seating in the church was promiscuous, consequently upon one very warm day, I found myself under the necessity of occupying quite a conspicuous place in front of the pulpit. It required unusual exertions to retain an upright position, but I did not become so sound asleep as to prevent my knowing when the minister closed his sermon, opened his hymn book and read distinctly from one of Dr. Watts' good old hymns,

"My drowsy powers, why sleep ye so?
    Awake my sluggish soul;
Nothing has half thy work to do,
    Yet nothing's half so dull."

---

* That part in brackets never appeared in the *Interior*, having been voluntarily withdrawn after being sent to the office, in order to abbreviate the article.

By the time the reading of the first verse was done, I was thoroughly aroused, and felt as though all eyes were upon me, but preserved a respectful demeanor. We walked home together, but the events of the morning were not alluded to until all were seated at the dinner table. Assuming a serious expression of countenance, for I really thought he had selected that hymn as applicable to my case, I said: 'Brother B., I think I have just cause to complain of you.' 'Why so?' said he with an inquiring look. 'Because, sir, you to-day took occasion to point out my infirmities publicly, when you could just as well have done it privately.' With a puzzled expression of countenance he said: 'I do not understand you, please explain.' 'Well, sir, at the close of your sermon this morning, seeing I had been asleep as usual, you could not wait until our arrival at home to reprove me, but under pretense of reading a hymn called aloud:

'My drowsy Powers, why sleep ye so?'

I then found that the selection of that hymn was entirely unpremediated on his part, and, therefore, will not attempt to describe what ensued, but any allusion to the subject after that, was sure to provoke the most unbounded mirth.]

One thing I want distinctly understood, I have thus far acted in self-defense, but now I assume the aggressive, become a missionary, and if I can prevent it no other person shall suffer as I have done. As long as I preach my sermon here, neither man, woman, nor child shall ever sleep under it, until they are dead, and then I shall do my utmost to prevent their bodies being carried away by vandal hands.   J. C. POWER, *Custodian.*

P. S.—We did not make anything by stirring up Bro. Power. However soundly he may have slept under his Hardshell pastor, it is evidently not easy to catch him napping now.   G.

The affair was so ludicrous that it attracted some attention, and I received a number of letters of congratulation. I will quote from three of them, from as many different States, the two first are from Presbyterian ministers of my acquaintance:

J. C. Power:

MY DEAR SIR—"I congratulate you on your answer to the *Interior.* It was first-rate good sense—ten times better than if you had clawed it. It was, moreover, Christian good sense. I shall vote for you to stay at the Monument."   G. H. F.

Bro. Power:

"Previous to receiving the papers which you had the kindness to send me, I read your letter to our Bro. G., and said to myself, Dr. G. has met more than his match, now that he has 'awakened' my brother, J. C. Power. I shall pin my vote with Bro. F.'s to continue you in a position where, I feel fully persuaded, the right man is in the right place. It is certainly a favorable school in which to study men and manners. May your bow abide in strength."   Kind salutations, etc.,

W. L. T.

J. C. Power:

"This, from one whom you do not know, and whose humble position in life will ever render him one of the 'great unknown,' is addressed to you, to tender you thanks for your efforts to entertain and interest those who visit the Lincoln Monument, of which you are Custodian. The attention paid by you to an aged relative while visiting the Monument, rendered the visit instructive and entertaining. He remembers Springfield as a pleasant place to visit, chiefly from the polite and considerate attention received from you while visiting the Monument. This is written because of an unjust criticism against you, which I noticed in a late Chicago paper."

It is not in a spirit of egotism, but strictly in self-defense, that I give two more specimens, in order to show how people feel and act who come with an honest desire to be entertained and edified. A lady-correspondent of the Detroit *Evening News*, closes a long and very carefully written letter with these words:

"It only remains to acknowledge the indebtedness of the writer for the information here given, to the intelligent, courteous and genial Custodian of the Monument, Mr. John Carroll Power, whose thorough knowledge of the duties of his position is only equaled by the fidelity, the readiness and the grace with which he discharges them."

Another, a lady correspondent of the *Cincinnati Commercial*, says:

"It is with no feeling of horror or gloom that I stand beside this Coffin. Everything is so sweet and clean and pure. The gray-haired man at my side has such friendly eyes, and is so kindly and pleasant. He has in his hand the keys that hold a Nation's priceless dead. Yet so gentle is he that I lay my hand unrebuked on the rich casket, while he tells me stories of the dead, and I tumble the perfumed blossoms in more sightly garlands over the lid. * * * How far away George and Martha Washington are from life, barred in their unwept, undecked tomb at Mount Vernon. We press our faces against the barred door. We wish we could brush away the litter of twigs that the sparrows have carried in. We would like to put a red rose above the fair Mistress Washington, but we cannot reach her. Lincoln's coffin we can stand by, we can touch, we can bend over, we can decorate. He is nearer, we are not shut away by bars. He is yet our neighbor and friend."

CHAPTER XXXIV.

Some points in the history of the Emancipation Proclamation may not be generally known, and I have given the matter sufficient attention to obtain the most essential facts. September 22, 1862, President Lincoln issued his preliminary Emancipation Proclamation, giving notice that unless certain conditions were complied with in less than one hundred days, he would issue a proclamation declaring freedom to the slaves in certain States and parts of States, then in rebellion against the authority of the United States. The final Emancipation Proclamation was issued January 1, 1868, by which more than three millions of slaves were liberated. At the instance of the ladies about to open à fair in Chicago for the sanitary commission, Hon. Isaac N. Arnold, then a member of Congress from Chicago, addressed a note to President Lincoln asking him to give them the original draft of the proclamation, that they might dispose of it with the understanding that it be deposited with the Historical Society of Chicago. Mr. Lincoln replied :

EXECUTIVE MANSION,
WASHINGTON, October 26, 1863.

Ladies having in charge the Northwestern Fair for the Sanitary Commission, Chicago, Illinois:

According to the request made in your behalf, the original draft of the Emancipation Proclamation is herewith inclosed. The formal words at the top, and the conclusion, except the signature, you perceive are not in my handwriting. They were written at the State Department, by whom, I know not. The printed part was cut from a copy of the preliminary proclamation, and pasted on merely to save writing. *I had some desire to retain the paper, but if it shall contribute to the relief or comfort of the soldiers, that will be better.*   Your obedient servant,

A. LINCOLN.

Having written to Mr. Arnold to ascertain who purchased it, and the amount realized by the ladies, I received a letter from him dated Chicago, March 4, 1882, from which the following is a quotation :

"At the Sanitary Fair it was purchased by THOMAS B. BRYAN, of Chicago, who paid into the treasury of the Fair for it the sum of $3,000. Afterwards it was deposited in the Chicago Historical Society, and burned in the great fire, October 9, 1871."

I wrote again to Mr. Arnold, calling his attention to an article in the *Century Magazine* for December, 1881, by the distinguished artist, Mr. Leonard W. Volk, of Chicago, on the Lincoln life mask, and how it was made. Mr. Volk had made a statue of Stephen A. Douglas, and when he measured the height of Lincoln, said to him :

"You are just twelve inches taller than Judge Douglas, that is just six feet and one inch."

I next quoted the last paragraph from a *fac simile* before me, of Mr. Lincoln's autobiography, written in 1859, at the request of Hon. Jesse W. Fell, of Bloomington, Illinois, who retains the original. It reads as follows :

"If any personal description of me is thought desirable, it may be said, I am in height, six feet four inches, nearly, lean in flesh, weighing on an average one hundred and eighty pounds, dark complexion, with coarse, black hair, and gray eyes, no other marks or brands recollected." Yours very truly,

HON. J. W. FELL.   A. LINCOLN.

I pointed out the discrepancy of the three inches and said that I preferred Mr. Lincoln's *fac simile* to Mr. Volk's memory, and asked Mr. Arnold if he could endorse me in the event of my making the same statement to the publishers of the *Century Magazine*. He replied :

CHICAGO, March 10, 1882.

J. C. Power:

DEAR SIR—"Mr. Volk is mistaken. Mr. Lincoln was six feet four inches. I will with pleasure endorse your and his—Lincoln's—statement to that effect." ISAAC N. ARNOLD.

As there has been frequent mention of how Mr. Lincoln came to cultivate whiskers, I deem it of sufficient interest to give a brief account of it.

Through the courtesy of Hon. George W. Patterson, of Westfield, New York, I was, in 1878, placed in correspondence with the "little girl" who suggested to Mr. Lincoln that he would look better if he would permit his beard to grow. I learned that her maiden name was Grace Bedell, but she had, "after the manner of womankind," changed it to Billings, and that her home was in Delphos, Kansas. She was then visiting relatives in her native State. I wrote to Mrs. Billings asking her to give me, in her own language, an account of the circumstances connected with her having made the suggestion. The following is her well written reply:

ALBION, N. Y., October 2, 1878.

Mr. J. C. Power:

Your favor of September nineteenth is before me, and I will with pleasure comply with your request, as far as the lapse of years and consequent forgetfulness will allow. It is indeed true, as you observe, that any incident connected with the life of this great and good man will always be of interest to the American people, and you have my permission to make use of this, should you consider it of sufficient importance. We were at that time residing at Westfield, New York. My father, who was a staunch Republican, brought one day to me,—who followed in his footsteps and was a zealous champion of Mr. Lincoln,—a picture of Lincoln and Hamlin, one of those coarse, exaggerated, *so-called* likenesses, which it seems to be the fate of our long-suffering people to have thrust upon them in such contests.

Those were days when every word or incident, however trivial, connected with the opposing candidates, was read and weighed as if heavy with import. So the personal appearance of the two men was discussed, and undoubtedly the low jeers and unworthy comparisons so current at the time, are as fresh in your mind as my own. You are familiar with Mr. Lincoln's physiognomy, and remember the high forehead over those sadly pathetic eyes, the angular lower face, with the deep cut lines about the mouth. As I regarded the picture, I said to my mother: "He would look better if he wore whiskers, and I mean to write and tell him so." She laughingly assented, and I proceeded to give him my name, age, place of residence, my views as to his fitness for the Presidency opinion of his personal appearance, and that I thought it would be much improved if he would cultivate whiskers, adding as an inducement, that if he would, I would try and coax my two Democratic brothers to cast their votes for him. In my heart of hearts I feared that this rather free criticism might give offense, and so tried to soften the blow,—a born diplomatist, you see,—by assuring him that I thought the rail-fence around his picture looked real pretty, and ended by asking him if he had not time to answer my letter, to allow his little girl to reply for him. I remember well one particular, the address. It burns within my memory yet:

'HON. ABRAHAM LINCOLN, ESQ.'

When I confided to a sister that I had written to Mr. Lincoln, she expressed a doubt as to whether I had addressed it correctly. To prove that I had, and that she might trust the evidence of things seen, I re-wrote the address and handed it to her for inspection. I was laughed at until I was speedily reduced to a more "umble" frame of mind than Dickens' Uriah Heep ever dreamed of.

His anxiety at that time must have been intense. The din of political strife, with its malice, threats and rumors of war, all the fore-runners of that day, not far distant when the "land should be red with judgments," when good men prayed, "Give us grace to keep our faith, and patience; wherefore should we leap on one hand into fratricidal fight, or on the other yield eternal right." But amid all the care and turmoil of his life, he still found time to answer the letter of a child. How this simple act shows the gentle, humorous side of the man's nature. In very truth he was a gentle-man, and the world will not soon see his like again. I am also obliged to depend upon my memory for Mr. Lincoln's reply, for although the original is still in my possession, it is at my home in Delphos, Kansas. I think, however, I can give it to you *verbatim*, as I have read it many times:

SPRINGFIELD, ILL., Oct. 19, 1860.

Miss Grace Bedell :

MY DEAR LITTLE MISS:—Your very agreeable letter of the fifteenth is received. I regret the necessity of saying I have no daughter. I have three sons; one seventeen, one nine, and one seven years of age. They, with their mother, constitute my whole family. As to the whiskers, having never worn any, do you not think people would call it a piece of silly affectation if I should begin it now?

Your very sincere well-wisher,

A. LINCOLN.

Nevertheless, my suggestion was not despised as you are aware, nor was the circumstance forgotten, as after his election, he inquired of Hon. G. W. Patterson, who accompanied him on his trip from Springfield to Washington, and whose residence was also at Westfield, if he knew a family bearing the name of Bedell. Mr. Patterson replying in the affirmative, Mr. Lincoln said that he had received a letter from a little girl, "advising me to wear whiskers, as she thought it would improve my looks, and you see I have followed her suggestion." He said further, that the character of the letter was so unlike many which he was daily receiving, some asking for office, and many threatening assassination, should he be elected, that it was a relief and pleasure to receive it. When the train reached Westfield, Mr. Lincoln made a short speech from the platform of the car, saying that he had a little correspondent at Westfield, called Grace Bedell, and if she were present he would like to see her. I was present, but the crowd was so great that I had neither seen nor heard the speaker, but a friend helped me forward, and Mr. Lincoln stepped down to the platform where I stood, shook hands with and kissed me, saying as he touched his beard, "You see I let these whiskers grow for you, Grace," shook my hand again cordially and re-entered the car; and that was the first and last I ever saw of this hero and martyr.

That he did not forget me, I received occasional assurances, though small would have been the wonder had I been forgotten in those dreadful years which followed—years of bloodshed and mourning, when

> " Fields of duty opened wide,
> Where all his powers
> Were tasked, the eager steps to guide,
> Of millions on a path untried,
> When the slave was ours !"
>
> Very truly yours,
> GRACE BEDELL BILLINGS.

Grace Bedell was less than thirteen years of age when she wrote to Mr. Lincoln. At my request she sent his letter to me, that I might have it photographed. I noticed that it was blurred, and upon inquiry was informed that when she received it, the weather was quite cold and a light snow falling. In her eager desire to read it, as she walked home with it open, some of the snow fell on it, and wherever it touched left its mark. She failed to tell me whether she induced her Democratic brothers to vote for Mr. Lincoln or not.

The personal magnetism of Mr. Lincoln was such as to put every one in his presence at ease and on good terms with themselves. Evidences of this are found to an almost ludicrous extent through central Illinois. Nearly every man, who ever saw and exchanged a few words with him, seems to want it understood that they were on *very intimate* terms, emphasizing the words italicised. Base ball had not been invented, or at most was not considered our National game at the time of his nomination for President, but to hear the statements of men who claim to have been playing "hand ball" with him when he received the news of his nomination, one would think that not only the city of Springfield, but all of Sangamon county, were assembled for a grand tournament of that game. Even the women and children tell about their husbands, fathers and brothers being engaged in the play with him when the news came. This grew monotonous with me, and I adopted the ruse of pretending to keep a record, and when a considerable number of visitors were at the Monument, and one of them would begin with the air of a man who thought himself fully as great as Lincoln, to tell that he was playing hand ball with him when the news of his nomination arrived, I would take a scrap of paper and pencil, and making a note, would carelessly remark that he was the nineteen hundred and twenty-seventh, or some other incredible number, who were playing with Lincoln on that memorable occasion. The visitor would generally lose his interest in the subject, and now I seldom hear of any person who makes such a claim. But the unkindest cut of all, to these boasters, comes from T. W. S. Kidd, the "Crier of the Court," when Lincoln practiced law in Springfield. He writes:

"It has been said that Mr. Lincoln was engaged in playing ball when the dispatch was handed him announcing his nomination to the Presidency in 1860, at Chicago, by the Republican party. This is a great mistake. Mr. Lincoln was as fully aware of what was going on that day as any man in Springfield. It would argue an apathy in regard to passing events never characterizing Abraham Lincoln, in anything political or professional. He was what the world would style a well posted man on nearly every subject claiming attention from public men particularly, and in a matter of such moment to *him*, and one upon which he had exchanged views with nearly every prominent delegate to the convention from this State, either in person or by letter, that it is out of the range of the probable to presume for a moment that he was playing ball or in any other way treating the matter with the indifference which some have endeavored to picture in this story. Allow me right here to diverge a little to give the true history of Mr. Lincoln's whereabouts when receiving the news. He had been in the telegraph office, at that time on the north side of the square, awaiting dispatches, and had quietly endured the suspense until the convention had begun to take the ballot. He then left the office and walked to the store door of Smith, Wickersham & Co., west of the square. While standing there talking of what he had already learned, a shout was heard and footsteps were also heard, coming down the stairway° of the telegraph office. This was taken up until cheer after cheer was heard all along the north side, and a messenger came running to him announcing the news. In a few minutes a hundred people had gathered around him cheering, while some wanted to know the particulars, others wanted to congratulate him. He wanted to get out of the crowd, and remarking in a loud voice to those around him, 'Well, there is a little woman who will be interested in this news, and I will go home and tell her,' started for home."

After the attempt to steal the remains of President Lincoln, November 7, 1876, Gen. J. N. Reece, G. S. Dana and the writer, became impressed with the importance of having some kind of an organization for the purpose of observing in an appropriate manner the anniversaries of his birth and death. Circumstances connected with that outrage upon civilization, kept the matter alive in our minds, and finally we three determined to act. In view of the fact that we are at the former home and tomb of Lincoln, to and from which all thoughts on his life, public services and death, naturally converge and radiate, and that we might at some time be entrusted with valuable property, it was necessary that we should be clothed with legal forms. The writer had it in mind that it would express a pleasing and patriotic sentiment to have thirteen members, corresponding with the number of the original States of the Union, but being desirous that the other two should take an equal part in selecting those whom we would invite to join us, the organization was effected with nine, and the number remains unchanged. We might just as easily have had fifty or one hundred, but we think the smaller number will be more efficient. The following is taken from our records:

On the twelfth day of February, 1880, the seventy-first anniversary of the birth of Abraham Lincoln, at a meeting in Memorial Hall of the National Lincoln Monument, the Lincoln Guard of Honor was organized and a certificate of incorporation issued the next day as follows:

STATE OF ILLINOIS, DEPARTMENT OF STATE, ⎱
GEORGE H. HARLOW, SECRETARY OF STATE. ⎰

To all whom these presents shall come, greeting :

WHEREAS, A certificate duly signed and acknowledged, having been filed in the office of the Secretary of State, on the thirteenth day of February, A. D. 1880, for the organization of the Lincoln Guard of Honor under and in accordance with the provisions of "An act concerning corporations," approved April 18, 1872, and in force July 1, 1872, a copy of which certificate is hereto attached:

Now, therefore, I, George H. Harlow, Secretary of State of the State of Illinois, by virtue of the powers and duties vested in me by law, do hereby certify that the said, the Lincoln Guard of Honor, is a legally organized corporation under the laws of this State.

In testimony whereof, I hereto set my hand, and cause to be affixed the great seal of State. Done at the City of Springfield, this thirteenth day of February, in the year of our Lord One Thousand Eight Hundred and Eighty, and of the Independence of the United States, the One Hundred and Fourth.

The original incorporators are J. C. Power, J. N. Reece, G. S. Dana, James F. McNeill, J. P. Lindley, Edward S. Johnson, Horace Chapin, N. B. Wiggins and Clinton L. Conkling, of whom G. S. Dana, is President; J. N. Reece, Vice-President; J. F. McNeill, Treasurer, and J. C. Power, Secretary.

There is on the Pacific coast a voluntary society called the Lincoln Guard of Honor. It holds memorial services at different points on the Lincoln anniversaries. The central point is San Francisco. The members of it take the most lively interest in everything transpiring about the tomb of Lincoln. After the attempt to steal his body in 1876, Mr. Edwin A. Sherman, who is the head of the movement on the Pacific, and is a cousin of Gen. W. T. Sherman, wrote a sonnet in honor of, and sent it with a beautiful testimonial to, the Custodian of the Monument. It is fully appreciated, but so highly complimentary that he pleads modesty for not publishing it here, as it would seem egotistical to do so. Recently the Custodian received a valuable testimonial from the same source, in the form of a collar, of the richest red, white and blue silk, lined with crimson satin. Gold fringe is pendant from all parts of it, and the entire surface is covered with patriotic emblems in gold. Accompanying the collar came a ring of massive gold. On the outside, in addition to cabalistic letters, the sun, and all-seeing eye; 57, the number they gave him in their local society, is inclosed in a triangle; 21, the number of Illinois in the Union, is in a five pointed star; 13, the number of the original States, 38, the present number, and 56 the number of the signers to the Declaration of Independence, and the number of the years of Lincoln at the time of his death, are each enclosed in a circle. Inside: "To Sup. Cust. G. G. C. John C. Power, Springfield, Ill. From his California Fraters.".

The Lincoln Guard of Honor of Springfield, being legally organized, has for its objects the raising of a fund with which to purchase and keep in repair the former home of President Lincoln; to open it under suitable regulations to visitors, and to hold the premises in trust for the people. It also proposes to hold memorial services upon suitable anniversary occasions, and to collect and preserve mementoes of his life and death.

The first memorial service was held at the door of the Catacomb of the National Lincoln Monument, April 15, 1880, beginning at seven o'clock and twenty-two minutes in the morning, corresponding with the time President Lincoln breathed his last, President Dana, of the Lincoln Guard of Honor, acting as master of ceremonies.

The services consisted of prayer by Rev. James A. Reed, of the First Presbyterian Church; singing by the Young Men's Christian Association Quintette Club—Messrs. S. T. Church, Edward A. Wills, Frank M. Wills, Frank L. Fuller and B. F. Ruth, Jr.; reading of Lincoln's farewell address to the people of Springfield, by Rev. Albert Hale, the oldest clergyman in Springfield; reading of Lincoln's letter to Eliza P. Gurney, by J. C. Power, Secretary of the Lincoln Guard of Honor; singing; reading of Lincoln's second inaugural address, by C. L. Conkling, a member of the Guard of Honor; voluntary addresses by Rev. W. B. Affleck and Governor Cullom, and the reading of Lincoln's favorite poem, "O, why should the spirit of mortal be proud," by Mrs. E. S. Johnson, wife of a member of the Guard of Honor; and the benediction, by Rev. J. H. Noble, of the First Methodist Church.

The following is the very brief, spirited and highly appropriate address of Rev. W. B. Affleck, of York, England:

"The sorrow and sympathy of the Guards of Honor, citizens, admiring friends, and of the many strangers whose cheeks are moistened with tears, who are assembled here on this momentously solemn occasion, leads me to repeat an ancient though appropriate question, "Is there no balm in Gilead, is there no physician there? Why then is the hurt of my people not healed?

Why, aye, why? Because no such wound as we are gathered here to commemorate was ever before inflicted, and no hurt was ever before so universally felt. In Abraham Lincoln's death humanity lost a loyal and beneficent representative, the oppressed colored race its champion, emancipator, and this great Nation its political and patriotic savior. He had love too ardent, sympathies too deep, a soul too large, a heart too tender and a mission too Catholic and comprehensive for any other country but this limitless and liberty-loving

"Land of the free
And home of the brave."

His great achievements inspired hope in the poorest of the poor. His honesty placed merchandise and law on a higher plane. His becoming and uniform humanity gave worthy example to the rich and the great. His willing and industrious hand gave dignity to honest toil. His graceful carriage and kindly demeanor under highest honors gave a lesson to all rulers, and his noble life, crowned with a martyr's death, gave testimony to a witnessing world that it is greater and diviner to die in a good cause, than to live and see a Nation's liberties sacrificed. For

"Whether on the scaffold high,
Or in the battle's van;
The fittest place for man to die
Is, when he dies for fellow man."

In this country's future the pure life of "Lincoln the Good," will inspire a spirit of Christian chivalry in tens of thousands of America's stalwart sons, and will give them a certainty that

"Freedom's battles once begun,
Bequeathed from bleeding sire to son,
Though baffled oft are always won."

Guards of Honor—May God bless you for organizing to guard the fair fame and the good name of honest Abraham Lincoln. Yours is a sacred trust. This is a fine Monument. Its sparkling granite making it imperishable but fitly symbolizes the enduring loyalty of our own Lincoln to truth, goodness and God.

In England we teach our children to love its Cromwell. In Scotland they teach their children to love its Wallace. In Ireland they teach their children to love its Daniel O'Connell. In Switzerland they teach their children to love its Winkelreid. In Italy they teach their children to love its Garibaldi. In America, humanity's refuge and freedom's hope and home, teach, oh, teach your children to love, ever love, its Washington the Securer, and Lincoln the Conservator, of a Nation united, prosperous and free.

> " Then heart to heart
> And hand to hand
> Bound together let us stand;
> Storms are gathering
>   O'er the land,
>   Many friends are gone.
> Still we never are alone,
> Still the battle must be won,
> Still we bravely march right on—
>   Right on—right on !"

Mr. Affleck's address was neither the first nor the last, and when the benediction was pronounced, the universal verdict was that the first effort to hold memorial services on the anniversary of the death of President Lincoln, was a most gratifying success.

The second memorial service was held at the same place and hour on the morning of April 15, 1881, President Dana of the Lincoln Guard of Honor again acting as master of ceremonies. It consisted of prayer by Rev. F. D. Rickerson of the Central Baptist Church; singing by the Young Men's Christian Association chorus; address by Rev. J. M. Sturtevant, D. D., ex-President of Illinois College; introductory address and reading of Lincoln's Gettysburg speech by Rev. T. A. Parker, of the First M. E. Church, Springfield; address by Gen. H. H. Thomas, Speaker of the Illinois House of Representatives, then in session; address and reading by Clinton L. Conkling, a member of the Lincoln Guard of Honor; address by Rev. W. B. Affleck, who had participated in similar services the year before at the same place. The services closed by singing, "The Roll Call on High," and prayer and benediction by Rev. Roswell O. Post, pastor of the Congregational Church, Springfield.

The exercises were exceedingly interesting in every part, but the address of the venerable Doctor Sturtevant was a résumé of a life-long acquaintance with his suject, and was studded with the richest gems of thought and oratory from beginning to end. No mere extracts could do it justice. The Guard of Honor hold it in reserve, expecting to publish it on some future occasion. Excepting that the weather was so cold and cloudy, the second memorial service was equally successful with the first, and the Lincoln Guard of Honor received words of commendation and encourgement on all sides.

The third memorial service was held at the monument, at half-past two o'clock, on the afternoon of April 15, 1882. The hour was thus changed in order to have the benefit of the warmer afternoon, for all our services have been held in the open air—and for the greater convenience of the people. President Dana, of the Lincoln Guard of Honor, for the third time conducting the services. The members of the Guard on all public occasions are distinguished by a neat badge worn on the left lapel. The services consisted of prayer by Rev. D. S. Johnson, D. D., of the Second Presbytern Church, Springfield; singing by the Double Quartette, Mr. George A. Sanders, Conductor, Miss Julia E. Holcomb, Mrs. W. L. Barlow, Miss Lulu Hibbs, Mrs. James F. McNeill, Mr. H. F. Velde, Mr. Fred Wilms, Mr. Harry M. Snape; Miss Minnie Goodwin, Organist; address by Shelby M. Cullom, Governor of the State of Illinois; reading reminiscences, extracts from a temperance address by Lincoln, an eulogy on him by an ex-Confederate soldier, by J. C. Power; singing; address by Hon. James A. Connolly, United States District Attorney; recitation by Mrs. Edward S. Johnson; singing, "America;" and prayer and benediction, by Rev. W. S. Matthew, of the Second Methodist Church.

26

Governor Cullom has been one of the speakers at each of the three memorial services, and the last with him is always the best. Mr. Connolly's address was patriotic, eloquent, and clothed in the most beautiful and polished language. It was listened to with the closest attention from the beginning to its close.

The Lincoln Guard of Honor keeps a carefully prepared copy of every utterance at these memorial services, and expects in time to publish them.

"Desiring to extend these services throughout the land, and to secure the coöperation of all patriotic citizens in its most laudable undertakings, this organization, regarding itself merely as a *standing committee* of the people, has provided for the admission of honorary members, and has procured finely engraved certificates of such membership. These certificates are printed upon fine paper, about fourteen by seventeen inches, and contain a medallion portrait of Abraham Lincoln, and correct views of his former residence in Springfield, and of the Monument beneath which lie his remains. Any person, upon the payment of five dollars or upwards, can become an honorary member, and receive one of these certificates, showing the name of the donor and the amount of his gift; which certificate will be signed by the officers of the organization, under its corporate seal. The Lincoln Guard of Honor, therefore, appeals to all who are in sympathy with its purposes, to assist in their accomplishment by enrolling themselves as honorary members, and lending their influence to the attainment of its plans. Neither personal nor mercenary interests are to be subserved, but the only object is to commemorate, in a fitting manner, the example and virtues of the immortal Lincoln."

The author being the Secretary of the organization and Custodian of the monument, takes the liberty to insert here his readings of the reminiscences, as part of the memorial service April 15, 1882. That part in brackets was not read:

LADIES AND GENTLEMEN:—The Lincoln Guard of Honor regard themselves merely as a standing committee to arrange for and conduct these Memorial Services. We are not a band of orators, but we propose to press into our service the best talent and patriotism we can find, that we may properly observe what we regard an important occasion. At the same time, however, we think it best that some one of our number should take part in the exercises of the hour, and the lot this time falls to me.

On the morning of March 6, 1879, a company of ladies, composing a committee of the Woman's Christian Temperance Union, under the leadership of the President of the Union, Miss Frances E. Willard, visited the National Lincoln Monument, and held a prayer-meeting on the Terrace, under the shadow of the statue of Lincoln.

As many of them had never visited the Monument before, I, at the close of the meeting, invited all into Memorial Hall. In explaining to them the circumstances under which the bust of Mr. Lincoln was taken, I showed them a cast of his right hand, and in giving an account of the manner in which Mr. Volk, the artist, obtained it, incidentally remarked that it was a cast of the hand that afterwards untied the hardest knot we ever had in this country, alluding, of course, to the writing of the Emancipation Proclamation. After a momentary silence, seemingly to divine my meaning, one of the ladies said: 'We understand you; slavery was a very hard knot, but it was only local. Whisky is a much worse one, for it is everywhere, no family is safe, we are trying to untie that." This impressed me as putting the question with great force. The ladies went from Memorial Hall direct to the State Capitol, and presented to the Legislature of Illinois, their great petition, supported by a hundred thousand names, asking for Home Protection, by giving the ballot to women, where the manufacture and sale of intoxicating drinks is the question. In view of later developments, their action in coming to Lincoln's tomb to pray for the success of the cause of temperance, was more appropriate than they at the time knew.

The full copy of an address on Temperance, delivered by Abraham Lincoln, in Springfield, Illinois, February twenty-second, eighteen hundred and forty-two, under the auspices of the Springfield Washingtonian Temperance Society, has recently been brought to light. Previous to that time he had served three terms in the lower house of the Legislature of Illinois. During those terms, he was remarkable for speaking little and listening much. If newspaper reporters had been as numerous then as they are now, there is little doubt that many wise sayings of Mr. Lincoln would have been preserved, that are now forever lost. I have not examined the subject myself, but a friend who has, informs me that this is the first speech by him that was ever printed. It appeared March 26, 1842, in the *Sangamo Journal*, of which the present *Illinois State Journal* is the successor.

At the time this address was delivered, prohibition of the manufacture and sale of intoxicating drinks, by legal enactment, was never mentioned, and perhaps, never thought of. Moral suasion was the only means by which the Washingtonians expected to achieve victory. All of Mr. Lincoln's arguments were based upon these principles. The wonderful faculty and spirit of fairness he always manifested, in first arguing every case from the standpoint of his opponent, was fully developed in this address. He first looked at the subject as seen by the manufacturer, the dram-seller and the dram-drinker. He drew parallels between the movement by the American colonies for political freedom which achieved its first great victory in 1776, and the Washingtonian Temperance movement, then in its infancy, battling for moral freedom. With a prophetic eye, he looked forward to the time when there would neither be a slave nor a drunkard on the earth; and of the proud position our own land would occupy as the birthplace and cradle of both revolutions. It may reasonably be presumed that Mr. Lincoln did not expect to live to see the consummation of either; but he did live to strike the death blow of one of these gigantic evils, thus writing his name so high upon the scroll of fame that it will never be effaced while time endures. Let us hope that the man or woman—for it ought to die by the hand of her who has suffered most by it—is now living who will strike the death blow to the other great enemy of mankind.

Talk about slavery and polygamy as the twin relics of barbarism! They were, and are circumscribed in their limits. Intemperance has no limits, and consequently towers high above them both ; no, it does not reach in that direction—but sinks so deep below as to fill, if it were possible, the bottomless pit with the souls of its victims. I will now present Mr. Lincoln's views on the then pending temperance revolution in his own words:

["But if it be true, as I have insisted, that those who have suffered by intemperance personally, and have reformed, are the most powerful and efficient instruments to push the reformation to ultimate success, it does not follow that those who have not suffered have no part left them to perform. Whether or not the world would be vastly benefitted by a total and final banishment from it of all intoxicating drinks, seems to me not now an open question. Three-fourths of mankind confess the affirmative with their tongues, and, I believe, all the rest acknowledge it in their hearts. ' Ought any, then, to refuse their aid in doing what the good of the whole demands? Shall he who can not do much, be for that reason excused if he do nothing? But, says one, what good can I do by signing the pledge? I never drink, even without signing. This question has been asked and answered more than a million times. Let it be answered once more. For the man suddenly, or in any other way, to break off from the use of drams, who has indulged in them for a long course of years, and until his appetite for them has grown ten or a hundred fold stronger, and more craving than any natural appetite can be, requires a most powerful moral effort. In such an undertaking he needs every moral support and influence that can possibly be brought to his aid and thrown around him. And not only so, but every moral prop should be taken from whatever argument might rise in his mind to lure him to his backsliding. When he casts his eyes around him, he should be able to see all that he respects, all that he admires, all that he loves, kindly and anxiously pointing him onward, and none beckoning him back to his former miserable wallowing in the mire.

"But it is said by some that men will think and act for themselves; that none will disuse spirits or anything else because his neighbors do; and that moral influence is not that powerful engine contended for. Let us examine this. Let me ask the man who could maintain this position most stiffly, what compensation he would accept to go to Church some Sunday and sit during the sermon with his wife's bonnet upon his head? Not a trifle, I'll venture. And why not? There would be nothing irreligious in it, nothing immoral, nothing uncomfortable—then why not? Is it not because there would be something egregiously unfashionable in it? Then it is the influence of fashion; and what is the influence of fashion but the influence that other people's actions have on our own actions—the strong inclination each ·of us feels to do as we see all our neighbors do? Nor is the influence of fashion confined to any particular thing or class of things. It is just as strong on one subject as another. Let us make it as unfashionable to withhold our names from the temperance pledge, as for husbands to wear their wives' bonnets to Church, and instances will be just as rare in the one case as the other. But, say some, we are no drunkards and we shall not acknowledge ourselves such by joining a reformed drunkards society, whatever our influence might be.

"Surely, no Christian will adhere to this objection. If they believe, as they profess, that Omnipotence condescended to take on himself the form of sinful man, and as such, to die an ignominious death for their sakes, surely they will not refuse submission to the infinitely lesser condescension for the the temporal, and perhaps eternal, salvation of a large, erring and unfortunate class of their fellow creatures. Nor is the condescension very great. In my judgment, such of us as have never fallen victims, have been spared more from the absence of appetite than from any mental or moral superiority over those who have. Indeed, I believe, if we take the habitual drunkards as a class, their heads and their hearts will bear an advantageous comparison with those of any other class. There seems ever to have been a proneness in the brilliant, and warm-blooded, to fall into the vice,—the demon of intemperance ever seems to have delighted in sucking the blood of genius and of generosity. What one of us but can call to mind some relative, more promising in youth than all his fellows, who has fallen a sacrifice to his rapacity? He ever seems to have gone forth like the Egyptian angel of death, commissioned to slay, if not the first, the fairest born of every family. Shall he now be arrested in his desolating career? In that arrest, all can give aid that will; and who shall be excused that can, and will not? Far around as human breath has ever blown, he keeps our fathers, our brothers, our sons, and our friends prostrate in the chains of moral death. To all the living, everywhere, we cry: Come, sound the moral trump, that these may rise and stand up an exceeding great army. Come from the four winds, O breath! and breathe upon these slain, that they may live."]

"If the relative grandeur of revolutions shall be estimated by the great amount of human misery they alleviate, and the small amount they inflict, then, indeed, will this be the grandest the world shall ever have seen. Of our political revolution of 1776, we are all justly proud. It has given us a degree of political freedom far exceeding that of any other nation of the earth. In it the world has found a solution of the long mooted problem as to the capability of man to govern himself. In it was the germ which has vegetated, and still is to grow and expand into the universal liberty of mankind. But with all these glorious results, past, present, and to come, it had its evils, too. It breathed forth famine, swam in blood, and rode in fire; and long, long after, the orphan's cry, and the widow's wail continued to break the sad silence that ensued. These were the price, the inevitable price, paid for the blessings it bought.

"Turn, now, to the temperance revolution. In it we shall find a stronger bondage broken, a viler slavery manumitted, a greater tyrant deposed. In it more of want supplied, more disease healed, more sorrow assuaged. By it no orphans starving, none injured in interest; even the dram-maker and dram-seller will have glided into other occupations so gradually, as never to have felt the change, and will stand ready to join all others in the universal song of gladness. And what a noble ally is this to the cause of political freedom. With such an aid, its march cannot fail to be on and on, till every son of earth shall drink in rich fruition the sorrow-quenching draughts of perfect liberty. Happy day, when, all appetites controlled, all passions subdued, all matter subjected; mind, all-conquering mind, shall live and move, the monarch of the world. Glorious consummation! Hail, fall of fury! Reign of reason, all hail!"

Mr. Lincoln did not make any allusion to the day they were observing, except in the closing paragraph:

"This is the one hundred and tenth anniversary of the birthday of Washington. We are met to celebrate this day. Washington is the mightiest name of earth—long since mightiest in the cause of civil liberty, still mightiest in moral reformation. On that name a eulogy is expected. It cannot be. To add brightness to the sun, or glory to the name of Washington, is alike impossible. Let none attempt it. In solemn awe pronounce the name, and in its naked, deathless splendor, leave it shining on."

In the subject eulogized, the words spoken, and the reverential bearing of the orator, in which he was too modest to call his utterances by their proper title, this eulogy is unique. Could Lincoln have looked down through the dark clouds, the surging billows, and the lights and shades of almost forty years, he might have heard,—which I almost think he did.—at his own tomb, words of equal grandeur, from a source apparently as humble, and far more surprising, when we consider the relation of the parties to each other.

About two years ago, just as I was dismissing a party of visitors from the door of the Catacomb, a very plain, modest looking man of middle age, approached and said he had come to see and learn all he could about the Monument and Lincoln. I proceeded in my usual way, when visitors are much interested, and completed my explanations on the Terrace, in front of the statue of the President. From the general bearing of the visitor, I should have taken him for a son of an original New England Abolitionist. When I left off speaking, he remained, and seemed reluctant to take his eyes from the statue. After several minutes spent in silent meditation, he astonished me by saying substantially:

"I was a soldier in the Confederate army, and spent four years doing my utmost to defeat all that Abraham Lincoln was trying to accomplish. He succeeded, and I have no regrets on that account."

The visitor then assumed a tragic attitude, and raising his right hand towards the statue, said, with deliberation and emphasis:

"He was an infinitely greater man than George Washington ever was."

With his eyes still fixed on the statue, and as though his whole soul was in his words, he continued:

"Washington had no difficulty in determining who were his friends and who were not. His enemies were principally on the water, on the other side of it, or officers and soldiers sent here to enforce the mandates of a tyrant. His friends were his neighbors, who, in addition to their struggles for existence in a new country, were oppressed by taxation without representation. The line was clearly drawn from the beginning.

"With Lincoln it was different. His enemies were in every department of the government. They filled the civil offices; they commanded his skeleton of an army; they trod the decks of his ships, such as they were. Where they could with immunity be open, they were bold and outspoken; where it was policy they were more wily, complaisant and cautious. It required two years, or half his first term, to learn who were friends and who were enemies; but he was equal to the emergency. And through it all a little child could approach him with perfect confidence; but the most wily statesman could not swerve him a hair's breadth from what he believed to be right!"

The Presbyterian church is governed by four judicatories or church courts: the Session, the Presbytery, the Synod, and the General Assembly. It is strictly a representative government, in which the majority rules. Some of the leading minds, in achieving our independence, both as soldiers and statesmen, are known to have been members of, and officers in, the Presbyterian church. It is claimed, with a reasonable probability of its truthfulness, that it served, to a considerable extent, as a model to the framers of our own National government.

During our Revolutionary period, but three of those courts existed in the colonies. The highest was styled the Synod of New York and Philadelphia. That Synod was divided into four Synods, and the Presbyteries composing those four Synods, in 1789, organized the General Assembly of the Presbyterian Church in the United States of America. Notwithstanding the divisions and re-unions that have taken place, the great body of Presbyterians in the United States, who are the descendants and successors of those represented in the first General Assembly, compose the Presbyterian church represented in the ninety-fourth General Assembly of the Presbyterian church in the United States of America, which convened in Springfield, Ill., in May, 1882.

Before the General Assembly settled down to work it became evident that the commissioners and others in attendance would visit the Lincoln Monument in such numbers as to render it impossible for all to register their names there. In order to obviate this difficulty, blanks were prepared, of uniform size with the pages of the register, so that by removing an equal number of sheets they will be inserted and form part of the register. Columns were prepared with suitable headings for the name, postoffice, and State of each commissioner, whether a minister or ruling elder, and the Presbytery he represents. These blanks were placed on the desk of the clerk of the General Assembly, and attention called to them by the Moderator. The names of nearly all the commissioners are enrolled. A beautifully printed title page reads:

"Autograph roll of the Commissioners composing the General Assembly of the Presbyterian Church, in the United States of America, to be deposited in Memorial Hall, National Lincoln Monument, as a memento of their ninety-fourth annual session, held in the city which was once the home of our martyred President, Abraham Lincoln. Convened, May 18, 1882; adjourned, May 29, 1882. Springfield, Illinois."

The next page reads:

Rev. Herrick Johnson, D. D., Moderator of the Presbyterian General Assembly, now in annual session:

DEAR SIR: This is done with the approval of the Executive Committee of the National Lincoln Monument Association, consisting of Hon. John T. Stuart, Col. John Williams and Hon. James C. Conkling.

As much would be done in connection with any other church court of national extent, should it assemble in Springfield, but this being a Presbyterian affair, the writer takes the liberty, without their knowledge, of saying who the members of the Executive Committee are:

Mr. Stuart was the preceptor, and afterwards the law partner, of Abraham Lincoln. He is the son of a Presbyterian minister, and is a regular attendant of the First Presbyterian Church, where Mr. Lincoln worshipped.

Mr. Williams is a member of the same church.

Mr. Conkling is a ruling elder in the Second Presbyterian Church of Springfield.

It may not be out of place to mention in this connection, as a coincidence, that your humble servant has served more than twenty years as a ruling elder in the Presbyterian church.

J. C. POWER, Custodian.

MEMORIAL HALL, NATIONAL LINCOLN MONUMENT,
SPRINGFIELD, ILLINOIS, MAY 24, 1882.

Upon the invitation of the Executive Committee, the members of the General Assembly visited the Monument on the afternoon of Saturday, May 27th, and were welcomed by the Hon. James C. Conkling, in the following well chosen words:

"The Lincoln Monument Association have thought it due to the patriotic attitude which has heretofore been assumed by the General Assembly of the Presbyterian Church of the United States of America, that they should be invited while here in the city of Springfield, to visit the tomb of our martyred President, Abraham

Lincoln, and they have, therefore, extended an invitation to you to be here on this occasion, in order that we may listen to some of those same patriotic utterances to, which many of us have heretofore listened during the darkest period of our country's peril. And to this end, we have invited some of your number to make a few remarks on this occasion, and I therefore now introduce Dr. Herrick Johnson," who spoke as follows:

"Gathered here to-day at the tomb of our first martyr President, it befits the place and the hour that we recall his death, catch, if possible, his inner spirit, and enter anew into the meaning of his sacrifice. We did well to rear this cenotaph* to his memory, and to weave amaranths for the brow of the beloved dead. Forevermore sacred will be this Monument that entombs him. * * * * But what of the dead to the living? We shall build better than monumental marble to his memory, if we build the meaning of his spirit and the meaning of his martyrdom into our hearts and lives. Let us emphasize, for one thing, a central truth of our holy religion that it is only by a crucified Redeemer salvation cometh. Apostles are stoned, prophets are sawn asunder—

> "Knowledge by suffering entereth,
> And life is perfected by death.'

"In looking over the field of strife, it seems as if men planted each new truth with blood, and shed much to set some truths. But in the end truth is set in hearts and homes, societies and States, and the fruitage is glorious. Is it too much to say that the plant of universal emancipation in all this land for the negro, was worth even the blood of Lincoln? Is it too much to say that even through that baptism of suffering and sorrow, which culminated in his death, the spirit of glory and of God nestled down upon this Nation, and we were left the richer for the baptism? Let us thank God to-day, that though

> 'Careless seems the Great Avenger,
> And history's pages but record
> One death grapple in the darkness,
> 'Twixt old systems and the Word;
> Truth forever on the scaffold,
> Wrong forever on the throne,—
> Yet that scaffold sways the future;
> And behind the dim unknown
> Standeth God within the shadow,
> Keeping watch above His own.'

"Here in this hallowed spot let us make room in our hearts for a larger and sweeter charity. Abraham Lincoln's heart was full of it. When the spirit of hate and passion murdered him, it murdered mercy. The calm, patient, often weary, but ever kindly and

---

*The use of this word would imply that he had been led, erroneously, to believe that the body was not in the Monument.

gentle soul, how he did plead with his wayward countrymen!
What gentleness was in all his speeches! With what brooding
tenderness did he watch over his great trust! His tears were bot-
tled, his prayers were registered, his love has conquered, his prophetic vision must have caught the glory of this glad hour, as he
said, 'The mystic chords of memory, stretching from every battle-
field and patriot grave to every living heart and hearthstone, all
over this broad land, will yet swell the chorus of the Union, when
again touched, as surely they will be, by the better angels of our
nature.' The hands of those better angels, hidden from mortal
eyes, have struck the last chorus. We listen here in the hush of
this holy hour, to the music of their vibration, and, blessed be God,
our dear dissevered, and so long alienated, Presbyterian church
takes step with the country to the music that finds its heavenly
expression and inspiration in the thirteenth chapter of first Cor-
rinthians. Let us go from this tomb praying to be bathed more
and more in the spirit of Christ's love and sacrifice, and to be
moulded more and more into the image of his divine passion."

Some of the colored commissioners and others were
prepared to speak, but the approaching rainstorm prevented carrying out the programme. There was a few
words by Governor Cullom, a prayer by Rev. Dr. Hat-
field, the singing of the doxology, and the benediction
by Rev. W. H. Roberts, all of which I omit, and give
only the brief address of Rev. E. P. Humphrey, D. D.,
of Louisville, Kentucky:

"I know of no reason why I should be expected to speak, except
the fact that I represent, in our General Assembly, the region in
which Mr. Lincoln was born. The Presbytery I represent covers the
region in which is the little town, near which Mr. Lincoln began life
in the world. 'Except a corn of wheat fall into the ground it abideth
alone, but if it die it bringeth forth much fruit.' And it will, perhaps, occur in the course of years, or of ages, as they revolve, that
the death of this man, under the circumstances, has been of advantage to the world, stimulating people, who love liberty, to sacrifice
themselves, if necessary, upon its altar, and inducing them to
declare that this government shall be preserved as a government
of the people, from the people, and for the people. If this man had
survived to this time, and had come out of his primitive dwelling
into the city now, he would have found here representatives of a
people who are governed, substantially, by the same great rules
which prevailed in the constitution of our country. There is, as
you know, such a resemblance between the constitution and the
government of this church and the constitution and government of
the country, that it would seem the one was specially indebted to
the other,—though not from the people, but from Christ, it is of the
people and for the people.

Now, let me suggest, also, that it becomes us as citizens of this country likewise,—because we are not only subjects of the church of Christ, ministers and working elders, but citizens,—to cherish the memory of this man in the work before us, and see to it that the great principles of liberty and philanthropy, for which he lived and died, are made permanent and eternal. I cannot continue these remarks, as I observe the rain is beginning to fall, but we are willing, even in the rain, to meditate a moment on these things. Astronomers tell us that from the most distant star in our system, light would require hundreds of years to travel to our earth. If, now, one of these stars should be blotted out, the light from it would still be coming down, long after the star had disappeared. So the light of this man's example shines upon the world, and will continue to shine, and shine upon the whole land and the whole earth, for ages and ages after his death—after even this Monument shall, in the course of years, decay and crumble, the example of that man and the light that flows from his example, will be perpetually falling upon the world. I feel as if my heart and mind, and body were full of the electric fire of liberty, and I seem a stronger, and I hope a better, man for having stood in this place, and for having communed with a heart and thought so pure, so simple and yet so grand,—so near and natural, he seems yours and mine as we stand here together upon this sacred spot."

DEATH OF MRS. LINCOLN.

After this volume was printed and the sheets placed in the hands of the binder, the people were startled by the announcement that Mrs. Mary Todd Lincoln, widow of Abraham Lincoln, late President of the United States of America, died at a quarter past eight o'clock, on Sunday evening, July 16, 1882. She died at the residence of her sister, Mrs. Ninian W. Edwards, the same house in which she was married November 2, 1842. Death to her was a merciful release after more than seventeen years of mental and physical torture. There seemed to be a spontaneous desire manifested on the part of the citizens of Springfield to do honor to her remains. Citizens' meetings were held for the purpose of making suitable preparations which resulted in the most elaborate and artistic floral tributes, both at the church and the Monument. Funeral services were held on Wednesday, the 19th, in the First Presbyterian church of Springfield, the same with which she united on profession of faith, April 13, 1852. A brief discourse, displaying rare good taste, was preached by the pastor, Rev. James A. Reed, D. D. The sermon was based upon the fourteenth verse of the fourteenth chapter of Second Samuel:

"For we must needs die, and are as water spilt on the ground, which cannot be gathered up again; neither doth God respect any person, yet doth He devise means that His banished be not expelled from Him."

"These admonitory words fell from the lips of a princely woman, pleading the common mortality to gain a merciful end with a princely man. They have their fitting repetition now, in the solemnities of this hour, when all that remains of the wife of a princely man lies before us. A poor, desolate, heart-broken woman, whose sorrows have been too great for utterance even, has at last yielded to the withering hand of death, and entered upon that 'silent bourne whence no traveller returns.' This is only the climax of a shock of years ago. Death's doings have only now ripened into maturity.

"When among the Alleghaney mountains last summer, I saw two tall and stately pines standing on a rocky ledge, where they, had grown so closely together as to be virtually united at the base

their interlocking roots entering the same rock cavities, and pene-
trating the same soil.   There they had stood for years with inter-
twining branches and interlocking roots, braving in noble fellowship the mountain storms.   But the taller of the two had, years
before, been struck by a flash of lightning, that had gone to its
very roots, shattering it from top to bottom, and leaving it scarred
and dead.   The other, apparently uninjured, had survived for some
years, but it was evident from the appearance of its leaves that it,
too, was now quite dead.   It had lingered in fellowship with its dead
companion, but the shock was too much for it.   In their sympathetic
fellowship and union, both trees had suffered from the same calamity.   They had virtually both been killed at the same time.   With
the one that lingered, it was only slow death from the same cause.
So it seems to me to-day, that we are only at death placing his
seal upon the lingering victim of a past calamity.

"Years ago, Abraham Lincoln placed a ring on the finger of
Mary Todd, inscribed with these words: 'Love is Eternal.'   Like
two stately trees they grew up among us in the nobler, sweeter
fellowship of wedded life.   They twain became one flesh.   Here
they planted their home, and in domestic bliss their olive
plants grew up around them.   Here they were known and honored
and loved by an appreciative and admiring community, and when
perilous times came, and the Nation looked forth among the people
for a steady hand to guide the ship of State, its heart went out
after this tall and stately man that walked like a prince among us.
He was their choice, and ascending to the chief place in the Nation's
gift, he stood, like some tall cedar, amid the storm of National
strife, and with a heroism, and a wisdom, and a lofty prudence in
his administration, that won the wonder and respect of the world,
he guided the Nation through its peril, back again to peace.   But
when at the height of his fame, when a grateful people were laud-
ing him with just acknowledgment of his great services to the
country, and when he was wearily trying to escape from their
very adulation, into the restful presence and company of his life
partner, to be alone awhile in the hour of his triumphant joy, like
lightning, the flash of a cruel and cowardly enemy's wrath struck
him down by her side.   The voice that cheered a Nation in its
darkest hour is hushed.   The beauty of Israel is slain upon the
high places.   The Nation, in its grief and consternation, is driven
almost to madness.   Strong men know not hardly how to assuage
their sorrow, or control themselves under it.   And when the Nation
so felt the shock, what must it have been to the poor woman that
stood by his side, who was the sharer of his joys, the partner of
his sorrows, whose heart strings were wound about his great heart
in that seal of eternal love.   What wonder, if the shock of that
sad hour, that made a nation reel, should leave a tender, loving
woman, shattered in body and mind, to walk softly all her days.
It is no reflection upon either the strength of her mind or the
tenderness of her heart, to say that when Abraham Lincoln died,
she died."

During all those seventeen years of living death, Mrs. Lincoln bore her burden almost alone, for she was not understood by her real friends, and the tongue of the slanderer never tired. It is more to be dreaded than pestilence, famine and the sword. Even after she was dead, some newspapers claiming respectability repeated statements known to have been slanderous in the extreme. Certain low and groveling natures have used every means to drag her and the memory of her martyred husband down to their level. St. James states the case clearly, when he says:

"The tongue is a fire, a world of iniquity; so is the tongue among our members, that it defileth the whole body, and setteth on fire the course of nature; and is set on fire of hell. For every kind of beasts, and of birds, and of serpents, and of things in the sea, is tamed and hath been tamed of mankind: But the tongue can no man tame; it is an unruly evil full of deadly poison."

A recent editorial in a religious paper, speaks of the case of a man who had been convicted of a foul crime, and sent to the penitentiary for twenty years, and who after four years' service, the loss of his property and a lucrative professional business, was proven, beyond a doubt, to have been convicted by perjured witnesses, and therefore innocent. Another, sentenced to the penitentiary for life, for murder, was proven to be innocent through the death-bed confession of the principal witness, that he had committed perjury. The editorial closes thus:

"Innocence is not the defense that it is generally supposed to be. The pure and innocent do fall every day before the tongue of malice, and they fall irretrievably, so far as this world is concerned. Fair fame is often assassinated with impunity.' Men and women, pure and upright, walk our streets, wearing the striped garb, and the ball and chain of ruined reputations."

Would there be a tithe of the business for our law courts if every witness told "the truth, the whole truth, and nothing but the truth?" The writer knows of a case where ten witnesses were all eager to swear falsely, and three of them did perjure themselves— the others being ruled out—and the whole amount involved was only five dollars.

How much better would it be, could all men and women be induced to act upon St. Paul's summing up of the attributes of charity or love.—*new version:*

"Love suffereth long and is kind; love envieth not; love vaunteth not itself, is not puffed up, doth not behave itself unseemly, seeketh not its own, is not provoked, taketh not account of evil; rejoiceth not in unrighteousness, but rejoiceth with the truth. * * * But now abideth faith, hope, love, these three; and the greatest of these is love."

. In the spirit of the latter speaks the wounded soldier. He says:

"At the first battle of Fredricksburg, I received a painful wound in the face; the bullet splintered the jaw and knocked out half a dozen teeth. I was taken to the Armory Square Hospital, of Washington. Among the many who came to the hospital to speak cheering words to the afflicted, none were more kind, or showed a nobler spirit, than the wife of the Chief Magistrate of the Nation. She called regularly, bringing with her, by attendants, flowers and delicacies, and bestowing them with her own hand, with a grace worthy the station she held. The cycle of time is ended with her. She is at rest with her sorrow. But though dead, she still lives in the memory of those whose agony she soothed with loving words."

In the same spirit wrote Mrs. Lincoln herself, in a letter before me, from Pau, France, in 1878, to a friend in this city. She had heard that her son, Robert T. Lincoln, was in failing health, and with the most tender and motherly solicitude, begged to be informed of the true state of the case. She spoke of herself as the most suffering and broken-hearted woman on earth, and prayed our Heavenly Father to bring no more sorrow upon her. She says: "This is a sunny, beautiful land, but it is not America. Wander where we . will, *our own flag* is always the dearest to us." Only the Thursday before her death, she conversed freely with a lady friend, of the habitual kindness and tender care of her departed husband, in times of affliction and sore trials. Her words were accompanied by a flow of tears through which she looked with joyful anticipation of meeting him to part no more. On the fatal night of April 15, 1865, when they were discussing plans for their future recreation, the bullet of the assassin cut short his last sentence: "There is no city I desire so much to see as Jerusalem." Have we not reason to hope that they may now together walk the golden streets of the new Jerusalem.

SECOND APPENDIX.

Fall and Reconstruction of Part of the Terrace.

On the morning of February 5, 1884, the Custodian came to the Monument earlier than he had done for several weeks, because there was a State organization called " Mutual Aid," to convene in the capitol that day, and he knew, from experience, that at such times the delegates visited the Monument earlier than visitors usually do. The sun had not risen, and there was barely sufficient light for him to see the lines in the register, and he was writing the heading for the day, when he heard a tremendous crash. Hastily lighting a lamp, he went through the back door of Memorial Hall, and found that a brick arch seventy feet long, spanning the five and a half feet space between the outer wall on the east side and the next one to it on the inside, had fallen, except about ten feet at each end, leaving the heavy flag-stones that formed the terrace without any visible support at the outer wall. A child walking on it would have taken all down, and yet it did not move. Fearing that visitors would come and get on it before supports could be put under, he hastened to carry lumber and used the pieces for barriers to keep any person from going on the weak place. He had labored with all his strength for about three-quarters of an hour, when a car on the Citizens' Street Railway landed twelve or thirteen of the expected delegates at the Monument. The Custodian is fully convinced that if he had been three minutes later getting to the Monument he would not have heard the crash, and would have led those men exactly on that weak spot, and they would all have gone down with him into a chasm fifty feet long, five and a half feet wide and twenty feet deep, where they would have been crushed and mangled together by those great flag-stones.

The stone covering was removed from one-half the terrace, the east side and the north end, during the summer of 1884, and it was re-constructed on iron beams and covered with copper at a total cost of about $8,400.

RECAPITULATION OF THE HISTORY AND REORGANIZATION OF THE NATIONAL LINCOLN MONUMENT ASSOCIATION, OUT OF THE OLD AND INTO THE NEW.

April 24, 1865, preliminary steps were taken to form an Association, which led to the organization, May 11, 1865, in the city of Springfield, Illinois, of the National Lincoln Monument Association. It was done under a law of the State of Illinois, entitled "An Act for the incorporation of Benevolent, Educational, Literary, Musical, Scientific and Missionary Societies, including societies formed for Mutual Improvement or for the promotion of Arts," and was approved February 24, 1859. All corporations under that law were limited to twenty years, without any provision for extending the time of their existence. The National Lincoln Monument Association was composed of fifteen members, and accomplished its declared purpose in building a Monument a the city of Springfield to the memory of Abraham Lincoln, late President of the United States. The Association provided for holding annual elections of officers, and although it filled vacancies, it never held more than one general election, and that was at the organization. The officers were elected for one year, or until their successors where chosen and qualified. Under the latter clause the same president, secretary and treasurer held their offices during the entire twenty years of the existance of the Association. The Association would have expired by limitation May 11, 1885, without any provision for taking care of the

Monument it had erected. Meantime the law under which it was organized had been repealed in connection with the enactment of another law on the same subject, with enlarged powers and duties.

Friday, May 1, 1885, pursuant to a call of the president, a meeting of the National Lincoln Monument Association was held in the city of Springfield, its main object being to take measures for reorganizing and continuing the Association. There were present, Gov. R. J. Oglesby, President; O. M. Hatch, Secretary; John T. Stuart. John Williams and James C. Conkling, Executive Committee; S. H. Treat, Jacob Bunn, Milton Hay, and John M. Palmer.

After the transaction of some financial business, and overlooking the fact that the two vacancies caused by the death of O H. Miner and D. L. Phillips had never been filled, the Association took notice of another fact or facts, that by the removal of Hon. Newton Bateman to Galesburg, and Hon. James H. Beveridge to Freeland, both in the State of Illinois, and Judge Charles S. Zane to Salt Lake City, Utah Territory, there were three vacant seats. On motion of Judge Treat, John W. Bunn, Lincoln Dubois and George N. Black were appointed to fill the vacancies thus made.

Mr. Hay offered the following resolutions, which were adopted:

Resolved, That in view of the fact that this corporation will expire by limitation on the 11th day of May. A. D. 1885, it is deemed necessary and expedient to take steps to promote and further the organization of a new corporation, to maintain, continue and preserve the Monument, constructed by this Association, and that when such corporation shall be formed, it is further

Resolved, That the president of this Association, and secretary, under the seal of the corporation, by proper conveyance or assignment, transfer to such new corporation the Monument, Monumen, grounds, and all other property, effects, money or choses in action belonging to this Association; and further,

Resolved, That the name of such new organization or corporation shall be the Lincoln Monument Association.

The following instrument of writing was then submitted in open meeting:

We, the undersigned, all being of full age, and citizens of the United States, and of the State of Illinois, certify that we do hereby associate ourselves under and by virtue of that part of an act of the General Assembly of the State of Illinois entitled, "*An Act Concerning Corporations*," approved April 18, 1872, and in force July 1, 1872, which refers to societies, corporations and associations not for pecuniary profit, by the following name, and for the purpose herein specified.

ARTICLE I.

This Association shall be called "The Lincoln Monument Association," and shall be located at Springfield, Illinois.

ARTICLE II.

The object of this Association shall be to preserve, repair and take all proper and necessary means to continue in existence the Monument heretofore constructed to the memory of Abraham Lincoln, and located at Oak Ridge Cemetery, near Springfield, county of Sangamon, and State of Illinois, as the successors to the "National Lincoln Monument Association."

ARTICLE III.

This Association shall consist of thirteen trustees, and the following persons shall be directors of said Association during the first year of its existence: Richard J. Oglesby, S. H. Treat, John T. Stuart, John Williams, James C. Conkling, John M. Palmer, Jacob Bunn, Ozias M. Hatch, Milton Hay, Shelby M. Cullom, George N. Black, Lincoln Dubois and John W. Bunn.

In testimony whereof, we have hereunto set our hands and seals this first day of May, 1885.

RICHARD J. OGLESBY,	[L. S.]
S. H. TREAT,	[L. S.]
JOHN T. STUART,	[L. S.]
JOHN WILLIAMS,	[L. S.]
JAMES C. CONKLING,	[L. S.]
JOHN M. PALMER,	[L. S.]
JACOB BUNN,	[L. S.]
OZIAS M. HATCH,	[L. S.]
MILTON HAY,	[L. S.]
SHELBY M. CULLOM,	[L. S.]
GEORGE N. BLACK,	[L. S.]
LINCOLN DUBOIS,	[L. S.]
JOHN W. BUNN,	[L. S.]

STATE OF ILLINOIS,   } ss.
SANGAMON COUNTY.   }

I, Clinton L. Conkling, a notary public in and for said county, in the State aforesaid, do hereby certify that Richerd J. Oglesby, S. H. Treat, John T. Stuart, John Williams, James C. Conkling, John M. Palmer, Jacob Bunn, Ozias M. Hatch, Milton Hay, Shelby M. Cullum, George N. Black, Lincoln Dubois and John W. Bunn, personally known to me to be the same persons whose names are subscribed to the foregoing instrument, appeared before me this day in person and acknowledged that they signed, sealed and delivered the said instrument as their free and voluntary act and deed for the uses and purposes therein set forth.

Witness my hand and seal this first day of May, 1885.

CLINTON L. CONKLING.

[SEAL]   Notary Public.

The Association then adjourned to meet Saturday, the ninth instant, at four o'clock in the afternoon. In the meantime the original paper, of which the above is a copy, was filed in the office of the Secretary of State, who accepted it as the basis upon which he issued the following:

STATE OF ILLINOIS, DEPARTMENT OF STATE. }
   HENRY D. DEMENT, SECRETARY OF STATE. }

To all whom these Presents shall come—Greeting:

WHEREAS, A certificate duly signed ond acknowledged, having been filed in the office of the Secretary of State. on the 9th day of May A. D. 1885. for the organization of "The Lincoln Monument Association." under and in accordance with the provisions of "An act concerning corporations," approved April 18, 1872, and in force July 1, 1872, a copy of which certificate is hereunto attached; now, therefore, I, Henry D. Dement Secretary of State of the State of Illinois, by virtue of the powers and duties vested in me by law, do hereby cetify that the said Lincoln Monument Association is a legally organized corporation under the laws of this State.

[SEAL.]
       In testimony whereof, I hereunto set my hand and cause to be affixed the Great Seal of State. Done at the city of Springfield, this ninth day of May. in the year of our Lord one thousand eight hundred and eighty-five, and of the Independence of the United States the one hundred and ninth.

HENRY D. DEMENT,
Secretary of State.

SPRINGFIELD, ILL., Saturday, May 9, 1885.

National Lincoln Monument Association, assembled. Present—Oglesby, Cullom, Stuart, Bunn, (Jacob) Bunn, (John W.) Williams, Conkling, Hay, DuBois, Black and Hatch. Absent—Treat and Palmer.

Minutes of the last meeting were read and approved. Mr. Hay submitted a deed of conveyance from the National Lincoln Monument Association, which was read and approved, and the President was directed to sign the same, and the Secretary to countersign it, and affix the seal of the National Lincoln Monument Association, which was done. It was then duly acknowledged on the part of the President and Secretary, before Clinton L. Conkling, a notary public. The President was then directed to deliver said deed to the Lincoln Monument Association, when its organization is completed.

All the arrangements for the change from the old to the new being finished, Hon. John T. Stuart offered the following preamble and resolution, which was adopted:

WHEREAS. The National Lincoln Monument Association will terminate its legal existence by limitation to-morrow, and that being Sunday.

Resolved, That it now adjourn *sine die*.

Mr. Stuart then made a brief statement of the situation, and that it was then in order to organize under the new certificate received from the Secretary of State. On motion of Hon. J. C. Conkling, it was

Resolved, That the gentlemen present who are named in the certificate from the Secretary of State, proceed to the election of officers for the Lincoln Monument Association.

The election terminated in the choice of

President—Gov. R. J. Oglesby.

Vice-President—U. S. Senator Shelby M. Cullom.

Secretary—Hon. O. M. Hatch.

Treasurer—John W. Bunn.

On motion of Senator Cullom, it was

Resolved, That the Executive Committee of the old Association, Stuart, Williams and Conkling, be the Executive Committee of the new one, and that George N. Black and John W. Bunn be added to that Committee.

As they were about to proceed to other business, the Custodian of the Monument, who had been present during the entire meeting, asked permission to speak, which was readily granted. He then said that nearly eleven years ago he had been appointed by the National Lincoln Monument Association Custodian of the Monument; that he had been on duty without intermission during all that time, but by the termination of the existence of that Association he found himself an orphan.

Hon. John T. Stuart, who, as chairman of the Executive Committee, had directed the movements of the Custodian and received all his reports, taking what the Custodian had said, as it was intended, merely as a hint that they were about to overlook the custody of the Monument, arose and said, in substance, that it was a self-evident truth that the Lord had made J. C. Power for the special purpose, and asked that by common consent of the members he be continued Custodian of the Monument under the new organization, to which they all assented.

The following, offered by Mr. Hay, was adopted:

WHEREAS, This organization has been effected for the purpose of taking care of the property of the National Lincoln Monument Association, whose corporate existence is about to expire; and for the further purpose of continuing the trusts and objects for which the said National Lincoln Monument Association was formed; and

WHEREAS, Said Association has, by its president, tendered a deed to this Association of all its property and effects, to be held upon the trusts and for the purposes in said deed expressed; therefore,

Resolved, That said deed be accepted, and that the same is hereby directed to be recorded, and that the secretary execute this order.

Resolved, That the president appoint a committee to prepare by-laws for the government of this Association, and report the same to the next meeting.

Messrs. Stuart, Hay and Conkling were appointed said committee.

Adjourned to meet Saturday, May 16, 1885, at 4 o'clock in the afternoon.

Thus the transition was made from the National Lincoln Monument Association, to the Lincoln Monument Association, the latter of which, under the law, may run for ninety-nine years, which is practically making it prepetual.

As will be seen in a preceding part of this appendix, a portion of the Monument was so defective in the original construction as to require reconstruction, which was done in 1884. It being found necessary to reconstruct the other half of the terrace, which is the west side and south end, in the same manner, and the

Monument Association having exhausted all the funds at its command, applied for aid to the Legislature of Illinois.   The following is a full copy of an act making the appropriation applied for :

AN ACT *making an appropriation for the repairs of the Lincoln Monument, near Springfield, Illinois.*

SECTION 1.   *Be it enacted by the People of the State of Illinois, represented in the General Assembly,* That the sum of ten thousand dollars, or as much thereof as may be required, be and the same is hereby appropriated out of any money in the treasury not otherwise appropriated, for the purpose of repairing the Lincoln Monument, at Oak Ridge Cemetery, near Springfield, Illinois.

§ 2.   The Auditor of Public Accounts is hereby authorized and directed to draw his warrant upon the State Treasurer for said sum, in favor of and payable to the order of the Treasurer of the Lincoln Monument Association, having the care and control of said Monument, upon bills of particulars certified to by the Executive Committee of the Lincoln Monument Association, approved by the Governor.

Approved June 13, 1887.

W. W. Boyington, architect, of Chicago, was employed by the Lincoln Monument Association to prepare plans and superintend the work of reconstructing the remainder of the building.   After preparing plans and advertising for proposals, the contract was let for the work designated, September 7, 1887, at $9,333. It will require an expenditure of two or three thousand dollars more to put all in good condition, making in all twelve or thirteen thousand dollars.   The work is now under way, and it is expected that the bulk of it will be done before the close of 1887.